The Shadow of Macedon

Iskandar's Game, Book One

Alexander Hill

To my father, who taught me to go my own way; to my mother, who inspired me to see the world; and to those who made my solo travels much less lonely.

Contents

CHAPTER ONE
The Banished Tiger

Tasnim shivered in the cold bite of midnight as she trudged through a field of dry wild grass. The desert was certainly colder, but the windy grasslands of central Morocco were an equivalent pain in the ass in different ways.

"Couldn't we have brought the car up?" she muttered at her client through gritted teeth and a tense jaw.

Henry Zhang was a self-professed graduate student at an American university's department of archaeology. Did she believe that for a second? Absolutely not. She had serious doubts that sneaking into the UNESCO heritage site of Volubilis in the dark was above board. Not to mention that nothing about his demeanor said "student." He dressed like a bouncer with his mandarin-collared black jacket, the sleeves rolled up to make his arms look bigger. He'd shaped the scruff on his chin into a trimmed goatee. Combined with his undercut, he looked like a villain.

He had an almost golden-brown complexion now. A week ago, he would've been unmistakably Chinese. But his tan and the scruff said Turkic. Maybe even Latino.

"I mean, I'm not super crazy about spending the night in prison," Henry said as he climbed over a boulder, dragging a large black duffel bag with him. "You can go back to the car and wait if you really want."

Tasnim narrowed her eyes. "And leave you unsupervised in Volubilis?"

Henry scoffed, crouching on top of the boulder. "There's nothing to steal but marble blocks. The Almoravids beat me to it a thousand years ago."

Tasnim took his hand as he offered it, pulling her onto the boulder. "If it's all the same to you, I'd like you to stay alive long enough to pay me."

Henry blew her off. What, was this a game to him?

"The guards have guns, you know." She frowned. "At least take this seriously."

He ignored her, starting up a steep hill.

Tasnim tsked. "Are you finally going to tell me what you're looking for?"

"I thought I was pretty clear that I wasn't," Henry said as they crouched down, overlooking the ruins.

"Look, we're bordering on some pretty serious legal consequences here. If you want me to go with you, I want you to tell me what the hell we're doing."

"Legal consequences." Henry chuckled. "You're a mercenary. Your whole profession is a crime."

"Right now, I'm a guide. And you damn well better tell me what I'm guiding you towards. I'll drive off with the car," Tasnim threatened, patting her pocket and the jingling keys within.

Henry sighed. "I...really? You've gotta be kidding me. This—it's...stupid. What I'm looking for is gonna sound stupid."

"So, not a big surprise, coming from you."

Henry gave her an unamused look. "Clever," he muttered. "I'm looking for a coin from Alexander the Great's tomb."

Tasnim furrowed her brow. "Now, that *is* stupid. You're on the wrong side of the Mediterranean."

"If the coin was still in Alexander's tomb, yes. But the Roman emperor Caracalla removed several pieces of his regalia when he paid a visit. And take a look at this." Henry pulled a small leather-bound journal from his jacket and pulled out a photocopy of some ancient scroll.

"Let's pretend for a moment that I can't read Latin," Tasnim muttered.

"It says Caracalla's advisor received the coin as a gift from the Emperor. And on his death, passed it onto his son, who was governor of Mauretania. Whose capital we're currently sneaking into. And he calls that coin a 'key'," Henry explained.

"A key to what?" Tasnim asked.

"To the tomb," Henry said nonchalantly, as if Alexander the Great's tomb hadn't gone missing hundreds of years ago.

"Didn't it sink under Alexandria?"

"That's what the stories say."

Tasnim scrunched up her nose in confusion. What else was there besides the stories? Was she carting a conspiracy theorist around? She began to rethink her commitment to helping this man.

But she'd already come this far...

Rather than pass through the tourist entrance to Volubilis, which was guarded at night, Henry and Tasnim had opted to climb up the hillside opposite from that entrance. After another steep climb, they had found their way to the remains of the Temple of Saturn, overlooking the limestone, marble, and restorative brick remnants of Volubilis, the ancient ruins of a Roman city.

Far from the nearest city of Meknes, Volubilis was wonderfully quiet at this time of night.

Aside from a few lights near the affixed museum, lack of pollution made the stars clear for all to see in the night sky. The moonlight on the ancient ruins gave an ethereal air to the city that had once been here. With lunar backlighting, the city's Triumphal Arch cast a shadow over the ruins of an old basilica. Both monuments towered over what used to be houses, baths, roads, and markets, the weathered old architecture performing its imperial function a thousand years after the city's abandonment.

Tasnim's gaze shifted from the majestic view to the irreverent tossing of Henry's black duffel bag onto the ground. She frowned as he unzipped it. "What's all that for?"

Her heart nearly stopped as he pulled out the synthetic black body of a pistol.

"*Bismillah*...How'd you even get that into the country?"

"Bribes, mostly. Have you ever been in a firefight?"

"Oh, *no*," Tasnim hissed. "I'm not getting into a shootout! What the hell are you expecting to find? Are you going to brute force your way through the guards?"

"Relax—" Henry started.

"I will *not* relax if your plan is to run in there and spray bullets everywhere!"

Henry looked at her, raising his eyebrows. "Are you done?"

Tasnim sighed, letting her arms fall limp to her sides. "Fine, then. Explain. Give it your best shot."

"I'm not the only one looking for this coin. And my competition would rather send this place sky high than let me have it. I'd rather have the means of stopping that," Henry said, loading a full magazine. "The only reason I'm out here tonight is because a certain...private collector has decided to make a move at some point tonight. I've been tracking their movements, and we're just barely ahead of them."

Tasnim's eyes widened. What kind of competition was he up against?

"I should be able to get in there and get out pretty fast, but things might go south. But if at any point you want to help me not die, I have a rifle."

Tasnim shook her head. "This is...absurd. I..."

"You don't have to, but I figure leaving whether you get paid or not up to chance can't feel too good."

She squeezed her eyes shut, realizing she really should've taken payment up front. "I...what rifle?"

He turned to his duffel bag and dug through it, pulling out a rifle with a wooden stock and a long, thin barrel.

She looked it over as he handed it off to her. "An M14? What, was this your grandpa's?"

"My apologies for not splurging on a Sig," Henry muttered as he pulled out a length of soft rope with a long metal dart tied to the end.

"What's your plan with that?" She gestured to the rope dart as he began to tie it around his left forearm.

"A contingency. In case I run out of bullets." He finished his elaborate knot.

Lastly, he removed a small bag carrying a pair of short swords with single-edged blades about as long as his forearm and knuckle guards that curved into upward hooks over the thumbs.

He pulled out a leather sheath for them as Tasnim picked up one of the swords. "And *these*? Do you plan on deflecting their bullets?" She twirled the blade around, nearly dropping it as her hand tried to account for weight that wasn't there. "*Bismillah*, these are light...What are they made of?"

"Good steel." Henry caught the handle of the sword as Tasnim fumbled it. He put the blade in a crossing sheath that belted around the back of his waist. "I'd rather not leave the ruins full of bullet holes if I can avoid it."

"How noble." Tasnim scoffed. Her tone shifted as Henry pulled out something that looked like a steel canister covered in electronics and wires. "What the hell is that?"

"A bomb." Henry looked up at her horrified expression. "For cars, not for the ancient ruins."

He pulled out a few magazines for the M14 and handed them to her before grabbing his last few items. Tasnim went to work loading the rifle, not bothering to ask about some weird slips of paper he pulled out of the bag.

As she finished loading, Henry grabbed an earpiece and an accompanying radio. He handed the radio to Tasnim. "Use this to communicate with me." He put the earpiece in. "You know how to broadcast?"

"I know enough. You have a callsign you want me to use or something?"

Henry shook his head as he stowed his sidearm away. "I had one. Not really a big fan of it anymore. If we don't have to run for our lives once I'm done here, dinner's on me."

Tasnim cocked her rifle and scoffed. "Oh, you'll be buying me a lot more than that."

She looked the weapon over. This was insane. Getting into a firefight? All for...what, a thousand US? The gun in her hands was probably worth a thousand on its own. And on the black market, she could get an extra premium.

She shook her head. Part of her felt bad just running off. But she wasn't going to close any doors if things got a little too hot.

Stealth wasn't something that came naturally to Henry. He wasn't an assassin or a secret agent. He was a Martial Magician—the loudest, most brutish type of Magician. So he wasn't going to duck-waddle everywhere under the pretense of sneaking. Though he did walk heel-to-toe to obscure his footfalls.

He made his way through the commons quarter of the ruined city and near the south gate on the opposite side of the ruin, characterized by a distinctly modern museum for tourists. Made of blank white stone in flat, geometric shapes with no texture, the entrance was flanked by two armed guards.

To be fair, modern styles of architecture had *some* appeal. At least, more so than modern art. But to Henry, that wasn't a very high bar.

"Check, check. Do you copy?" he whispered into his earpiece as he crept through the piles of ruined stone and bricks.

"I read you." Tasnim's voice patched through. "Aside from the guards at the museum, your coast is clear."

Henry pulled out a *fulu* charm, a small yellow slip of paper covered in red-ink scribbling that vaguely resembled Chinese characters. He pulled off a strip of paper covering a bit of adhesive and stuck the charm to the tail of his jacket. The charm turned the polyester fabric to silk of the same jet-black color. It was the upper limit of what he could do with written magic.

The talisman used a small bit of Confucian magic, but goaded Solomon's Wisdom into effect, hiding all magic from unawakened eyes.

Henry stood up, in full view of the guards, and let the ancient worldwide spell do its work. He waved at them, but even as they were looking in his direction, their eyes were glazed over in boredom before they started some idle conversation with one another.

Tasnim wouldn't be able to see him either.

Unburdened by any need to be stealthy, Henry trudged to the west, towards the ruin's characteristically Roman triumphal arch.

So far, everything was going according to plan. That said, his plan was missing a few things—namely, someone able to detect magic. Henry's arcane senses were...blunted. He'd always relied on his squad to sniff out targets for him in the past. To say he was paranoid about being snuck up on now was the understatement of the century.

His head on a swivel, he ducked under a lopsided arch belonging to the entrance of a block-size pavilion. Down a few stairs, he wove his way around tufts of weeds and foundational stone blocks. He climbed up a small incline to a few ruined columns just as Tasnim patched into his radio.

"Eyes on the museum," she warned.

Henry glanced over a waist-high stone wall and crouched.

A small group of westerners passing by the oblivious guards stuck out like a sore thumb. Henry frowned. If the guards weren't seeing them, how could Tasnim?

Maybe she had the makings of a Magician. He'd let the Society of the Setting Sun find that out for themselves.

As for the interlopers, he was under the impression that every Magician's Circle in Europe was out for this coin. They could be from any Circle. Latins, Germans, Slavs, Greeks. Likely the Latins, since they were the ones who had his information first before it passed hands to him, but he'd cross that bridge when he got to it.

For now, they didn't know he was here.

Henry crossed a beaten path that had once been a proper road past the despondent ruins of houses that should've belonged to richer members of the settlement, leading up to the governor's Gordian Palace.

The palace was a symbol to him, like treading the last steps of the thousand-mile journey he'd been burdened with these last eighteen months. Relief and terror flooded into him at the prospect of making it this far. Just before him lay the chance for vindication. With the key to the tomb, he could finally be done with this nonsense. Weiying's lies would be revealed, and he could get his life back.

But a seed of doubt wiggled its way into his mind, sending a burning tingle to the spot between his shoulder blades.

A series of three arches, surrounded by columns implying the continuation of the pattern, marked the Gordian Palace. He stepped over the shin-high stacks of stone that were once walls and onto a patch of ground just outside one of the palace's mosaics, for which the entire settlement was known.

Pulling off his shoes so as to not damage the mosaic, Henry stepped onto it and pressed his palms against the carefully arranged artwork, focusing on his arcane senses, trying to search for any sign of magic.

There was nothing he could feel. But his fingers grabbed at the mosaic anyway.

He searched columns, walls, other mosaics, and every inch of floor not yet consumed by the overgrowth. He looked for mechanisms, hidden compartments, shifted rocks, anything.

And he came up with jack.

It could be that it wasn't here. But it could also be that it *was* here, and its hiding spot was buried under two thousand years of history. Or someone lost it. Or literally any of the near-infinite possibilities that could have occurred since that coin last appeared in recorded history.

Henry pinched the bridge of his nose. He couldn't afford to spend time worrying about whether or not it was here. But if it wasn't, he'd be wasting that much time, and possibly more.

He closed his eyes and breathed, calming himself. "Alright," he muttered. "Just think."

The coin had been a gift to the governor from Caracalla, later passed onto his son...

"Tasnim, do you know when different parts of this city were constructed?" he asked over the radio.

"Why would I know that?"

Henry grimaced.

"Best I can do is say the Triumphal Arch was built...I think sometime in the two hundreds. I don't know, it was a school trip."

The third century? That would've been right at the time of Caracalla's final years in power.

Henry pulled out his journal, filled with notes from his research on this place. Research that neglected to date every quarter of the city. But the arch *was* built in Caracalla's honor. It was a plausible hiding place. And his best lead aside from the governor's house.

Footsteps on the beaten gravel just beyond the arches made him grab his shoes and dive for cover behind a block of stone.

The four westerners had their backs turned to him as they split up. They held gold talismans out like Geiger counters to extend the range of their arcane senses. Two women, two men. All around his age. Maybe a little older.

Henry waited in the shadows, listening as they spoke to one another.

It was...Latin?

He had figured the Coven of Latium, being a multinational Circle between France, Spain, and Italy, would use English or French as a common tongue. But it seemed Latin served the same purpose. Henry's expertise was in Mandarin and Arabic. His Latin translations had come from the internet. So he wasn't getting any of what they were saying.

Slowly and quietly, he maneuvered around them, heading south for the Triumphal Arch, as they continued north.

Once he was out of earshot, he broke into a jog, but stopped as he caught sight of another figure sneaking out from behind the Arch. He was expecting more manpower from the Latins, and in any other circumstance, he would've dealt with them then and there. But the coin was top priority.

Henry sprinted towards the Arch and turned the corner of the massive monument to find a hole in the marble. His eyes met the surprised glance of a brunette woman a head shorter than him. She looked like she might fall in with the Latins, with long, wavy hair and broad, more European features with lightly tanned skin. But if she were with the Latins, she would've called for help by now.

Maybe she was German or Slavic.

Henry caught a glint of light as she shoved her hand into her pocket.

Without a moment's hesitation, she threw a punch at him. Henry blocked the strike and countered with an admittedly arrogant flurry of blows with a single hand, trying to reach for her pocket with the other.

She was able to hold her own with some basic boxing skills, but was hardly trained to fight off a Martial Magician. Henry managed to sweep her legs out from under her. Like he was wrestling with his brother over a toy, he tried to shove his hand into her pockets, which she viciously defended.

He was starting to think she was definitely in the same boat as himself.

"Stop being so...stubborn." Henry grunted, trying to get past her arms. Grappling was the one combat skill he was lacking in, and it was really showing right now.

"Get...off!" she hissed, planting a surprising kick in his sternum. He stumbled back, the wind flooding out of his lungs as the woman scrambled to her feet and ran. He fell to one knee to catch his breath.

Henry pushed himself off the ground, stumbling again in the process. Before he could chase after the woman, he heard shouts in Latin coming from behind him.

The weathered arch was at least two stories high. Probably higher. There weren't a lot of hiding places around the wide-open space surrounding the arch, but he *could* hide up top.

That was his best chance to avoid being outnumbered. He quickly scaled a portion of worn stone before throwing himself up to a handhold provided by a missing block. He pulled himself over the top of the arch just as the Latins sprinted down to it.

"Tasnim." Henry patched into his radio. "I could really use some support down by the Arch."

He waited for a response, but nothing came.

CHAPTER TWO
The Heaven and Earth Society

"Tasnim?"

There was no way he was out of range.

"Tasnim, do you copy?"

"You!"

Henry glanced down at the redheaded woman pointing at him.

"Get down here!" Her French accent was as thick as her hair. Her three companions—a willowy, bearded man, a blonde woman, and a man with a pencil-thin goatee that looked like it came out of the 1600s—pointed pistols at him.

"Shit..." Henry muttered to himself.

"Who are you?" the French woman asked.

Henry peered down at the Latins. "It's typically polite to introduce yourself before asking another to do so."

"You deal with Trajan Squad. Now, get down here if you know what's good for you."

The redhead must've been Trajan 1. Callsign Josephine, if he recalled. He had heard of a Slavic Magician who'd taken his own life with just a few words from her.

There was no talking this out.

Fine.

Taking a deep breath, Henry forsook oxygen to cultivate it all into the life energy commonly known as Qi, allowing him use of Five Elements Fist, the Heaven and Earth Society's arcane martial art.

He channeled the Qi through his veins into Fire Style, giving his muscles a boost of explosive strength.

"I do not like to repeat myself, Defector," Josephine said, goading him.

Henry leapt off the Arch with superhuman strength, throwing a spinning kick, with two stories of freefall to build up, into the goatee man's head. His enemy's neck snapped upon impact.

Henry landed with a shoulder roll, grabbed the blonde woman by her shirt, and threw her over his hip and into the ground. Before Josephine could even react, Henry closed the distance and threw a punch straight to her sternum, stealing the air from her lungs. As she collapsed, coughing, he turned and grabbed the willowy man by the hair, pulling the man's head into his knee.

Henry sprinted towards his objective once he finished dealing with the Latins.

Down the gravel path that used to be a road, he ran towards the museum, finding the woman who'd stolen the coin attempting to be stealthy.

He rushed up from behind her, wrapping his arm around her neck as his hand shoved its way into her pocket. He yanked out a small, circular object wrapped in purple cloth. It was kind of large for a coin, but he could feel something arcane coming from it, even with his blunted senses.

The woman took him by surprise, slamming her elbow into his ribs and pushing him away, ready to fight before she noticed the coin in his hand.

"You're not with any of the Circles, are you?" she asked. "We can talk about this, can't we?" Though her accent was light, it was definitely German.

"Pass," Henry said, pocketing the coin. He couldn't let her get another shot at him like that again. The coin was distracting him from being properly aware.

The woman opened her mouth to speak again, but fell silent as her gaze went past him.

"Hanying."

Henry's whole body went cold as a familiar voice reached his ears.

What were they doing here? Now? Of all times?

The Tiandihui had months to interrupt him. And they had to pick now? How had they even gotten the information? He had stolen it from them before they got the chance to read it.

His fists clenched as he turned to face three figures approaching his standoff with the woman. On either flank of the central figure stood a Magician wearing a Beijing opera mask, obscuring their faces. The central figure had the face of a kindly man in his later years, but a smug expression of superiority written over it. With only humble black robes and a white brimmed hat, Fang Sima—better known to Henry as Mr. Fang—stood with his arms folded behind his back.

With half of Zhao Squad.

Judging by the green mask on the woman with him and the yellow mask on the man with him, Henry was looking at his old comrades, Guoxing Min and Tao Shen.

He wondered where the other three were—specifically, where Weiying was.

Shen, in yellow and black, rested his hand on the pommels of his double Chinese broadswords. Min, in black and green silks, readied her metal fans for a fight.

"Who's this?" Fang asked, pointing out the German woman with his chin. "You were never one for impulsive team-ups, Hanying."

"The Tiandihui has never been one for inserting itself into foreign affairs," Henry growled. "Don't you have Chinese artifacts to look for?"

"Don't give me that. You have even less reason to be here than us." Fang gave Henry a knowing look to punctuate his point. "Is this going to come down to a fight?"

"Depends." Henry sighed. "Are you gonna fuck off?"

Fang pursed his lips. Henry tensed his legs, ready to spring into action. He met the gaze of the German woman, whose face betrayed her anxiety.

His eyes darted between Min, Fang, and Shen. He could take Min and Shen in a fight. But Fang? That was a whole other can of worms.

He could hear footsteps behind him, the remaining Latins having recovered from the beatdown he dealt them. Maybe they could take care of Fang.

The old man broke the silence. "Go."

Shen and Min leapt into action, closing the distance between the Chinese and the Latins like thunderbolts.

The Europeans responded with gunfire and spell-slinging.

Henry flinched out of the way of a bullet from Josephine's gun before he rushed in to take her out of the fight again.

"*Stop.*" Her voice echoed in his head as his body locked up against his will.

She began to say something else before a bolt of golden light from the still-glowing palm of the German woman sent her to the ground.

Henry turned on instinct, only to get kneed in the ribs by Mr. Fang. His old mentor backed away rather than following up, dancing on the balls of his feet.

Henry breathed through the pain and drew his butterfly swords, fueling his body with Qi, increasing his speed and agility with Five Elements Fist's Metal Style.

He descended on Fang with a storm of slashes as fast as a machine gun, but the old man swayed around his flurry of strikes as if he were dodging clumsy punches from a shitty boxer.

Henry backed off, panting slightly.

"Hanying," Fang said, aggressively neutral.

"I don't like repeating myself," Henry said. "Fuck off."

"That's no way to talk to a teacher, pupil," Fang said. "Past or otherwise, show due respect."

"I'm done learning from *you*!" Henry spat.

While not as fast as his last assault, he attacked Fang with a more diverse array of strikes, making it harder to evade. Fang, in turn, started parrying with short, snappy, efficient Wing Chun ripostes.

"You can't keep this up forever!"

"Nor can you, Hanying. I highly doubt you've managed to match your stamina with mine in the last year and a half."

This contest wasn't remotely fair. Even unarmed, Fang had taught Henry everything he knew about fighting. Henry would keel over from exhaustion before Fang took a scratch.

At least, so long as this kept up.

Henry tossed his left sword to his right as he undid the knot of his rope dart with his teeth and threw the dagger out.

The blade flew forth, scraping Mr. Fang's cheek. A gash the size of a paper cut appeared on his face as Henry pulled the dart back.

He stowed his swords as Fang blinked in genuine surprise. "You like it? Made it myself." He spun the rope dart, keeping it moving as he glared.

Henry threw the dart underhanded. Fang ducked under it. So he wrapped it over his elbow and shot it again, missing a second time. But Fang was barely dodging, still somewhat shocked by the revelation.

Was it that unthinkable that Henry would continue learning without the Tiandihui?

Henry kicked the dart out, slicing Fang's arm as he tried to parry the soft weapon.

He pulled the dart back and started to spin it as his tunnel vision towards Mr. Fang faded. The Latins were on the ground, taken care of. And he spotted the bright violet silk dress adorning Lu Ying, Zhao Squad's resident Daoist caster. Not far, of course, was Chen Bo, clad head to toe in modern body armor, aside from his opera mask, and carrying a rifle.

So Zhao Squad *was* here in full. Almost.

Henry canvassed the area in less than a second, keeping his eye out for Weiying.

He spared a glance back to find Min and Shen cornering him and the German woman together.

"Swords, miaodao, guandao, and now this?" Fang chuckled. "Don't you remember my first lesson? Don't be the rabbit that drops the carrots he's picked to pick up another."

"Shut up!" Henry hissed as he shot the dart from around his back. He pulled it back and tossed it under his leg before kicking it out.

This time, Mr. Fang caught the dart and pulled, reeling him in. Before he knew it, Henry's own weapon was strangling him.

He choked for air, but Fang's grip was like iron, though his old mentor never pulled so tightly he couldn't breathe at all.

He didn't need Fang's sympathy. He didn't need anyone's charity.

Henry slammed his elbow back, but Fang just took the chance to bind his arm to his back in the process.

"You're not ready for soft weapons, rabbit."

"*You're* the herd of rabbits. A tiger hunts alone." Henry struggled to no avail in spite of his bravado.

"Rabbit or tiger, you're still a beast. Stop being so stubborn," Fang said. "I'm trying to let you leave here alive."

"I don't need you..." Henry strained. "To go easy on me!"

"Then do better or give in."

A flash of light flooded Henry's vision. Even though it seared his retinas, he managed to slip out from Fang's grip and disentangle himself before stumbling away, half-blind.

The German girl grabbed his wrist and dragged him away as the other members of Zhao Squad chased after them.

Henry yanked both himself and the girl around a corner and into a somewhat-intact stone building housing an ancient oil press.

He kept his eyes on the road until Zhao Squad ran past him, letting out a sigh only once they were headed towards the governor's palace. Glancing at the German girl, he narrowed his eyes. "Why did you help me?"

"Is the squad of Magicians hunting us not a good enough reason?" She raised an eyebrow. "I made a mistake before. I'm on my own as well. I'd rather have you as a friend."

"Friend? We're half-strangers at best." Henry tried to patch into his radio. "Tasnim. Tasnim! Come in, dammit!"

He sighed. He might as well make sure he actually got the coin he was looking for before making a break for it.

He untied the twine holding the cloth wrap in place and unraveled it.

His breath caught in his throat as he gazed upon the perfectly polished gold sheen of the coin. There were plenty of images, words, and symbols dotting the abnormally large coin. Lots to analyze once he got out alive.

Henry grabbed the coin and held it before him.

The German girl gasped. "Wait, don't—"

His heart dropped as a wave of intangible power exploded from the coin, rippling across Volubilis.

It was like a giant, blinking arcane sign that pointed to his exact location.

He cursed under his breath, wrapping the coin back up. Thankfully, the cloth seemed to obscure the signal. But the damage was already done.

"Run!" the girl hissed.

Henry wasn't going to question that. He leapt from the shelter of the mill and sprinted towards the museum.

He half-ran, half-tumbled down the hill of ruins towards the museum. He scrambled to his feet at the bottom, only for Shen to land in front of him, having leapt off the roof of the museum.

Henry moved to slip past him, but his flank was cut off by a spray of bullets from on high. Chen Bo stood atop the museum's roof. Min and Lu Ying blocked his escape to his right. He turned to find Mr. Fang helping Shen to his feet.

His mind scrambled for an answer to his current predicament.

"Henry," Min called out to him from behind, "you've got nowhere to go. Give up the coin." She undid her mask, letting her face wear another, more deceitful visage shaped like concern. He knew she hated him, believing Weiying at his word. Of everyone here, she had the biggest grudge.

He was surrounded again.

"Tasnim!" Henry roared. The radio had to be malfunctioning. If he yelled, maybe she could hear him.

They waited a few seconds. Nothing.

"Tasnim...is that the Moroccan girl you had posted up with a rifle?" Lu Ying chuckled.

"What did you do?" Henry demanded.

"Touchy, aren't we?" Lu Ying's condescending tone mocked him with vicious poison. "Were you two friends?"

Mr. Fang sighed. "Your Moroccan friend took off with the slightest threat from Lu Ying. You should really keep better company."

Henry gritted his teeth. His ego bruised and his skills outmatched, he became desperate, searching for something to get himself out of here.

Chen Bo called from the rooftop. "Hand over the coin. For old times' sake, we may let you live, traitor."

He remembered the bomb hidden under his jacket.

"'Old times?' Fuck you, Chen Bo." Henry scoffed. He pulled the canister out from his jacket and threw it at his former ally.

But he should've known Fang would be fast enough to throw a knife from under his sleeve at the bomb.

Dangerously close to both Henry and Fang, the bomb exploded. The blast ripped through Henry's ears and threw him back. His head bounced off a wall, causing his consciousness to vanish.

CHAPTER THREE
Achilles' Dilemma

"I s this some kind of joke to you?"

Zhang Hanying leaned against the detailed wooden railing between himself and a vast panorama of cliffs and peaks, deep in Daba mountains. The morning mist filled the air with a chill thickness and cast a haze over the sheer cliffs and verdant slopes. The cliff faces all around the monastery were marked by streaks of black or grey rock straight out of a Chinese ink-wash painting. Hanying stared at the tree roots reaching down over the temple from the overhang of packed soil and rock.

"No..." Weiying muttered, voice full of shame.

Hanying spared a glance at his younger brother and the welts on his face. A less-than-satisfactory repayment for the stinging bruises on Hanying's own skin.

He and his brother were both clad in the white-and-black wool uniforms of the Heaven and Earth Society's Magician academy.

He didn't know why both of them were out here. Weiying had clearly instigated. Weiying always instigated. Hanying only ever did anything to defend himself.

"I don't think that's the crux of the—" Hanying began.

"Be silent!" Fang snapped, looming over the two boys with an aura of sternness. "You must be tired of me disciplining you. I know I am. So, no matter how often I punish you, why do you two insist on fighting?"

Hanying felt the cut on his cheek tingle.

It had been less of a fight and more of a delusion-fueled assault. Hanying had refused to refill Weiying's water at the pump for him over a week ago, and Weiying found that act so insulting that he felt it was justified for him to break the rules of sparring and actively try to hurt Hanying. Not that he could explain that to Mr. Fang.

"I don't recall being the one who attacked someone with a sword." Hanying shot a look at his brother.

"I don't care who started it."

"Why?" Hanying asked, shooting an indignant look at his instructor. "Isn't the point of you mediating to dispense justice?"

"No. I am not mediating. I am disciplining you," Fang said. "I don't care because all that matters is that you two don't fight. You have been given a very generous opportunity by the Heaven and Earth Society to be trained in the arcane arts and to put those skills to use in the service of our country. You both will be part of a combat squadron soon. In the field, if you two fight like this, people will die! You'll die!"

"This isn't my country," Hanying dared to murmur.

"What was that?" Fang shot a glare his way.

"Why are you even putting kids into military squads? Isn't that a war crime or something?" Weiying asked before sheepishly adding, "Sir..."

"Don't be a smartass. You know damn well why," Fang growled.

According to the Tiandihui, other Magicians' Circles the world over had been enjoying a boom in young people breaking through Solomon's Wisdom. If the Tiandihui didn't deploy their young members in combat, the other Circles would outnumber them ten to one.

Fang sighed. "What boggles my mind, Weiying, is that you're the most gifted student we have. You completed the basic Confucian Sorcery set in a month. Why do you fight with your brother over the result of a simple sparring match?"

Hanying scoffed. "Because he can't imagine the idea of me being better than him at anything."

"No! You're just a coward!"

"The match was over! You tried to attack me after you tapped out!" Hanying shouted.

"You're a moron who won't spar with magic!"

"I can barely use magic! And let's talk about how you had the gall to get mad at me just because I wouldn't fetch you water!"

"What's so hard about it?"

"That was a week ago! You're still holding that grudge!" Hanying's face twisted with anger.

"I'm in the intermediate class! Your senior! You should get me water when I tell you to get me water! You shouldn't even be here, you—"

Hanying drew his fist back.

Fang put himself between the two of them. "Stop!"

Hanying sighed and returned to leaning over the railing.

"Look...if you two can't get yourselves under control by the end of the month, one of you is going to have to leave," Fang said. "And whoever does is not going to enjoy that experience. So, to give you time to think on it, Weiying, after dinner, you will run to the peak of the next mountain and back before sunrise."

"What?" Weiying exclaimed. "But it's gonna rain tonight!"

"Hanying." Fang turned to him. "You still haven't passed the Confucian beginning set. If you don't pass, we won't have to spend time deciding on who leaves."

Hanying grimaced.

"He gets to study?" Weiying moaned, throwing his arms around limply as if trying to give the impression of helplessness. "That's not fair! Why doesn't he have to run?"

"Believe me, I'd rather run," Hanying muttered. He didn't even want to look at those books anymore.

"This is favoritism!" Weiying jabbed an accusatory finger at his teacher.

"I'm being more than fair." Fang glared at him.

"It's because I'm a better Magician than your daughter, isn't it?"

"What does that—"

"You're all just jealous!" Weiying snarled, storming away, stomping across the stone floors.

Fang sighed, shaking his head.

Once Weiying was well out of earshot, Fang pinched his nose. "I mean...where does he get off..."

"My parents never really disciplined him. Would you believe me if I said he's always been that way?" Hanying sighed.

Fang nodded. "Unfortunately. I think I was being fair."

"Yeah, well, anything that isn't exactly what he wants is unfair." Hanying's weak smile vanished.

Fang leaned against the railing with Hanying. "I ought to record him the next time he has an outburst. Show High Command their star prodigy is an asshole, since they seem eager to take his word over mine."

"He only acts that way when he thinks he can get away with it." Hanying scoffed.

"He's a hard worker, nonetheless. Just...equally hard to work *with*." Fang gave Hanying a side-eyed glance. "I'm serious about the punishment, by the way. You really need to pass that beginning set."

"I don't know what to tell you, sir." Hanying shrugged. "I just...wasn't made for civic sorcery. I'm good at the martial stuff."

"You can't confine yourself to only what you're good at, Hanying. Only by holding yourself to a standard that makes you push yourself will you improve. Otherwise, you'll lose control over even what you're good at."

"I know that, sir." He sighed. "I just don't..."

Mr. Fang's stone face was starting to come back.

"I'll try harder, sir," he muttered, dreading this evening. "If it means making Weiying shut up..."

Fang shook his head. "If you let him drag you down to his level, you're no better than him. Let go of all this with your brother. Don't let it stop your growth as a Magician. Or a martial artist. I'm his master. Leave him to me."

Hanying grimaced. "Yes, sir..."

Henry's eyes flickered open. The last vestiges of his breath escaped his throat and bubbled up to the surface.

He thrashed around through rushing water as he tried to pull himself up towards a light. His head broke through the surface, and a breath of fresh air filled his lungs. The several feet he'd been submerged in had been replaced by a riverbed. The water barely rose above his ankles as he sat.

But the stream was wide, surrounded by a large bank of stones and silt.

Steep mountains covered in short grass rose high enough to vanish into the thick fog that had settled over the river. The bends of the gorge twisted around the mountains as if a giant snake had burrowed through the rock.

His head was foggy, a jumble of fighting, explosions, and...well, not much else. How did he get here? That was a useless question, since he couldn't even answer where he'd come *from*.

The silt banks of the river faded into soil, meeting a sharp border between the mountains and a massive field of wild golden grains stretching as far as he could see. A setting—or maybe rising—sun cast the meadow and sky in brilliant colors. But the moment they reached the mountain mist, each ray of sunlight was reflected and scattered into an ambient glow amongst the fog. The grandiose size of everything around him filled his chest with a sense of expanding wonder.

His gaze was drawn by the crunch of sediment under hooves. He glanced at the bank of the river, spotting a man on horseback. The rider's bronze Corinthian helmet shrouded his face, with a crimson plume and detailing resembling a ram's horns on its sides. The horse itself had a coat of jet silk with a leopard skin draped over its back in place of a saddle. The rider was outfitted with iron armor, wielding a spear longer than even a Chinese *qiang*.

But it was his shield that revealed his identity. The bronze-coated aegis depicted a Macedonian sunburst.

Henry's eyes widened as the rider's horse walked past him. "E-excuse me!" he called out, his voice echoing in the gorge.

The rider continued on. Not knowing what else to do, Henry clambered to his feet and waded to the bank of the river.

Fog seeped in around them as he broke into a jog towards the horse so as to not lose the rider in the mist. But as he picked up his pace, the fog seemed to be more intent on obscuring the man in the haze. He broke into a sprint, only for the mists to wrap around him, completely blocking his vision.

Henry's face slammed into a sheet of bronze.

His butt hitting the silt, he collapsed with a grunt. He cursed, looking up at the Macedonian soldier staring down at him. The horse had seemingly vanished.

"What the hell is going on here?" Henry grumbled, getting to his feet.

The soldier stabbed his spear into the ground, eliciting a flinch from Henry. The bronze-clad man drew a curved sword from his hip—a kopis. He raised the weapon as it began to glow with vibrant golden light. A wave like sunlight pushed the fog back, revealing more gorge and something *really* strange.

Smooth as glass, some kind of massive wall blocked the gorge, rising into the sky beyond what Henry could see. The wall shined either from some kind of metal or wetness of stone.

"Jesus Christ..." Henry muttered.

Engraved in the wall were two massive inscriptions in...Syriac, if he was reading it right.

Syriac script was close enough to Arabic that he could understand it.

It was two words. *Yajuj* and *Majuj*.

Gawg and Megawg.

The last time Henry had read the Book of Revelations—a weird bit of required reading for his profession—he'd taken note of those names. They were cannibal tribes and enemies of the Israelites who were supposedly the forerunners and heralds of the Apocalypse.

The rider sheathed his sword and began to approach the wall. Henry, unsure of what else to do, tentatively followed.

The closer he got to the wall, the more detail revealed itself on its seemingly smooth surface. Every inch was covered in nearly microscopic script, but the letters kept shifting every second between different variations of Semitic languages, Cuneiform, Greek, some Minoan scripts that hadn't been deciphered yet, and plenty of other ancient writing systems.

As he and the soldier approached the massive wall, Henry noticed that it was not, in fact, a wall. Rather, a small line ran straight down the center of the edifice, dividing it into a gate. And it was slightly ajar.

On the ground at the small opening, something dark and ambiguous seemed to be leaking out, swirling and tangling itself around Henry's ankle. He took a step back, realizing he was looking at nothing.

He looked at the soldier, whose gaze was obscured by his helmet, but solely focused on the gate. At his own risk, Henry moved to peer into the gap, but the rider put a gauntleted hand on his shoulder, stopping him.

"What lies beyond is still contained. And better not thought of at all," the rider said. "Stare into the abyss, and it will do more than stare back. It will follow you. It will know you. But the fortune you seek lies there, in the void."

"What do you mean?" Henry asked.

The soldier presented an ultimatum. "Glance at the truth and seek the king of conquerors. Or step away and be conquered. There is shame in neither. But glory in one."

Henry furrowed his brow at the rider. Was this the coin's magic? Was it someone else? But the thought dominating his mind was simple and unquestioning.

"Achilles was offered this choice, if I remember correctly," he said, his voice grave as he stared at the crack in the gate. "Live a long life of obscurity...or die with honor."

The soldier nodded, solemn in his demeanor. "What I offer is not a glorious death followed by relief, but a future of strife and a legacy of honor."

"'A future of strife?'" Henry grimaced. "Well...I don't have much of a peaceful life to lose, do I?"

He stepped forward and peered into the void behind the gate.

What he saw was...nothing. Wisps of a shadow, abstract in its form, like an idea trying to manifest itself into material.

And a pair of eyes. Shining, brilliant eyes full of cold white light staring at him.

Let go...

His eyes snapped open.

Henry smacked his head against an aluminum bar, sending him straight back onto a cheap, sweat-soaked pillow he'd just torn himself from. He heaved through the pain, clutching his forehead. Images of his dream started to fade away as ringing shook his skull.

"Son of a bitch!" he hissed.

When the pain wore off, he sat up, maneuvering *around* the metal this time. He swung his legs to the side of an aluminum bunk bed. One of eight in this room.

Sunlight streamed through blinds at each window, making patches of illumination in the mostly dark room. The popcorn ceiling was at least twelve feet high, and each bed had a set of lockers next to it.

Henry tossed a thin sheet off of himself and stood, expanding his body with a stretch. As he took a few steps in place, he was surprised to find no noticeable injuries. Hadn't he been hit by a grenade? No, it was a bomb. His bomb.

That was...embarrassing, to say the least.

Maybe he was dead. Though he seriously doubted heaven or hell would look like a hostel dorm. Just to make sure, he stumbled to the en suite bathroom, which smelled of a recent shower, and stared at himself in the mirror over the tiny sink. He was covered in scars and a few bruises, but nothing major.

"What the hell?" he muttered to himself, voice scraping against the dry, sore, mucus-ridden mess that was his throat.

With a blast like the one he remembered, his entire front side should've been lacerated and scorched. Someone must've done something.

He looked at the faucet below him and had an impulse to drink from it. But he had no idea where he was. If he was still in Morocco, he'd best wait for bottled water.

With a sigh and some exertion, Henry left the bathroom and headed for the door. He opened it to a brightly lit hub between his room and half a dozen rooms just like it, with some kind of absurdly smooth stone on the floor that felt good on his bare feet. He'd bother with shoes later.

He squinted in the glow of the skylight overhead and followed the stone walls towards a stairwell, nearly bumping into a waist-high potted plant on the way. He made his way down the stairs and around a corner to a set of windows facing a stone brick street. Across from them was a front desk with the words *LoL Hostel* on it.

In spite of the name, Henry sighed in relief.

"Long night, huh?" The guy working the desk grinned knowingly at him.

Henry nodded slightly before heading past the desk and into the hostel's common area. Were he not injured or running from...well, it had to be two Magician's Circles now—he would've definitely stayed at a place like this. He'd always had an architectural soft spot for stone brick, so seeing the long wall that extended from the left of the front desk all the way to the bar put him at ease. The common room was filled with brightly colored beanbags and plush chairs, including a sofa in front of a television. Along the edge of the room, there were several desktop computers lined up like in a school library. Somewhat random décor, such as metal beams and a weirdly ornate mirror, dotted the stone wall, and the lights hanging off the ceiling cast everything untouched by the sun in a warm glow.

"You're awake."

Henry glanced behind him at a circular table in the corner between the front desk and the common area.

"I figured that blast would've put you down for at least a week."

Sitting at it was a girl no older than he was, looking up from a laptop. She was willowy in almost every feature, with shoulder-length curly brown hair and slightly suntanned skin. She wore a tight-fitting multicolored dress that really screamed "on vacation," but suited the unassuming facade she put forward. It took Henry a good minute, but he slowly started to recognize her.

"Analise..." he muttered.

"Good to see you again, Henry."

Anna-Lisa Abt—or Analise—was an old contact from his days in the Heaven and Earth Society, being willing to betray the Palatine Order of Cologne. Henry would often correspond with her for information as Zhao Squad's representative. And she wasn't the one who had intervened in Volubilis.

"What do you mean, 'a week?' How long has it been?" Henry got to the real crux of his concerns. "How did I get here? What—"

Analise held a finger up, silencing him. "Let's slow down. Sit and relax first." She gestured to a chair next to her with a thin hand. "It's a rare opportunity."

Henry gave her a look of disapproval, but sat down to alleviate his frankly exhausted body. Leaning on the table, he asked, "Where are we?"

"Syracuse. Sicily."

Henry squeezed his eyes shut. He was in the Coven of Latium's territory. Analise had betrayed the Germans to defect to the Latins. *Of course.* He'd been caught.

"It's not what you think," she said, reading his dismayed expression. "I'm not with the Latins."

Henry furrowed his brow.

"It's a long story."

"So, who *are* you working for?" Henry asked.

Analise frowned. "Hey. I don't always have to work for someone. I'm working *with* someone?"

"Yeah? Who?"

"I don't see how that's any of your business right now." She grimaced. So, either she didn't know, or she had a reason to keep the information from him.

"'Working with,' my ass." He scoffed.

"You should be thanking me. I watched over you for two days!"

"Two days." Henry sighed, trying to convince himself that it wasn't so bad. "I...I had a coin. And my weapons. Where are my—"

"You had your short swords on you, but that's about it," Analise said.

Henry noticed a violet cloth wrap next to her laptop. He reached for it, but she slid it away from him. "Not a chance. I know what this is."

"Analise..." Henry tilted his head, letting a stressed grin creep onto his face. "Don't do this. I don't wanna cause a scene."

"Then don't," she said nonchalantly. "You'll get it back once I'm done with it."

Did she expect him to believe that? That she wouldn't spike his drink with some paralysis concoction or charm him into a deep sleep before running off?

But in spite of his threats, he was in no position to take the coin by force. Even if he overcame his exhaustion, Analise could alarm the people he'd just stolen that coin from in a heartbeat.

Henry squeezed his eyes shut and sighed. He might as well try to play nice. For now.

"Alright," he muttered. At least he knew where the coin was. "Then can you...tell me how I got here from Morocco?"

Analise chuckled, lounging back in her chair. "You were already dozing off upstairs when I got here. My partner said you were the newest addition to our team."

"I'm what?"

"You're getting recruited." She shrugged. "It's a smart choice. You're good at what you do. But you need a linguist like myself." She unwrapped only part of the coin, allowing the wrap's magical suppression to continue working. "Look closely. There's a riddle here in ancient Greek. You'll need my help."

Henry peered at the coin. Indeed, there was ancient Greek scrawled on the edge, surrounding an image of some temple.

He sat back in his chair. "You're not the only one in the world who knows Ancient Greek. Why would I need *your* help?"

"Because my partner and I already know where to go next." Analise pulled out her phone and showed him a screenshot of a news article.

The headline read *Wealthy Medici Descendant to Host Fundraiser for National Archaeological Institute*. The photo was of a young Italian man proudly showing the camera a collection of artifacts.

Analise tapped her finger on the table next to the phone. "This fundraiser is a cover for a big party with all the Magicians' Circles who want to hunt for the tomb. I don't know how, but your little scuffle in Morocco caused a different coin to fall into the Coven's hands. The Latins have had a rough go of it recently. The Japanese managed to intercept their communications about their biggest lead, which I assume is the information that got into your hands. Calling that a loss of face is an understatement. You and Zhao Squad jumping them in Morocco was the straw that broke the camel's back, I guess. They intend to release the clues on the tomb to all interested parties as a sign of good sportsmanship."

Henry's eyes widened. "Which means every Magicians' Circle with resources and manpower will have the first step on a silver platter. So people like us will be locked out of the competition."

Analise nodded. "Exactly. But the Coven is going to keep the coin. And that's the only part that really matters."

Henry glanced at his coin sitting on the table. "What do you mean?"

"These coins aren't identical. Each of them has different writing and different images," Analise said, flipping the coin over while still having it touch its violet wrapping. "What tipped me off was this side."

The proverbial "heads" side of the coin had two profiles of men facing one another. Henry's Greek was poor, but he could still sound out names. On the edges, the leftmost face had the marker *Achilles*. The right face was named *Ptolemy*.

"The Latins' coin has someone else on it. The image was kind of small, but I think it was Lysimachus."

"The coins are a set. One for each of Alexander's heirs. The Diadochi," Henry voiced his epiphany as it came to him. He sat up. "Why are you telling me all this? I could take this information right now and leave."

Analise smirked. "Oh? And what exactly do you plan to do with that information? You have no connections to draw on except me. And you aren't exactly famous for your ability to pull heists."

"You wanna steal it?" Henry furrowed his brow. "From under the noses of that many Magicians?"

"Well, they aren't selling it." She scoffed. "My partner wants to meet us in Athens. She has a plan to get us to the coin."

"What does your partner want with the tomb?" Henry asked. "What do *you* want with it?"

"I can't answer that first one. But at the very least, she sounds...inexperienced. If it were to come down to it," Analise said. "As for the second one...let's just say I think it would be really stupid for *one* Circle to get all that ancient magic for themselves. I'll consider going into specifics if we have a deal."

"Better you than them, huh?" Henry huffed. "You're really strong-arming me here."

"That's kind of the point, Zhang. You're stubborn, but you're not stupid. Trying to do this alone would be suicide." Analise smirked. "But if it's any consolation, better me and my partner than your old squad and the Tiandihui, right?"

Henry grimaced. That *was* part of what he was here for—to make them realize the mistake they made in making an enemy out of him. Besides, it wasn't the first time he'd worked with people he didn't trust.

"Fine." He sighed. "But...I have a logistical issue. A good chunk of my money was in Morocco. So right now, aside from a four-hundred-dollar pair of butterfly swords...I'm flat broke."

"I figured as much." Analise sighed. "I'm not overflowing with cash myself. So, there's one other thing you'll have to help me with: I have a job with the Egyptians I have to deliver on."

"The Egyptians? Aren't they our competition? I'd figure they'd be hot contenders for Alexander the Great. We should...avoid them." Henry furrowed his brow.

Analise wrapped the coin back up in its purple cloth and golden thread. "Well, they're the only source of quick cash we have. If you'd like to go *beg* for a ferry ticket and try to win a shootout with your toy knives, be my guest. I, personally, have an affinity for firearms. Expensive, untraceable firearms."

CHAPTER FOUR
Arming up at Arethusa

Wind swept through the runway of the Tangiers airport as Min followed her squadmates out to the pavement. Her hands clamped on her ears, she squinted through both her billowing strands of hair and the dust kicked up by the jet engines on the plane in front of her.

She slowly let go of the vice grip on her temples as the engine wound down. The plane's door folded down, creating a staircase to the runway for the jet's passengers. She bowed at the waist with her squadmates, her left hand covering her right fist, proffered in salute.

Seven men and women in black-and-white combat silks disembarked, their faces obscured by opera masks and their chins parallel with the ground as they took each imperious step down to the runway.

Min had only ever laid eyes on Qin Squad once. They were named for the dynasty that first united all of China, as opposed to other squads like Zhao, who were named after the defeated kingdoms of the Warring States period. Foremost among them was their squad leader, callsign Huangdi, after the Yellow Emperor. He wore an appropriately yellow mask and carried a single broadsword at his hip, a Confucian spell scroll on a bandolier, and a Daoist talisman on a necklace. The leader of the Tiandihui's most elite squadron was a master in all three branches of Chinese magic, needing only to carry the bare essentials of each branch. The other members of Qin Squad were all named for emperors, heroes, and gods, but no one knew their real names. The only one Min did know was Qin 7, callsign Kongming. To her and the rest of Zhao Squad, he was Zhang Weiying.

"Good to see you, Zhao 1," Huangdi said, voice muffled by his mask.

"The pleasure is all mine." Mr. Fang stood from his bow. The other members of Zhao Squad followed suit.

"High Command has decided that due to the nature of our interloper, someone ought to share the burden in overseeing you," Huangdi informed him. "That way, one leader can focus on the pursuit of the tomb. The other can prevent us from losing face."

"As requested, we've also brought a resupply of spell components and weapons," said Qin 2, callsign Zetian, after the Tang Empress. Her stark white mask, tinted with blush eye shadow, looked back to the jet as former People's Liberation Army soldiers, now turned private soldiers for the Heaven and Earth Society, unloaded crates from the plane. The soldiers set the crates down and broke them open with crowbars.

"Germans, Latins, Egyptians, Greeks, Slavs, English, and even a few Defectors?" A mountain of a man with a red mask of Guan Yu, the god of war, chuckled. "This is gonna be a hell of a fight. It's a shame they didn't let us participate."

"The prospects for this quarry are too small to justify turning this hunt into an arms race," Huangdi said. "If we gain a better understanding of the tomb's contents...perhaps we might see combat ourselves."

The more Min heard about the circumstances of their mission, the more she dreaded it. It was bad enough that they had to run up against all these other Magician squads. It didn't help that Henry seemed bent on getting in the way.

She understood why he was angry, but it would be smarter just to let this go.

"One of us will join the fray at the very least." Huangdi glanced back at a lean man wearing a blue mask. "Kongming. You know our Defector, right?"

Weiying stood a little straighter as he spoke. "I regret to say that he is my older brother. Callsign Wukong."

Huangdi took a deep breath, not quite sighing. "Wukong, huh? He's the one who got in your way in Morocco?"

"He was an...unexpected element, yes," Mr. Fang said. "We were distracted by a squad of Latin Magicians while he made off with the coin. One of the Europeans actually provided an escape for him."

Huangdi paused. "Kongming, you take partial command here. You are to be a co-leader and focus your efforts on capturing Wukong when the opportunity arises."

"Capture?" Weiying asked. "The punishment for treason is typically death."

"Keep him from competing in this race. I won't make you kill your brother," Huangdi said. "Traitor or not."

Weiying nodded. "Thank you, Huangdi. But even though I was born of the same blood as this filthy mutt of a traitor, I do not consider him my brother anymore. The fact that he's lived this long since his conviction is spitting on the Tiandihui's honor."

"Your dedication is noted, Kongming." Huangdi nodded. "The rest of Qin Squad will begin setting up bases of operations around the Mediterranean and will assist in communication and intelligence during the hunt when we can. Stay in contact, Qin 7."

Weiying stood at attention until the rest of Qin Squad walked into the airport proper, followed by their soldiers.

Mr. Fang smiled at him. "It's good to see you again, *Xiao Wei.*"

Weiying tore off his mask, smiling at Min as Fang hugged their former member. She gave him a half-smile in return.

"You've really moved up in the world!" Shen chuckled, slapping him on the back. "How is it? Being on Qin Squad?"

"Stressful." Weiying sighed, tying his hair up in a bun. "But once all this is sorted out, they want me to start a new department for domestic arcane security. I'd be the head strategist."

"You've really left us behind, haven't you?" Min said.

"I mean, I think I've earned it." Weiying shrugged, as if suddenly realizing the inherent power imbalance here. "But with the new department...I could bring some people with me."

"Showing favoritism is generally frowned upon, *Xiao Weiying.*" Mr. Fang smiled.

Weiying scoffed. "So is going easy on my brother."

"'Going easy?'" Chen Bo towered over the lot of them before Lu Ying held him back.

"We didn't go *easy* on him, dear. I assure you." Lu Ying fluttered her lashes. "We just...underestimated him."

"Underestimate? Hanying? That's not possible." Weiying chuckled. Shen laughed with him. "What is there to underestimate? Aside from how insistent he is on making himself our problem."

"It's been two years, Weiying," Min said. "Hanying...he's improved. A lot. If he weren't working against us..."

Weiying sneered. "Well, last I checked, you wanted nothing to do with him."

She furrowed her brow. She *had* been among the most furious when she found out about Henry's betrayal. But in the months since his exile, she'd found herself doubting the conviction.

Still, the Tiandihui took Weiying's side. So Min's opinions would remain very private.

"Well, let's get you a room in our Riyad." Mr. Fang put an arm around Weiying's shoulders. "And get you into a less sweltering uniform."

Weiying pushed Mr. Fang's arm off. "I'll stay in uniform, thanks. A professional dresses appropriately if he's to do his job effectively. In that interest, I suggest the five of you put on your own uniforms. Else High Command will know how you've been representing us."

Out of sight of the others, Min scowled.

Weiying had always been this way. It had always been ignored for his aptitude for magic. Now that Zhao Squad was partially under his command, she couldn't help it if a shiver ran up her spine.

Henry let out the first sigh of true relief he'd had in over a year. He was clean, he had nothing to do until tonight, he had just finished a pizza, and was idly eating away at a Styrofoam cup of the snow-cone-esque dessert called granita as he drew oracle-bone script onto yellow *fulu* charm paper, his legs resting on the cast-iron chair across from him.

Stretching out before him was the Syracuse lagoon and a beautiful array of fiery orange and deep violet in the sky caused by the sunset. He'd even managed to find a spot with no tourists to disturb him.

Rows of sailboat masts filled the marina further down the coast of Ortigia, the tiny island that hosted the Syracusan old town, as the pleasant sea breeze ruffled his hair a bit. Someone on this sea-level walkway was playing a slow, relaxing tune on the piano, adding to the near-perfect ambience. It was almost as if he was on vacation. Almost.

Dressed in a loose shirt covered in flowering pink-and-orange patterns, Analise waved to Henry from a ways down the coastline strip. She was holding a manilla folder under her arm as she sat down at his table.

"I just finished translating." She grinned.

"Why, yes, my day's been lovely. Thank you for asking. How has yours been?" Henry smirked, glancing at her over a pair of aviators.

Analise frowned. "Oh, I'm sorry, would you like me to waste your time asking about frivolous bullshit, or would you like to know how to find the tomb of Alexander the Great?"

"You must be great at parties." Henry sighed. "Fine, spill."

"So, the coin." Analise pulled out a beat-up leather-bound journal not unlike Henry's own and flipped to a detailed sketch of both faces of the coin. She pointed to the face with the temple on it. "The inscription along the edge says, *The Fearful cannot believe in an honorable world. And The Honorable know the world kills the Fearful.*"

Henry raised an eyebrow. "Is that it?"

Analise spread her hands. "It's a coin. What else do you want?"

"Well, what about the image on the back?" Henry tapped his finger on the drawing of the back face. "Is there nothing about it?"

"It's...a temple. It could be any temple from here to Lebanon." She sighed.

Henry grimaced. "Let's shift focus a little bit and assume that we need all the coins to make sense of anything. We know where the second one's going to be. Did you get the information from your client?"

"*Partner,*" Analise insisted.

"*Client.*"

She scoffed and set the file folder on the table, sliding it to him. "Don't get any granita on it."

Henry muttered a random noise, opening the folder and looking over building plans, schedules, guest lists, and manifests for the artifacts being displayed at the event.

"The Latins are hosting this gala in tandem with the Greeks at the Acropolis Museum," Analise said. "Aside from them, the Germans, English, Slavs, Levantines, Egyptians, and Chinese will be sending representative combat squads to attend."

"Eight Circles...Jesus," Henry muttered, shifting through the papers. Mention of the Germans made him wonder if they had similar plans for either the girl from Morocco or Analise as the Chinese likely had for him.

"It's not...*that* bad," Analise insisted, though she didn't sound like she believed her own words. "Each Circle will only be sending one Squad. They can't risk losing more numbers than that over one treasure trove."

"Thank God we live in this time. Imagine twenty years from now. If this boom of Magicians keeps up, the Circles could send Magicians into battle like a meat grinder. They could take over their governments. Maybe the world," Henry said.

"Let's not think too far in the future." Analise pulled out a map of the museum grounds. "Any plans coming to mind?"

"What, you got nothing up there, Brainiac? I thought you *had* a plan. That was one of your selling points."

"We have means, not a plan. I'm not a combat Magician. This is your field."

Henry scoffed as he took the map from her. He began to scour the other documents, including details on the security system and the schedule for the event. "I mean, we can probably find the coin wherever it's stored before it gets put on display. As long as we can get ourselves on the guest list, things should go smoothly. If we can get by without magic, even better. They're probably looking out for magical threats, anyway."

"Hm...I don't know about forging our way onto the guest list, but I do know that my partner has her name on the list," Analise said. "You could go as her plus one."

Henry grimaced. "I don't know...I'd have to meet this partner of yours, who seems reluctant to show her face. Why is she even on the guest list? Doesn't that seem suspicious to you?"

"You can ask her yourself before we get to Athens. She wants to meet you as well." Analise pulled out her phone. "I'll...wait, I don't have your phone number."

"I'm just saying, anyone who has their name on that list is either being led into a trap or is dragging someone else into a trap." Henry opened his phone. "Fuck. I need to buy a sim card."

"Get an international plan," Analise said. "Do you have Signal? We don't want the other Circles being able to hack our communications."

"Oh, no, I've just used Whatsapp this whole time. And WeChat! Did I mention I'm a fugitive from the Chinese?" Henry's voice dripped with sarcasm as he exchanged contact information with her. "I'll see what I can divine from this client of yours. Any word on the Egyptians? What exactly is this job?"

"I'm selling some Minoan texts to them. They're willing to pay for any leverage over the Greeks they can get right now," Analise explained. "We'll get about fifteen thousand US for the ordeal, plus an order of firearms. Five for you, ten for me."

"Whoa, what?"

"I found the texts, I set up the deal. I should get a bigger cut."

He was *going* to ask why he was getting five grand, but he decided it was best not to bring that up. Maybe Analise had worse business sense than he gave her credit for. Especially considering her relationship with this mysterious client of hers.

"Which squad is doing the deal?" he asked.

"Atum Squad. Know anything about them?"

Henry grimaced, racking his brain. Egyptian Squad leaders always inherited the name of the god their squad was named for. So callsign Atum could be a different person every year. That said, Henry was familiar with Atum in an operational context.

"I think Atum 1 is a Tomb Walker. Can't die of age or...half the shit that makes people die. But I think he can only use baseline Hieroglyphic magic beyond that," Henry said. "And they have to have a Lectorist."

Lectorists could almost mind-control you if they knew your true name, along with several other true name-based magics. It was the whole reason Magicians used callsigns and pseudonyms in the first place.

"You need something for me to call you if they have a Lectorist," Analise said. "Your callsign...wasn't it Wukong? Am I pronouncing that right?" She wasn't.

"My true name is Chinese. You should be fine calling me Henry."

Analise sighed. "Alright...Well, we'd best hope things don't go south."

"The deal should be simple enough," Henry muttered. "But if they're here, no doubt they're looking for Alexander's tomb as well."

"I figured the Egyptians would have a head start over anyone else, considering the tomb's last sighting was in Alexandria," Analise said.

"It sank centuries ago," Henry said. "Until the Latins dug up that manuscript, there wasn't a magical way to find it. For whatever riddles we have to solve, the Egyptians will be our competition. They don't have any inherent advantages we know of. But that does mean they'll fight harder."

"Hm...I'll see what else I can dig up." Analise lounged in her chair. "We have until midnight, so we might as well enjoy the view. Things are going to get much more frantic after we hit Athens..."

Hours later, Henry and Analise climbed the short way up to the Fountain of Arethusa, a premier tourist site in old Syracuse, but almost completely devoid of people at this time of night. The ramparts that turned the island of Ortigia into a fortress split to make room for this odd freshwater spring only a few meters from the ocean.

Henry leaned over the iron fence between himself and the ten-foot drop into the water, admiring the palms and other plants growing on a small island in the middle of the fountain. "This is the meeting place? Really?" he asked.

"These are the coordinates." Analise shrugged.

"You'd think they'd want it to be a bit more secretive," he muttered.

"This is to our advantage," Analise said. "The more risk there is of people seeing us, the more dangerous it is to use magic."

"Yeah, that's exactly why I'm worried," Henry said.

"You know, this fountain is legendary." Analise gestured to the pit surrounding the spring, changing the subject.

"Yeah? How so?"

"Oh! I finally get to teach *you* something, history major."

"I'm a college dropout, and legends aren't exactly history."

"Don't take this from me," she said before clearing her throat. "This spring is thought to be the home of a nymph named Arethusa, who was a patron figure of ancient Syracuse. It's also one of only four places in Europe where papyrus grows." She pointed at the reeds surrounding the palm trees down below.

"Huh. Maybe that's why the Egyptians wanna meet here," Henry said. "They'll, like...walk out of the papyrus plants or something."

"I wouldn't hold your breath for that." She tapped him on the shoulder.

Henry turned to face the old town.

Headed by a black man in a trench coat, darkened spectacles, and a hat out of the thirties, a team of three men and two women walked out of the labyrinthine streets. Like many Magicians' Circles, the team was overwhelmingly young aside from the leader. Most Circles only sustained about five to ten concurrent members during the last few hundred years. Only recently had their numbers exploded.

Henry didn't quite have a solid theory as to why that was, but as far as he could tell, it was a reaction against an increasingly digitized and globalized world. The understanding required to break Solomon's Wisdom, which once took a lifetime of study and access to scarce knowledge, was more accessible than ever, if lacking in nuance and true mastery. Even though his time in China had left a bitter taste in his mouth, he didn't want its culture becoming a commodity to be cheapened and besmirched.

The other four seemed to be of Arabic-speaking Egyptian descent, with olive skin. Henry figured the leader must be Nubian or part of a Bantu ethnicity. He potentially had access tot he magic of a second culture.

The streetlamps provided fitting illumination for this midnight deal.

Henry and Analise approached, meeting them halfway across the plaza in front of the spring.

"Moneta." The bespectacled man smiled as he shook Analise's hand as he used her callsign. His accent was thick, yet Henry couldn't tell what kind of accent it was. The man glanced at Henry. "And friends." He looked back to Analise. "Birds of a feather flock together, I suppose."

"Atum. Good to see you."

"Is the information secure?"

Analise nodded. "Is my payment ready?"

"Ramses?" Atum looked to a tall, lean Arab man, no more than three years Henry's senior.

Ramses held aloft a briefcase handcuffed to his wrist before opening it. Analise got a look at the piles of money before he closed it again. Half of it was U.S. Dollars, the other half Euros.

Upon seeing the money, the tension in the air seemed to dissipate. Henry had never really been involved in non-combat situations in the Magicians' world. He was expecting them to be far more antagonistic.

"You're that Chinese Defector, aren't you?" said a girl with heavy eye makeup and a rather eccentric black-and-gold dress that looked like it belonged in a sci-fi novel.

"Oh, yeah!" The third man of their team said in far more accented English than the others. "If you ignore the beard..."

"Now, Cleopatra. We aren't here to pry," Atum said. "Though I don't think in all my days, I've ever seen two Defectors of different Circles work together."

"Really? Never?" Ramses asked.

"Maybe once...back during Ottoman times," Atum muttered. "But it takes an un-trustworthy soul to know one, so I doubt the prospect is often enticing."

"I heard you were a Tomb Walker, Atum. What's the time frame for 'all your days?'" Henry asked. "If you don't mind."

"Oh, I was born sometime during the Fatamid Caliphate. What, three hundred years ago?"

Henry's eyes widened. "Try a thousand. You're really that old?" Beyond Atum's immense age, Henry was happy to know that the immortal's mental faculties weren't all there.

"Tomb Walking is powerful. It can theoretically go on forever, so long as you do the ritual once every eighty years. Though I've lost count of how many times I've done it. I even remember trading with Chinamen like yourself on the Silk Road."

Henry blinked.

"Atum, you can't say 'Chinamen,'" Cleopatra hissed in Arabic.

"What, really?"

"It doesn't exactly have a positive connotation." Henry shrugged, joining them in speaking Arabic.

"My gods, I'm sorry. You have to understand that language changes happen really fast for me. I mean, it seems like yesterday you would've been speaking Anglo-Saxon."

"I'm not torn up about it. But is that why you dress like a jazz musician from the thirties?" Henry chuckled.

"I just really like this style." Atum grinned as he looked down at his trench coat.

For being the premier sortie squad of the Egyptian Circle, Atum Squad was surprisingly friendly.

But that was exactly what was putting Henry on edge.

Atum gestured to the unused tables sitting on the patio of a closed restaurant with an overhanging roof of red tiles. "Shall we conduct our business?"

As Atum Squad took up positions around the patio, as combat squads usually did during a tradeoff, Henry juxtaposed himself to Atum as Analise and the Egyptian Magician sat at the cast-iron table. Analise pulled a laptop out of her tote bag, along with a hard drive. She logged onto the computer and plugged in the hard drive.

Henry's eyes moved between the members of Atum Squad. His fingers grazed his butterfly swords tucked into his belt, since he'd somehow lost his sheath between here and Morocco. Analise spared a glance behind her, giving him a death stare like he'd never seen. He responded with his own, refusing to accept her apparent insistence on being gullible.

Ramses uncuffed his wrist from the money, setting the briefcase on the table as Analise put her laptop next to it and opened it.

A smile crept onto Atum's face as he looked over the texts. "Very nice..." he said. "And very fine work. I'm glad there were no issues. Nefertiti?"

The girl whose callsign was apparently Nefertiti came over to the table and placed a backpack on top of the money.

"Now, we did fulfill your request for ten thousand dollars' worth of your payment in the form of weapons and ammunition. But we do have to be candid that the weapons are enchanted, so they may not be used against the members of our Circle," Atum said. "Is that acceptable?"

Henry furrowed his brow. "Hang on a minute—

Analise cut him off. "It was expected."

"Moneta! We—" Henry hissed.

"We'll discuss later," Analise said. "Now, get our things."

Analise handed Atum the hard drive while Henry begrudgingly picked up the backpack and briefcase.

"Have a good night, Moneta. Hopefully, we'll meet again and continue our...profitable business together." Atum stood and tipped his hat as his squad filed out of the patio towards the fountain.

Ramses lifted his hand, as papyrus plants grew out of the fountain's walls and wrapped around Atum Squad. The plants closed up, then opened, starting to return to normal.

Atum Squad was gone.

"Huh. I guess you were right." Analise chuckled.

"Analise, what the fuck? These weapons are enchanted! They could be—"

"It'll be fine, Henry. I can strip most of the enchantments on my own." Analise sighed. "And they call *me* high-strung..."

"Well, you said it yourself—I'm a combat Magician, so..." Henry shrugged. "Let's just get to bed. We have an early train tomorrow."

Henry squinted as the sun blasted his face with heat, accompanied by fresh air. Having spent the last twenty-six hours on a car ferry, forced to sleep in the seat of a restaurant booth, he felt like a cave-dwelling creature stepping into light for the first time.

Both he and Analise were covered in a mix of sea grime, their own sweat, and grease. And in Henry's case, he was about to collapse.

Funny how an extra-long ferry could exhaust him as much as an all-out brawl with a squad of Magicians.

Magicians often had to take things like buses, trains, and ferries in order to avoid confrontations with other Magicians. Being trapped in an airplane for hours on end was the perfect circumstance for an assassination. More than one plane had gone missing over the ocean thanks to Magician conflicts. It was also far easier to smuggle weapons across borders by land and sea than by air.

Compared to the ferry, the bus ride was a breeze. Only three hours, and they'd gone from the port city of Patras across the Peloponnese and into Attica.

Not to mention that the buses in Greece were pretty nice. Especially compared to the one Greyhound Henry had ever taken, where someone had gotten stabbed halfway through.

This time, he was the most dangerous one on the bus, given the slew of handguns, shotguns, and rifles that the Egyptians had given him and Analise.

They'd had no time to wash up after the ferry ride, and as such, were both disgusting. That grime was starting to get...crusty was the best word he could think of.

The Athens Bus Terminal was only a ten-minute walk from the nearest metro station, and within the hour, Henry was heaving his backpack up into Monastiraki Square, right on the edge of ancient Athens.

The afternoon sun was sweltering, as it usually was, but thankfully, not many tourists were out and about at the moment, leaving the multicolored tiles visible and the Ottoman mosque and Orthodox church right across from each other unswarmed.

Cast in shadow by the sun, Henry caught the magnificent sight of the Parthenon's silhouette between the mosque and the metro station. The plateau-shaped hill dominated the skyline. "Holy shit..." He couldn't help but smile.

He wanted to go up there. Once they washed up, he wanted to go see it. And he wanted to see it at sunset. That would be perfect.

Henry flinched as Analise snapped her fingers next to his ears a couple times. "I know you're creaming your pants over those old rocks, but let's try to focus." She frowned.

"Yeah. Yes. Let's, uh...where are we staying?" He started following her away from the square and towards less colorful winding streets of stone brick.

"A hostel," Analise said. "It's clustered around a bunch of other hostels, so there'll be plenty of witnesses. Solomon's Wisdom won't be able to hold if we're attacked."

Cars carefully made brazen attempts to get through the streets while bikers and pedestrians owned the roads. Henry's stomach squirmed as his nose caught the scent of grilled meat from a gyro stand. The bus stations only had pastries and the ingredients for what he called "Out of Options," which consisted of a bag of chips, a bottle of water, and an ice cream from one of those little freezer units.

"Any word on squads in the area?"

"I haven't heard anything." Analise shrugged.

"Well, keep your guard up. The Hecatean Circle's headquarters is probably less than a half-mile walk from here. Plus all the visiting squads for the gala. We're in the belly of the beast."

Henry glanced to his right and found three massive windows that had been opened like garage doors, allowing him to look directly into a bar mixed with a common room filled with early twenty-somethings on their laptops. Undoubtedly a hostel.

He followed Analise around the building to the front, which had been covered in some strange mix between graffiti and street art depicting two lounging humanoid figures with photorealistic fox and raccoon heads on their necks. He frowned at the painting before entering through the glass door.

They checked in and unloaded their things in a room with six beds. The other four occupants were missing, probably out sightseeing.

Just before the two of them got ready to shower, Henry froze. "Wait...I only have one pair of clothes."

"I'll shower and then go buy you something while you wash up," Analise said. She immediately grabbed her things and locked herself in the room's en suite bathroom.

Henry sighed, claiming one of the lower bunks. He looked at himself in a mirror hanging on the wall over a long table. He poked and prodded at his face and hair, disgusted with his own visage.

He didn't consider himself a germaphobe or paragon of hygiene, but he had standards. To think he was travelling with a woman and looking like this…It was a bit embarrassing to say the least. Analise didn't come off the boat unscathed, but he looked like a feral dog compared to her.

As Analise showered, Henry went about setting up an account with a food-delivery app and ordered himself about thirty euros' worth of souvlaki and gyros.

The moment she stepped out of the bathroom, he moved past her and claimed the shower for himself.

"By the way, I'm washing my clothes in the sink!" Analise's shout was muffled through the door.

He scrunched up his nose at the sink, which was full of Analise's clothes, soaking in slightly soapy water. The severe discoloration of the water made him wary of his own clothes.

"Just get me something to wear!" he replied.

"What do you want?"

"Black shirt, nice shorts! And boxers!"

He took off his mandarin jacket and plunged it into the discolored soapy water, hoping whatever laundry strips Analise was using would soak up some of the filth from his favorite piece of clothing.

He spent twice as long as he usually did in the shower, making sure every speck of grime left his body. Now was his only chance to get clean. He had managed to arrange a meeting with Analise's "partner" for this evening. And this afternoon, he had plans.

He was *going* to see the Acropolis.

CHAPTER FIVE
Pub Crawl

Henry sat cross-legged, staring up in awe at the immense splendor of the Parthenon. Backlit by the setting sun, the Acropolis's megalithic structures towered over the few tourists left during the final hour of opening for the day.

Even covered in scaffolding for restoration and in ruins, the Parthenon's grandeur was more than anything Henry could express with words.

He could imagine it. How flawless the stonework was before time weathered it. How smooth the columns would've been. How vibrant the paint must've been. How mere men, over two thousand years ago, had put this together with iron-age machinery and bare hands.

What would it have been like to be a citizen of Athens, watching this building be constructed?

Greek and Roman culture had always been too mainstream for Henry's tastes. But sitting here in front of the epitome of Classical Greek architecture, he understood why it was so admired.

He returned to reality from his drug trip on sheer wonder alone to glance behind him at Analise.

Under the blue and orange of the setting sun, the city of Athens stretched out behind her in all directions. Wind rippled through both their hair, tossing it up.

Henry looked over the top of his aviators at the map of Athens that Analise had scribbled on a napkin she'd pinned down with a few rocks. She pulled a thread from a spool of what looked like gold, drawing an outline of the napkin with it to create an Arcane Detection Zone, just in case anything went sideways. An ADZ, prepped in advance, would let them track the movements of almost any Magician across a wide swath of the city.

Conveniently, the Acropolis was the best place to do it.

"When I was a member of the Tiandihui, they always used computers and phones for the ADZ. Why the napkin?" Henry asked.

"Computers and all their components mess with the integrity of the spell. Analog maps will always be more accurate."

"Okay...then why didn't you get, like...a tourist map? There were plenty at the hostel."

Analise fell silent for a moment. "I...didn't think of that."

Henry scoffed, laughing.

"Ass," Analise muttered.

She pulled a small circular device made from brass filigree from her tote bag, a polished gemstone inlaid with the centerpiece. She twisted the radar, causing the mechanisms inside to start spinning as she laid it next to the map.

Eventually, the whirring of the gears slowed down, causing the gemstone to glow a faint green.

Analise held the glowing gem over the map, lighting up the golden thread. Beams of light concentrated from the thread to several pinpoints on the map.

At least, the city side.

Henry snapped a photo of the radar projection.

"Shit. The Hecatean Circle has a countermeasure in place, lowering the range," Analise muttered. "I need to get a view for the historical city's side. I'm going to go find a better-placed cliff."

"Want me to go with you?"

"And tear you away from the 'Epitome of Classical Greek architecture?'" Analise asked. "I couldn't bear to break your heart like that."

"Wait...was I speaking out loud?"

"The wind carries your voice." She scoffed. "Turn your radio on."

Henry put his radio in his ear as Analise picked up her components and moved.

He stared out across Athens, trying to reconstruct the ancient city in his mind and thinking about the fact that ancient Athenians from two and a half millennia ago had walked the same ground he sat upon.

It was his opinion that, in the modern day, too many people found the world to be a mundane and boring place. Especially with how popular fantasy media was. Not enough people had enough appreciation for the wonders of their own world.

Speaking from experience, Henry would much rather not know that Magicians existed. It had only served to rip his family apart and make him a fugitive.

However, solving a puzzle crafted by Alexander the Great himself was kind of the dream for an ancient and medieval historian like himself.

Should he even consider himself a historian? He was educated, yes. But on his own time, not by an institution. Then again, most college graduates he knew were morons.

In the midst of a thought, he was interrupted.

"Beautiful, innit?"

Whoever was speaking had a thick Irish accent.

Henry glanced over his shoulder at a lanky, clean-shaven man, likely around his age, wearing an olive-green polo shirt. The Irish accent had really put a different image in his mind, because this guy looked as Greek as the sun was bright.

"That it is." Henry looked back at the Parthenon.

The man took a seat next to him. "Yianni." He held out a hand.

"Henry." He shook it.

"Where're you from, Henry? California? New York?"

"Iowa." Henry smirked. "We have corn for days, a creative writing program, and 'Oh, Christmas Tree' as our state anthem. How about yourself?"

While Henry was acting chummy, he had a script in his head for whenever he needed to talk to a stranger while travelling. He wasn't the kind to be all standoffish. Mostly. It paid to make others feel a false sense of security, whether or not he intended on exploiting that.

"Right, Henry. I gotta ask if you seen a friend o' mine. Wanna make sure he stays outta trouble."

"I don't think I'd know any of your friends..." Henry muttered. "But I—"

"Oh, no, no, no. You'd know this lad for sure! Got an...impressionable mug, he does." Yianni pulled a folded photo out of his pocket and showed him. "Look familiar, right?"

It was a picture of Henry.

"Motherfucker..." He sighed.

"Look at 'im...so serious..." Yianni chuckled, flicking the photo.

"Be careful what you say next," Henry growled. "I can rip you to shreds in—"

"In more time than it'll take to activate the Triskelion behind you. Move a muscle I don't fancy, including turning to look at it, and you'll learn what it's like to be two places at once."

Henry clenched his fists in his lap. A Triskelion? That would make this guy Celtic. Not that the accent wasn't already tipping him off.

"I can't imagine you're here to collect a measly five-thousand-dollar bounty," Henry muttered. "Unless you're just that broke."

"They didn't tell you? Your bounty's gone up! Two hundred fifty thousand."

Henry's eyes widened. "Fifty times?" he hissed.

"As much as I'd like to cash in on that payday, I've got my eyes on a different prize," Yianni said, plucking Henry's earpiece out and tossing it off the edge of the Acropolis. "The one in your pocket."

Henry bit his tongue as understanding hit him. "I see..." He started to chuckle.

"This is funny, huh? You don't wanna fuck with me, Yankee."

"Maybe." Henry sighed. "So, I can add the Celts to the people who have me on their shit list."

"Lie low, and you might just find yourself off it."

"Tell Belgae 1, or whatever squad your higher-ups sent, to focus on their real enemies. Every Circle on this side of the world is after the same thing, so don't play coy."

Yianni blinked as if falling asleep for a second before responding. "Maybe you can tell him that yourself when I drag you to him."

If the Celts were keeping an eye on him, they might pin the target on his back the moment he stole the Latins' coin. Half the reason he could even work as a single Defector was because the Circles constantly underestimated him.

But stealing that coin would naturally pin a target on his back regardless.

That said, this Yianni fellow looked biracial. And typically, a biracial Magician had access to abilities from both parents' cultures, which made people of every Circle look upon you with suspicion, regardless of your loyalties. So there was a fair chance of that being the case.

Now was no time for timidity. Or so Henry thought. As Sun Ce always said, "If you are weak, appear strong to the enemy." Yianni was trying his damnedest to follow that, but Henry could see through it.

If he outed Yianni as a Defector, that might lead to him panicking, acting irrationally, and causing a scene. If Henry had the actual power here, the potentially explosive spell behind him notwithstanding, perhaps he should play this looking weak.

"Hand over the coin, Wukong," Yianni demanded.

"I would if I could." Henry shrugged, ignoring his old callsign. "I don't have it."

That was true. Analise had it. He had planned to ask her for it back, though.

Yianni furrowed his brow.

"Turn out my pockets if you want," Henry said. "Just don't make me go get it from its hiding spot. Otherwise, that Triskelion threat of yours becomes useless. And I can silence you in a heartbeat."

"I don't think you'll have to move a muscle." Yianni patted him on the shoulder before standing up and walking in the direction in which Analise had headed off. He knew. Or guessed. Didn't matter.

Henry cursed under his breath and cultivated a small amount of Qi before expelling it into Metal style as he launched himself into a backflip. He rolled away from where he'd been sitting, prepared for an explosion.

But when he stood, he found nothing that looked like a Triskelion. He'd been duped.

He gritted his teeth and sprinted after Yianni, who had already gotten a head start on him. Without the time to take any more cultivating breaths, he had to get by on his prowess alone. He leapt over a set of uneven stairs, and as Yianni rounded the corner of the second, smaller edifice on the Acropolis's peak, he screamed, "Moneta!"

Henry slid around the corner of the temple, spraying gravel off the side of the mountain as the Celtic Magician he was after pulled a Shillelagh, a thorny walking stick topped by a large knot and a mainstay of Celtic martial magic, and grabbed Analise, threatening her.

Henry froze, unsure of how to proceed.

"Hand me the coin, and no one gets hurt, lass," Yianni growled.

Analise's breath was panicked, though her composure somehow maintained itself on her face.

If Henry took a cultivating breath, Yianni's arcane senses would notice the Qi unless he was distracted.

He met Analise's eyes and nodded. "Give it over."

She gave him a wary look in return, but obliged. "Front pocket. On the left."

Yianni shoved his hand in her left pocket, giving Henry an opening to take a cultivating breath. Energy flowed into his lungs, empowering his muscles with the quick-twitch speed of Metal Style.

He closed the distance in less than an eyeblink and grabbed at Yianni's wrist to control his weapon. Analise threw herself out of the fray as Henry trapped Yianni's free hand before he could switch his Shillelagh over.

Dry, brambly vines burst out of the ground around Henry's foot as he went to sweep Yianni's legs out from under him, the magic throwing his balance off. The Celtic Magician took the opening to pin Henry to the ground, pressing the length of the Shillelagh onto his throat.

Henry struck both of Yianni's elbows, freeing his windpipe, before grabbing the man by his hair and bashing his skull into the ground hard enough to make him go limp.

He pushed Yianni's unconscious body off him, scrambling to his feet and breaking his ankle out of the bramble.

"Holy...did you kill him?" Analise hissed.

Henry shook his head. "Probably concussed him, though. I thought we could get some info..." He panted, rubbing his sliced-up ankle. "Shit..."

"I still can't believe he snuck up on you like that." Analise shook her head. She sat at the one chair in their dorm room in a pair of tight jeans and a green top made up of a network of overly complicated straps, a coffee in hand and her laptop open. "I also can't believe I thought you were actually going to hand the coin over for my safety."

"It's not like he *really* got the drop on me. A hundred bucks says he's a Defector," Henry said, tightening some very improvised paracord bindings around Yianni's wrists. "Plus, you would've worn my guts for garters if I actually let him get away with the coin."

"You know people aren't supposed to be unconscious for this long, right?" Analise asked.

"Eh. You get like...three freebie concussions." Henry clipped their one and only Nullifier band around the Irishman's wrist. It was a golden bracelet with a ruby in the center that cut off one's access to magic. It was a talisman of Levantine make, since Hebrew magic was the only type of magic close enough to Solomon's Wisdom to do such a thing.

"So are your arcane senses really that bad?" Analise scoffed. "I thought you were exaggerating."

"I think I underplayed it more than anything," Henry said. "If someone, say...shot a fireball directly at me, I'd feel the heat before I felt the magic strongly enough to notice."

"Hm...that might be a problem."

"No way, really?" Henry asked, deadpan.

"What do you sense from this?" Analise pulled out their wrapped coin, which had almost been stolen an hour ago.

"Only a little buzz. I can't even feel it when I'm more than ten feet away."

"I mean the pattern. The beat. The magical resonance."

Henry sighed, but closed his eyes. He tried to listen for the magical energy radiating off the coin. He put his all into it until he gasped. "It's..." he started.

"Irregular, right?"

Most magical objects gave off a resonant pattern like music bars. It could be a constant pattern, it could be like a heartbeat, it could be three beats like a waltz, or even like jazz.

But while there seemed to be a four-beat pattern, the pauses between them were different each time. The first time, the pause was after the first beat. Then the third beat. Then the fourth beat, then the second.

"There's an incredibly complex magic here, but it doesn't seem to do anything," Analise said. "I'm thinking it's a scent for us to follow. When you steal the coin, look for this pattern. That way, you know it's real."

"I'm less worried about the actual stealing of the coin," Henry said. "I just hope this partner of yours is trustworthy."

"We're Defectors, Henry." Analise sighed, pulling a pendant out of her bag. "Take this before you go. We don't need any more surprises."

"Thanks," Henry said, taking the paracord with a smooth white stone dangling off a hole bored in the center. "What is this?"

"A river stone," Analise said. "It'll heat up when significant magical resonance aside from your own gets near you. That way, you can actually sense when someone's using magic."

"So, I take it you're going to watch him?" Henry nodded at the unconscious Celt sitting on his bunk.

"I think we should just kill him." Analise shrugged. "He'll be a liability otherwise."

"We have enough on our plate right now. I think adding 'murder coverup' to our to-do list is gonna be a bigger problem," Henry said, fastening the paracord around his neck. "And I'm telling you, that guy doesn't have any friends in high places. I know the type, and he is *not* it."

"All the more reason for him to rat us out to anyone." Analise sighed. "Fine. I'll watch him. I have a book I wanted to finish anyway."

"You're the best!" Henry flashed her a grin before slipping out of the dorm.

He headed down to the common room, then looked up the location on his phone as he left the hostel. Analise's partner had told him to meet her at the Circus City Hostel and to sign up for the pub crawl there at nine o'clock.

It was only a five-minute walk, and he barely had time to pick a song to listen to on his earbuds before he got there.

This hostel was much cozier than his, with the décor feeling less like an industrial garage mixed with a Starbucks and more like a family home—lots of wooden furniture, cushions, wooden floors, and warm lighting.

Unsure of who he was supposed to meet, Henry discovered that a thirty-something Greek woman was getting people together for the pub crawl. So, after he forked over fifteen euros to sign up, he indulged in some idle conversation. Or, at least, he tried.

He introduced himself to everyone, but quickly nosedived a burgeoning conversation with a group of four guys when he found out they were all part of the same fraternity. Groups were bad enough to penetrate, but any variety of the "lads-on-tour" group archetype was best avoided in general.

Instead, he struck up some idle conversation with a pair of British-Indian sisters, which went well at first.

But once they stopped talking about travel plans and where they'd been to already, he told them he was from America, which somehow prompted them to ask about a recent school shooting.

How was he supposed to respond to that? Practically speaking, he hadn't lived in America for almost five years now. He kept up to date with current events, but only the stuff that mattered on a large scale, like the Turkish elections this year. Furthermore, it would be somewhat hypocritical of him to chastise American gun control when he broke many of those very laws in several countries to ensure he wouldn't die due to other people breaking those laws. Even in America, it was illegal for a civilian to buy an automatic rifle, and here he was hiding a cartel boss's wet dream in a duffel bag under his bunk bed. And all that was assuming he was in favor of such policies, which could only be the case if he hadn't been living in an authoritarian hellhole like China.

And then came the dread-inducing realization that aside from history, geopolitics, travel, and magic, he had nothing to talk about. He couldn't even talk about his job without risking a break in Solomon's Wisdom.

He could talk a little bit about the alternate-history manuscript he had been passively working on, but the sisters proved to have little interest in it.

As his conversations died, the river stone under his shirt began to heat up.

He threw a glance behind him and widened his eyes.

The German girl from Morocco—she was right behind him, talking to someone else. She didn't seem to have noticed him. It was hard to recognize her at first, since last time, she hadn't been wearing glasses. Not to mention that the dark red blouse and jean shorts she'd worn in Morocco were a far cry from the long black pants and the patterned green-and-orange feathers covering what Henry could only presume was a swimsuit top she was wearing now.

She was shorter than him by half a head or so, with wavy brown hair that got lighter at the ends and soft features that seemed inviting and approachable.

Who was this woman? Why did she want the coin? Was she an enemy or an ally?

Was *she* the partner?

She met his eyes, and he could see recognition spark in her gaze.

Henry kept his eyes on her as he let the blade of his rope dart slip into his hand from the wrap around his wrist. Weaving through the small crowd, he listened in on her conversation as he came up next to her. They were talking about sightseeing—something about an all-in-one ticket.

"There's an all-in-one ticket? How much is it?" Henry jumped in.

"Oh, only like thirty euros," the girl said. "But it's not really worth it if you've already been to most of the sites."

"I just got in today, so that'll definitely be worth the money." Henry approximated a smile. His heart slammed into his ribcage, full of anxiety, as he tightened his grip on the dart.

"Where are you from?" she asked, not showing any sign of recognizing him after the first instance.

"America. The Midwest, corn-growing area. How about yourself?"

As they began talking, the person she'd been previously talking with found a new conversation to join.

"Southern Germany. Right near the border with France," she answered.

Henry touched her side with the tip of his rope dart. She glanced down at it before looking back at him, slightly irritated. Not what he was expecting.

"There's no need for that," she whispered.

"I'm inclined to disagree."

"I'll scream."

"I'll knock the wind out of you. Unless you'd rather I cut your throat," Henry said. "Who are you?"

"I'm happy to answer all your questions. But only if you play nice."

Henry narrowed his eyes, hesitating as he tempered his defensive instinct. Unfortunately, diplomacy was needed here. He could burst into a whirlwind of physicality if needed, but it wasn't getting him far right now.

He folded the dagger back into the wrap of rope on his arm and shifted around, facing her. "Volubilis, Morocco. Five days ago. You were there."

"As were you."

"You brought me to Syracuse?" He waited for her to nod. "Why? I don't like having outstanding debts."

The girl laughed, startling him. "It's not a debt. You don't have to pay me back."

Henry blinked. Was she fucking with him? "So, what, you just saved my life out of the goodness of your heart? Not so you could recruit me into...whatever arrangement you have with Moneta?"

She shrugged. "Couldn't I have?"

Henry scoffed. "We're Magicians. Kindness gets us killed."

"You know...the least you could do, if you're so intent on paying me back, is offer an introduction." She sighed.

Henry gave her a side-eyed look. She probably already knew his name. But she held the cards, so he offered his hand. "Henry Zhang."

"Marion. Marion Gutenberg." She shook it. Her touch was warm and soft, nothing like the firm, begrudging handshake he'd been prepared to give and receive.

As their eyes met, Henry felt something odd. Or, rather, an odd absence of something. She wasn't scheming behind her hazel eyes. At least, he couldn't tell if she was.

Both were terrifying prospects in different ways.

"So, what do the Germans want with the tomb? Or me, for that matter?"

Marion shrugged. "I wouldn't know. I don't work for the Germans. I'm as much a Defector as you are, Heinrich."

"Heinrich?"

"I think it's a cooler version of your name." She grinned.

"The only kind of people who associate more German-ness with being cool are kink-club enthusiasts and neo-Nazis." Was she trying to get in his head by saying his name wrong? Was she trying to be condescending and assert her authority?

She laughed in response. "I don't think it's *that* narrow."

"Funny. Act like we're buddies if you want. But don't think I've forgotten about how you tried to steal the coin away from me," Henry said. "What's with that?"

"It was an honest mistake." She pursed her lips. "I thought you were with the Chinese, not a Defector."

"Does that matter?"

"More than you know. Why do you think I asked Analise to offer you a job?"

That had been less of an offer and more of a browbeating. Henry hardened his eyes. "I don't work for anyone. Especially not on this job."

"I'm not asking you to work *for* me. Just *with* me." Marion sighed. "Did you have any...particularly vivid dreams before waking up in Syracuse?"

Henry thought it wasn't possible to furrow his brow any further, and yet he managed. "You had it too?"

Her inscrutable expression broke into a smile. "Thank God..." She chuckled. "I thought I might've been wrong."

Should he also feel relieved? "What are you talking about? What do you know about it?" He interrogated her, getting closer with each question, as if worried she'd try to run.

"If you've had the dream, I don't know much more than you. But that was Alexander the Great himself, trying what I can assume is his best to communicate with us and lead us to his tomb."

Henry frowned. "Why would Alexander want us to dig up his tomb?"

Marion shrugged. "Not sure. But it seemed like fun."

Henry scoffed. "You need to come up with a better lie for your motive."

"Oh, and you're going to be all transparent with me?"

"Just some advice for winning me over." He raised his hands in surrender. "I won't pry."

"I know as Defectors, we're supposed to be independent actors and rogue Magicians, but...I don't know, I felt like we could help each other out," Marion said. "I mean, we're already working together. So? Let's make an alliance."

Henry grimaced. "You just called attention to how we aren't being candid with one another. Temporary truce. That's as much as you're getting."

Marion sighed, looking disappointed. "I suppose I'll have to take that."

After shaking hands with her again, Henry recalled very little about how he got from there to twelve drinks in, at the third bar on their crawl. The bottomless sangria at the second bar, however weak it was, might've had something to do with it.

"So, what made you break Solomon's Wisdom?" Henry asked, trying not to yell, but also striving to be heard over the pounding music of the third bar. In a desperate attempt to be a club without being a club, this bar insisted on slamming techno trash into his skull and hitting his eyes with a flashbang of strobe lights.

The cave-like interior and fake foliage gave off a completely discordant atmosphere. Henry and Marion sat at a wooden table on a terrace looking over the dance floor and bar below as they talked.

"Honestly? It's a little silly."

"Come on!"

"Oh, fine. I...read too many fairy tales. And mythology books. I haven't even started university yet."

"Really?" Henry chuckled. "The world-encompassing ancient spell that hides all of the Magician world from humanity. And you broke it with fairy tales?"

She scoffed. "Oh, yeah? How did you do it, genius?"

Henry broke into full-bellied laughter. "History books! I dropped out of college!"

Marion gasped with faux outrage. "Ass!"

"Hey, even if I did have room to talk, you shouldn't give a shit. You're a Magician. That's what matters," Henry said. "So, that makes you a Religion Wisdom? Or Occult?"

"Religion," Marion said. "Though I could've been a History Wisdom. I *love* Greek and Roman history."

"Greek and Roman? That's so basic!" Henry scoffed, leaning back in his seat.

"'Basic?' What do you mean, 'basic?'" She feigned offense. "What are you into?"

"Ancient China. The Bronze Age Collapse. Mesopotamia. The older it is, the cooler it is for me."

"So, what, you're a hipster historian?"

"Oh...oh, I don't like that." Henry pinched the bridge of his nose, still grinning.

"Yeah?"

"Yeah, no...that...that's way too accurate for comfort." He chuckled. Marion laughed.

A waitress came over to serve them and a larger table of other pub crawlers complementary shots. Henry and Marion knocked their glasses together, though he was distracted by a sudden beat drop from a nearby speaker.

"Wait, wait, wait! Do it again! You have to look me in the eyes, or it's seven years of bad sex!" Marion insisted.

They did it again before drinking. The liquid was really sweet, with just a hint of alcohol behind it as it went down his throat.

She scoffed. "What is this, orange juice?"

"Even for me, that was weak," Henry said as Marion took both their glasses.

She tapped them twice against the table, magically causing them to refill with a clear liquid.

Henry's eyes widened. "Holy shit!"

"Here, again!"

They toasted and drank.

Henry coughed once the last of it went down, his throat burning. "Oh, what the hell was that?"

"Really? It was just vodka."

"What kind?" He hacked.

Marion laughed. "I forget America's drinking age is so high!"

"That"—Henry got the last of his coughs out—"and I'm not much of a drinker to begin with."

"Don't worry. I'll make sure you don't end up pissing in an alleyway if you get shitfaced."

"That little trick you did with the glasses. Can all the Germans do it?"

"It'd be on theme, that's for sure." She chuckled. "But no, it's because of these."

She held up her hands, wiggling her fingers as two Germanic runes shimmered into existence as tattoos on her palms.

"What kind of Magician are you, then? Got anything else in your arsenal?"

"I broke Solomon's Wisdom with religion, so my specialized practice is Script magic. But I dabble in everything," Marion said. "How about you?"

"I know you must think I'm an incredible magical artist," Henry said with theatrically inflated confidence, "but would you believe that I'm actually really shit at magic?"

Marion shook her head. "You don't want me to answer that. I saw you fight in Morocco."

"Well, I'm not exactly a star pupil," Henry said. "I was always better at fighting. And I broke in with history. So, naturally, I'm a Martial Magician. I specialize in southern styles."

"What does that mean?"

"You remember the Chinese Magicians from Volubilis? They were my old squad."

Marion scoffed. "No offense, but they didn't really have their heads in the right place for that sortie."

"No, they did not. But most of them, except the old guy, Mr. Fang, use northern styles. Very flowy, graceful, lots of jumps and acrobatics," Henry explained. "Southern styles have taller stances, way more hand movements. We're more about power, brutality, and speed. I mostly practice Wing Chun, which is probably among the fastest styles."

"My God, you're a nerd." Marion giggled.

"I'd rather be a nerd about something useful than...I think my brother broke Solomon's with art," Henry said defensively.

"Fair enough. Every time I try to cast something, I end up with my ass on the floor because some Martial Magician just flips me over his shoulder," Marion said.

"That's how I win fights most of the time. Giving a Magician time to think or cast is just a bad idea," Henry said. "Though once a squad has a body to put in front of me, the long-range spells do me in pretty quick. Opposite problems, I guess."

Why had he told her that? He knew when magic was being used *on* him, at the very least. Maybe...

He was just having a good conversation. For him to attribute that to magical manipulation was somewhat worrying.

"That's why we should work together!" Marion said. "I'm a defensive caster! We cover each other's weaknesses!"

"We'll see about that." Henry leaned back, crossing his arms. "So...do you have a plan?"

CHAPTER SIX
A Hellenic Heist

"Check, check. This is your WAC, callsign Moneta. Do you copy?" Analise's voice came in over the radio in Henry's earpiece.

"Copy," Henry said.

"Callsign Sunna. Copy," Marion followed.

"Henry, who's copying?" Analise asked. "What's your callsign?"

"You don't need to know it."

"Damnit, just make a new one."

Henry took a moment. "Uh...how about Nezha?"

Analise hesitated. "Fine."

Henry and Marion were sitting in the back of a limousine. The gala's attendees were a mix of well-to-do philanthropists, renowned scholars from the Archaeological Society, journalists, and Magicians.

The Magicians would stand out with traditional or historically-based clothing. To blend with the lay people, Henry and Marion had opted for more modern styles.

Henry's clothing was something between a tuxedo and traditional *hanfu* clothing, being made up of several layers of black robes, though they had cuffs on the arms instead of traditional loose sleeves. He had also opted for pants.

Meanwhile, Marion wore an expensive-looking dark red silk dress adorned with small bits of gold jewelry to go with the sunburst pendant hanging down to her chest from a chain necklace.

"Who's Nezha?" Marion asked, fiddling with her hair, tied up in the back of her head.

"A Chinese guardian deity." Henry shrugged. "I like the story."

"You'll have to tell it to me sometime."

The last thing Henry wanted to do was tell her anything else. Likely due to the alcohol, he had ended up spilling way more about himself than he was comfortable with last night, and he didn't think he got the same amount of information in return.

"I'll keep watch on the Arcane Detection Zone. Until I have eyes on the storage room, stick to your roles," Analise said.

Henry glanced out the window at the streets of Athens. "You managed to get an invite to this thing in spite of being a Defector. How'd that happen?"

"That's because as much as the Order of Cologne doesn't like me, they can't exactly afford to lose me," Marion said, gazing out the window on her side. "Every so often, they'll invite me to a function or a negotiation or what have you in an effort to win me back."

"Really?" Henry turned to her and raised an eyebrow. "And what is it about you that makes you such a valuable asset?"

"I can make infinite beer." She smirked.

Henry scoffed. "Oh, yeah, you must be priceless to High Command. Don't let the Slavs hear about your vodka trick."

"For your information, that 'trick' saves me upwards of a hundred euros per month." Marion frowned.

Henry furrowed his brow. "Well...that's *one* symptom of alcoholism you can solve with magic."

Marion sat up as she glanced out the window. Henry followed her gaze. They were almost at the venue. The Acropolis was lit up by spotlights, the sun having set, and tourists were starting to mingle with the locals as rivers of pedestrians made their way to bars and clubs for their Saturday night.

"You know, the coin we're after was mine," she said. "The Latins stole it from me while I was trying to get you out of Morocco."

"Wait, what?" Henry sat up, his brow furrowed. "Why didn't you tell me that before?"

"Well, I didn't want to, like...guilt you into helping me."

"Then why tell me now? How else am I supposed to react to that?"

"Okay, I wanted to guilt you a little bit," Marion admitted. "I figured it'd be less embarrassing if you heard it from me."

"'Embarrassing?' I...whatever. We'll get it back, alright?" Henry assured her.

"The museum is heavily warded, so don't think about trying any magic, no matter how small," Marion warned.

"What about enchantments?"

"You're risking it, but as long as the magic stays inactive, it should be fine."

"The only time it would be active is if we had to get into a fight." Henry put something from the folds of his suit into the crook of his ear.

Marion activated her radio. "We're pulling up to the venue, Moneta."

The Acropolis Museum was a massive glass-and-metal square with sections that had been shifted diagonally ajar like a Rubik's Cube to give viewers the impression it wasn't just a cube with extra steps. Flat panels of glass and synthetic-looking concrete as tall as three houses stacked on each other dominated the building. Henry's nose scrunched up at the abhorrent modern architecture being used to house pieces of far superior classical architecture.

The limo pulled up a ramp and entered a line of other limos, but it seemed all the cameras were focused on the philanthropist subset of attendees. Luckily, all the journalists were kept outside by a pair of armed guards in front of a row of glass doors.

Henry opened the car door and offered his hand to Marion. She took it and linked her arm around his, as was typical for formal events. The two of them headed for the entrance across a polished stone walkway and under an oddly-shaped veranda dotted with spotlights. They avoided the carpet rolled out for the famous attendees and passed under a pair of thick, featureless white columns holding the veranda up.

They maneuvered around a small hole in the ground, the opening showcasing the foundations of an ancient building, now in ruins. Two Greek men with tac-vests and assault rifles stopped them at the door as a woman with a metal detector asked them to spread their arms. The woman ran the detector over every surface but their heads before patting them down.

"Name?" asked another woman holding a clipboard with the guestlist on it.

"Marion Gutenberg." She tilted her head to gesture at Henry. "He's my plus one."

"Ah. Welcome, Ms. Gutenberg. Have a pleasant evening." The woman bowed her head and swept an arm out. With that, they were allowed inside.

The museum's entrance was marked by another, much larger hole that peered into the level beneath it, which was covered in blocks and pieces of the structures on the Acropolis. Mostly the Parthenon. Glass railings and concrete columns lined the opening and the spotlights illuminating the artifacts used warm light to try to contrast against the cold, clean building.

Partygoers in more usual formalwear roamed the main hall in front of a massive stage while some kind of electronic dance music spewed from a sound system. But there was also a noticeable presence of either very young adults or very old people, the former outnumbering the latter by a significant margin, dressed in traditional clothing for a myriad of cultures.

"We're inside, Moneta," Marion reported.

"Copy. I'll get back to you with the coin's location."

"Why are they playing club music?" Henry asked as they waded into the crowd. "It doesn't really mesh well with the historical costumes."

Marion chuckled. "Most people here are under the age of thirty, so…we're bound to hear stuff like that at some point."

Henry grimaced. "Gross."

The two Magicians waded through the crowd, finding themselves standing at a small table in front of a big portable stage covered in metal scaffolding and lights. A projector cast the logo of the Archaeological Institute of America on the blank back of the stage.

Marion sighed, leaning on the table. "Well, we have some time to kill before Analise locates the coin. I take it your idea of fun is looking at these old rocks."

"Don't throw shade at me, Ms. I-Read-Percy-Jackson-Once." Henry scoffed, catching sight of a bar. "You want something to drink?"

"Yes, but we're far too unfamiliar for me to begin trusting your taste in wine," Marion said. "I'll be right back."

She pulled away and headed towards the bar. In that dress, he could hardly resist watching her walk away. He shook his head. No. He met this girl *yesterday*.

Well…technically not yesterday, but their first meeting was a fight. She was far from trustworthy in his eyes.

Henry felt something poking into his back. "And that's twice this week I've caught you off-guard."

Henry recognized the voice immediately. "Min?"

Min circled around him, joining his table. "You're losing your edge, Zhang."

"Sure, I am." Henry smirked.

His heart skipped a beat upon seeing her. She brushed a strand of wavy hair aside, as she'd forgone the traditional headdresses and robes for a simple bun and a black, green, and gold qipao. Seeing her delicate features in person, without the presence of a mission in his mind, brought several complicated memories bubbling to the surface.

She, like everyone else, had sided with Weiying. But less than the others. So, if she could remain civil, he could.

"You know, if it weren't for you, we wouldn't have had to go to this event in the first place." She narrowed her eyes, crossing her arms over her chest.

Henry chuckled. "How awful. I hardly recognize you out of your silks."

Min tilted her chin up. "Come on, Hanying. Do you mean to tell me you *didn't* steal that coin to see me all dolled-up?" She flourished her hand down her side, her deadpan face giving the move a sarcastic edge.

Henry smoldered, that comment picking at an old wound. "Give me more credit than that."

"Interesting choice, by the way." Min pinched the sleeve of his suit. "Did you make this yourself? Looks sharp."

"You're not so bad yourself."

She scoffed. "I don't feel it. This is worse than that function we had to go to in Shanghai."

"It's the music. Sets the completely wrong tone," Henry said. "You come here with the rest of Zhao Squad?"

Min nodded. "They're...somewhere around here."

"Who'd you partner up with? Shen?" Henry laughed. "Mr. Fang?"

"Ugh, no. Mr. Fang would never." Min chuckled. "And Shen...I'd rather go with you, Defector or not, than go with that douchebag."

"I...I'll choose to take that as a compliment. So, you flying solo?"

"Not quite," a different, colder voice said from behind.

Henry froze, goosebumps breaking out on his neck. The patch of skin between his shoulder blades burned. He tensed his back muscles.

Hair pinned in a traditional crown and dressed in a white shirt, a navy inner robe, and a pale blue outer robe with aquatic designs embroidered into the silk, Zhang Weiying walked up next to Min, chortling.

"Hanying." Weiying wore a smug grin, offering his hand. "How've you been?"

Henry gulped. He was slow to take it, but he did. "Weiying."

"How long has it been? Ten months? A year?"

"A year and a half," Henry muttered, keeping his face dead to hide the cauldron of emotions boiling in his gut.

His every organ felt ready to burst. Not only was his brother here, but he was with Min. Something about that felt like salt in that old wound, even if he knew it was just for the event.

"I missed you in Morocco," he said, managing to keep up his facade.

"That was Zhao Squad's mission. I'm on Qin Squad now."

Henry's eyebrows raised. Qin Squad was the Tiandihui's elite combat squad, named after the first dynasty of a unified China. They took the most talented and skilled Magicians from each squad and put them into one super squad of ruthless killers.

"Really? Congratulations on your promotion." He tried to sound genuine. "The pay must be nice."

"It is. I can send way more back to Mom and Dad now."

"How are the old folks?"

"Oh, you know. They're making it through. It's not easy in America when you only have one child to rely on."

Henry pursed his lips, trying to play nice. "I'll visit them once the hunt's over and done with."

"Tell me, Hanying, who did you convince to let you in as their plus one? There's gotta be a story involving you and an old lady I'm gonna want to hear." Weiying chuckled. "Oh, or maybe it was a guy!"

As if on cue, and much to Henry's relief, Marion appeared next to him with two glasses of white wine. "Care to introduce me, Heinrich?" she asked, handing him a glass. "Er—Nezha...sorry."

"'Heinrich?'" Min frowned.

"'Nezha?' That's a rather presumptive callsign," Weiying said.

Henry nodded, sipping his wine. He smirked into his glass at Weiying's barely suppressed indignation and confusion.

He rarely liked to play Weiying's little power games, but sometimes he found himself in a "winning" position. And it'd be a shame to let it go to waste.

"This is callsign Kongming, my brother, and callsign Guanyin, a former associate of mine," Henry said, keeping names out of the picture. "And, guys, this is Sunna. My company for tonight and my current associate. Guanyin, you've met her before. In Morocco."

"A pleasure." Marion shook both their hands.

"Uh...we have a problem," Analise said over the radio.

"Well, we don't want to keep you from the lively conversation," Henry said. "I'll see you two around. You have fun tonight."

"Hold on just a second, brother," Weiying said, tugging on his sleeve. "How'd you know about it?"

Henry raised an eyebrow. "Guanyin, you might wanna watch what my brother drinks. He can get a little—"

"Don't fuck with me!" Weiying hissed, swatting Henry's glass onto the floor. The shattering drew the attention of several people in the room. "I don't know what you

Defectors do, squirming around with the other worms, but if you even try putting your hands on that coin tonight, I will make sure you leave this place in chains or a body bag—"

"Weiying." Min grabbed Weiying's shoulder, using his real name. Although it seemed he cared less about that than he did about the people staring.

Henry's little brother scoffed. "You know what? I don't need to say it."

"See you around, Weiying," Henry muttered before he and Marion turned their backs on his old comrades. They slipped around a corner and a few steps down the stairwell. He scanned the area before patching into his radio. "What's the problem?"

"Someone's locked onto you. Magically," Analise said. "IDing them now. In the meantime, I have eyes on the coin. Turn left, then head down to the catwalks through the excavation beneath this floor. The artifacts are being stored on the north side. Just watch your step."

Henry caught sight of the stairwell to his left. "Got it."

"ADZ is online."

Arne Moritz, callsign Barbarossa, took a deep breath as he turned to his teammates in the third-floor women's bathroom of the Acropolis Museum. Small lights appeared in his vision, coalescing into a magical heads-up-display.

"Listen up, Staufer squad." He addressed the five other members of his squad as they all pulled pistols out of a small bag they'd smuggled in. "Looks like Sunna has some new friends. Once our WAC gets eyes on her, we need to move quickly. Notably because of this man."

A very mugshot-esque image of a Chinese man with an undercut and a goatee appeared on the side of the Arcane Defense Zone interface in his vision.

"Callsign Wukong, former Tiandihui," Hegel, Staufer squad's Warning and Control officer, explained. "The Tiandihui doesn't seem to think much of him, but the Latins had an encounter with him a week ago. He's a fast and deadly Martial Magician. So, until you've put a bullet in his head, don't consider him or Sunna secure. Understood?"

"God, these Defectors are coming out of the woodwork like termites." Konstanz shivered as she tied her raven hair back. "First Moneta, now Sunna. This is absurd."

"Keep your head on straight, Staufer 4," Barbarossa said. "We have a shot to smother the problem now. Come on."

The six Magicians of Staufer squad filed out of the bathroom, tucking their guns into their formalwear.

"Hey, Faust." Gisela, their ginger-haired Runecaster, addressed the squad's resident alchemist. "Weren't you and Sunna, like...a thing?"

"For two days. I don't wanna talk about it," Faust grumbled as he started drawing an alchemical circle on the back of his hand. "I'd rather ask why we went so far as to use this party as a trap, but still have to sneak in. If we sent a missive to the Chaldean Court, everyone in this building would be helping us."

"If *you* want to sit through the Court's wait times for audiences, be my guest." Hegel scoffed. "I'd hate to pay your phone bill."

"Everyone shut up. We're here now. Let's focus." Barbarossa started down the stairs to the second floor. "Where are they, Hegel?"

"I got her. First floor by the Caryatid statues."

As a red highlight appeared in his vision, Barbarossa hurried down the steel stairs and sprinted across the glass floor.

"Take a left down the hallway."

He lightly gripped the gun in his suit jacket and slowed into a power walk as he passed through a light crowd of partygoers, the red highlight in his vision growing larger.

"Right in front of you. Green dress."

Barbarossa glanced to either side, nodding at Faust and Gisela before they veered off to the sides, intent on flanking Sunna. He spotted her, a woman in a green dress with her back facing them.

Not wanting to be noticed, Barbarossa suppressed his magical aura as best he could and prayed Sunna didn't have a WAC watching her back.

Having a Defector come out of your squad wasn't only humiliating. Your standing in the Magician's Circle suffered for it.

Moneta's departure hardly affected Ottonen Squad, since she was just a WAC. But Sunna had been Staufer 3. If he and Faust were taken out, she would've been next in the chain of command.

As one of the youngest squad leaders in the Palatine Order of Cologne, High Command already gave him a hard time. After Sunna left, Staufer squad had been forced to *beg* for more than the bottom-of-the-barrel work.

Even if not for himself, Barbarossa wanted to assure he didn't hinder any of his squadmates' careers as Magicians.

Right when Faust and Gisela were in arm's reach, Barbarossa grabbed her by the shoulder.

He blinked, staring into the blue eyes of an equally bewildered middle-aged woman. Barbarossa grabbed her face, trying to disrupt any illusion magic, but she shoved him away and started angrily yelling at him in Greek.

Gisela tried to settle the woman down as Barbarossa patched into his comms. "It's not her," he muttered.

"What? Of course it is." Hegel scoffed.

"No, it isn't."

"I'm telling you, her aura is a compl—" Hegel fell silent.

Barbarossa frowned. "Hegel, do you copy?"

"*Fickt mich...*" the WAC muttered. "Wait, I have her again!"

"Sunna's fucking with us," Barbarossa snarled. "Staufer. Teams of two. Split up and canvass this place top to bottom. Move!"

Analise chuckled as she continued tampering with the German ADZ. With her legs up on the dashboard of her rental car, she fiddled with the dials on her brass Detection Zone compass, swapping Marion's magical signature to a new location across the museum. She had three laptops and a map open, each set up with an ADZ. The map was hers, but the digital ones were the ADZs setup by the Latins, Greeks, and Germans.

"Hey, Sunna." She patched into her radio. "You wouldn't happen to have burnt some bridges after you left the Order of Cologne, would you?"

"Why do you ask?"

"Because those friends of ours who locked onto you were from Staufer squad."

"Shit," Marion hissed.

"They're from what?" Henry exclaimed. "I thought you were still in their good graces!"

"I thought I was! I was invited to this damn thing!"

Analise sighed. "Did you not investigate the possibility that they invited you so they would know where you are and could hunt you down?"

"Well, I...I...not at the time—"

"Damnit, *this* is why I fly solo."

"Calm down, Nezha. It's under control," Analise said before her new partners could start arguing. "I sent them on a wild goose chase. But it won't keep them busy forever. Find that coin."

"Copy."

"So, this is what you WACs get up to while we're out there riskin' our necks?" Yianni scoffed from the backseat, his hands still bound.

"Maybe you shouldn't have become a combat Magician." Analise shrugged. "Ever given that any thought?"

Yianni narrowed his eyes, giving her a death stare in the rearview mirror. "Some of us aren't afforded the luxury of choice."

Analise returned his menacing glare with an appraising look of her own. "So *that's* why you're a Defector, isn't it?"

Yianni's face twisted in confusion. "Who said—I'm not a Defector!"

"Guess I owe Henry money..." Analise sighed.

"I'm tellin' you, I'm not—"

"And I'm telling you I know you're lying. I mean, look at you! You're Greek as the Parthenon! There's no way the Celts wouldn't cut you loose as soon as they could." Analise scoffed.

"What would you know about it, German? You had a perfectly fine position in the Palatine Order! I know what happened with you, Moneta. You threw it all away because the grass looked greener on the other side of the Alps!" Yianni fired back.

Analise sighed, refusing to meet his gaze in the mirror. Barely loud enough for herself to hear, she muttered, "Some of us are burdened with choices we didn't know we were making." She turned to him in her seat. "Don't make me come back there and gag you. I need to focus."

"Focus away, lass." Yianni threw his bound hands up in defeat.

Analise turned back to her screens, monitoring a little of everyone's ADZ, but keeping her eyes primarily on her own. She didn't always brag about her spellcraft, but ADZ displays ran on something like magical software. And hers was military-grade amongst amateur intro-to-computer-science projects.

A blue ping went off on her map. But then it was gone before she had the chance to look at it. None of the other screens even registered it.

Analise furrowed her brow as she spoke a Latin command to her interface. "*Monitus.*"

A log made of light of all the pings in the last hour appeared, hovering over her map. "*Audite Primum.*"

The latest ping expanded, with a spectrogram of the ping's Magical frequency while it appeared for that split second.

"*Continue Audire.*"

Nothing. Her ADZ couldn't get a lock on it again.

She looked more closely at the spectrogram. The spikes of magical energy, although there were only three, had uneven space between them. The only other uneven frequencies would be the coins. Her ADZ tracked Henry's coin and Marion's coin, so it had to be something else. Maybe something...getting faster.

Analise's eyes widened.

It could be a bomb. An arcane bomb soaking up just enough magical energy to stay off everyone's radar. Everyone's but hers.

Should she tell the other two? No, they were already trying to grab that coin and evade Staufer squad. Besides, if they got to it, they were both combat Magicians. She could disarm it faster herself.

Analise folded up her map and stepped out of the car, onto the crooked sidewalk just outside the Acropolis Museum.

"Oi, what's this?" Yianni asked.

Analise squeezed her eyes shut. Right. She was babysitting. She walked back to the car and opened the door, dragging him out by the ear as she drew a knife.

"Hey, hey! I'm not a fuckin' Amazon package."

She sliced through his bonds before removing the Nullifier Band. Then she placed the muzzle of a handgun to his head.

The Irishman froze up. "Is this because of the Alps comment?"

"There's a bomb about to blow off this museum's top and everything around it, us included. You're gonna help me disarm it, or your brains are going to paint the sidewalk," Analise said.

"Alright, alright. Just...careful with that thing." Yianni's mouth became a thin, stressed line. "Why do you want my help?"

"Because I'd rather you be more than dead weight." Analise nodded towards the museum. "Now, come on. Move!"

Henry gripped the metal railing along the stone catwalks crisscrossing a whole neighborhood of ruins from ancient Athens just a meter below.

"I don't get it..." Marion said.

He whirled around, gesturing to the empty storage closet before them. "What isn't there to get?"

"I meant why Ana—I mean, Moneta—isn't answering comms," Marion grumbled.

Henry felt kind of bad for yelling. But it just made his disposition worse. They'd both tried several times to get in touch with Analise. One more couldn't hurt.

Henry sighed and patched into his radio. "Moneta, do you copy?"

After a brief second of radio static, Analise's voice came through. "Sorry, what is it?"

"The coin's gone!" Henry exclaimed.

"What?"

"Why aren't you answering?" Marion asked.

"Sorry, I just...I ran into a little trouble with Yianni—"

"Do you need help?" Henry asked.

"No. I've got things handled. Just...I can't be your eyes in the sky much. The coin..." Analise drifted off. "Looks like the coin's on the first floor. Maybe they're showing it early. Also, Staufer squad's wisened up. They're about to sweep the basement."

Henry cursed as Analise hung up.

"What do we do?" Marion pinched the bridge of her nose.

"What, you have nothing, team leader?"

"I just brought us together!" Marion hissed. "*You're* the Martial Magician. Strategize!"

Henry sighed, rubbing his temples. He calmed himself with a few breaths. He just had to think clearly.

Their immediate threat was Staufer squad. The labyrinth of ancient roads and walls beneath them, covered in catwalks, would be a good hiding spot.

Without a word, Henry hopped over the railing and landed on one of the excavated roads. The catwalks and walls were just high enough for him to pass under them while standing.

"Get down here before the Germans find us." He held out his hands towards Marion as she peered over the railing.

"Alright, alright, don't rush me!" she hissed.

"Why shouldn't I?" Henry scoffed as she vaulted over the railing. He caught her before she hit the ground, since her shoes were not made for jumping.

"Thanks."

"Maybe we just leave the shoes behind for good measure," Henry suggested.

Marion nodded. "I came prepared. Watch for Staufer."

Henry did that, but kept an eye on her as she pulled off her heels and held them up in one hand. She pulled a small rock or a pebble out of her…whatever that something between a wallet and a purse that girls carried when they went out was. Putting the rock in the right shoe, she closed her eyes. The air around the heels seemed to distort for a split second as the shoes collapsed in on themselves, then were replaced with a pair of sneakers as quickly as they had vanished.

"You have teleportation magic for your *shoes*?" Henry asked.

"It's not *just* for my shoes." Marion sighed. She pulled out another one of those pebbles from her new shoes before she started putting them on. "I need two of these to swap two objects. I can throw one and swap myself and one other person with the runestone's location. But once I use them, they're dead."

"How many do you have?" Henry asked.

"Only two. I haven't been able to stock up since Morocco," she said. "I'm done. Let's move."

Henry nodded. The two of them began navigating through the maze of walls and ruins just as they heard hurried footsteps hit the catwalks.

As they did, some guy shouted something in German. Henry wasn't sure what, having never learned the language except the important bits—notably swearing.

"So," Marion whispered as they turned a narrow corner between two limestone walls still partially encased in dirt, "do you have a plan for the coin?"

"One pain in my ass at a time, please." Henry sighed.

He raised his fist, causing both of them to freeze under a catwalk as two sets of feet ran overhead. "There're four," he muttered.

"Then there should be two more somewhere," Marion whispered.

They kept moving, winding through the eroding limestone under the dim light of a few industrial Edison bulbs. Henry had never really thought about the smell of dirt before, but it was certainly coming to mind now. It was overwhelmingly dry, thank God.

Dust and dirt were sprinkling the sleek black sheen of his suit like a mess involving flour. He glanced up to find the steel grate of the platform linking the stairs to the catwalks. The Germans seemed far enough away. They were out of sight, at the very least. He pulled himself up over the railing before helping Marion up, his head on a swivel. The two tried to make as little noise on the grate as possible as they rushed for the stairs and headed up to the first floor.

"I feel it," Marion said as they got to the top of the stairs. "Not strong enough to place, but it's still here."

"We'll head for the lobby," Henry said. "But that's good."

They started down a hallway filled with artifacts on pedestals that Henry would've really liked to look at in his downtime.

He was walking fast enough to get some weird looks from partygoers, but not enough to cause suspicion. Even if he did, he didn't really care at that moment. He needed that coin as much as Zhao squad needed to fuck off. Gritting his teeth and clenching his fists, he shifted his weight forward as he started to jog, like he was about to get into a fight.

Suddenly, a hand grabbed his wrist. He grappled that hand in turn, but was pulled around a corner as Marion's hands placed his around her waist. She wrapped her arms around his neck as Henry furrowed his brow at her, the tension from before vacating his body for confusion. He followed her darting eyes, catching sight of a man and a woman in European historical clothing as they walked past them.

"Sorry," Marion whispered. "Had to act fast."

Henry nodded, consciously letting his breath go. "Hey, it worked."

When it was clear, they let go of each other.

"I sense it!" Marion exclaimed, causing him to flinch. "The coin's over by the stage."

Henry breathed a sigh of relief. They hadn't been beaten. They'd just taken the coin out to show early.

But that naturally led to the question of how the hell he was going to steal it out from under the noses of a room full of witnesses.

CHAPTER SEVEN
Pursuit through Athens

Following her map, Analise had led herself and her new tagalong to the second floor of the museum, having snuck in through the many open entrances to the excavation site beneath the building. In hindsight, that would've been so much easier to go through. They could've brought guns that way.

But it was too late for that. Next time they had to infiltrate a building, she was going to scour *all* the Google Street View images.

"Who the hell puts a bomb on the second floor?" Yianni asked.

She scoffed. "You really are a solo act."

"And you're a bit of a feckin' gobshite."

"I'm not even gonna ask what that means." Analise glanced at her map. The last ping had come from the other side of a set of marble statues right in front of the staircase. "The basement is loaded with wards. Though I figured they'd try to hide it better."

She circled around the pedestal they stood on and gasped as she laid eyes on the explosive.

The bomb was *big*. It was at least three meters long and made of a metal casing with some kind of alchemically amplified explosive material inside. Even if it weren't strapped to the ground, it would be impossible to carry.

Analise calibrated her ADZ display to measure the bomb's magical heartbeat and estimate a countdown. As the number appeared in her vision, she groaned. Three and a half minutes.

She took a deep breath.

This had to be some kind of diversion. No one sane would dare try to kill so many Magicians at once. Even Defectors were still beholden to the rules of Magician society at large.

"What *is* this thing?" Yianni furrowed his brow.

"I haven't seen anything like this before. But I think I know how it works. It's been soaking up magical energy for the last few hours, I'd guess." Analise grimaced. "Once it reaches full capacity, it'll all come spewing out as fire and explosions."

"'The last few hours?' Then that thing's got the juice to level everything from here to the Parthenon," Yianni muttered.

"You're not helping." Analise sighed. She knelt down next to the bomb. "Help me check it for wards."

Yianni's hands glowed with a soft aura of green magic as Analise's glowed blue. They probed the device for any charms, wards, or other spellcraft. The strange thing was that there was nothing. In fact, there wasn't even any magic fueling the device. The pings came from it absorbing a bit of magical power from the atmosphere. Like a car slowly filling itself with petrol. One pump at a time.

"There's nothing." Analise grimaced. She touched the metal casing and the flat steel sheen shifted slightly, creating imprints of...

"Is that Arabic?" Yianni asked.

"No, it's...I think it's Syriac. Or maybe..." Analise's eyes flickered to the countdown. "Three minutes. Shit." There were so many Semitic languages, she didn't know them all. She barely knew Hebrew, the one she actually studied.

She pulled out her phone and took a photo of the text. The Circles could hack her all they wanted. It wouldn't matter if she didn't defuse this thing. She sent it to Henry.

"Nezha, what language is this?"

"What?" Henry patched in.

"The photo. It's a ward that's in my way."

"I...whatever. It's Aramaic." He sighed.

"What does it say?" she asked.

Henry was silent for a moment.

"Nezha, do you copy?"

"It says...it says your name," Henry stammered. "Your real name. It says *We know what you fear. We know what makes you cry. We know what makes you want to live. And what will make you want to die. Are we correct?*"

A chill ran up Analise's spine as she looked back at the bomb.

"What is it?" Yianni asked.

She squeezed her eyes shut. Thank God she could compartmentalize.

Upon opening them again, Analise attributed each of the letters spelling out her name to a sound. She looked up an Aramaic dictionary and quickly associated the letters to sounds in her mind so she could transcribe them.

"You don't know me; you're a bomb," she muttered.

As she said that, the script shifted. She quickly translated the phrase.

"*What do you fear more? Weakness, danger, or confinement?*" She repeated the phrase aloud. "What?"

"I think that's how you disarm it," Yianni said. "Whoever made this thing is trying to psych you out."

Analise sighed. "Weakness."

The script shifted again, and once again, she had to waste precious seconds translating.

"*Where does your pride come from? Achievement or love?*"

"Achievement."

The next question really sent her stomach roiling. "Where does your anger lie? In dominance, in sleep, or in fury?"

Analise furrowed her brow. "In sleep. I'm not angry."

The script didn't change.

"Did you lie?" Yianni asked. "Maybe it can tell."

"No, I just..." Analise looked back at that timer. A minute thirty. "Shit, okay, fury! I don't even know what the hell that means..."

She clenched her teeth. This piece-of-shit bomb was being controlled by some smug asshole safe in his hotel, making her spill her...whatever it was he wanted.

"Who do you hate more? Your father or your mother?"

Analise punched the casing, wincing in pain. "My mother," she admitted through gritted teeth.

She would kill whoever made this thing.

Did you kill your father?

She didn't read that question aloud, simply staring at it with contempt.

"Yes..." She would reverse-engineer this bomb, trace it back to its maker, and string them up by their Achilles' heels with fishing hooks over a volcano.

The lights in the museum suddenly went out, then turned back on again, flickering to life as quickly as they'd gone off. But it seemed to have nothing to do with the bomb.

"The hell was that?" Yianni asked.

"Nothing. Focus."

The script shifted.

"The final answer," it said. *"Say my name."*

A completely different script from Aramaic appeared on the surface of the bomb. It was Cuneiform of some kind.

Analise started to panic. There were so many languages that used Cuneiform. It was the only script around for a large portion of history. How was she supposed to know which one it was?

She had thirty seconds.

It could be Persian, Hittite, Akkadian, Babylonian, Elamite, Assyrian, or any number of undeciphered languages.

"No, no, no, no!" she muttered to herself as sweat dripped off her nose, scrambling to piece the symbols together.

She scoured the surface of the bomb for some kind of clue as the timer kept ticking down.

Twenty seconds. Ten seconds.

Seven.

"Wait, here!" Yianni said. "What's this?"

Four.

Analise moved next to Yianni and peered at the side of the bomb. An Anatolian Sun Disk. It was Hittite. She glanced at the Cuneiform again.

Two seconds.

"*Hepom Nepots*! *Hepom Nepots*!" she exclaimed.

The countdown stopped.

A moment passed before the bomb started to disintegrate into dust. She collapsed onto the floor in relief.

She'd gotten it.

Henry stared at the photo on his phone for a moment before squeezing his eyes shut and refocusing on the issue at hand. Whatever Analise was dealing with, she could handle it.

"Any ideas?" Marion asked as two men in suits brought a display case onto the stage.

Henry shook his head. "Not yet."

"Good, because I think I have something. The coin sets off a huge burst of magic when it stops touching the purple cloth. It'll get the attention of every Magician in the venue, and by proxy, the guards. But it'll only buy us a few seconds," Marion explained. "You're fast enough to snatch it, right?"

"Yeah, but that means..." Henry eyed her. "You'd have to take *my* coin."

"If you have any other ideas, I'm all ears."

Henry glanced back at the coin sitting on stage. The normal attendees wouldn't even see him, thanks to Solomon's Wisdom. But there were Magicians crawling all over the place. If he wanted to steal the coin, he needed the distraction.

But what if Marion took the Ptolemy coin and left him to die? If he handed it to her and she didn't set off the distraction, he'd be just as coinless as the other Magicians here.

That said, he needed all four to get anywhere.

He sighed. "Okay. I need you to take this. But hand it back *right* after, alright? Immediately."

Marion nodded. "Understood."

Henry still hesitated to hand the Ptolemy coin to her, but he did. He took a breath, turning back to the stage as he cultivated oxygen into Qi.

He spared a glance back at her. "We'll meet up on the second—"

A thunderclap of industrial noise reverberated through the museum as everything went dark. People gasped and screamed as someone from the stage announced, "Please remain calm, ladies and gentlemen. Backup power will be on shortly."

The lights flickered back to life.

The coin was gone.

Henry whirled around just in time to see the blue tail end of Weiying's robes slip through the front doors.

He rushed to chase after him, but two guards with assault rifles stopped him. "Hey, hey! He has the coin!" he tried to explain, but the guards only admonished him in Greek and shoved him back.

They needed to find another way out.

Henry patched into his radio. "Moneta, come in."

"Ye-yeah?" Analise answered, panting from her end of the radio. "Copy."

"Zhao Squad stole the coin. We need you to track their location and find us a way out that isn't the front door," Henry reported. "Basement's a no-go. Staufer squad is still down there."

"Right. Give me a second," she muttered.

Henry put his hand on Marion's shoulder and started guiding both of them towards the staircases. But guards were starting to close in on all exits from the lobby. "I think we might have to take crashing this party in a more literal direction," he muttered.

"Try the second floor. You can get out onto the veranda and drop down from there," Analise said. "The coin's traveling north, towards the Psyri district."

Henry sprinted towards the stairs with Marion right behind. The two guards posted there barely noticed him before his Qi-fueled legs launched him towards them. In one lightning-fast strike, he stole both their consciousnesses away.

Henry and Marion rushed past and up the stairs as shouts echoed from the hall.

"Security's scrambling. Stay on your toes," Analise said.

The two Defectors sprinted past three stone statues and a myriad of other exhibits, only to be met by two security guards as they turned the corner.

The guards shouted at them in Greek, aiming their guns.

Henry tried to play off his appearance. "Wait, wait, I'm lost—"

They fired first, with no intention to ask questions.

Marion ducked for cover.

Henry managed to evade the shots with the remains of his Qi and grabbed the item from his ear. Its magic activated as the item, no bigger than a paperclip, grew into a six-foot-long guandao, a massive, bladed halberd with serrations on the back end of the blade and a spike on the reverse end of the shaft.

He swung the reverse end across, knocking both guards unconscious in one sweep, then shrank the guandao back to its storage size and placed it in his ear before stealing one of the guards' rifles.

Marion grabbed the other as they approached the massive floor-to-ceiling windows overlooking the front of the museum.

Henry managed to hit the glass with the butt of the rifle enough to make a small hole, barely big enough for his head, before a bullet hit the window next to him.

"It's Staufer!" Marion cried as he turned around.

He forced the Germans to dive for cover as he fired at them. Scattered around the room, there was no way for him to stop firing at their multiple hiding spots before one would try to peek out and take a shot at him.

Marion grabbed his hand as she threw one of her runestones through the small hole in the glass. He blinked, and they were both falling towards the white veranda.

They managed to land softly enough, though Henry's gun slid out of his grip, clattering off the edge of the veranda. The drop from the third floor to the veranda was a third of that between the veranda and the ground.

Marion reported their position to Analise as Henry pulled a sharpie marker from the folds of his suit. On the veranda's concrete, he drew the necessary characters in meaning to pull a five-meter-long silk rope out of the concrete as the material transmuted, then did the proper combo with his hands for a Martial spell calling on Chiyou, the god of weapons. From the metal scaffolding, he pulled out a chunk in the form of a perfectly shaped rope dart head.

He hastily tied the weapon together, breathing through the fatigue that those simple spells caused him, and stuck it in the concrete. Adrenaline fueling him, he used it like a grappling hook as he jumped off the veranda. His feet hit the ground just as Marion began making her way down the rope.

"Where's Zhao Squad?" Henry asked Analise over the radio.

"Gimme a sec. I'll be there to drive you over," Analise said.

"I can move faster on my own. Mark it on the ADZ."

"You want to go after it alone?"

"We can't let them escape!" Henry snarled.

"Jesus, fine," she muttered.

Henry took several cultivating breaths, replenishing his energy as Analise sent the information his way. A marker for the coin and each of the members of Zhao Squad lit up in his vision on the other side of the Acropolis.

He finally took a normal breath, gasping for oxygen. Filled to the brim with Qi, he knelt in a sprinter's stance. He channeled Metal and Fire Styles at once, imbuing his legs with both explosive strength and supernatural speed.

He thought he heard Marion's voice for a moment.

Henry launched, leaving a small crater in the ground under his foot. Moving northward, he sprinted faster than any human had the right to. With just Metal Style, he could sprint as fast as Usain Bolt's best time. With just Fire Style, he could squat the world record for powerlifting. With the two combined, his muscles could push him to forty miles an hour on foot.

He shoulder-checked a wall of hedges and ran over stone brick roads, his eyes on the nearest historical landmark, the many stacked limestone arches and seats of the Theater of Dionysus.

Just past the theater's semicircular rows of seating, he could see the reinforced sheer wall of the Acropolis.

He leapt over the back of the stage and climbed the seats two rows at a time, breezing past and continuing up the slope of gravel leading up to the megalithic Acropolis.

The grass and gravel beneath his feet turned to white limestone as he started to climb the steeper incline of natural stone around the bottom of the Acropolis's walls.

He barely gave himself time to breathe before throwing himself up onto the sheer stone brick walls, finding holds in the weathered gaps between bricks. He pulled himself up onto the top of the Acropolis, rolling onto a few tufts of grass at the base of the Parthenon.

Getting to his feet, he sprinted through the spotlights illuminating the Parthenon at night.

There was no way in hell he was going to jump off the damn Acropolis, so he took the path down to the Beule Gate, an edifice that, though ruined, was fit to be the entrance to the Acropolis proper.

He passed under the gate and hopped over the metal railing that guided tourists up and down the winding path of the stone brick road from a grove of trees sloping down the steep limestone hill.

He broke off from the road, heading north through trees, hedges, and over green metal fences as he half-ran, half-slipped down the uneven, inconsistent slopes of dirt and limestone making up the bottom of the Acropolis and the top of the Agora.

He could see the Stoa of Attalos, a long, thin walkway covered by columns and a roof going all along the east side of the Agora's smattering of ruined foundations. He leapt down to the Agora proper and sprinted by the facade of the building, marble columns rushing by like the green blinders on highway dividers.

He leapt over a wide pit of foundational ruins between the Stoa and the metal railing dividing the modern city's streets from the ancient sites. He grabbed the railing, slamming his body into the stone wall supporting the raised roads, and pulled himself over them.

"Holy shit," Analise muttered over the radio. "You just crossed four hundred meters in twenty seconds..."

"That's Martial magic for you." Henry grimaced as he navigated through the crowds of tourists and locals seeking entertainment for the night. If he tried to go as fast as he'd gone out there in the urban streets, he'd definitely break Solomon's Wisdom for someone who wasn't meant for it.

But the coin was *so* much closer.

Marion scoffed. "I don't appreciate being left behind, you know."

"You want me to get your coin back, don't you?"

"You're alone with no weapons! You're not going to get it back, *Arschloch*! You're going to die!"

Henry scrunched up his nose. "I'm getting it back."

He made it past Monastiraki square and into the nightlife district, full of clubs and bars, where he had been last night. The markers for Zhao Squad and the coin headed into a building just a block away.

Then they vanished.

"Shit," Henry whispered. He pushed his way through the crowds, trying to get to the building. He prayed they hadn't managed to get away. Though to whom, he didn't know.

He burst into the building, even though its windows were boarded-up and it was dark inside. It was some kind of abandoned restaurant or bar.

And they were waiting for him.

Was he confident he could take on Zhao Squad? No. Did he have an escape plan if he failed? No. Did he have a plan of what to do next if he succeeded? Also no.

But he couldn't let them have the coin. Anyone but them, he would let it go.

He could see Weiying looking down on him through his Beijing opera mask from the other side of the room. There was no option for diplomacy here. Either he had to defeat them, or the tomb of Alexander the Great would forever be a regret and a humiliating loss in his dreams.

Henry willed his guandao to return to its normal size as he took it out of the crook of his ear.

"Looking for this?" Weiying held up the violet-wrapped coin.

"As much as you want the one I have." Henry glowered.

"Honestly, I thought I could just pick it out of the rubble when my bomb leveled the museum."

"*He* set the bomb?" Analise exclaimed through the radio.

"Bomb? What bomb?" Fang asked.

"Just a distraction, nothing more," Weiying said to their former mentor. "It pulled their WAC's attention long enough for us to steal the coin."

"But part of you wishes it would've gone off. Why would you do that?" Henry asked. "You wouldn't have the chance to beat me."

"Because the prospect of sending you into despair by blowing up a couple old rocks is almost as tempting as killing you myself," Weiying said.

"So, we're just dropping any pretense of familial bonds now?" Henry glanced around the room as the other members of Zhao squad emerged from the shadows. He'd hoped for a split second that Weiying would insist on a one-on-one fight.

"Hand over the coin, and we'll let you leave," Min promised.

Maybe he'd bitten off a bit more than he could chew. Even with his guandao, he couldn't hold off six simultaneous attackers. Especially when Fang was his martial superior.

Before he could even say yes or no, something from his left slammed into his gut. In a flash, his entire body bloomed in pain as he crashed through the plaster wall of the building and then through the window of the building across the street with a nasty crunch.

Screaming agony stabbed into his wrist and ribs from all sides as he collapsed to the ground. He cursed a thousand different ways as he righted himself and cradled his wrist.

"Nezha, are you alright?" Analise asked.

Henry had to keep breathing. His father always told him pain came from not breathing enough. He gritted his teeth.

"Nezha, do you read?" Analise's voice was growing panicked already. "Nezha!"

"My wrist...fuck. I think it's broken..." He heaved. "No...no, I'll be alright...just—" He growled as he tried to do anything other than cradle his wrist.

"Chen Bo!" Min screamed from outside. "What the hell did you do?"

"He deserved way more than that for what he's done! Besides, I just did all of your jobs for you."

Henry tried to stand, but the agony flowing through his body made him want to curl up like a dead spider.

"Alright, my ass." Marion knelt next to him.

Henry furrowed his brow. "What the hell are you doing here?"

Marion held up a runestone as the bright blue marking faded away from its surface. She gingerly picked up his arm, eliciting a hiss from him. "Your wrist is broken."

"No shit, Sherlock. What are we supposed to do about it?" Henry asked.

Marion grimaced, her face full of conflict, before she cupped his wrist. Zhao Squad was getting closer.

Her right palm began to glow. A warm, nostalgic feeling blossomed in his chest as golden light seeped into his broken bones. It was the comforting feeling of cozying up to someone next to a fire in the middle of a snowstorm.

Henry sighed in relief as Marion removed her hands. He flexed his wrist, blinking in disbelief. It was good as new.

"You can...heal people?" he muttered.

"Remember when I said I was too valuable for the Germans to let go?" Marion pressed one of her hands to his ribs while she pulled down the neckline of her dress slightly, exposing the patch of skin above her heart, marked by a rune that was reminiscent of the letter S.

Once she removed her hands, Henry got to his feet, feeling good as new. He still felt the injuries, but they weren't hindering his movement.

She handed him the sheath holding his butterfly swords.

"I can see why..." he muttered as he drew his weapons. "I'm gonna get the coin. Are you ready to help?"

"As I'll ever be."

CHAPTER EIGHT
The Zhao Dragon

Henry planted a push kick on the door to the building, slamming it open so hard it nearly came off its hinges. A volley of golden bolts of light held Zhao Squad at bay as the two Defectors claimed their half of the road.

"How the hell are you walking?" Weiying demanded, looking at Chen Bo.

"Looks like I was right." Fang grinned, staring at Henry from under the brim of his hat. "Defectors are working together."

Henry brandished his swords. "I take it you aren't about to make this a fair fight."

Min shrugged. "If the coins weren't at stake, maybe."

"What's the plan?" Marion whispered.

"I can only take them one or two at a time. I need you to occupy them." Henry met Marion's eyes, and something between them morphed into an understanding of one another. An understanding on the battlefield, at least.

Golden light carved runes all along Marion's arms. Her hands took hold of a staff as it materialized from nothing. It was sleek and lacquered, with a gold idol at the top in the shape of that rune over her heart. "I'm with you," she said.

Henry glared at his former comrades as he flexed his grip on his swords.

He broke into a sprint as Marion covered him with volleys of concussive bolts, leaping at Chen Bo.

His tunnel vision zeroed in on his enemies. Whatever it was Marion would use to help him, he would take, but as far as he was concerned, he was on his own.

As Chen Bo was the most physically imposing of the squad, Henry made sure to slash his arms and clock him in the head with the butt of his sword. He couldn't afford more than Fang in terms of martial challengers.

As the blindness wore off and Marion was occupied by showering the other members of Zhao Squad in magic, Shen pushed the attack, forcing Henry to parry or die.

With dual weapons, Shen's strikes came so much faster, even with drunken fist.

"Eight o'clock! Break!"

Analise's warning over the radio came in time, but Henry's focus shifted too late, and a metal fan sliced through his left forearm.

He gritted his teeth through the pain, knocking Shen out with a sudden tornado kick to the head, then parried another of Min's fans, which returned to her as she pulled out another to dual wield.

She threw out a fan that trailed silk behind it. The fan missed him, but as she caught the weapon on its return, she pulled him in with a silk rope now wrapped around his neck. She threw him into the electric sign of a closed gyro stand, sending sparks showering down on impact.

Henry landed painfully on the cobblestone path, his weapons clattering beside him. But he found the strength to get back up as Analise warned him of an incoming attack.

"Evade!"

He threw himself into a butterfly twist, evading two gouts of azure flames from Lu Ying.

The Daoist closed the distance between them in a flash, getting a free strike with the sharp claws at the tip of each of her fingers. Stripes burned in Henry's cheek as his head snapped to the side.

Although unarmed, Henry used rapid trapping and parrying to get the upper hand on Lu Ying. He soon found his situation reversed as she countered and slammed her bent wrist, an ox-jaw strike, into his nose.

She whirled around into a kick, but her leg slammed into a shield of light as it flickered to life around him for a moment, bending her joints in a nasty-looking way for just an instant. "Fuck!" she screamed with uncharacteristic-yet-reasonable vulgarity as she collapsed to the ground.

Henry only had a fraction of a second to pick his butterfly swords up off the ground as Mr. Fang's silhouette closed in on him, appearing like a shadow.

Henry had ever only felt true horror twice while fighting hand-to-hand. Once when Weiying had tried to attack him in a breach of sparring rules. And once in middle school, when he fought the kid who had been giving him a hard time for almost a year.

This was a very sobering third.

As he filled his body with as much Qi as he could cultivate in that moment, he realized this was the only time Fang had ever come at him without holding back. At least in Morocco, his old mentor had been mocking him.

Now...it seemed Fang wanted to know how far Henry had really come in their mutual weapon of expertise.

Henry committed every ounce of Qi to Metal Style.

It was as though time slowed as Mr. Fang's right sword flew towards him. A moment of tranquility. A breath before...

Their swords clashed. The crash of metal on metal rang throughout the battle like shots from a minigun. He struck faster than a strobe light could blink.

The blood in his arms rushed to his knuckles and fingertips as each impact between their swords created sparks and ever-so-slightly caused his grip to slide.

His muscles strained to keep up with his teacher's speed. Every joint felt ready to fall from its socket as he lost track of his own arms and hands, flashing through the air.

But he was stronger than before. He could tell Fang wasn't going easy on him. And he could take it. At least a little.

He roared, half in agony, half in rage as the winds produced by their duel kicked up dust and gravel.

Their knuckle guards knocked against each other, sending each of their swords flying out of their hands. They stumbled back from each other.

Marion ran up to Henry from behind. "Are you alright?"

Fang was unbothered. He even grinned under the brim of his hat.

"I have to admit," Fang said as he picked up his lost sword, "our contests are much more enjoyable this way. I'm glad to see you've kept up with your training. Excellent precision."

Henry could barely move his arms. His throat and lungs were ice-cold. With each breath, he recovered some strength, but he was no match for Mr. Fang. Still, he was happy to hear that his former mentor was impressed.

Fang kicked Henry's sword over to him.

He stared at the blade, unsure.

"Pick it up. You can go another round." It was like he was back in Fang's gym, sparring.

No, Henry wasn't even close to matching his old teacher. And this wasn't a class. The stakes were much higher.

He turned slightly to Marion. "I think we need to retr—"

"Why don't you let me take over from here, Mr. Fang?" Weiying walked up to the old man. "I trust that in my...spry age, I'll be able to scratch him."

All of a sudden, Henry didn't feel so tired. He gritted his teeth as his fingers curled into a fist.

Weiying was so sure of himself. He had never beaten Henry in a sparring match. Not fairly, anyway.

Years and years of verbal abuse and fury welled up in Henry, revitalizing his muscles.

"When I heard you'd teamed up with other Defectors, I was surprised no one had thought of it sooner. But I also didn't believe it to be true." Weiying grinned. "Mostly because the thought of you having friends is...alien. I have to say, I'm impressed."

It occurred to Henry that for the first time, he didn't just have to lie down and take Weiying's insults. He no longer had to play the part of the responsible older brother. They were enemies now. There was no oath binding them to one another as comrades and no bonds of blood that Weiying considered sacred. He could fight back.

Henry kicked his fallen butterfly sword into his hand.

"Don't make this harder than it has to be. Give me the coin." Weiying held a hand out expectantly.

"I'd rather make you work for it."

Weiying sighed in exasperation as if he'd been pestering Henry for hours. Or, rather, as if Henry had been the one pestering him. "Why? Why can't you just make things simple?"

Henry scoffed. "'Why?' You did me a favor, exiling me. I can finally put my dignity as a person above your whims. For the first time in your life, I'm not responsible for you. Doesn't feel good, does it?"

"Well, it's not *my* fault you betrayed us. Why should I have to make concessions for your mistakes?"

Henry's face contorted in rage. Even as the anger was consuming him, he knew it would cloud his judgement. "We both know damn well who betrayed who! Or have you finally started to believe your own bullshit?"

"Is that...your brother?" Marion asked.

Weiying smirked that insufferable twisting grin of superiority he loved to wear. "Allow me to introduce myself properly. Weiying Zhang. Hanying's much more intelligent younger brother. I'm surprised to see he managed to rope someone as pretty as yourself into this," he said. "I'm not here to cause any trouble. I just need the coins, and I'll be on my way."

"The others are down, Heinrich. I think it's best we take the chance to leave. They've sustained too many losses," Marion said. "It's a grudge match at this point."

"And give him the satisfaction of watching me run away?" Henry growled. "I don't think so."

"Listen to your friend, Hanying. Remember that your little team is probably much smarter than you."

He wasn't going to let Weiying keep running his mouth. "All bark and no bite! You're a petty coward, Weiying! I'll do the world a favor and sear your fucking mouth shut!"

"Heinrich!" Marion protested.

Weiying scoffed, drawing his jian. "I'm not afraid of you."

Henry roared as he launched a flurry of strikes against his brother. Admittedly, his form wasn't quite up to par. It was Weiying's fault for enraging him.

His brother parried each of the blows and made a thrust, attempting to run the length of his blade through Henry's sternum. He parried the strike with the flat of his left blade.

Weiying drew a character in the air with his sword, and a rope of silk wrapped around Henry's ankle, pulling him to the ground and dragging him across the stone street. It brought him in just for Weiying to crack a crescent kick on his temple.

He crashed into the ground, his jaw on fire and his head spinning.

"Heinrich, stop. This is stupid! Let it go!" Marion's words fell on deaf ears as Henry pushed himself to his feet.

"She has the right idea."

Henry gripped his swords as he rushed in to close the distance. He swatted Weiying's jian aside and struck at his chest.

The blade of his sword barely scraped the fabric of his brother's suit. He swung for Weiying's neck instead, but received a push kick to his gut.

Henry stumbled backwards as two tendrils of silk lashed out at him. He slashed through both, but not in time to catch a third before it wrapped itself around his head, blinding and suffocating him.

Henry let out muffled screams as his sword clattered to the ground while he tried to pull at the magically bound fabric. He gnashed with his teeth and struggled against it to no avail.

The silk loosened only as Weiying swung the flat of his blade against the side of Henry's head, sending him to the ground as the metal rang off his temple like a bell.

Every inch of his skull rattled with pain.

Weiying laughed as he squatted over Henry. "That was your one thing, wasn't it? You were good at fighting? Well, look at you now. Falling behind, like usual. I've beaten you again."

Henry squeezed his fist so tightly his wrist started to hurt. But he didn't have the strength or the balance to stand back up. Especially as Weiying grabbed his hair and slammed his head into the stone.

Henry's vision exploded with stars as his consciousness began to flicker in and out. He groaned, trying to push himself up.

"Oh, suck it up," Weiying said. "You can at least have some dignity while I rob you blind."

Marion moved in the corner of his vision, but Min closed the distance in an instant, holding a bladed fan at her throat.

Henry tried to push himself up, but even as he persevered through his own exhaustion, Weiying's foot pushed him back to the ground. His eyes locked with Fang's from under the brim of his hat. Henry's teeth gritted at the disappointment in the old man's eyes.

"Poor Hanying. Always sticks his neck out. Fails every time. You know no one cares how angry you get or how hard you try, right? If all you do is fail, what's the point of all this? Just stay outta my way from now on, alright?" Weiying started digging around in his pockets. "Now, where are those—"

Weiying flew through the air, walloped by a gnarled, thorn-covered root that had burst through the ground.

Henry glanced up, his consciousness flickering, as his presumed savior flourished a glinting blade.

CHAPTER NINE
The Companions

Henry slouched in his seat as Marion placed her glowing palms on his side, repairing the damage dealt to his ribs by his younger brother.

His eyes flickered between Analise across from him and Yianni at the other end of a table definitely not meant for four people, situated just in front of a late-night falafel-and-gyro stand. They sat in silence.

This late at night—or early in the morning—the only crowds around were exceptionally drunk people. Their gyros sat untouched, still wrapped in foil as the scent of sizzling meat wafted through the air and the cooks yelled at one another in Arabic. Well, except Yianni's. He was almost done with his.

"What the hell is *he* doing here? Unbound?" Henry pointed his chin at Yianni.

"I'll go wherever I damn well please, you dickhead." Yianni scoffed.

"He...helped me disarm a bomb," Analise said. "Not to mention he saved you and bought me the time to snatch this off your brother." She held up the second coin.

"Oh, and...I figured I oughtta say this now. I'm actually a Defector," Yianni said. "Not involved with the Celtic Circle. At least, not anymore."

"I never would've guessed." Henry cocked an eyebrow. "What do you want from the tomb, then?"

"I should know the same from you," Yianni said. "I'm not just spilling everything."

"Regardless of motive, we all want the same thing," Marion said, playing arbiter. "We're also all completely isolated from the rest of Magician society. We either have bounties on our heads or have abandoned our Circles. The only people we can trust are other Defectors."

After having been told countless times that Defectors were untrustworthy, the other three squirmed at least a little at hearing that.

"But...that means we've all been traitors," Yianni said.

"I've had my eyes opened to the...benefits of numbers. Regardless of our individual sordid histories," Henry said. "You must see it too, if you went out of your way to save us."

Yianni tilted his head. "Meh."

"So...what, should we make an alliance of Defectors?" Marion asked. "We have a Martial Magician, a healer, a WAC, and...I don't know, I guess you're something of a warlock?" She looked at Yianni.

"'Warlock?' Sweetheart, do I look like I wear robes and a pointy hat? I'm a Pact Magician," Yianni said. "But...I do specialize in area control, so I guess I round out the roles on our little squad. Like a Dungeons and Dragons party or something."

"Magicians were thinking about combat specialization and combined-arms warfare *centuries* before Dungeons and Dragons." Analise spat the roleplaying game's title.

Henry considered for a moment. "I think before we go calling this an alliance, we should outline specific terms of this agreement. Just so we're clear about what's expected."

"There's four of us and four coins," Analise said. "I say we help each other at least find all four coins, so each of us can hold an equal part of the key, then see what the coins lead to. We can figure things out from there. Sound fair?"

"I've made some estimates," Henry said. "They say the tomb's priceless, more a collection for human heritage than a monetary asset. But...I could see its contents going for...sixty billion, maybe. USD. Fifteen billion each way. And then whatever ancient magic happens to be in there, let's just agree to work that bit out peacefully."

Everyone murmured in agreement.

"Then it's settled!" Marion exclaimed. "Now, all we need is a name."

Henry gave her a look. Why was she so enthusiastic? He, Analise, and Yianni were teaming up out of necessity. She looked like she was drafting a perfect fantasy football team.

"A name?" Analise raised an eyebrow.

"Yeah!" Marion seemed to have no knowledge or no concern for the fact that Analise was judging her.

"We *should* figure out our obligations in the event that one of us is in danger of death," Henry said. "Since splitting the gold kind of incentivizes leaving each other for dead."

"You just got your head cracked open like an egg, and you're fine. I'll cover it." Marion waved his concern away. "Now, come on. Names."

Henry grimaced. "Well...considering that we're going after Alexander the Great's Tomb, we could be cheeky and name ourselves the Hetairoi."

"The Greeks would string us up by our balls for that," Yianni said. "Or other similarly painful parts."

"If it'll put an end to the frivolity of this conversation, what about the Companions? That way we have some plausible deniability when the Greeks accuse us of cultural appropriation," Analise offered.

"Sure." Henry shrugged.

"Companion Squad..." Marion muttered, cupping her chin. "I like it."

"Henry, you're Companion 1. Marion, Companion 2. Yianni, Companion 3." Analise assigned them their squad numbers.

"Alright! I declare this the official founding—" Marion started, raising her finger.

"Do you really want our official founding to be in front of a gyro stand? Assuming this is anything more than a temporary alliance." Henry raised an eyebrow.

Marion frowned as her arm came back down. "Fine. We'll wait around, I guess."

"Speaking of gyros, I'm gonna go order another one," Yianni said. "I'm famished."

"I need to get some updated rubbings from the coins so I can compare them better. Figure out our next steps, at least." Analise held out her hand as Yianni left the table.

Henry sighed, but fished out his coin and handed it to her. "Just...do it out of sight."

Analise nodded before she walked off.

With only themselves left, Henry and Marion looked at each other, an unspoken tension in the air after their confrontation with Weiying.

"Feel better?" she asked after a moment of quiet.

Henry nodded.

"I won't pretend to know what kind of history is there with your old squad, but...don't be afraid to talk to me about it," Marion said. "I want this squad of ours to work out more than anybody."

Henry had to stop himself from laughing. He would *never* think about telling anyone on this earth for at least another twenty years, when it was far enough in the past. Especially not this girl he met in a fight a week ago.

"Maybe someday." He chuckled. "But don't wait around for it."

The most concerning bit about all of it was how much he *wanted* to put his trust in her. Her innocent eyes, her well-meaning attitude, her enthusiasm—it was all too convincing. She was undoubtedly capable of scheming. Maybe she was so good he couldn't even tell when she was doing it.

She *had* brought Analise and Henry together to work with her without them even knowing.

If he let that facade deceive him, he would pay for it dearly.

Analise returned to the table, handing Henry one of the wrapped coins and opening her journal to images of the new coin just as Yianni returned with his second gyro.

"I still have a lot to analyze, but we have a location for the next coin," Analise said. "Crete." She pointed to the tails side of the new coin, which had a small map of the island, with a marker on the south end.

"That looks like...Plakias," Marion muttered.

"I wouldn't say it's far, but I think it's somewhere in the White Mountains. Somewhere with Minoan Ruins," Analise said. "I suspect we'll get another location from the third coin. Likely to the last if...Marion, where did you find this coin to begin with?"

"Um...it's kind of a long story, but...under the ruins at Babylon," Marion said. "I got a dream telling me to go there, and..." She waved her hands as if her explanation wasn't important.

"So, are we all having the dreams?" Analise asked.

Yianni's eyes widened. "You...you three are gettin' them?"

"That's...disconcerting," Henry muttered.

"Marion, what did this dream say? What did you find there?" Analise pressed her.

"I...It just said I would find what I was looking for, okay? It was very vague." Marion shied away from Analise as she answered. "And I didn't stick around to sketch everything I saw down there. It's...I almost died."

"Recognized this?" Henry unwrapped his coin, ensuring it was still touching the wrap that suppressed its signal. He showed her the tails side.

"I...Wait, yeah. That was the facade of the ruin I was in," Marion muttered.

"So then, the guide on this coin is moot. And the clue on the Cretan coin should lead us to the last one," Henry said, grinning. "And then we'll have all four."

"I've been meaning to ask," Yianni muttered. "How do you know there are four?"

"The coins each have one of the Diadochi on them—Alexander's heirs. Not to mention three points of a Vergina Sun at the bottom of each one. A Vergina sun only has twelve points," Henry said. "We think that since there were four heirs, there are four coins. And those coins are keys of some sort to the Tomb."

"Which brings me to our next problem," Analise said. "We need to figure out where the proverbial lock for this key is. Or at the very least, we can't let the other Circles catch up to us while we're figuring it out."

Henry looked at the drawings again. Both coins had two faces staring at one another. One was Alexander's general. But the other...on Ptolemy's coin, it was Achilles.

On this one, it was Diomedes.

Figures from the Trojan War.

"Analise, what was it you said the riddles on the back said?" Henry asked.

"The coin with Ptolemy on it says *The Fearful cannot believe in an honorable world*. And *The Honorable believe the world kills the Fearful*. The second coin says *The Fearful run from what they cannot grasp*. And *The Wise grasp at what they can see*."

"Honor and Wisdom...juxtaposed to fear," Henry said. "I think...Alexander's trying to tell us something. The names of the other faces are from the *Iliad*."

Marion muttered. "The Achaean names make sense. Diomedes was literally the goddess of wisdom's chosen champion. And Achilles' honor eventually killed him. So the generals must carry the same trait."

Henry shook his head. "No, the generals don't. Ptolemy would go on to steal Alexander's corpse and take over Egypt with a web of lies and propaganda. I would hesitate to call him honorable. And Lysimachus was plagued by domestic issues during his reign, and everything he did only made them worse."

"Not the wisest man in the world, I take it," Analise said.

Henry shook his head. "Not enough for Alexander, it seems."

"So, you think Alexander is trying to make a point against his generals?" Marion asked.

"I do. Because we're missing two. And one of them bears Cassander's face. After Alexander died, Cassander spat on his memory. He killed Alexander's family and couldn't walk by a statue of him without feeling woozy. I take it whoever is on that coin contrasts that personality quirk," Henry said. He shook his head. "Whatever point Alexander wanted to make after his death, all these references to the *Iliad*, not to mention Alexander's own admiration of Achilles, makes me think we need to go to Troy."

"Troy?" Yianni asked. "Doesn't that take us through Thessaloniki?"

"Shit," Analise muttered.

Thessaloniki was the main headquarters for the Hecatean Circle, in spite of Athens being the capital of Greece. Ironically, the city was founded by Cassander. But the Hecatean Circle had based itself out of Macedonia ever since the Spartans forced them out of Arcadia in the Classical Period.

And like it or not, they would have to go through that city.

Magicians had a list of what forms of transportation were most dangerous. Top of that list was air travel. The only time a Magician would dare to fly would be between the new and old worlds, since the Latins and English had agreed to peaceable cooperation when it came to trans-Pacific and Atlantic air traffic and enforced that peace quite heavily. Boats had similar issues, but they were still better than flying.

In the case of getting to Turkey, ground travel was best. Even though both a ferry and a bus would go through Thessaloniki, the Hecatean Circle would know exactly where to look if they stopped in port.

"If we aren't careful, the Hecateans could take all the work we've done and use it to find the Tomb for themselves. And we'd be helpless to stop them," Yianni warned. "We need time to secure a path, either through the city or around it.We need to know the ins and outs of their surveillance network. Or shut the whole fucker down, if possible."

"Give me a few days, and I can come up with something that can let us backdoor into their network," Analise said. "We just need to capture a connection point for whatever magic they use."

Henry grimaced. "Alright...what do you say we split up? Marion and I will go to Crete as the advance team and do some reconnaissance. They know our faces, so they'll be after us instead of looking for you. Analise, you and Yianni do what you need to on the mainland, then come join us."

Yianni nodded. "That could work."

"And who will be the one to let you know when you're about to be barbecued by a pyromancer?" Analise asked. "If any of them catch wind of your whereabouts, the Circles will dogpile on you."

"We can lay low," Marion assured her.

Analise sighed. "Alright, well...you should get the tickets for your ferry. The longer we stay in Athens, the more likely we'll be spotted by what I can imagine are *very* vigilant Circles."

CHAPTER TEN
Good Company

"Magic is culture."

Hanying wiped beads of sweat from his forehead as his horsehair brush moved with caution over a slip of stiff yellow paper.

Mr. Fang patrolled up and down the rows of stressed-out students at old Qin Dynasty calligraphy desks in a small, cloistered room made of dark wooden planks. The only light came from flickering candles and through the paper stretched across the wooden frame of the sliding door.

Hanying sat cross-legged at one of these desks, his legs starting to hurt as he had trouble recalling what he hadn't studied.

He knew the principles of talisman-crafting, though.

"That is why only stewards, scholars, and pioneers of culture can become Magicians. You are all historians, artists, sociologists, or disciplined in some form of the Humanities. Because you understand our culture, you have the ability to understand our magic."

Using one hand to hold his uniform's loose sleeve and keeping a tense grip on his calligraphy brush with the other, Hanying drew the final stroke of his sixth character. Sixth of thirteen.

"And like culture, magic is endlessly complicated, yet devilishly simple. Your mind racks over the nuances for a lifetime, while your intuition understands them from the moment you come of age. It lies beneath consciousness. But without discipline, it cannot be controlled." Mr. Fang continued his lecture. "Language, art, dance, writing—these are the ways in which culture expresses itself. These are your weapons. Master them before they master you."

Nine characters done. They were supposed to copy something from a book. But Hanying hadn't read it. Nonetheless, he was confident he could pass. His idea for a charm was advanced, yet practical. As long as it worked.

"Lose yourself, and not only will you be under threat from your own powers," Mr. Fang said, "but you will be under the sword of every other magician who has succeeded where you failed. You are Chinese. You are Han. And therefore, every magician whose culture's nature stands against ours will try to see you dead. Europeans. Africans. Muslims. The Japanese. Their Magicians wouldn't hesitate to kill you if given the chance."

Eleven. Now was the home stretch. Hanying dipped his brush in his shallow ink tray again, waiting for excess ink to drip off. It had to be perfect.

"Your talismans will be symbols of your values, your discipline, and your will. Talismans are Daoist magic. They are more forgiving than celestial incantations, but they are just as unpredictable. Learn to master what you can control. Learn to let go of what you can't."

Thirteen.

Hanying put his brush down.

"Finished?"

Mr. Fang was looming over him.

"Uh...I think?" Hanying said, unable to keep eye contact with his teacher for more than a split-second at a time.

He looked over his talisman. What was wrong with it? Had he missed something?

His little brother set his brush down loudly to signal his completion.

Mr. Fang glanced over at Weiying. "Hm...very nice, Weiying. You and your brother will be our first pair. Zhangs, go to the front."

After having finished his talisman with such bravado, Weiying seemed nervous all of a sudden.

Despite being unsure himself, Henry gave his brother a confident nod before standing. Weiying followed him up to the front of the room.

They stood facing each other.

"Why don't you tell us what your talismans are designed for?" Mr. Fang said. "Weiying, why don't you go first?"

Weiying hesitated, slightly bouncing on the balls of his feet. "Uh...my talisman draws on traditional Daoist and Wudang symbols for internal *qigong*. It's like the Wuxing Quan charms in our books. This one gives me power over water," he said.

"Very good. Hanying?"

Hanying held up his talisman. "I designed this to draw on the Confucian concept of the Mandate of Heaven."

Mr. Fang blinked. "The Mandate of Heaven? Hanying, these are Daoist talismans."

"I thought that—"

"You were meant to memorize and recreate one of the charms from the book," Weiying said.

"But...I mean, if this works right, this could—"

"Did you read the book?" Fang asked.

He *had* grasped the main concept.

"Y-yes." He nodded, trying to keep his eyes from darting around.

Mr. Fang sighed. "Alright. Fine. What's it supposed to do?"

"Reflect any opponent's magical attack."

The rest of the class chuckled as Henry narrowed his eyes. Fine. He'd show it in action.

Weiying and Henry both tucked their talismans into their belts.

"Salute your opponent," Mr. Fang said. "Let's see if these work as intended."

Both brothers offered a salute to the other with their left hand covering their right fist.

Weiying sat into a high empty stance, pushing his right palm forward and hooking his left hand behind him.

Hanying pushed his hands forward, one further than the other, in a basic Wing Chun stance, sliding his feet apart on the wooden floor.

Immediately, his younger brother broke into a series of long, graceful strikes that only hit air, but sent water rushing forth from nothing. They were slow, so Hanying managed to dodge all of them.

The class clapped for Weiying's success in making his talisman. But Hanying could see that his brother wasn't quite satisfied.

Had he wanted to hit him? That wasn't the point of the exercise.

"Now, Hanying. Weiying, attack him. Show us your talisman, Hanying."

Adrenaline pumped through him as he focused on the magic in his talisman, bringing the presence of arcane energy to his forearms. Or, at least, he tried.

The magic wasn't budging. It was like trying to drag someone out of bed.

Weiying punched before he was ready, launching a bolt of water. Hanying made a move to parry the attack, but he hadn't accounted for how close Weiying had gotten, and he slammed his younger brother in the chest and forced him onto his behind.

Silence permeated through the room before their classmates began to murmur among each other.

"What was that for?" Weiying demanded.

"I wasn't ready! You attacked me!" Hanying said.

A bolt of water slapped him in the side of the head, sending Hanying to the ground.

"Shit!" he cried, cradling his head. "What was *that* for?"

"To teach you not to hit me!" Weiying jabbed an accusatory finger at him.

"Are you serious? It was an accident!" Hanying got to his feet, as did Weiying.

"I'm not losing to you!"

"This isn't a competition!"

"Boys, boys." Mr. Fang tried to break them up. "Calm down, both of you."

"I will if he does," Weiying said. "And if he apologizes."

"Apologize? For what?"

"Quiet!" Fang snapped. He took a deep breath. "Hanying, why weren't you ready?"

He shrugged. "I'm not sure. The magic just...wouldn't listen to me."

Fang snatched the talisman away. "Because you've constructed it wrong. Confucian talismans do not use Oracle Bone Script. You lack attention to detail, Hanying. Your magic suffers as a result. I know it may seem tedious to you, but without the basics, there *is* no innovation. You can't just jump to the abstracts because you don't want to deal with the concrete. This is a product of all theory and no technique."

"But it would've worked if it was—"

"It wasn't," Weiying said. "Next time, try to put in more than the bare-minimum effort."

Hanying clenched his fists. He wasn't slacking off. He wasn't trying to be lazy. He was better at martial magic than any of them could ever hope to be.

"That's not your judgement call to make, Weiying," Mr. Fang said. "But Hanying, life cannot be about doing solely what you enjoy or are comfortable with. In order to grow, you can't let failure deter you from putting in the work."

Hanying clenched his fists. He wanted to protest, but Mr. Fang's lecture was telling him what he already knew. Anything he said would just draw more mockery from his classmates.

"It's as if you assume you'll fail if you do things the right way, so you try something different without even giving the conventional way a chance. Your creativity has no discipline. Have you ever thought there might be a reason we—"

Mr. Fang's flip phone rang. The old man refused to carry anything made after 2005. He answered. "*Wei?*"

Hanying took a calming breath, exchanging a glance with Min in the second row before his eyes returned to Fang.

Their teacher was dead silent as someone on the other side of the line spoke.

"Thank you. Goodbye," Fang muttered before hanging up. He turned to the students, hesitating before he spoke. "Let's end class."

Chen Bo furrowed his brow. "What happened?"

"Classified." Fang sniffed. "Ready."

The students put their fists on their hips.

"Salute."

They saluted. Mr. Fang was the first to let his hands down as he left the classroom, almost fleeing.

And Hanying could have sworn he saw a shadow slip through the door with him.

He would eventually learn that was the night Mr. Fang lost his only daughter. In a misguided, hasty attempt to reclaim some lost relics taken by Imperial Japan, the Tiandihui's high command lost two full combat squads to the Japanese.

Henry blinked and found himself sitting in silt, watching from the grey banks as the wide, shallow river flowed from the gate somewhere beyond the twisting pass through the mountains.

He glanced to his left, finding the bronze-clad warrior sitting next to him.

"Who are you?" Henry asked.

"Not who you seek," the warrior responded simply. "Asking such questions wastes what little time we have. Try to avoid that from now on."

"What's so important that you need to show me?"

The warrior stood. "Come."

Henry figured he might as well play along until he woke up, so he stood and followed the warrior in wading into the river.

Then the ground vanished beneath him. He stumbled as he fell out of the water as quickly as he fell into something else entirely, landing on stone. He squinted in the sunlight as his eyes adjusted from the misty pass he'd just come from.

He was back in Athens. But not modern Athens.

The Parthenon had no signs of erosion. Statues lined the street he stood on, their white marble painted over. People had set up wooden stalls in the Agora, actually buying and selling things. An orator spoke Ancient Greek from a podium in the center of a small crowd.

"Tell me what you see. As you see it."

"Athens..." Henry muttered. "Classical Athens."

"No. Be more specific."

Henry frowned at the warrior. Specific? About what? He didn't know the exact year this would've taken place. How was he supposed to be more specific?

"What do you see?" the warrior repeated.

Henry sighed and looked around the Agora.

On a second look, he caught sight of a cart filled with bodies being pushed past the entrance. He noticed how angry the crowd around the orator was. He noticed the merchants and their customers arguing. Undoubtedly about something's price.

Plague…instability…economic troubles…

"We're in the second year of the Peloponnesian War. During the Plague of Athens," Henry guessed.

The scene before them shifted. The city around him was distinctly late medieval with colored walls on each of the tightly packed houses, cobblestone streets, and cold weather.

Pike-and-shot formations rushed through the streets as civilians with improvised weapons attempted to defend themselves on a bridge. The soldiers were waving a blue flag with a golden cross on it—the Swedish banner. This was the Thirty Years' War, the capstone to a century of global cooling, religious wars, and societal collapse.

"What do you see?"

"The final battle of the Thirty Years' War," Henry said. "The Battle of Prague."

The scene changed again to Caesar's military takeover of Rome, then to the French Revolution, then to the World Wars.

"What is the point of showing me this?" Henry asked. "That history repeats? Because it doesn't."

"Does it not?" the warrior said as the two of them gazed upon the muddy, charred, horrific hellscape of No Man's Land.

"No. History rhymes. It's all about allegory and comparing time periods to one another. You might find some similarities. You might find a scary amount of similarities. But you will never get a perfect repetition," Henry said.

"Hence why I sought you out. Your understanding of the grand epic of mankind…it suits you to this task."

"What task?"

"A crisis is coming. Collapse is on the horizon for the West."

"So? That sort of thing is inevitable. It's been almost eighty years since the end of World War II. That's how these things go."

"Only a fool would ask you to stop history in its tracks," the warrior said. "But you must understand that there are an opportunistic few who would take advantage of the coming troubles. A few who would seek to make the suffering greater. To make the death tolls higher. To scorch the earth of not just civilization, but culture. Gawg and Megawg."

"Those names were on the gates. I can't imagine you're here to tell me that cannibals are about to overrun the Earth. So, what are they?"

The scene shifted to a distinctly medieval city. From the sheer number of bodies and the bulbs on their flesh, Henry identified it as the period of the Black Death.

"Before the Bubonic Plague, Europe had no understanding of germ theory," the warrior said. "Families slept in the same bed, naked. There was little to no connection between hygiene and health. Overpopulation from the medieval warm period made cities cramped and crowded. Hands would go through the day touching poisoned water, fecal matter, dirt, food, clothes, cleaning water, and more."

"Yeah. And a third of the continent paid the price," Henry said.

"They had set themselves up, unknowingly, for a plague to disproportionately dec-imate their population. Only later did we realize what had gone wrong." The warrior snapped his fingers, changing the scene to Times Square in New York. "The people of your time have done the same to their souls. Your time's abandonment of the spiritual and esoteric, in whatever form one wishes to see them, has set the world up for a psychological plague of the spirit on the scale of the Black Death. The Megawgs are the ones who set you up for this catastrophe."

"What reason do I have to believe you?" Henry asked. "You seem to be asking a lot of me here, burdening me with some...task, as you very specifically described it. If this is supposed to move me to some kind of action, it's failed. I'm ambivalent at best. So, tell me specifically what you're trying to get through to me."

"This is a fight for survival. For the future. You are one of the few with the skills to outflank the enemies of mankind. When you find the tomb of Alexander, you must do so committing yourself to that destiny."

Henry furrowed his brow. "Oh, must I now?" he muttered, crossing his arms. A fight for survival? What was there to survive for? More humiliation? Despair? Not to mention all the material conditions of the world plummeting.

The warrior scoffed. "You act as if you've come to peace with an inevitability. Do not let your own fear disguise itself before it kills you in your sleep."

Henry slowly, groggily, blinked himself awake. His hand fumbled, trying to get a grip on the table over him. He lifted his head from a lumpy, makeshift pillow made out of his waist pack wrapped in his mandarin jacket as he sat up in the cushioned restaurant booth he'd been sleeping in. He'd once again snuck into the ferry's onboard eatery to get something approximating a mattress.

Glancing out the window next to him at the pitch-black Aegean Sea, he figured it was way too early for him to be awake. He checked his phone and confirmed that it was another three hours before the ferry was due to arrive in Crete.

Deciding he needed some fresh air, he stepped through the boat's lobby and staircases toward the upper decks, carefully walking around passengers sleeping on the carpeted floors and in chairs until he reached the metal hatch door to the highest deck accessible to passengers.

The full moon reflected off the calm waves of the Mediterranean, the only source of light in a void of blackness. Salty sea wind blew through his hair as he leaned against the metal railing across from the door. He wasn't sure if he was warm or cold, his sweat combining with the humidity to make him feel both.

His head still ached from his encounter with Weiying.

He had relied on martial prowess until now. But that too had failed him.

It was the one thing he could match the greatest Magicians with. The one thing that he could rely on.

And Weiying had taken that from him, too.

He stared at the four-story drop onto the lowest of the decks below, his hands quivering. The warrior's words echoed in his head.

"Do not let your own fear disguise itself before it kills you in your sleep."

He wasn't afraid. He wouldn't be out here in the first place if he was afraid.

But another thought occurred to him. What business did he have going after Alexander's tomb? When Alexander was his age, he was already king of Macedon.

Meanwhile, Henry was a college dropout and a flunking Magician, not to mention a Defector.

He squeezed his eyes shut. The more he felt sorry for himself, the more useless he was. *Quit whining,* he told himself.

It had only gone wrong because he had let his emotions get the best of him. But a part of him was indignant at the idea of having to control his emotions while Weiying had been the one at fault.

His back tingled with the resonance of an old wound.

How had he been so stoic when receiving it?

It was the worst pain he'd ever felt in his life. And yet he remembered staring at High Command, at his brother, with nothing but sweat and a silent promise of retribution on his face.

The hatch door to the deck creaked open. Henry glanced back as Marion stepped out onto the metal.

"What are you doing out here?" she asked, stretching in that expansive way after waking up.

"Just...admiring the sights." Henry nodded at the moon.

"You're pretty sweaty from moon-watching." She chuckled as she joined him on the railing. She pulled out a cigarette and stuck it between her lips before offering him one.

"It's the saltwater," he said. "And I don't partake."

"No, for *me,* it's the saltwater. I'm sticky. You're soaked." She said, lighting her cigarette.

Henry grimaced.

"Didn't sleep so well, did you?"

He shook his head, leaning on the railing. "Those dreams are a pain in the ass."

Marion nodded as she blew out a jet stream of smoke. "I don't think they're designed to remind us of pleasant moments."

Henry had half a mind to ask her what she'd seen, but he knew that would come with revealing his own past—something he was very invested in avoiding.

"I take it yours have something to do with your brother."

Henry didn't confirm nor deny it, but his shifting posture told her all she needed to know.

"I can't believe that coward beat me in a fight," he blurted out. "Fuck, uh...just forget I—ugh..."

"You can speak freely with me," Marion assured him.

That wasn't the problem.

"Look...next time, I won't let my brother get to me. I almost got us killed. It won't happen again," Henry said. "I'm just...not used to working with other people. Sometimes I forget there are more lives than mine at stake."

Marion shrugged, tapping her ashes off the side of the deck. "Well, I suppose I can forgive a few counts of reckless endangerment."

Henry scoffed, leaning away from her. "You are *way* too nice to be a Magician."

She grinned.

"That's not a compliment. It freaks me out." Henry was serious, but her unapologetic demeanor was about equal parts impressive and off-putting. "Don't expect me to spill anything in return, but...you don't seem like the type to be participating in this kind of race. And didn't you say you were the one who brought us together? Why?"

Marion grimaced, her lips thinning out as she considered the question. "If I'm honest," she started, "it's a little too personal for my liking."

Henry nodded. "Guess we're in the same boat." He glanced at the deck below them. "Heh, get it?"

Marion scrunched her nose up in faux disgust, though she was still grinning as she rolled her eyes. "And what about you, Mr. Broody? What's the plan for your fifteen billion?"

"Didn't I just say I wouldn't spill anything?"

"What, are you too shy to talk about your hopes and dreams about...I don't know, buying a house in Istria?" She mocked him, putting her cigarette out on the metal railing.

"Bold of you to assume I wanna move to Europe," Henry said. "No, it's...it's not about the money for me. It's deeper than that."

"Hm. Well, you and I may have our secrets..." Henry almost yelped as Marion dug her hand into his pocket and fished out the Honor coin. "But I'll still let you in on a little something: these coins are more than just keys." She planted the wrapped coin in his palm. "See you at sunrise."

With that, she walked off towards the hatch door, heading back below deck.

Henry unwrapped the coin, raising an eyebrow at the face of Achilles as he clutched it with its shielding cloth.

The coin began to glow with a soft red light as he held it to himself. Particularly towards his armpits. Towards his swords.

He lifted an arm and moved the coin closer to his blade. The light became more intense.

"What the hell..." Henry drew the sword.

He kept moving the two items closer, spurring the light to brighten until the two touched. The coin spewed out a jet of sparks as it touched the flat of the sword's blade, almost causing Henry to drop them as he pulled them apart.

Hesitating, he pushed the edge of the coin against the blade again. He touched the weapon, and it screamed with the crisp noise of red-hot iron being quenched, spraying crimson sparks all over the deck.

Henry drew the coin up the flat of the blade. A series of old Chinese characters appeared on the metal, flaring red before cooling to a darkened etching.

The characters read *Gan Jiang*.

Henry quickly did the same to his other sword. Its markings were different, reading *Mo Ye*. Both names were from a Chinese myth.

The river stone under his shirt felt near-to-burning against his skin. He could even feel something emanating from the weapons with his own senses before the presence faded with the glow. Almost like...like a tether—a thread of fate binding him to the swords.

He wrapped the coin back up and pocketed it before holding his swords aloft.

Slowly, he uncurled his fingers from the handles and...removed them.

The swords hovered in the air.

With a thought, the handles zipped back into his palms, causing him to stumble.

"No way..."

CHAPTER ELEVEN
Sea Snakes

Through a pair of sunglasses, Analise glanced over top of her magazine, staring across the waterfront plaza of Aristotelous Square. The coastal breeze of Thessaloniki managed to counteract the ruthlessness of the Macedonian sun, offering a pleasantly temperate climate.

She stared at a door to a small souvenir shop far across the plaza—almost a hundred and fifty meters, by her estimation—with magically enhanced eyesight. Keeping her eye on it, she waited.

But the longer she waited, the more her mind kept drifting to those dreams she'd been having. Two of them.

If these were going to become a constant, she would really prefer it if Alexander's emissaries were clearer about what exactly she was getting herself into. Especially if she had to watch herself make that damned stupid mistake again. It was like the dreams were taunting her, dangling the promise of that bitter memory in front of her like the season finale of a particularly stressful TV show.

Maybe she should ask if the others saw anything different. Once she was out from under the oppressively watchful eye of the Hecatean Circle.

She could feel the ever-present static of their surveillance network in her arcane senses, like a weight just barely hovering over her chest.

She shook her head. No use in her worrying. Even if she was caught, it was worth it to shoot out the proverbial kneecaps of the Hecateans. But she wouldn't be caught. Because she was ready for this. That was the whole point of this.

She'd lied by saying she was only in this hunt because she feared for the balance of power between the Circles. Undoubtedly, part of her truly believed that was a present danger. But her real reason was so much pettier.

She was fairly sure that she didn't have to save the world to get what she wanted. But what better way to prove herself?

The thought of it sent a small thrill jolting up her spine. Just like the prospect of the hunt for the tomb itself.

Analise sat up as magic burned her senses like a huge whiff of petrol from a car exhaust.

The hell was going on in that shop?

She stared at the door across the plaza as it burst open, nearly coming off its hinges.

Yianni, carrying a large duffel bag, stepped out of the shop, rolling his shoulders as if trying to get a kink out.

Analise pressed her earpiece radio as civilians backed away in shock.

"Sétanta...what the hell was that blast of magic I felt?" she asked. "Detection enchantments are all over the city. Your usage was not to exceed two meters of sensitivity."

"Do you not think I heard you the first fifty times you said it?" Yianni said. "It was either that or a gunshot in a public square."

Analise squeezed her eyes shut, whispering a curse under her breath.

"Look, I was compromised, but I got the apparatus."

She sighed. Her mind raced. They had the apparatus, but at what cost? When would the Greeks descend on them? Would she have time to shut down their network?

"We're going to have to move fast," she muttered.

"Are you pissed? You seem pissed." Yianni's voice was like a squawking bird in her ear.

"I gave you specific instructions to avoid drawing attention," she said as Yianni finished his walk across the plaza and joined her with the bag as she gathered her things.

They started north, away from the waterfront of Thessaloniki.

"You really shouldn't expect that much of me. Are you always this miserable?" Yianni asked, hovering over her shoulder as they walked. "Or does sunlight make you cranky?"

"I am *not* miserable," Analise growled, crossing the street.

"Coulda fooled me. Just because you gave me instructions doesn't mean everything's going to go right," Yianni said. "How have you gotten this far with that attitude?"

"How have *you* gotten this far?" Analise snapped. "With your constant complaining! Do you even care about finding the tomb, or are you just here to crack wise?"

"Oh, right, that's me. Mister Class Clown! Resident chucklefuck! Not miserable, huh? I've never met someone as cranky as you. You stress me out, lass," Yianni hissed as they turned a corner and started down a sunbaked sidewalk along one of the main roads. "And for your information, I *do* care. I seem to care much more than you do. If I really want something, I don't give a damn how it happens!"

Analise pinched the bridge of her nose. Her first instinct was to fire back again, but she couldn't afford to psych herself out of the mood to dismantle the apparatus. Especially if they were going to be on a clock.

"Look, sorry I couldn't pull it off exactly the way you wanted." Yianni sighed as they turned right, down one of the side roads next to an Orthodox church. "But I took out those Hecatean lackeys before they could call for reinforcements. We're deep in it. Can't afford to be perfect. Or fight too much."

Analise shook her head. "If any of us slips up, it could lead to us not waking up tomorrow. We can't afford to take those kinds of losses."

"Well, we'll just have to agree to disagree." Yianni sighed. "You can think I'm a brute or a moron, but caution is a luxury. The Circles want us to play close to the chest."

"If you want to leave yourself open like that, fine. But try to consider other people, tough guy. I'd rather not make any stupid and avoidable mistakes."

By the time they'd finished slinging mud at one another, they had returned to their hostel, *Zeus is Loose*. It was certainly...a name.

The hostel was a seven-story tall baby-blue building with a bar at the top. For all the amenities it had, it wasn't the most sociable place, something Yianni had spent the last night lamenting.

They passed the front desk and took the elevator to the fourth-floor kitchen, covered in large windows and giving the modern interior a pleasant dose of sunlight.

Yianni set the duffel bag on the table farthest from the elevator, in front of the full-size kitchen island.

The area was devoid of anyone, allowing Analise to open the bag and pull out a wheel of solid brass and copper with concentric circles loose within its bounds. Stripes of ivory along each wheel had sets of symbols carved into them.

"So...what is this thing?" Yianni asked.

Analise scoffed as her fingers ran along the symbols. "I thought you were a Greek Magician."

"I'm not exactly the most studied Magician in the world." Yianni shrugged. "Only got my first burst of Greek magic a month ago."

She sighed, though she couldn't really blame him. It wasn't like other Circles welcomed Defectors to learn their magic with open arms.

Analise had gotten lucky. She would often trade information for information with other Circles, exchanging intelligence for understanding of their magic.

In fact...she *could* teach Yianni a little.

"From how I understand it, at least, Greek magic is split into three types: Homeric, corresponding with the Achaeans, Classical, and Hellenistic, for everything after Alexander the Great," she said.

"Wait, how do you know this?"

She gave him an unamused look. "You could afford to open a book once in a while. Now, pay attention. Homeric magic channels power through magical objects, rare plants, and divine theurgy. This is what we have here—a codex wheel connected to a bunch of other wheels that create a network all over the city," she explained, setting the wheel down. "The key to breaking Homeric magic is not with a countercharm or other arcane solutions. There's typically a weakness that can be puzzled out."

Yianni nodded. "In this case, it's literally a puzzle, right?"

"Well, not exactly." Analise chuckled.

She picked up the wheel and smashed it into the table, causing the concentric rings to scatter everywhere.

"Jesus!" Yianni flinched as metal flew past him. "How the hell is that supposed to help?"

"The codes and symbols were a red herring. The arcane wiring just serves to alert the other wheels of its position. Fiddling with it would've been our downfall," Analise said. "Odysseus defeated Circe by threatening her and making her swear an unbreakable oath. Often, the simplest answer is the correct one." She let out a sigh of relief as the omnipresent static washed away, the presence of the network gone. "See? And now we can make our own link in the chain out of its pieces."

She grabbed a clay tablet from her backpack. With a small amount of Theurgy, she wetted the tablet enough to write on, turning it into a Katadesmoi—a Roman curse tablet.

Granted, she never used it for curses. They took too long and were too convoluted.

"What's that for?" Yianni asked.

"It's for scripting," Analise said. "It's like programming, except with...you know, magic."

Yianni chuckled. "Well, would you look at that? Seriously, how do you know so much about this stuff?"

She grimaced. "A mix of opportunity and curiosity."

"Well, that curiosity of yours is fuckin' something."

Analise scoffed, embarrassed to take the praise. "It's not so...Anyone could've..." She sighed. "I'm glad you see it that way."

"Guess we can finally use our phones again," Yianni said, pulling his out.

"*And* I can access the last few days of communications on our opponents' side." Analise knelt down to the wreckage of the disk and plucked out a small green gemstone humming with arcane energy. She focused on it, synthesizing the traces of data into her ADZ display.

"Shit," she hissed.

"What is—oh. That can't be good." Yianni looked at his own display in his vision.

And a message about assassins deployed two days ago to Crete.

"I don't believe you." Marion chuckled as they were dropped off in a small parking lot on the coastline in Plakias, a small beach town on the southern side of Crete. "You mean to tell me the moment I left, that coin started casting spells?"

The parking lot sat just off the main and only real road in front of a car rental. The sun beat down on Henry's brow as he scanned the horizon, finding nothing but mountains to the north, east, and west. All the way down to the pier in the west and as far as he could see to the east, the main road was lined with restaurants claiming half the road with outdoor seating, supermarkets with sunbaked signage, souvenir stores built like labyrinths of postcard stands, and tourist offices using repurposed janitorial signs to advertise their services.

"I'm serious. My swords have enchantments on them that weren't there before. I can call them back to my hands and shit," Henry said. "But if the coins can all do something like that, they might balance the playing field for us. Did you know they could do that?"

"I didn't know they could do *that* with your swords. I just thought it would've taken longer for it to manifest."

"You really need to tell me this stuff," Henry insisted. "Stop being coy about it."

"But where's the fun in that?" Marion threw her hands up. "Besides, I...kind of forgot."

"You forgot." Henry frowned. "Brilliant save."

"I'm serious! I'm really bad at keeping track of this stuff!"

He was about to accuse her further, but as he thought about it, nothing he'd seen contradicted her explanation. Actually, travelling with her just these few hours had proved what an impulsive and disorganized person she was.

It wasn't always a bad thing. He himself wasn't huge on details, but still preferred to plan ahead. Marion was on another level. And they were in a possibly life-or-death situation here.

Henry's stomach roiled as it groaned for food, interrupting his thoughts. "Well...let's get to the hostel first. I need breakfast." He sighed. "But at some point *today*, you tell me everything. I'll note it down in my journal."

"I need a shower." Marion grimaced after toying with a strand of her hair. It was oily, but nothing compared to the clumped strands atop Henry's head. But food was more important than cleanliness right now.

"We both need sleep, too. I think in the past three days, I've gotten a grand total of five hours."

Marion groaned. "Oh, I would kill for a nap. I hope this place is nice."

"Well, it looked decent when I booked it, and it has good reviews," Henry muttered.

He and Marion made their way past the main town, which had proved to be no more than the one main road, and made the journey towards the single hostel in Plakias, going across dirt roads, old pavement, and gravel pathways, weaving through resorts and hotels.

In spite of how remote this place was, tourists accidentally seeing through Solomon's Wisdom was probably their biggest problem.

Well, if he was lucky.

The two of them turned off their maps as they glanced to the left, where the hostel was supposed to be.

In front of them, off the gravel pathway, was a two-meter-tall white plaster wall. Under a small arch, they entered onto a small cobblestone pathway that wound its way through a grove of olive trees and white stucco cabins dotting either side of the path, shrouded by the grove's shade.

A cat pranced across the path in front of them as Henry spotted a central pavilion at the end of the grove. The patio was occupied with a few tables flanked either by white lawn chairs or wooden benches.

"You sure this isn't a campground?" Marion frowned.

"Well, it's called Youth Hostel Plakias, so I'm guessing the owner would disagree," Henry said.

"It's unique, if nothing else." She glanced to the left as the grove opened up into a small field of grass with a row of trees around the edge of the property. Each of the trunks supported a hammock. "Oh, those look like the perfect place to read!"

"I can actually practice here." Henry stamped on the dirt beneath his feet. "Instead of bashing my knee against concrete every time I do a butterfly stance."

The central pavilion also happened to be home to a kitchen, creating a unique open-air atmosphere for pretty much everything.

Five or so girls around their late teens and early- to mid-twenties were occupying said kitchen, making something for breakfast.

"Excuse me, do you know where we can check in?" Henry called out.

"Oh, the office is just through there." A girl with braided blonde hair, wearing shorts over a red two-piece bathing suit, pointed to a doorway in the back of the pavilion. "But the owner's out right now." She had an English accent, but Henry wasn't too good at placing the region.

His nose caught a whiff of whatever was in their pot. His mouth watered. "Uh...second question: Do you guys mind if I have some of...whatever you're making? I haven't eaten in like...two days."

"Sure!" The girl smiled. "It's pasta for breakfast, but if you're fine with that, we have enough for everyone."

Henry turned to Marion and jabbed his thumb at the pavilion. "Imma go eat."

"I will get a shower, then. Which..." Her eyes landed on another building made of white stucco and separated from the cabins, pavilion, and pathway. She sighed as she set her backpack down and fished out a change of clothes, toiletries and a towel. "Stow my bag away, will you?" she asked as she headed towards the bath house.

Henry grabbed both their backpacks and their gun bag, stowing them in the owner's office through the doorway in the pavilion. When he emerged, one of the girls handed him a paper bowl filled with pasta with some kind of pesto and a fork.

"Thanks." He grinned.

He wandered over to one of the many plastic tables surrounding the edge of the patio with an empty white lawn chair.

"Mind if I join you?" he asked the current occupants of the table, which included a man with a wispy beard, a shaggy haircut, and large, round glasses, and a woman with suntanned skin, a pleasant smile, and silky blonde hair.

"Sure thing," the man responded with a quirky smile and an Australian—or New Zealander—accent. Henry could never tell the difference.

"I'm Henry, by the way," he said, shaking both their hands, eager to get the pleasantries out of the way so he could eat.

"I'm Sahara," the woman said, also in an Australian accent. "That's Percy."

"Nice to meet you," Henry said, already stuffing his mouth. "Sahara like the desert?"

"Yes, like the desert." She chuckled.

Henry nodded, barely swallowing before wolfing down more pasta. "I haven't eaten anything but saltine crackers for the last day and a half."

"No worries, mate." Percy grinned. "Where're ya from?"

Henry swallowed before answering this time. "The Midwest. Iowa, if you know where that is."

Percy gave him a so-so gesture.

"How about you two?"

"New Zealand," Percy said.

"Sydney," Sahara added. "Did you come in on the ferry?"

"This morning," Henry mumbled. "Took a bus straight here from Chania."

Percy laughed. "That explains your appetite."

"You didn't stick around to see Chania?" Sahara asked. "It's worth the visit."

He shrugged in response. "You guys been travelling long? What can you recommend around here?" Henry asked between bites. He wasn't just talking to talk. He was looking for a lay of the land from a tourism perspective in case he had to worry about spectators when he went after the coin.

"We're just here for a few weeks, though this is one of Sahara's favorite spots to come back to. We're on more of a work trip, so we haven't gotten out to see much," Percy said. "But there is a hike from here to a gorge about halfway up the island that was a real treat. Oh, and the Hidden Beach is nice. How about yourself? Is this your first time abroad?"

"Well, I never really had anything to spend money on. I've been working for the last two years. Had a lot saved up and thought, *Fuck it, Europe trip*. Not my first time going international, though," Henry lied.

"Oh, yeah? Where have you been so far?"

Henry pursed his lips. "Um...Morocco and Italy so far. Not counting Greece. Planning on going to Turkey, and I'm gonna see if I have the cash to get to Egypt."

"Egypt? Oh, I *loved* being there. Just make sure you don't let the shopkeepers rope into buying anything you don't wanna pay for." Sahara smiled, clasping her hands.

Henry raised his eyebrows. "I dealt with that plenty in Morocco."

He glanced to his left as Marion walked into the courtyard from the bath house, drying her wet hair and wearing a swimsuit top and shorts. She caught sight of him and joined their table.

"That was fast," Henry muttered.

She scoffed, a hint of defensiveness in her voice. "I'm clean."

"And this is?" Percy asked.

"This is Marion. She's from Germany," Henry said. "Marion, this is Percy and Sahara from New Zealand and Australia."

"Nice to meet you." Marion grinned.

"Are you two travelling together?" Percy asked.

"I wanted to go to Santorini at first, but Santorini is Santorini. Not too budget-friendly. Plus, all the flights were super early, so I decided to just tag along with Marion," Henry lied.

"And what brings you all the way out here?" Percy directed the question to Marion.

"Just taking a year off before I start uni next semester."

"Oh! Wait, so, then...how old are you two?" Sahara asked. "If you don't mind."

"Twenty," Marion said.

"I'm nineteen," Henry said.

"Nineteen? You're only nineteen?" Sahara exclaimed.

"Well...she's only a year older." Henry nodded towards Marion.

"Yeah, but she's twenty. It just...sounds different than nineteen." Sahara pursed her lips. "You're a baby."

"I've been mistaken for thirty once," Henry claimed defensively.

Sahara scoffed. "Is that something to be proud of? I'd give you twenty-two. Max."

"It's the beard, I think." Henry scruffed up his goatee. He wasn't really able to grow much facial hair on his cheeks, so he settled for what he could get.

"Yeah, no. I see it." Percy chuckled. "Still, thirty's a stretch."

"How long are you guys staying here?" Sahara asked.

"A few days. We're taking things slow..." Marion said.

"Oh! Well, if you have the time, you should come out clubbing with us!" Sahara offered. "A group from the hostel is going as well."

Henry met Marion's glance again. "Well...we didn't exactly get to experience the pub crawl in full last time," she said.

"Hm...I don't know. I've never been clubbing before," Henry said.

Sahara let out an excited gasp.

"Plus, I'm not much of a drinker. It's not legal in America until you're twenty-one."

"I forgot about that!" Sahara exclaimed. "Oh, now, you *have* you go. I'll buy you some drinks. I want to see you shitfaced."

Henry felt dread start to creep up his throat. He didn't really want this distraction getting in the way of his hunt. But then again...it wasn't like he had much else to do while Analise and Yianni were taking care of things up north.

"Don't worry. We'll take care of you if you can't hold your liquor, right?" Marion smirked, glancing at Sahara.

"Without a doubt," she said with an almost-predatory tone.

She and Percy left the table with their dishes scraped clean as Henry leaned towards Marion. "There's a place nearby called the Hidden Beach, apparently," he said. "Wanna head there to do a sweep?"

Marion shrugged. "I could do with a change of scenery. If that's not private, I don't know what is."

"Seems fairly public to me." Henry said as he and Marion landed on the gravelly shores of a beach closed in by several weed-infested rock formations.

There were several families and couples littered around the beach and in the coastal waters. The searing-hot pebbles would've hurt, but one perk of knowing Fire Style Wuxing Quan was an increased resistance to heat.

Marion tiptoed across the pebbly beach and was quick to lay down a towel and step onto it.

Henry drew the character for silk in the pebbles and grabbed onto the edge of a silk cloth, which he lashed into a blanket for him to lounge on.

"It's pretty empty, all things considered," Marion muttered, toying with the golden sunburst on her chain necklace.

They had both changed into beach-worthy attire. She was sporting a two-piece bathing suit with a top patterned with something akin to tile mosaics, while Henry sat with an open button-down shirt and a pair of solid-color trunks.

Marion grabbed a folding map of Crete she had swiped from the Rethymno bus station and laid it out on the pebbles. Henry helped pin it down with his butterfly swords. She took a spool of golden thread and lined the map with it. "Can I see your river stone?" She held out her hand.

Henry pulled the paracord off his neck and gave it over. "Don't you have a radar?"

"They're too expensive." Marion sighed. "My sunstone is a good alternative. I can still cast the spell. It just needs a conduit."

She unclipped the sunburst necklace from behind her neck and held it up to the actual sun. She placed the river stone under it like a lens, and the sunstone in the middle of the golden pendant seemed to refract the sunlight into the visible color spectrum before the river stone cast it over the map, highlighting sources of magic.

Henry fiddled with the silk knot on his left forearm, hiding a rope dart in his sleeve. The dart's blade was now enchanted with the Honor coin's power, which turned it into a much more versatile tool, able to launch at any target he willed and retract into a perfect wrap around his arm in under a second. It was different from the swords in that there was only one axis of movement: wherever his arm was pointing.

"We have two big hits," Marion said.

Henry stopped messing with his weapon and pulled out his phone to take a picture of the map. He showed her the photo as she returned the two necklaces to their rightful places. There were two heavily saturated splotches of blue in their area, with smaller dots splattered across the map.

"We have one in the gorge just north of here, where I was suspecting it might be," Henry said. "And one to the east at...Kleidesi beach."

"The people at the hostel called it...One Rock, right?"

"Yeah. Something about an underwater tunnel," he muttered. "What do you think?"

"It'll be much easier for people to go to One Rock," Marion said. "We might encounter problems. But it's probably the first place any of our competitors would check."

"I don't know. I think the gorge is more likely to have it," Henry said.

Marion pursed her lips, considering. "I suppose One Rock would be better to cover at night. For the sake of avoiding tourists and all. We'll go to the gorge tomorrow, then. Hopefully, Analise and Yianni can find a boat to get here before then. Assuming everything went well for them..."

Henry's phone buzzed with a notification. He pulled it out of his bag to find a message from Analise. "Speak of the devil..."

"Is it them?"

Henry's eyes scanned the message. "*On our way south. Should be there by tomorrow. FYI, it looks like the Hecateans employed some mercenary help and they're on Crete right now. Watch your backs.*"

"Mercenaries?"

"Shouldn't be too big of a problem. Mercenaries can be negotiated with," Henry said. "Plus, they typically come in much lower numbers." He pulled out the two coins wrapped in violet cloth. "In the meantime, you can explain these to me. In full."

"Right." Marion sighed. "Let's see...I guess I don't have much to tell aside from—"

"Tell me everything," Henry said. "Let's be thorough. Even stuff I already know."

She frowned at him. "Will it coax the stick out of your ass?"

"Only one way to find out."

She rolled her eyes, so Henry rolled his back.

Marion blew a raspberry. "Okay, the beginning. So, I got kicked out of the Palatine Order and had to scrounge up some money, so I did a job for the Greeks. They were digging up some old rocks in Bulgaria. The South Slavs weren't happy about it. But they were excavating this old Macedonian tomb, and...one night, I got a dream from that armored man in front of the big gates. He directed me to Iraq and the ruins of Babylon, where I found my coin, and then had a second dream from that, which led me to Morocco—"

"*Your* coin?" Henry asked.

"Yes, *my* coin." Marion snatched the Wisdom coin out of his hands. "That one is yours."

Henry narrowed his eyes at her.

"What? Don't you know how to share?" Marion said. "We need all four, so stop being paranoid."

He sighed. "What does your coin do?"

"It creates a huge amount of sunlight that destroys illusions and some enchantments. It also makes the undead dead again and banishes creatures not of this world. It's helpful that the spell looks the same as my Kenaz rune. It's the thing I do when I blind people." On her forearm, she showed him a tattoo shaped like a wide arrow without a stick. "But that's about all I know. See? Not much."

Henry blinked. "You could've explained it to me before."

"You must've been a delightful child. Just enjoy the beach." Marion sighed, propping herself up on her elbows as she laid back.

Henry frowned. "I've never really been one for beaches, personally."

"Why not?" she shot a look at him.

"I...I'm not a huge fan of the ocean," Henry mumbled.

"You're afraid of the ocean? We were just on a ferry."

"I didn't say I was afraid. I just like to avoid it if I can help it. It's fine if I'm on a boat or...if it's a lake or a river," he said. "I mean, have you *seen* the shit that lives down there? The abominations? Do you know what a telescope fish is?"

"Those are so far down," Marion protested.

"Well, I didn't exactly call it a rational aversion."

"'Aversion?'" She scoffed. "That's unfortunate. Because now, you and I"—she pushed herself to her feet—"are getting in the water."

Henry gave her a glare.

"Come on." She held her hand out to him. "Just the water. I'll teach you how to swim. I don't want to be exploring that cave at One Rock alone."

"I can swim." He took her hand, but didn't draw on her help when getting to his feet. "I became the fastest swimmer in my middle school so I could get out of the ocean faster."

Marion giggled, a sound he wasn't used to hearing from her, but one that put him at ease more than he expected.

"For all of human history, mankind has feared the ocean and its unfathomable depths," Henry said as Marion grabbed his wrist and dragged him down to the shoreline. "You're a mythologist; you should know. I see no reason not to adhere to that wisdom."

"Tradition is not a valid argument. Just because something has always been done doesn't mean that it should continue being so."

"Oh, no?" Henry scoffed. "Tell me, Marion, are you a fan of democracy?"

"Yes?" She quirked an eyebrow.

"What greater democracy, then, is there than the democracy of the dead? All the dead people that came before us voted and did things a certain way that worked for them, more or less. Granted, democracy isn't perfect. But compared to an oligarchy ruled by the tiny minority of those still alive? I think dead democracy is the morally righteous option."

"Well, societies tend to self-proliferate. Most people had values instilled in them before they got the chance to vote on whether or not they liked said values over any others," Marion responded.

"Ah, the blank-slate argument. I think it's going a bit overboard to say people were brainwashed into participating in a culture. Doesn't that justify authoritarian regimes to program people with 'correct' values?"

Marion scoffed. "You're such a nerd, Heinrich." She turned to him, hands folded behind her head with a sly smile on her face. "And all this to justify your fear of this beautiful sea."

Henry glanced down. He was standing in the coastal waters, the pleasantly chill waves lapping at his feet.

"See? That's not so bad, is it?" She put an arm around his shoulders.

"Alright, you don't have to patronize me." He shrugged her off, but smiled—though some of his anxiety returned upon looking out into the bluer waters not far from where they stood. "This is the Mediterranean Sea, anyway. It's not really an ocean."

She scoffed again, punching him lightly in the arm.

CHAPTER TWELVE
Minoan Marauding

Henry sat at the bar in a dark room full of flashing and swirling lights. Music pounded into his skull. It was too loud to hear anyone unless they yelled directly into his ear.

But despite all the stimulation, his eyes were glued to a metal cage in the back of the club, where Sahara and two other patrons were dancing, eliciting cheers from the crowd on the dancefloor.

He and the others from his hostel had drunk quite a bit before coming here, so he was well into the realm of tipsy. But even if he were sober, he'd be willing to bet that his reaction would be the same.

"Do you wanna go in there?" Marion asked over the music.

"Over my dead body!" He shook his head.

The bartender passed three drinks to them. Henry picked up his gin and tonic, while Marion and Percy each grabbed a beer. "A gin and tonic?" Percy asked.

"He hasn't learned to love beer yet!" Marion said, drinking a quarter of her glass in a matter of seconds before scrunching up her nose in disgust. "Ugh! Six euros for this?"

"Everything is six!" Henry said. "Why'd you get a beer?"

Percy scoffed. "What kind of system is that?"

"*Ein* stupid one!" Marion finished the rest of her drink before Henry could even get halfway through his. "Come on! Finish up, and let's dance!"

Henry squeezed his eyes shut and downed the rest of a pretty damn strong cocktail before throwing himself off his barstool and half-walking, half-stumbling into the center of the dance floor, mostly following Marion around, since she seemed to know what she was doing here. He glanced around self-consciously as she started moving to the beat of the very, very loud music.

No surprise, but Henry had never really been much of a dancer. And for as much as people compared dance to martial arts, especially Chinese wushu, it wasn't a style of dance even remotely suited for club music. Still, he couldn't just stand around.

A lot of the other guys were just kind of bobbing their shoulders and heads, which seemed easy enough.

Him and Marion facing each other offered some illusion of privacy, as if they were partners in a ballroom, but if that were really the case, he at least knew how to waltz.

And they said alcohol was supposed to suppress anxiety.

Get out of your head, he told himself. *If you wanted to, you could kill everyone in the room in under a minute, no contest.*

Somehow, that made him a bit more comfortable.

He began to get more into it, moving more of his body and doing so more enthusiastically. Marion matched his energy, and for a moment, he actually found the appeal, so long as he just forgot about literally everything else on his mind, which seemed to kind of be the point.

Henry felt himself get pushed off-balance as someone moved past him.

The perpetrator was a man who had to be at least thirty, with a receding hairline, but all the enthusiasm for dancing in the world as he not-so-subtly tried to take Henry's place as Marion's person-she-looked-at-while-dancing.

As he realized this, something strange manifested in Henry's chest.

Defensiveness?

Why?

He'd only known her for...what, three days? Two and a half weeks if he counted their run-in in Morocco.

And this was a club, not an ADZ. She could do whatever she wanted. He was in no place to tell her otherwise.

But it was kind of weird that this guy was in a club full of twenty-somethings. And pretty rude, all things considered.

And then again, it wasn't often he found himself with company he enjoyed. Keeping that company around seemed to be a subconscious priority of his.

Should he do something?

Would it be weird if he did something?

Would she think he was being courageous or chauvinistic?

Why did that matt—

Before he could finish that last thought, he was already moving, cutting the other guy off from getting into an imaginary circle he'd designated in his mind.

God, it took him that long to *walk* in front of him?

The guy was trying to move in to get between them before he could continue his thought.

Christ, am I getting myself into a fight? This is stupid, right? Right?

This time, Henry grabbed Marion's hand and spun her around in a sort of impromptu and drunken ballroom dance move, maneuvering them away to another part of the dance floor.

But she was smiling.

He'd take that.

A chill ran up his spine as a hand planted a firm slap on *his* ass.

Without thinking, Henry threw an elbow strike over his shoulder. His elbow crunched against flesh and bone. People gasped and scattered as whoever had violated his space fell to the ground and Henry dropped into a fighting stance, ready to kill.

"Ah, shit!" It was the older guy. "What the hell, man? I think...fuck, you broke my nose!"

Henry froze up. Everyone was staring at him.

"Hey, no fighting!" One of the bouncers at the door started pushing through the crowd.

Marion grabbed him by the wrist and pulled him away. "Sorry, everyone! They're drunk!"

Before he knew it, Henry was leaning over a small wooden balcony next to the stairs to the club, his ears stuffed with the deafening cotton of silence and his lungs full of clean air.

"Hey, are you alright?"

"Wanting to vomit is normal, right?" Henry slurred.

"Yes, very normal. Do you want to go to the bathroom?" Marion asked.

Henry shook his head. "I...I like the air outside."

"Okay...um...why don't we head back to the hostel? It's pretty late already. Two in the morning," Marion said. "You're good to walk back with me, right?"

Henry nodded. "Ugh...yeah, I think so."

"Alright. I'll help you." Marion put a hand on the small of his back as she guided him down the wooden steps to the paved surface of the main road.

"The hell was that?" Henry muttered. "I mean...I thought he was going for you."

"Who, the...the older guy?"

"Yeah...I...I kinda wedged myself in the way between you two. Was that...was that weird?"

Marion shook her head. "Not at all. I mean...you'd figure he'd have a family to go back to. That on its own is pretty strange."

"Right?" Henry shuddered. "And then...ugh, I feel filthy."

"He should not have done that," Marion said.

"I mean...I did nail him in the nose pretty good, so...I'm not too hung up about it." He chuckled.

"You shouldn't have had to do that in the first place."

Henry shrugged. "You can't stop shitty people from existing. Best you can do is protect yourself with your own strength."

"That explains a lot, actually. Is that your life philosophy?" Marion asked as the cool night air blew past them.

"Sure," he said. "But it's mostly from experience. People will always put their self-interest above other people. It's not a good or bad thing; you just...can't let it blindside you. I learned that lesson the hard way with the Tiandihui."

A moment of silence passed between them as they slowly made their way towards the entrance of the old town.

"Maybe...maybe I should've..." Henry trailed off. He regretted it before the words even had a chance to leave his mouth. "No. No, fuck them."

"What...what exactly happened? Why do you want this tomb, of all things?"

Henry shook his head.

"Come on. We're allies, aren't we?"

"Do you have any idea how many people have told me that? Seventeen. Seventeen people have told me 'we're friends' or 'we're allies' or 'we're squadmates' to get me to tell them things. How many of those people do you think used those things against me later on?" Henry asked.

Marion glanced down. "I...how many?"

"Sixteen." Henry scoffed. "Number seventeen wasn't convincing enough."

"So, what, you're just going to curl up into a cocoon? Not let anyone else in? Ever?"

Henry shrugged. "I don't know about *ever*, but...yeah. It's worked so far."

Marion stopped moving, giving him a shockingly potent look of pity and agony. "Listen to me when I say this, Henry. That way lies madness. If you close yourself off, you won't realize you need someone you can rely on until it's too late."

Henry narrowed his eyes. "Sixteen times, Marion. I may be an idiot, but I'm not a pushover. I will drop *anyone* who wastes my time trying the same lie."

Marion sighed and hefted more of his weight onto her shoulders as she muttered, "You're not an idiot..."

They stumbled out of the old city, leaning on one another as Henry, with strange coherence, recalled the directions back to the hostel.

"Did you ever have something like that happen?" he muttered in a moment of silence. "When you closed yourself off?"

Marion shot a glance at him and sighed. "At one point in time, yes. I had some...disagreements with my family, which led me to the Order of Cologne."

"Damn...that sucks."

"At least my family isn't actively belligerent." Marion shrugged. "But...everyone has their bad side."

"True." Henry nodded.

The journey back to the hostel was kind of a blur. Was he getting drunker? How?

Marion sat him down on one of the benches under the pavilion. He didn't realize she was calling his name until she was yelling it. "Heinrich!"

"Huh?" Everything was starting to swirl around him.

"Shit, I think someone might've slipped you something."

Henry laughed. "Why?"

"Nothing magical..." Marion muttered.

"I don't know...this is pretty magical to me." He let out a strange-sounding chuckle, though everything sounded strange right now.

"Is he alright?"

Henry glanced to the side. "Are you an angel?"

"No. I think someone drugged him," Marion said.

"Henry? Henry, it's me, Sahara." Her image cleared up as she knelt in front of him. "We're gonna fix you up, alright?"

"Can you get some food into him?" Marion asked. "I'll get some water. Make sure he doesn't fall asleep. The alcohol plus this might make him overdose."

"Got it," Sahara said.

Either a few seconds later or a few days later—they felt the same to Henry—Sahara knelt in front of him.

"Pity." She cupped his chin. "That friend of yours has downright freakish drug tolerance. Had it worked on both of you, things would've gone very differently tonight. You get to slip away this time, Zhao 4."

"Where am I?" he muttered.

"I'll make you a grilled cheese or something."

Henry's head felt like a ringing bell. He didn't remember much of anything after Marion helped him leave the club, but whatever had happened was showing off its consequences in full.

He'd downed at least three liters of water since waking up, but it wasn't helping things, in spite of Marion's insistence.

She told him he'd been drugged.

Why? How? It could have been one of the mercenaries Analise warned him about. But if they wanted him dead, they would need to take both him and Marion out.

Kourtaliotiko Gorge was one of several canyons and rock formations dotting southern Crete among the White Mountains.

The only footpath near the arcane signal Henry and Marion had gotten was a stone ramp off the side of a road that took them to a small white plaster church hidden under jagged cliffs of white limestone dotted with dry shrubs and moss. They could hear the rumbling of the gorge's main attraction, the waterfall, before they even got off the road. And the mist rising up from its location cast a cloud of fog into the otherwise-sunny and clear sky.

Analise and Yianni had shipped into Chania early in the morning, having finished their business in Thessaloniki. Thankfully, it seemed as though none of them had run into these hired guns of the Hecateans.

"Check, check. Everyone copy?" Analise patched in, having stayed in the rental car with her maps and a Finnish Sako TRG sniper rifle.

"Nezha, copy," Henry said.

"Sunna, copy."

"Sétanta, copy."

Out of all the guns in the bag, Henry had opted for a .44 Magnum revolver. Overkill? Definitely. Cool as shit? Absolutely. Besides, the only shotgun the Egyptians had gotten them was a monstrosity of a bullpup semi-automatic shotgun. Disconnecting the trigger from the firing mechanism and trying to stuff twelve-gauge shells into a magazine made it a breeding ground for jamming. As a frontliner, Henry figured a battle rifle would be dead weight for him more often than not.

Being the American in the group, the other two looked to Henry for what guns they should use, so he showed Marion how to use a low-recoil MP5 and managed to get Yianni to wrap his mind around a Glock when he refused to carry a proper rifle. He gave the Irishman credit on enthusiasm, as he didn't have to spend half an hour talking him into picking the thing up like he did for Marion, but it was really hard to teach him anything.

Marion and Yianni followed Henry as he trekked down the small flights of stairs towards the church. With his abomination of a shotgun slung over his shoulder, he was grateful there weren't any tourists here today. At least, not within sight. He *could* hear people talking from upstream. But that was a ways off.

"Damn, that water looks nice." Analise sighed. "I wish I could go for a swim."

"Once we're all richer than any person has a right to be, you can come back here as many times as you want, Moneta," Yianni said.

Henry glanced back at him as they stopped on the church's grounds. "Speaking of swimming, what's the plan with the kilt?" He nodded at the multicolored wool wrapped around Yianni's shoulder and waist. "Plus, aren't those a Scottish thing? I thought you were Irish."

"They're a wider Gaelic thing now," Yianni said. "And this isn't a kilt. It's a belted plaid, and it's gonna save someone's life today."

Henry raised an eyebrow, wondering how well a piece of wool could really be enchanted, but let it go.

The three Companions started on the stone bridge to their right, which overlooked the many waterfalls into the gorge that this place was famous for. A chorus of running and crashing water filled the air with an earthy freshwater scent.

"Oh, there it is!" Yianni exclaimed.

"I feel it too." Marion pointed down at the waterfalls. "It's coming from behind the big one."

Henry had no other choice than to take their word for it, unable to feel the arcane presence of the coin for himself. He stuck the dagger of his rope dart into the stone bridge and hopped onto the edge. He glanced down at the water below. It was shallow, and way further down than he'd initially thought.

"Can't we just take the stairs?" Yianni asked.

"I would recommend not doing that," Analise said over the radio. "We have bandits incoming. Bearing three-oh-two."

Henry whirled around as several silhouettes of light appeared in his vision thanks to Analise's interface.

"It's Staufer Squad."

"Again?" Henry glanced at Marion as if it were her fault. These were the consequences of not being thorough.

Cursing in Chinese, he rappelled off the bridge and down to the turquoise water below, under the shadow of the gorge's cliffs.

He landed in the knee-high water as the other two used his rope dart to follow him down. Water rained down from all directions, though only the roaring waterfall behind him had the mass to be called such.

Once all three were down in the gorge, Henry willed the enchantment on his rope dart to wrap itself perfectly around his arm again and turned towards the waterfall through a procession of dark cliffs and trickling streams.

"You guys said you saw something about assassins?" Marion asked. "Were they not talking about Staufer squad?"

"Didn't look like it," Yianni muttered.

"How much time do we have, Moneta?" Henry asked.

"If you're quick about it, enough."

"Let's haul ass, then, aye?" the Irishman said.

The three Companions waded deeper into the water, trudging towards the falls. Henry was starting to sense the coin too, if just a little.

Following the other two, he dove under the surface to pass through the waterfall, careful to avoid the rocks at the bottom. He broke through the surface in the middle of a cave.

He couldn't help but stare for a moment at the massive stone structure filling the cave, illuminated by what few streaks of light made it past the rocks and the waterfall.

"Holy shit," he muttered as he pulled himself out of the pool of water and onto the mossy rocks.

The structure looked like a Minoan palace, with red-and-black columns supporting overwhelmingly square stone architecture whose walls were stained with millennia-old paint. The faded reds and blues on the walls swirled around the white limestone to create foliage patterns and bulls out of the negative space. It wasn't quite large enough to be a proper palace complex. It might be more accurate to call this thing a temple.

"How has no one discovered this place?" Henry wondered, scanning the edifice.

Marion held up her fingers as if feeling for wind. "Must be Solomon's Wisdom keeping it hidden. This place is soaking in magic."

"Let's go, people. We don't have all day!" Yianni insisted.

There were only six known palatial sites from the mysterious Minoan civilization. To find something that not only brought that number of sites to seven, but something so intact...archaeologically speaking, this was more valuable than Alexander's tomb.

"Companion 1?" Analise asked.

"Heinrich?"

Henry turned back to the silhouettes. Inevitably, they would have to fight the Germans and their soldiers—soldiers who didn't give a damn about historical preservation.

"What'd I fuckin' tell yous?" Yianni spat.

Henry pulled his shotgun around to his front and pulled the bolt, chambering a round. "Still sure we have enough time, Moneta?"

"Still sure. Even if you don't, I think you three can take them. Wouldn't recommend it, though."

"Let's try to finish in time." Henry turned to the temple. "It's all you, Moneta."

At Analise's instruction, Henry veered off to the left, moving towards the stone stairwell that sloped up the temple's three floors. Even though only the first two floors had full reign over the complex, the third still had a lot of ground to cover. Analise assured him that the coin was on the first floor.

They entered the first floor, going into a maze of chambers and halls before turning right into one of said chambers. The room was small, with Henry's head almost touching the ceiling as he stood on the weathered rocks that made up the floor. The walls were stained red like every other wall in the complex, with murals of muted white and beige depicting fields and animals.

A rotting wooden door hung off the remains of a frame made from planks. Henry pushed past the door as gently as he could, stepping out into a long stone hallway with openings over the side towards the interior of the cave.

He couldn't help being starstruck by the intact architecture. Such perfectly preserved ruins from one of the world's oldest civilizations. The historian in him began to hyperventilate. He was getting to see what was probably the last example of intact Minoan architecture left in the world.

Eventually, Analise's instructions took them to a half-destroyed chamber that faced a courtyard in the center of the complex. Henry hopped over the ankle-high wall between him and the central courtyard's limestone brick floor. The Companions passed under a ring of roofing around the inside edge of the yard, held up by black columns. The rectangular space was flanked along the longer sides with stone podiums holding up pots, vases, and jars.

The art on them was all made up of black figures, popular in classical Greece and hitting a resurgence in the decades after Alexander's death. Notably anachronistic.

"It's here..." Marion muttered. "In one of these jars. But I can't tell which one."

"My ADZ is going ballistic in the courtyard. I'm not sure either," Analise said.

Henry turned and flinched as his eyes landed on a skeleton dressed in distinctly Ottoman armor. The skeleton's arm was propped up on one of the podiums, pinned by arrows covering any part of the body that could still hold them. The hand was covered in smashed pottery, and the podium noticeably lacked a piece to showcase.

"A puzzle plus, uh...death trap." Henry approached the skeleton, hands on his hips. "Great."

"Christ..." Marion examined the skeleton, tracing the trajectory of the arrows with her fingers. "It looks like the two walls on the far ends are rigged to fire a whole volley. I don't know if my defensive magic could take that kind of blow from two angles."

"How are we supposed to figure out the right jar?" Yianni asked. "That's just...fuckin' dandy."

"I think not being able to is kind of the point."

"Hey, the Germans crossed the waterfall. You guys need to hurry," Analise warned.

"No one would construct this if they *didn't* want someone to find it. They just want the right people," Marion said.

Yianni furrowed his brow. "Hang on..." He approached one of the jars.

"Don't smash anything you're not sure of, Companion 3!" Analise shouted.

"Mother of Christ, I'm not gonna fuckin' smash anything!" He sighed. "I just...these jars all have scenes on them. Scenes from the *Iliad*, I think."

Henry frowned and approached the same jar.

"Look. That figure is labeled Achilles. And Paris. This is the sacking of Troy," Yianni said.

Henry walked to the other side of the dead Ottoman and peered at the pot, although he had no idea how to read Ancient Greek or what any of the figures were doing.

Marion joined him and seemed to understand the pot in seconds. "Philoctetes slaying Paris..." She backed away from it. "So, our smashed pot is Achilles's death. Paris shot him in the heel. Which coin had the map to this place again?"

Holding it with the wrap so as to not alert every Magician in a fifty-mile radius, Henry unwrapped one of the coins, which turned out to be the right one. "Wisdom," he said. "Lysimachus and Diomedes."

"Forget that," Yianni said. "Both coins mentioned fear. Surely that throughline means something. Look for...I don't know, a scene of fearlessness."

Marion nodded. "Okay..." She started walking around the edges of the courtyard, taking note of every single pot. "Here we go..."

"What'd you find?" Henry asked, wrapping the coin back up.

"Hector killing Patroclus," Marion said, explaining the vase before them.

Henry raised an eyebrow. "You think this one embodies fearlessness?"

"Why not?"

"There are plenty of scenes with acts of heroism and great warriors and...I don't know, anything Achilles does."

"Achilles is already on your coin, remember? He's out," Marion said. "I believe both Patroclus and Hector are exemplifying fearlessness here. Patroclus, in this moment, by fighting Hector. But Hector has been unwavering in fighting the Achaeans this whole time."

"I think it's a pretty obvious red herring, and I'm not really interested in seeing if we can escape the hail of arrows that will skewer our bodies if—"

"Uh...guys?" Yianni grabbed Henry's shoulder.

He turned just as a pair of footsteps echoed off the stone from the southern hallway, letting his gun fall on its sling as he went for his swords.

A low whistle came from the intruder as he stepped into the courtyard.

Henry furrowed his brow. "Percy?"

Percy gave him a smug grin as he looked at the two of them. "How ya going?"

CHAPTER THIRTEEN
Nosophoros

"Shit! Shit, shit, shit!" Analise hissed over the radio. "Where the fuck did he come from?"

"How'd, uh...how'd you find this place, Percy?" Henry asked, wetting his lips as his fingers curled over the tennis grips wrapped around his butterfly swords.

"Oh, you know. Not much else around here that's radiating with magic." Percy shrugged as an outline appeared around him, courtesy of Analise. "Plus, you two leave quite the paper trail." He held up two ticket stubs from their ferry.

"Getting straight to the point, huh?" Henry sighed. "Not even gonna try to play coy?"

"And waste our precious time?"

Henry whirled around as Marion kept her eyes trained on Percy. Sahara leapt from the second floor, landing on the other side of the courtyard.

He could hear Analise in a rage on the other side of his radio, cursing and demanding to know how they slipped past her radar. His chest sank as he was reminded that yes, in fact, everyone was out to get him.

"Maybe if we were paid hourly." Sahara grinned. "But you're worth a flat fee, Zhang."

"You're outnumbered," Yianni said, brandishing his cane.

Henry's heart started to pound in his chest, preparing to fight.

Being a bounty hunter meant that you not only needed the power to Defect without people chasing after you, but also had to be powerful enough to hunt down the best of the best.

Suffice to say, these two were not to be trifled with.

Sahara pursed her lips. "Are we?"

Henry's eyes flickered to the silhouettes of the Germans just as they reached the courtyard. But it was just the six Magicians. The mercenaries had to be posted up outside.

"Alright, everyone, hands on your heads," ordered a tall blonde man in plate armor as he and the rest of Staufer Squad pointed rifle muzzles at them.

"The hell are you doing, Barbarossa?" Percy started towards the man in armor, but was forced back as a black-haired woman in violet swim attire pointed her gun at him.

"Sunna, you're coming with us." Barbarossa lowered his gun. Henry noticed the sword and mace at his hip and felt some amount of magic coming off them. He was a Martial Magician.

That drew his attention to a wooden stick strapped to Percy's back. He was *also* a Martial Magician.

The Companions were outgunned, especially if the Germans and bounty hunters decided to work together.

Henry needed an opening. He needed to create chaos.

He lashed his wrist out, causing all guns in the room to aim towards him. His rope dart shot out and shattered one of the pots lining the room.

Arrows filled the courtyard as the Magicians scrambled for cover.

Henry hid behind one of the podiums and pulled his shotgun around, hitting one of the Germans in the chest as he tried to hide nearby.

When the arrows stopped, Henry abandoned the gun and drew his butterfly swords. He leapt out from behind the podium as a red-headed Runecrafter let a shield of azure light dissipate from around herself and Barbarossa. He threw a side kick at Barbarossa, denting his gun and throwing him back.

"Nezha, what the shit?" Yianni yelled as he came out from behind his podium and was nearly stabbed by a giant needle being wielded like a sword by Sahara. The needle sparked off the Irishman's kilt as if the wool were made of metal before he retaliated with his Shillelagh.

Marion fired off a volley of golden bolts at the redhead, labeled as Gisela on Henry's ADZ display.

It seemed everyone else had been done in by the arrows.

Henry, Barbarossa, and Percy each raised their weapons. Percy's was a Taiaha, a Maori quarterstaff. The flaring wooden weapon glowed with turquoise markings in the bounty hunter's hands. Barbarossa, in turn, brandished his longsword.

Henry's eyes flickered between the two Martial Magicians. Barbarossa whispered a prayer, and Percy snarled something in Maori, causing the symbols on his weapon to flare up. Henry took a cultivating breath, filling his muscles with the ice-cold chill of Qi.

All three Martial Magicians were wary of one another. In a fight against a different opponent, a Martial Magician's overwhelming physical ability was enough to execute their techniques almost perfectly. But when three Martial Magicians, all from different traditions, were face to face, things were bound to get messy.

Henry, Barbarossa, and Percy paced around one another, each waiting for the others to act.

If no one else was going to, Henry decided to strike first. He rushed at the more heavily armored Barbarossa.

The German man tried to intercept the attack with his sword, but Henry leapt up, leaping off a column to get around the weapon and plunging the length of his butterfly sword into a gap in Barbarossa's armor.

Barbarossa threw him over his shoulder, slamming him into the stone. His breath evacuated his lungs as armored elbow strikes rained down on his guard. He kicked Barbarossa off in time to roll out of the way of an overhead strike from Percy's taiaha. The wooden staff made a crater in the stone courtyard.

Henry stumbled to his feet and launched his remaining butterfly sword at the bounty hunter like a throwing knife. As Percy dodged it, Henry threw a Qi-powered haymaker that would've shattered the jaw of any normal person.

Percy hit the ground hard, but before Henry could follow up, Barbarossa threw all the weight of his body and his armor into Henry's side.

Henry rolled to his feet as his enemies hesitated to close the distance.

One of his butterfly swords was still embedded in Barbarossa's shoulder. He pulled on the tether between himself and his swords, ripping the sword out of Barbarossa's wound and forcing the German to his knees as they both returned to his hands.

Percy's eyes widened as he realized this fight was more than he'd bargained for. Henry would never have admitted it, but it gave him a perverse satisfaction to see Percy desperately recalculating his situation.

"He...he couldn't do that before," Barbarossa said, heaving as he pushed himself to his feet.

"Chinese Magicians can't do that, period," Percy said. "Not without a somatic motion. I think..."

Henry threw his swords at Barbarossa before jumping into a tornado kick at Percy. The brunt of the blow was taken by the taiaha, so he yanked the weapon down and threw three swift punches at Percy's teeth through the opening, then backed off and pulled on the tether between him and his swords, causing them to zip back to his hands.

Barbarossa's pommel crunched against Henry's knuckles, disarming him of his left sword. He parried the following thrust with his right sword and slammed the metal knuckle guard into the German man's jaw.

Henry gritted his teeth as the wooden taiaha cracked against his ribs, sending him stumbling over.

The only reason he was able to climb to his feet was because Percy and Barbarossa attempted to finish him off at the same time, resulting in the two colliding. Before anyone could realize it had been an accident through their adrenaline, Percy struck back, and the two began fighting with one another instead of Henry.

He called his swords back to his hands and, fueled by Metal Style Five Elements Fist, leapt back into the fray.

The free for all quickly began to show what each Martial Magician was capable of. Percy was ridiculously strong, while Barbarossa, even while wounded, was precise to a hair, as if he knew where his opponents would be in the next second. Henry, of course, was fast and agile.

His enemies tried to team up against him, but they got in each others' way more often than not. Not that his own allies were being particularly helpful.

As Percy launched at him, Henry grabbed the Maori Magician's arm and redirected the immense force into Barbarossa's cuirass, denting the metal and throwing the German man onto his ass.

In the brief moment of respite, Henry saw Yianni smash a pot. He ducked, expecting another volley of arrows.

But none came, and Yianni snatched something from the pile of shattered ceramic. "I have the coin!" he shouted over the radio. "We can—"

Caught off-guard, Yianni didn't see Sahara poised to gut him like a fish. Henry rushed to his ally's defense, only for a field of golden light to pull up in front of him. He slammed into the golden force field of Marion's design, which only staved off the first of Sahara's attacks before being broken through. Yianni was able to react to the follow-up, but was on the back foot as Henry held his nose, stars filling his vision.

"Damnit, Sunna!" he snapped.

"Sorry!" Marion cried.

Henry sensed someone behind him. Still dazed and operating on instinct, he threw all his weight and all that remained of his Qi into a spinning back kick. The blow hit Percy in the side with flawless timing. With all the force behind it, the kick sent him crashing through three of the stone columns lining the courtyard.

The walls starting to crack was all the warning he got. In an instant, the entire temple complex collapsed under its own weight—with Henry caught in the disaster.

At some point, he lost his footing as dust and rocks rained all around him. And at another point, something pinned him down.

He blinked vertigo and dizziness out of his head as the dust settled, finding a fallen column pinning him against a jagged piece of stonework.

For a moment, he strained against the column, but stopped and cringed as he felt a sharp edge push farther into his body than it already had. The left side of his torso felt cold and hot at the same time, wet with blood. The adrenaline pumping through his system dulled most of the pain, but he could still feel it.

This would've been a great time for Earth Style.

Fire could give him the strength he needed, but he would make whatever impalement was going on in his side ten times worse in the process.

His breath picked up in pace as panic set in, but he managed to calm himself before his composure escaped him.

A groan drew his attention to a half-conscious Marion, hanging almost halfway off the edge of the remains of the floor as it had caved in to reveal a deep cellar.

"Marion! Marion, wake up!" He grunted through the pain.

She came to, thankfully. "What the...what happened?" She groaned, cradling her side. But she stood up just fine, so she was probably alright.

"Marion." He got her attention again. "Marion, I need your help with this..."

"Oh, my God..." She gasped.

"Yeah. Yeah, I know." Henry groaned.

"Okay..." Marion approached the column and flexed her fingers as she tried to find a good spot to lift from. She gripped the column and strained, gritting her teeth as she tried to pull it up.

The column didn't so much as budge, and she let go. She tried again and got the same result. "*Fickt mich...*" Marion heaved. "I...I—I can't lift it if you don't help, Henry."

"There's a rock stabbing into my back. I can't lift without making a giant hole in my torso," Henry explained. "Otherwise, I'd be free by now."

"I...I...maybe I can...no." Marion shook her head. She was starting to break under the pressure.

"Marion, whatever you've got, you need to try it!" Henry cried.

"I—I can't! Not that! What if I get Yianni?"

"I don't...we don't have time." Henry groaned. "Please, just—" He glanced behind her as Sahara stumbled out from under a fallen piece of debris. "Marion, look out!"

Marion screamed as a metallic spike erupted from the ground and stabbed her through the leg. She stumbled, clutching the wound, as Sahara brandished her needle-sword.

"God, you small-time Defectors are like roaches," Sahara spat. "We've had targets worth five times as much as you who at least had the decency to die quickly."

Henry gritted his teeth as Marion writhed on the ground. He threw his hand out and hoarsely belted out a Chinese couplet, calling on the god of the wind with Daoist magic.

A strong gust made Sahara take a few steps back, but that was it.

She grinned at him. "Really?"

He shouted the couplet again, but nothing happened. He cursed the god's name before a bullet hit the column he was pinned under. It was the Runecrafter girl, Gisela.

Henry could do nothing as Marion dragged herself over to him and tried to put a shield between herself and the two women. Two shots from Gisela's rifle shattered the magic.

A glint from the pile of rubble in his periphery him caught his eye. He craned his neck in spite of the pain in his back. The handle of his revolver stuck out of the crumbled stone.

Henry stretched, reaching for the gun. The metal grazed his fingertips. He let the stone dig into his back a bit more as he pushed himself up, wrapping his hand around the gun just as Sahara placed the tip of her needle-sword at Marion's throat.

He fired at Gisela, the recoil nearly sending the gun flying from his hands. His shot elicited a cry of pain as it grazed her leg. The rifle clattered to the ground as she clutched her wound.

Henry tried to do the same to Sahara, but the bounty hunter was too fast. She grabbed his revolver and threw it aside.

With a condescending grin, she towered over him.

"Three bounties for the work of one with you, Sunna, and Sétanta. And if I can find that coin...that'll be a nice bonus. Don't you think, Wukong?"

"Don't..." Henry coughed, his fingers going cold from blood loss. "Don't call me that..."

A scream split Henry's ears.

"*Scheiße!*" Gisela cried. "She bit me! The bitch—"

Henry blinked as a rush of blackness slammed into Sahara, throwing her backwards. "Yianni?" he murmured.

No.

It was Marion.

The color had drained away from her tanned skin until it looked like she'd spent the last month inside. A trail of blood made its way down her chin from the corner of her lips. Her fingernails had grown into claws, painted black by...something. It sure as hell wasn't nail polish. When she opened her eyes, they were black. Her pupils shone golden, piercing through the cave's shadows. Black smoke seemed to trail off her arms, and as she snarled at the bounty hunters from afar, Henry noticed two fangs in place of her canines.

"M...Marion?"

She screamed something in a language Henry couldn't understand. If he had to guess...Romanian?

For a moment, her expression morphed into something more like his friend's—something more human.

"I can't...I can't control her for long..." Marion cringed. The vampiric features returned as she snarled.

Her voice had gone deeper, with a Romanian accent rather than a German one. Almost as if a different person was speaking. "Where the hell are we? What is this trifle, girl?"

Henry had heard of the Impaler's Curse before. More than simple vampirism, Romanian Magicians burdened with the curse often found themselves acting in unusual ways as other, older, more primal parts of their personality were amplified.

Marion grabbed onto the column. It shifted a little, but even her vampiric form struggled before setting it down.

"This isn't worth the blood!" Her head twisted on her neck as she stumbled.

Her human features fought with the vampiric ones for dominance as what Henry assumed to be the Marion he knew tried to convince her alter ego. "He's my friend! Please...please help him."

Her vampiric side growled. "Coward!"

Henry struggled to breathe through the cold pain in his back, racking what was left of his brain function for a way to help. His mind went to Jiangshi, Chinese vampires.

He held out his hand. "Take it."

Marion peered at his hand as he held it out. She sighed, but grabbed onto his forearm.

She gasped as Henry breathed through the pain to cultivate Qi. He channeled the flow of his Qi into her, causing her to let out a shaky breath as her eyes rolled up in sudden satisfaction. "What...what was—"

"That was Qi. It should give you the life energy you need to...motherfucker." Henry heaved as the pain started coming to him in waves. "To lift the thing..."

Marion scowled, hissing at him.

"Come on!" Henry pleaded.

She bared her teeth at him, but her fingers dug into the column, and she lifted again. She grunted through the process, but his body actually felt some relief as she lifted the column. He pushed himself off the jagged rock behind him and slipped out from under the column.

He staggered and lost his footing, allowing the stranger in Marion's body to catch him.

He glanced behind her as Sahara was starting to recover. But before they could do anything, she vanished as a geyser of water erupted from the ground.

Henry's fists clenched, the only way he could express his frustration as Marion slowly fell to her knees, heaving.

While their enemies were making a retreat, it didn't really feel like a win for the Companions, as Henry continued to bleed out.

CHAPTER FOURTEEN
Burning Treachery

M arion startled awake. She squinted, groaning as her hand went to clutch her forehead. Her head was stuck in a vice of temple pain, and she could feel her blood pounding behind her eyes.

"You alright?" Henry sat up in the sand. The sun seemed to have set a while ago, meaning they were the only ones on Plakias beach, facing the pitch-dark waters and starlit sky.

"I feel like someone hit me in the head with a pipe..." she muttered. "Why are we at the beach?"

Henry pursed his lips. "Figured it would be a nice place to wake up. Well, it would've been seven hours ago. Being unconscious for that long is really bad for you."

His voice was deadpan. Even more than usual. His eyes stared off into nothing, despondent.

Whatever happened after her transformation, it couldn't have been good. Marion prayed that she hadn't done anything to hurt anyone.

"Your face says aesthetics weren't on your mind." She propped herself up on her elbows. "What happened?"

Henry shook his head. "Yianni lost the coin to the bounty hunters. Analise is trying to track them down, but so far, we're clueless." His fists clenched around handfuls of sand. "I can't believe I didn't see it before. Not to mention the temple…"

Marion thought he was trying to joke and lighten the mood at first, but she soon realized that losing that Minoan temple hurt just as much to him as losing the coin.

"It's my fault…" Henry muttered. "We…we acted like amateurs."

Marion huffed. "Unfortunately. You're not hurt, are you?"

"Aside from this guy?" Henry pulled up his shirt. His abdomen was covered in burn marks where the wound had been.

"*Mein Gott*…did you ca-caut—did you burn that shut?" She scrambled onto her knees, losing a bit of her English in the process.

"I was about to die of blood loss, so…yeah." Henry shrugged. "Could you, uh…look at it?"

"*Mist*," she muttered, softly hovering her glowing hands over the wound. "I don't think I can even heal this all the way."

"Well, I'm not dead, so I think my organs are fine."

Marion calmed herself and slowed her breathing as her hands glowed to life, her brow knitting in concentration. Healing wasn't something she had ever cultivated, unlike her abilities with runes. It was an inherited power. But it was better than her *nosophoros* transformation, which had come out of nowhere when she was a child. Too often, she was deprived of what she felt was a reasonable amount of control to ask for.

Healing was more of a curse and a burden than a gift. It made her valuable to people who were too used to puppeteering others. It made her nothing more than a prize—something to be fought over and won. A trophy at worst. A useful tool at best.

But among the Companions, she was an equal. Not a subordinate. Not a young girl beholden to the whims of the village. So, for them, at least, she didn't mind using it.

"So…what's up with your Jekyll–Hyde situation?" Henry chuckled, though it was cut off as it agitated the wound Marion was working on.

"Sorry." She sighed. "I don't typically enjoy talking about it."

"I get that, but…most Impaler's Curses I've seen don't have that bad of an alter-ego issue."

Marion nodded. "I can't really explain it, but she's been a burden since I was young. My father got a Romanian Solomonari to draw up a sigil to prevent the transformation from happening without my consent."

"You never should've had to bring her out," Henry muttered. "I didn't think that there might be bounty hunters after us. And I didn't think *they* would be the mercenaries."

"We got out of there intact," Marion said.

"We failed," Henry growled. "*I* failed. I didn't call out to you before I activated the trap. No one went for the coin except Yianni. We all got tied up in our individual battles. We let two competing pairs of people defeat three of us when we could've turned them against—"

"Thinking about every way it could've gone differently won't change anything," Marion said.

"But it *will* change the future. I hope." Henry's head hung slightly. "That's assuming I have reason to make it that far."

Marion frowned, glancing up at him. "Why do you say that?"

"Never mind." He turned away from her, even as she was healing him.

"Why are you so desperate to find Alexander's tomb?" Marion asked. She knew she was prying, but slow-moving trust was no longer a luxury they could afford.

Henry pulled away from her, wincing at the consequences to his wound. "Look, as someone who's been fighting since they were four years old, I don't think me spilling my heart out to you is going to offer us any tactical advantages."

"You said we acted like amateurs. That's because when it comes to working together, we *are* amateurs. I know nothing about you. How are any of us supposed to trust each other?" she asked. "Every well-functioning family communicates these sorts of things for a reason."

He glared at her with a sudden burst of fire in his eyes. It was almost as if, for that moment, he saw her as an enemy. "What we have here? This isn't a family. Family, for me, is back in Iowa or trying to kill me right now. Family for you is back in Germany. We are business partners. Friends, at best."

Marion furrowed her brow in frustration. She hadn't meant to call it that, but why did he have to be so callous? Did Alexander really expect her to work with someone like him? A brutish killer?

She caught herself. That was unfair of her. By that logic, she was no more than a childish coward. She wasn't exactly sure what his deal was yet, but he surely had a reason to act the way he did.

"Why do *you* want the tomb?" Henry asked. "You've never struck me as the ambitious type."

Marion pursed her lips. That seemed like a fair trade. She crossed her arms. "If I tell my story, you have to tell yours. Fair?"

Henry narrowed his eyes, considering. Marion believed she was beginning to understand him and his...stinginess. Not with money, but with knowledge and power. He was like a hoarder, if useless trinkets were swapped out with skills and information.

"Fine. You first." He sighed, collapsing onto the sand. "Regale me."

"Ass," she muttered, letting out a little hesitant sigh before continuing. She hated talking about this, but...this relationship was a two-way street. She had to take what little control she had and be the first to offer an olive branch. "I...well, it's not easy to sum up in a sentence or even hook you, but...there's this little town in the Black Forest in the south of Germany. Maybe two thousand people live there. And every single one of them is a Magician."

Henry blinked. "Wait, two *thousand*?"

Each Circle barely had a hundred Magicians, and less than half would be trained as combat Magicians. So, relative to the Magician world, her small town was kind of massive. But it wasn't like those people went around advertising their existence to the Circles.

"I guess you might call it a...mystery cult?" Marion frowned. "Wait, no. That makes it sound bad. They aren't a cult. They don't, like, sacrifice people to pagan gods or anything. But they believe they're direct descendants of the Alemanni confederation and Gibuld, the last king of Alemannia. They even call themselves Suebi, after the main tribe of the Alemanni."

"I take it this is your hometown?"

Marion nodded. "I was born there. All Suebi are born with the Sowilo rune marked over their hearts. It's what allows us to heal people. No German Magicians are capable of that ability except for the Suebi."

"And the Suebi are separate from the Palatine Order?"

"Yes. They practice nearly complete isolation from the outside world."

"So, how'd you end up here?"

"I had to leave the Suebi. Permanently," Marion muttered. "I never intended to do it at first, but before I was born, a group of people settled in my village. They came from Bulgaria and Romania and called themselves Cathars. They were Magicians too. And they had the same healing abilities. Or, at least, we thought they did."

Henry frowned. "I thought the Cathars were all killed off in, like...the thirteenth century."

Marion shrugged. "I don't know the wider history, but my father was one of them. My mother and father did something of a Romeo and Juliet, but actually managed to stay alive, unite the two groups, and integrate the Cathars. I was trained by the Suebi at first. They taught me with Lutheran doctrine, as had been the case since the Reformation. But then my father's side of the family insisted on sharing responsibility in training me, and they taught me about Cathar doctrine. And it was...different."

"From what I hear, Gnosticism is pretty gnarly." Henry scoffed. "Just from an atheist's perspective, it's, uh...interesting. Pretty cool, even. Conceptually."

"Maybe." Marion shrugged, not voicing her disagreement to its full extent. "But I think their teachings are full of it. They told me I had a spark of God inside me. And that the world was...holding me back. That I was inherently divine, and that they understood a hidden truth called the *Gnos* that they would teach me. They said if I accepted the *Gnos* and my own divinity, I would become stronger. I would become free."

She stared out into the blackness of the sea, remembering the feeling of emptiness those teachings gave her—the worthlessness spurred on by fantasies of utopia and delusions of grandeur.

"My mother's side had taught me that humans were weak and that there were many forces beyond our control that I had to understand. And I always reflected on my actions as a result of that. I always tried to understand my limitations."

Her voice darkened with her memories, remembering what she suffered under Perfecta Natalia. To think that Cathars called their priests Perfect. She should've known better.

"But the Cathars told me *I* was God. That I was perfect. That I had no limits. It was nice to believe, but it wasn't real. It was an opiate to pacify me while they slowly converted my entire village to their way of thinking. When I realized what happened, the Cathars were calling for a war of expansion—a violent revolution to make the whole world Gnostic. When I tried to argue, they just said I hadn't understood the *Gnos*. I was little more than a figurehead to them, a puppet whose strings they could pull when I inherited the village's leadership from my mother. I refused to be their tool. So, I left."

Marion pushed out her next breath, having finally gotten past the part she dreaded. She reminded herself that Henry needed to hear this as much as she needed to hear his story. The next bits hurt her pride, but…it wasn't much compared to leaving her family and community behind.

"I take it the Order of Cologne had its own issues," Henry muttered, shifting in the sand to do away with some of the distance he'd put between them.

"It went fine at first. I was trained in the modern fashion. I ran sorties, lived in the city. But…the more time I spent there, the more I felt like an object to them. My healing abilities made me a prize for the Order. A tool again. Barely a soldier. And it wasn't just the Magician life. Life in the city was so…isolating, as ironic as that sounds. Like I was a lab rat in a maze. I couldn't go to see my family. I had no one I could really rely on. The churches were empty most Sundays. Most of my work never contributed to anything real. I just…partied until all the bad feelings went away. But eventually, that wasn't enough." She sighed. "No matter where I am, I'm never a person. Never a real member of the group. I'm just a means to an end for someone else's game."

She looked at him, letting the sound of the crashing waves fill the silence as he mulled her story over.

"I'm sorry that happened." Henry put a hand on her shoulder. It was warm and strong in the wake of the cool coastal breeze. "I know what it's like to be treated like…a cog in the machine. I hope…I hope this hunt will turn out differently for you."

Marion offered a soft smile. Not that she could help it as it spread across her face. "I didn't really believe the dreams when they said I could find what I was looking for here.

But so far, so good. I'm glad I'm friends with you, Henry. No matter what the people from your old Circle say, you have my respect."

Henry blinked as if shocked. He cleared his throat and glanced away from her as his hand moved away. *How strange*, Marion thought.

"Okay. Your turn."

He returned from his thoughts with a start. "You know that's not normal, right?" He frowned. "Your little mood swing there."

Marion gave him a half-smile. "Well, if I let it get me down all the time, we'd probably die from despair. So come on, spill."

Henry pursed his lips.

"Hey, remember our deal—"

"I'm thinking..." he said before letting out a glum sigh. "I...I don't like to think about this at all, if I can help it."

Marion nodded, accepting his aversion. She had a tendency to do the same.

Henry was silent. Uncharacteristically so. He drew his arms and legs towards himself. His eyes stared intensely at the ground. He twitched, the impulse seeming to have stemmed from his back.

"I...I didn't Defect from the Tiandihui."

Marion blinked. Her mind immediately jumped to the assumption that he was Damnatio Memoriae. But if that was the case, the Chaldean Court would be after them.

"I was exiled," Henry muttered. "Left for dead. My only chance at penance is to find Alexander's tomb and give it to them."

Marion furrowed her brow, drawing herself closer to him. "But...then, why are they sending people to compete with you? Why do you fight them?"

"Well, aside from the fact that they don't think I can do it...I hate them." He gritted his teeth. "I would rather see every artifact in that tomb be crushed into dust than let them get their hands on it."

Her eyes widened at that. This was the man who had been so distraught over the destruction of an archaeological site not ten minutes ago. What kind of hatred would spur him to abandon his one passion?

Henry got to his feet, still staring at the ground as he rested his hands on his head. He paced as he spoke. "My brother...he's a prodigy. Magic, academics, art—it all comes to him like second nature. Compared to him, I'm nothing. They never let me forget that. My mother always put her hopes and dreams for our future onto him. Me? Well...she barely gave me a second look before giving up. For the Tiandihui, it was the same. No matter what I did, I knew they would never give a damn about whether I lived or died. Except for Mr. Fang."

"The old guy?"

Henry nodded. "He trained everyone on Zhao Squad. But he and I were a lot alike. He taught me everything I know about magic."

"How were you exiled?"

"We were sent out to recover some relics stolen from us by the Japanese in World War II, and...it went poorly. Weiying and I were the only ones who made it inside the castle where they were keeping them. I watched the door while Weiying grabbed the relics. When High Command found out that most of the relics were fake, I was blamed. When I tried to tell them that Weiying handled all the artifacts, he lied and scapegoated me. And they believed him when he said I colluded with the Japanese, warning them in advance. I was accused of treason. It was only thanks to Mr. Fang that I managed to escape alive. But I can never go back."

Marion flinched as Henry pulled his shirt over his head in one motion. She gasped as her eyes landed upon the scarred red flesh of a brand. From shoulder blade to shoulder blade, a Chinese character had been burned into his skin.

"Oh, my God..." she whispered, choking slightly. Whether it was from gagging or the urge to cry, she wasn't sure.

"*Zéi*. It means 'traitor.' Thief. They did this to me because my brother refused to admit a mistake," Henry snarled. "And even if he did, he wouldn't have been punished like I was. Because my brother was born with some devil's luck that I don't have." He pulled his shirt back on and stared at Marion, eyes boring into her soul with cold fire.

Her heart slammed in her chest. Maybe it was fear. Maybe it was something else. But she could plainly see the icy rage that she'd coaxed out simmering under his skin.

He bared his teeth, fists curling. "But here's the thing, Marion. I don't need his luck. I don't want it. I've fought tooth and nail for everything, and that makes me stronger than any of them could hope to be! I don't care if they treat me like trash or throw me out like nothing! I want them to sleep with one eye open! I want them to never have a moment of peace, knowing they fucked with a sleeping tiger! I'll make them respect me! I won't let myself be their victim! I won't let them hurt me again!"

As if he hadn't been awake, he shook his head, blinking. His gaze returned to something akin to normal as he stumbled back.

"The worst part is, no matter how much I try to come to peace with the truth of things, it still hurts. No one gives a damn. And when they do listen, it's so they can use it against me later," he muttered, rubbing his fingers together, a guilty expression plastered to his face.

The waves were deafening in the wake of Henry's chaotic spill of emotions. Marion tried to display as much kindness as she could. Not because he had it any worse than her. Comparisons like that only served to divide people. She felt pity because he was so much more lost. Gratitude for at least knowing what it was she was looking for, filled her chest.

Henry...in spite of his attempts to re-establish his stoic facade, she could see it on his face: he didn't believe there was anywhere in the world for him. Hence why he doubted his future. He felt guilty, like a burden, for making anyone listen to his problems. He hated himself for being vulnerable.

"I give a damn," she said, to start.

Henry scoffed. "They all say that, but their actions always—"

"I won't have you doubt me, Henry Zhang. I care." Marion stood up from the sand and jabbed a pointer finger into his chest. "Look me in the eyes and tell me I'm a liar. Tell me this is some elaborate scheme to manipulate you. Then, maybe I'll join your pity party."

Her muscles relaxed as her hand moved down to cup his still-tight fist in her hands.

"We're all looking for something by going after this tomb," Marion said, gently feeling each aching tendon and tight bone under his skin. "More than what's inside it. You'll help me find what I need. I'll help you find what you need."

His fist loosened slightly as she stared at him with unwavering conviction.

"This isn't some transaction. We're friends. If I know one thing about you, it's this: you don't have anything to prove to anyone," she insisted. "You have a future. You may just not see it yet. But...don't give up on yourself. You'll regret it."

Henry offered her a half-smile and a handshake. "Deal."

She took it. But upon doing so, both their hands flared up with light that gave off no arcane signal. They fell back from each other onto the sand.

Marion looked at her hands as they glowed with brilliant white light that illuminated the beach around her like a tiny sun. She peered at Henry, whose hands were ablaze with crackling flames.

"Holy shit..." he muttered. "This is because of the coins, right?"

"I...I hope."

Henry tilted his head, seemingly rolling with the punches as he squeezed his fists shut, extinguishing the flames. "We...should have more midnight discussions."

Marion shook her head, scoffing.

Hanying's eyes flickered nervously to his left as he knelt on hard rocks and dirt in the cold winds of night.

He and Min met each other's gaze, both stripped down to nothing but their underwear. Their eye contact was all they could do to reassure one another, as they had to keep their heads down.

Mr. Fang, dressed in Ming Dynasty garments, faced towards the edge of a cliff overlooking the Daba mountains, chanting in an ancient Chinese dialect that Hanying could barely understand.

All of Hanying's classmates had been violently woken up at an ungodly hour of the night and forced to strip down before making the run all the way up to the top of the mountain. Doing it every morning for training should've made the run easy, but without shoes, it was an entirely different ballgame.

Hanying's goosed-up skin pined for the warmth of his blankets as his breath made small puffs of steam in the air. It was late October, after all. But he couldn't do so much as clutch himself without ruining the ceremony. The only source of heat he could rely on was the slowly burning incense clasped between his praying hands.

He spared a glance to the altar in front of him. The statue of Guan Yu, the patron god of the historical Dragons of Fujian gang, was rather small for such an important ceremony. The Central Dragons, now renamed for their role as the Tiandihui's military branch, put much more focus on religion than the other branches.

Whirling smoke from bundles of incense drifted into the air, casting the mountaintop in a strange, smoky fog that obscured the men and women dressed in black who had woken them. They were now wielding Chinese broadswords as they watched the ceremony from the tree line of the clearing.

Fang finally spoke words that Hanying understood. They were still in the ancient dialect, but he and his classmates had practiced them and knew what they meant.

"I shall never betray a brother," Fang said.

"I shall never betray a brother," Hanying and his classmates repeated in unison.

"I will never steal from a brother."

"I will never steal from a brother," Hanying repeated. Weiying would have to stop some of his habits quickly if he didn't want to break his oaths.

"I will never covet nor lie with a brother's wife."

Hanying repeated the oath, feeling kind of silly, but it was tradition.

"*Da ge*," Fang called.

Hanying almost moved, not being used to being a younger brother.

But among the six of them, Chen Bo was the oldest and largest. He got to his feet, incense clasped between his hands, as the darkly clad men and women stepped forward, thrusting their swords up and creating a tunnel of blades for him to walk under.

Hanying didn't pay attention to what Chen Bo was doing, waiting to hear his call. He remembered Fang telling him that he fell asleep during his own ceremony, squashing some of his anxiety. Still, his heart felt like it was about to burst.

"*Er ge.*"

Hanying took a deep breath and got to his feet. Keeping his hands from shaking by pressing them together around his incense, he started forward. He forced his eyes on Guan Yu and ignored the rocks jabbing into his feet as he passed under the arch of swords.

When he passed the arch and approached the altar, he found Chen Bo's incense stuck on the statue's back like a war flag. He did the same with his incense.

He glanced at the bloody knife, a stack of *fulu* talisman paper, and then the pitcher of wine on the stone table, knowing what was required of him.

Hanying picked up the knife and made a quick gash in his left palm, trying not to wince. As the blood pooled in his hand, he closed his fingers and let it drip off the edge of his fist and into the wine.

He put the knife down and dipped a finger in his still-pooling blood. He wrote his name, Zhang Hanying, on one of the talisman papers before taking the slip and touching it to his incense stick. The paper caught fire, quickly burning to ash as he let it go in the wind.

"With that, your old name becomes a secret known only to your family by blood, oath, and bond," Fang said. "And with this, I give you a new name."

Hanying held his hand out, the open air stinging his wound. Mr. Fang pulled his right sleeve back as he readied a horsehair calligraphy brush.

Hanying grimaced as Mr. Fang dabbed the brush in his blood and began to write in it upon his chest. The blood was actually a welcome warmth to his shivering body. He tried to focus by drawing the characters in his head as Mr. Fang drew them.

Mr. Fang stepped back, having finished his work. "I dub thee Wukong. Renew your oaths under your new name."

Hanying raised three fingers of his left hand, even as it continued to bleed, and recited the oaths from earlier.

With that, he saluted his teacher and lined up with Chen Bo, whose hand was still leaking. Eyes forward and hand bleeding, he waited as Fang called for Lu Ying with "*San Jie.*" Chen Bo was the oldest brother, Hanying the second-oldest. Lu Ying was the third, Weiying was the fourth, Min was the fifth, and the sixth was Shen.

Hanying started breathing as if he were cultivating Qi, but used it only as a technique to regulate his body temperature. Meanwhile, each of his teammates placed their incense, cut their hands, contributed to the wine, then got their new callsigns written on their collars or chests.

Wukong was not what Hanying had been expecting. Each of them had some amount of choice in the matter, and he had wanted to be called Nezha, after the guardian deity who bravely stood against the Dragon Kings. While he enjoyed *Journey to the West*, Wukong was an impetuous rebel who was strong, but impulsive and undisciplined—an animal.

If High Command saw him more as a Wukong than a Nezha...well, it was a deeper cut than the one on his palm.

As Shen took his place in the lineup, Fang took the pitcher of wine and poured each of them an iron cup of the bloody mixture.

Six of the sword-wielders took the cups and handed one to each of them before filing back into the arch. The cup, having spent hours in the cold, was sticky and slightly painful on Hanying's fingers.

"Drink of your shared blood," Fang told them in the ancient tongue, "and become brothers in arms of the Heaven and Earth Society."

Hanying and his classmates drank from their cups. The sweet wine warmed his body with a slight burn in his throat as it went down. A hint of iron reminded him it was practically half blood.

He threw his cup against the ground almost at the same time as the others.

"*Fan Qing! Fu Ming!*" they shouted, promising to destroy the Qing and restore the Ming, as the Shaolin monks who began the Society had sworn.

A smile crept onto Mr. Fang's face. "Welcome to the Tiandihui."

Hanying sighed in relief, breaking out into gasps of laughter with the rest of his new squadmates. His new siblings. In spite of their half-nakedness—or maybe because of it, combined with the cold—Min wrapped her arms around him, squealing with joy. Though shocked for a second, he returned her embrace, and soon enough, the rest of classmates were piling on.

No. No, not classmates.

His brothers and sisters.

His new family.

A place where he finally belonged.

CHAPTER FIFTEEN
The Great Meteoron

"**N**orth? Yeah, okay. We've already arrived..." Marion said, on the radio with Analise.

Henry and Marion had woken up at dawn and hiked up from Kalambaka, the small town at the base of the mountains the Meteora monasteries were built on. Meanwhile, Analise and Yianni were driving to the north side.

Analise's tracking efforts had brought them here, to mountainous Thessaly. The bounty hunters' trail had gone cold at the bus station in the nearby city of Trikala, allowing the Companions to make an educated guess that they were headed for the monasteries. Yianni had helpfully pointed out that, for some time now, the Celts had believed the site to be a hidden fortress of the Hecateans.

They'd done a sweep with a map, at least proving that there was a massive web of tangled magical energy surrounding the Meteoron Monastery, the northernmost of the five. When Henry had asked about it, the owner of their hostel had said it was closed for restoration.

Henry peered through a pair of binoculars at the small array of black vans, trucks, and cars gathered outside the base of the monastery's stone steps.

The monastery's defensive position was doing exactly what it was supposed to be doing. It was only intended to harbor monks who had no intention of fighting back, after all.

That left the Companions with very few routes for both ingress and egress.

And considering the fact that he was seeing signs of the Egyptians, Latins, and Germans among an overwhelming presence of Greek mercenaries, Henry figured they had guessed right. The last he'd heard, a scarce few Circles had managed to acquire a true paramilitary wing beyond a few sortie squads of combat Magicians. And he didn't expect the Greeks to be among their number. It seemed the men guarding the gala at the Museum were not just hired security, but the Hecatean Circle's private army.

"Come in, Companion 1, Companion 2."

"Go ahead, Moneta," Marion muttered from behind him.

The two were situated on a small balcony, part of an outcropping of the nearest monastery, which overlooked a steep chasm of grey stone and greenery between this peak and the one the Meteoron monastery was situated on. Medieval walls and mossy green built up the foundation of the newer white stone complex, built for tourists and bordered in red tile roofing in place of railings.

A Greek flag on a pole in the center of the circular, open-air porch flapped in the breeze as Henry handed the binoculars off to Marion.

"Companion 3 and I are about to make our way up the west-side stairs as we speak," Analise said.

"Since when do you fight?" Henry asked.

"Since I was a sitting duck last time," Analise replied. "I'm not going to let you three muck it up again."

"That's hurtful, Moneta." Marion frowned. "We're improving."

"Then let's see some results," Analise said.

"Just to check, Nezha, we're *not* taking your new set of flaming hands into account for this operation?" Yianni asked.

"Learning to use new magic doesn't really fit into our tight schedules, Sétanta," Henry said. "So, no. At best, I could warm up your seat in the rental car."

"Ooh, please do. That'd be nice."

"Can we focus? Please?" Analise interrupted. "Once I'm done briefing, we need to go."

"Roger." Henry checked all his equipment, including his weapons, some light explosives, and cartridges to reload his revolver.

"By my count, there are upwards of thirty guards patrolling the monastery," Analise said. "And based on the communications we intercepted, it seems our worst fears have come true. Our alliance has spurned Trajan Squad of the Latins, Staufer Squad of the Germans, Atum Squad of the Egyptians, Zhao Squad of the Chinese, and the Greek Alpha Squad to join forces."

"That's ironic..." Marion sighed.

"They're fairly disorganized, and we're unlikely to see reinforcements. Still, we have sightings of the Germans, Latins, Egyptians, and three Greek squads. We're outnumbered in magic and firepower," Analise said. "Additionally, all trackable scouting parties have stopped searching since last night. I believe this to mean that the alliance has the fourth and final coin in custody as well. Only issue is, we don't know where. As such, we need to canvas this place thoroughly, so we can't just make a break for it once we have the third coin. We'll have to win a conventional victory. Nezha, you're Companion 1. You're in command."

"Is everyone clear on the plan?" Henry asked.

"More or less." Yianni chuckled. "I will say, though...it's kind of insane."

"Well, you gotta be insane to send four people in against...what, sixty, seventy opponents?"

"Something like that," Analise muttered. "Can't keep count because of those damn ADZ jammers..."

"Well, if we're all set...Companions, engage," Henry ordered.

Marion handed Henry a runestone. He channeled Qi into Fire Style and launched the pebble across the chasm before them with supernaturally explosive power. She grabbed his hand before they swapped with it.

The ground vanished beneath him, and he barely registered that he was falling before he threw his rope dart out at the sheer face of a four-story stone tower. He grabbed onto the silk and Marion's arm as the slack tightened, and he got his footing against the limestone tower wall.

He sighed in relief as he looked up at the wooden facade and balcony hanging over them, the point of entry being infrastructure for a rope lift that had since been uninstalled.

"Throw me up to the window," Marion said. "I'll clear it out from the inside, and you can climb to the top."

Henry pulled and tossed Marion up towards the wooden sill of the third story window. She grabbed on with her fingertips and pulled herself inside.

"It's clear." She poked her head out, wavy locks falling around her face.

"Don't head to the top yet. Just clear the lower floors," Henry whispered. He grabbed his rope dart with both hands and started to walk up the face of the tower.

At the top, he wedged himself in the frame and supports of the less-than-stable centuries-old balcony, then retracted his rope dart with magic. He peered through the gaps in the planks to find four guards sitting on top of the tower. Two were playing cards. One of them was smoking. And one was leaning against the support of the facade, near the edge of the balcony.

The sides of the small overhang were walled off, and the front was fenced in. If he wanted to get the drop on these four, he couldn't do it from down here. He pulled himself onto the clay tile roof, which was thankfully surrounded by closed buildings and no guards.

He ran to the front and jumped off the edge, grabbing onto the roof and putting all that momentum into a two-footed kick to the nearest guard's chest, sending him careening into the table at the back of the lift's cabin. He sent his butterfly swords flying towards the chests of the two playing cards before slamming the smoking one into the wall and throwing knees and elbows into him until he slumped over.

He called his swords back to his hands and flicked the blood off before sheathing them.

As Marion climbed up through a small staircase, Henry began stripping one of the men of his fatigues and gear.

"This is...grisly," Marion muttered.

"Most of these guys are mercenaries. Odds that they've committed some kind of atrocity are higher than not, so...don't feel bad."

The first guard Henry had kicked started groaning, but Marion whacked him in the head with her staff, knocking him unconscious. "Rope lift tower is secure, Moneta," she reported over the radio.

"Roger that. I think I've found myself a decent perch," Analise responded.

Henry fitted the unconscious man's fatigues over his mandarin jacket and tightened the straps on the body armor.

"Stay safe," Marion said.

"Right back at you." Henry picked up the mercenary's cheaply made Armalite 180 rifle, pulling the canvas sling onto his shoulder. "Don't get caught."

From the rope lift tower, Henry started down a polished wooden staircase to the east entrance of the monastery. He tried to navigate in a vaguely central direction, but every corridor seemed to lead to three different artifact-filled chambers or chapels. Following sunlight was never helpful, since the lattice windows let plenty of it into secluded chambers and every building seemed to have some kind of boardwalk wrapping around it.

"This place is a damn maze," he muttered. "Why didn't we get a map beforehand?"

"I don't think they have them," Marion said. "Lord knows I tried to find one."

"Really? Isn't this place a tourist attraction?"

"I guess that's kinda supposed to be the charm or something." Yianni sighed.

Henry finally managed to find his way into a roofed intersection of walkways and doors to other chambers, with one of the paths leading into an open courtyard. "Thank fuck." He walked out into the sunlight, questioning the choice to have the guards wear all black in summer weather.

Built from stark white limestone with flat, narrow red bricks for accents, the courtyard was defined by a strangely subtle carving in the far-left corner with iconography of an angel etched into marble, a small bell hanging over it. The carving was flanked by rose beds and shaded by a singular spear tip-shaped cypress tree. In the far-right corner was another icon, though it was unclear who the carving was meant to represent. It didn't help that it was covered in water stains from the fountain right above it. A tower with an orthodox cross and a larger bell in the middle stood watch over the courtyard a ways behind the fountain.

The Byzantine architecture was certainly something to marvel at, and, were he not looking for the coin, Henry would've liked to have taken in all the stonework, elaborate gold icons, and gardens.

"Is that you, Companion 1?" Analise asked.

"Yeah. Just came out into the courtyard. Where to from here?"

"Take a left from your position, down the pathway towards the cliffside."

Passing a knee-high wall lined with potted flowers, Henry started down the pathway, which narrowed as towers and sanctums demanded more space.

"Take a left towards the stairs."

Henry glanced left at a low-incline ramp and few stairs that brought him to a much smaller courtyard surrounded by architecture rather than greenery, with several labyrinthine staircases, doors, and decks heading in three different directions.

"Take the stairs on the right that head down and go inside the building at the bottom."

Henry followed Analise's directions and found himself inside a miniature museum with plenty of artifacts from the monks' daily lives on display in glass cases.

"From there, just keep heading down until you reach the crypt."

"'The crypt?'"

"You'll know it when you see it."

He moved through the monastery with the same tactic as before, just trying to head in a vaguely downward direction.

He nearly passed one of the chambers before he spotted a skull through the cracked door in his periphery. Stopping for a moment, he pushed the door open and found himself face to face with a seven-foot shelf full of skulls with piles of bones stacked up on the limestone-and-mortar walls that boxed in the claustrophobic chamber.

"I believe the proper term for this place is 'ossuary,'" he muttered, pacing around the edge of the tiny space.

"Whatever. You found the shelf, right?"

"Yeah. Now what?"

"I, uh…" Analise's voice started to crackle over the radio. "I'm not exactly sure. You can figure it out, right?"

"Oh, yeah, I watched plenty of Scooby-Doo back in the day. I'm an expert."

In spite of his sarcasm, the first thing he did *was* something that'd do the trick in a cartoon: he started pulling or pushing on anything that wasn't a bone, including the low-hanging lamp, candlesticks, icons of the Virgin Mary propped on the top shelf, and even some of the tourist-born litter around the edges of the room.

Nothing.

Henry looked at the shelf of skulls and shuddered. He wasn't as superstitious as his mother, but considering the fact that magic existed, disrespecting the dead couldn't be a cosmically favorable move.

Coming up with a clever workaround to pure trial and error, he gave the shelf a light kick, rattling the bones—all except one on the third layer. Hesitant, he placed his hand on the skull and pushed. It clicked.

The shelf ground against stone, receding into the wall behind it and revealing a small, medieval-person-sized hole under where it had been.

Henry dropped down into it, ducking his head under the five-foot ceiling of the dark stone tunnel below, lit only by old incandescents, like a mineshaft.

"I'm in," he whispered. "Let me find a hiding place."

Analise's voice came across, even more garbled than before. "Roger. Give us the signal once you do."

"I think my radio might lose signal, so if you don't hear from me in five minutes, go ahead with the plan anyway," Henry said.

He crept through the tunnel, taking off the gear he'd stolen, since it would only slow him down and make noise. He pulled his rifle around in front of him and racked it.

The tunnel eventually ended at a very conspicuous metal door bolted into the rock. Even more conspicuous was the metric fuck ton of arcane wards on it.

From his pocket, Henry pulled the gold pendant Analise had given him that morning. If she had her usual command of the battlefield, the wards would have been broken before he got there. Instead, he had to use this.

He licked his lips, staring at the small, polished garnet gem hanging off the bottom of the circular talisman, and tried to read the etchings made in the gold surface as though he knew any Latin magic. This had been drafted entirely based on speculation. Wards could be finicky. Any of them could trip an alarm, so it was always better to get a look at a ward and disassemble it on the fly. But here, there weren't that many options.

"Going in with the countercharm," Henry whispered, hanging the pendant onto the door's handle by a paracord.

He barely had time to anticipate before the door cracked open. He slipped inside and shut it behind him.

Voices on the other side caused him to pick out a stone column and rush to hide behind it before he could really get his bearings. From what little he could gather, he'd found himself in a winding underground church. He was shrouded in shadows cast by fire braziers and candles, even worse than the archaic electric lights in the tunnel.

The temple couldn't be too complicated, considering the massive monastery that sat overhead made every hollow inch an additional risk.

"You think we can use the coins to track the others?" asked an unfamiliar woman's voice.

"If we can scale a radar, it'd be child's play."

Was that...Atum?

They sounded somewhat far from him, so Henry risked patching into his radio. It was all static.

Shit.

He couldn't just sit here and wait for five minutes. Not with two magicians in the same chamber as him.

He peeked out from around the column. The two were busy with their conversation, allowing him to make his way around the edge of the cave tentatively, moving under stone arches and past wind-weathered columns.

As long as he stuck to the shadows, the space was dark enough to hide his movements.

He could probably set off an alarm, and the other Companions would pick up on it. It may put them at a slight disadvantage, but it was the only way to let them know they had to draw attention without slipping out through the door again.

He could try and—

"You two!" a voice shouted from among a mob of quick footsteps. "Defectors have infiltrated the monastery! They're after the coin!"

"What?" Atum scoffed. "They're only four in number, Josephine! How'd they get past the guards?"

"Get your squads! Keep them out of the ossuary." That was Barbarossa's voice.

As the Magicians evacuated through the door, Henry stepped into the light, readying his gun.

The cave continued through a doorway to the left that led into a carved-out hallway covered in Orthodox artwork on the ceilings. He began checking inside all the doorways that lined the sides of the cave. There were barracks to sleep in, an armory, a component chamber, a chapel, and a number of other rooms meant for military activities and the creation of magical items.

Henry poked his head into a small, cloistered shrine just as the door at the end of the hall burst open. He slipped into the shrine and held the door shut as ten, maybe twenty Magicians poured into the hallway, rushing towards the exit.

He turned to survey the chamber he'd have to hide in for the time being, catching sight of a woman with eyes the size of dinner plates kneeling before the altar.

Before she could scream for help, he rushed towards her and clapped a hand over her mouth. Assuming she was an enemy Magician, he held the muzzle of his gun to her abdomen. "Don't you dare make a sound," he snarled under his breath.

The girl nodded, her curly black hair bouncing as she agreed to follow his instructions. Slowly, he removed the hand over her mouth, but kept the gun in place.

He furrowed his brow as he felt a small buzz of magic coming from the front of the shrine. He peered over the girl's shoulder at a small golden icon of the Virgin Mary on the altar. "What the—"

A gout of sparks and flames shot out of the icon, throwing Henry through the door and into the cave wall across the hall. He collapsed to the ground, aches flooding into his body as he groaned.

The girl ran out of the shrine and through a door at the end of the hall, yelling in Greek. So much for staying quiet.

Henry scrambled to his feet as a large Greek man burst through the door with a gun. He rammed the stock of his rifle into the man's sternum, hitting him with force enough to send him crashing back through the same door.

Devoting his Qi to Metal Style, Henry rushed over the body and fired five shots at other defenders before he dove for cover behind a metal desk.

The entire room was full of desks, papers, and screens, all tapped into the Hecateans' surveillance network across the country.

And the two coins sat on a podium in the center of the room, warded by three layers of spinning gold rings.

Henry knew the ward well. It was Archimedes's Armillary, a spell for emergencies, and as such, it was easy to break if they had the time. All it really did was prevent people from directly touching it, so theoretically, he could just pick up the gyroscopic assembly with the coins inside and make a break for it.

But there were at least four people firing back at him, minus the girl.

He waited for a lull in the shooting to peek over his cover and pump half his magazine into his enemies' cover. He stood and slowly made his way towards the Armillary Ward, firing at anyone who dared to move.

But halfway to the coins, he pulled the trigger of his gun, and nothing happened.

Jammed.

He threw the gun aside and dove behind a file cabinet as the Greeks returned fire. Mind racing, he grabbed one of his swords and threw it to his left. The sound of the clattering metal drew their fire as he whirled around his cover and lashed out his rope dart.

The dagger buried itself into the chest of a lanky man before Henry yanked the dart and the man attached to it towards him. He put the man between himself and the next hail of bullets as he closed the distance. Discarding the body, he unloaded a flurry of chain punches into an older female Magician.

He lashed out his rope dart at another man and threw a Fire-Style-fueled side kick into his ribs as the man was being pulled in. He felt the man's bones crumble under the blade of his foot like a stale pastry.

The girl from the shrine tried to grab one of her fallen comrade's guns, but Henry whipped the back of his fist across her jaw, sending her to the ground. His sword flew into his hand before he flipped his grip and plunged the blade towards the girl's neck.

Something made his hand stop before the sword dealt the lethal blow—a small memory of his conversation on the beach with Marion, perhaps. The girl's eyes were squeezed shut, her breath quivering with the fear of death.

She's right to be afraid.

He slashed her throat before flicking the blood off his blade, refusing to leave her to report his position to her comrades above ground, then grabbed the Armillary Ward and started back towards the surface, hoping things were going more according to plan for his teammates.

CHAPTER SIXTEEN
In Pursuit of Honor

The Great Meteoron Monastery was a bloodbath of close-combat magic. Any pretense of encrypted communications and secrecy to this operation had been dropped as radio chatter in English, German, Latin, Greek, and Arabic swarmed in Henry's ears.

Guns weren't an option with this mess of a battlefield, since no one seemed keen on receiving friendly fire. Especially since it was four against twenty.

And yet the four seemed to be doing unreasonably well. Magicians ran all over the towers surrounding the courtyard, firing spells off like a fireworks show on Independence Day. The ground was swarming with Martial Magicians or those playing at being Martial Magicians, who fought with Yianni and Marion using steel weaponry like a brawl out of Late Antiquity.

But notably, there didn't seem to be any Chinese Magicians.

As he reached the courtyard, Henry took a breath, filling his veins with Qi, and hooked the Armillary Ward onto a belt loop before he rushed into the fray.

"Reporting an unidentified Chinese in the ADZ! Is the Tiandihui here too?" One of the enemy WACs broadcasted across an open channel. Or more likely an encrypted channel, that Analise had broken into.

"Negative. Identified as fugitive Defect, formerly Zhao 4."

"This is Atum Squad WAC to ALCON! Marking the Defectors! Stop their escape by any means necessary! Engage at will!"

Henry cursed under his breath as he threw himself into a butterfly twist, narrowly dodging the swipe of an Egyptian khopesh. He trapped the khopesh and slammed his elbow into its wielder's neck. Then, with a quick combo, he slashed the man's legs and throat open with his butterfly swords.

"There's too many damn hostiles, Moneta! Got any of your contingencies ready?" he asked.

"They were designed to be doable *before* the alarms went off!" Analise screamed in his ear.

"That's on you, then!"

He turned to fight another Magician, but she slumped over as a rifle round made a hole in her head, courtesy of Analise.

"Alright, I'm clearing a path," Henry said. "We need to get out! Now!"

"Did you find the fourth?" Analise asked.

"Yeah! They were a bit haphazard with it, since they found it *yesterday*."

"Let's hijack one of their armored transports," Marion suggested.

"Good thinking, Sunna," Analise said. "All Companions, make your way down the peak to the south roadside."

"Moneta! I have three bandits on me!" Yianni cried.

Henry spotted Yianni's silhouette and three Latins chasing him.

"I see 'em!" He threw his swords through the air, each hitting one of Yianni's pursuers.

Yianni lashed out with some kind of shadow magic at the last one.

"Nezha, evade!"

Henry felt his river stone grow hot just before a bolt of lightning crashed into his chest, sending him spinning through the air. He crashed into a cypress tree and landed on the cobblestone courtyard. His entire abdomen ached with stabbing pain and burns.

"Companion 1, report!"

Henry squeezed his eyes shut as he tried to breathe through the impact. "I'm...I'm hit..."

"Sunna, do not rally!" Analise cried. "Sunna!"

"Damnit," Henry muttered. "Companion 2, keep your distance! I'm fine! Focus on clearing the way!"

"Companion 1, the perpetrator's tagging you. He's bringing friends."

"Shit." Henry summoned his swords back to his hands as he struggled to stand.

Marion was suddenly there, hoisting his arm over her shoulder as she ran. Yianni lagged behind to cast a cloud of shadowy mist over the courtyard, and the three of them ducked into the winding halls of the monastery. They headed downwards and nearly crashed into the waist-high wall between the stairs and a hundred-meter drop down the forested chasm below.

There were at least three really long flights of stairs between them and the myriad of black vehicles parked below. Analise was already down there somehow.

Marion pulled out a runestone. "Last one...shit, I can only bring two people."

"Don't worry about us." Henry pulled the softball-sized gyroscope and the coins it contained off his belt. "Take this. And this." He fished out the Honor coin and handed it to her. "Go with Analise. We'll be right behind you."

Marion stared at the coins in disbelief.

Henry didn't think it was that surprising, given their current situation. *"Go!"* he snapped.

She snapped out of her shock and threw her runestone, swapping with it as it landed on the roadside. She got into a low-to-the-ground blocker car with Analise before they drove off.

"Come on, man. Let's get you down there." Yianni supported some of Henry's weight as the two tried to make it down the stairs.

Henry could hear the mob of enemy Magicians before they turned the corner at the top of the stairs. He drew his revolver and fired, clipping one of the Latin men in the shoulder. He yelped and hid behind the stone wall.

The two men managed to get onto the roadside and piled into a four-by-four.

"I'll drive." Henry groaned.

Yianni furrowed his brow. "You're injured!"

"Do you even have a license?"

Yianni sighed and got in the passenger seat as Henry took the wheel. As bullets dinked off the car, he made a series of hand signs, using Buddhist magic to call on the Chinese God of Vehicles. The car magically hotwired itself before he slammed on the gas.

Once he had the two of them on the road, he found the time to breathe through the burns and wounds inflicted on him.

But they had barely started down the mountain before the Hecateans and their allies piled into their own vehicles and sped after them. In the rearview mirror, Henry saw several trucks and armored cars veer off in a different direction at a fork in the road.

"Shite. They're gonna try and cut off the girls," Yianni muttered.

"Not if we can help it." Henry took a hard turn around the bend of a mountain road, causing the car to tip dangerously towards the cliffside.

"This is Companion 3. Sunna, you got seven...no, eight enemy transports on your six!" Yianni shouted into his radio. "We're comin' up from behind, just don't let them catch you!"

The road would take them east about half a mile before they could start downward. Henry could cut through the rocks and green between the bend.

"Hang on."

"Hey, what are you—" Yianni started as Henry turned the car away from the road.

"Oh, calm down. We have a four by four."

"Fuckin' Christ, you chancer!"

The car lurched as it hit rock, but Henry slammed his foot on the pedal, giving it enough speed not to get caught on the boulders between them and a smoother incline of dirt.

He pulled onto the road below, nearly slamming into the car of some poor tourist.

"Henry! *Henry!*" Yianni screamed, twisting towards the road behind them.

Henry glanced in the mirror to find a mass of black metal and armor careening towards them over the boulders. The massive turret mounted on top of the armored truck fired not bullets, but a hyper-concentrated bolt of raw arcane energy. The impact of the blast rattled Henry's skeleton, frying his arcane senses with the magical equivalent to tinnitus.

Swerving in an attempt to be evasive, Henry veered right, going through a break in the guardrail as they passed another monastery. The car half-tumbled, half-drove through the path of a stream down the mountain, carving the depth of one of the many chasms.

The armored truck kept to the road.

"Oh, this is just fuckin' brilliant!"

"Would you like to drive?" Henry yelled.

"While you're doing so fierce a job?"

"Shut up and hang on!"

Their bumpy ride down the mountain nearly ended, as they had a coinflip's chance of just slamming into the boulder between them and the next stretch of road. The car popped into the air for a moment before slamming back onto the road.

Henry winced, as no suspension in the world could make the impact feel better on his scarred torso.

"Holy Mary, mother of God. Pray for us sinners now and at the hour of our death," Yianni mumbled as Henry drove.

The roar of an engine grew louder behind them, and a beam of turret fire scraped against the car's body, barely grazing them.

"Bullshit!" Henry snarled.

"Leg it, man!"

"The hell do you think I'm doing?"

Henry took a sharp left into some kind of vineyard, barreling through wood posts and grapevines as they neared the bottom of the mountain, putting some distance between them and the massive arcane cannon looking to turn them into soot stains on the wind-shield.

The car skipped as it ran over a thin wall of vegetation and skidded across a dirt path. He sped towards a gravel-covered drop and pushed on the brake, slowing them just enough to slide down the gravel and the steep slope ahead. The car managed to skid its way down to another dirt drive that led to a hotel and the main road to town.

Henry barked a laugh. "I'd like to see them try to follow us through that!"

"Holy shit..." Yianni gasped.

Henry pulled onto the main road, heading towards the outskirts of Kalambaka.

In all honesty, he wasn't sure why he was so intent on taking risks to get to the girls. They could probably make it away on their own. They'd done a swell job of it so far. A part of it felt out of character for him to rush to their aid, but another, more insistent side of him had to help Marion. And he wasn't going to start asking that fire in his belly any questions.

"Down there!" Yianni pointed to their right as Analise's stolen blocker car raced down a parallel road half a mile or so ahead of them, followed by a whole convoy of armored cars and trucks.

Maybe they weren't doing as great as he thought...

Henry slammed his foot on the brake to turn and speed after the girls' car as they and their pursuers veered left. He didn't hesitate to take the car off-road as their path took them towards a bulbous rock formation as tall as a skyscraper.

As he drove, Yianni spared a glance back and cursed. "What's the plan here, Zhang?"

The other road was starting to dip down, leaving their car rolling through a patch of green with a very steep drop approaching fast.

"Henry!"

He kept his foot on the gas, his eyes glued to a black truck in the back of the convoy whose open-topped back was full of soldiers.

"Take the wheel!" Henry shouted.

"Fuckin' what?"

"Take it!" Henry let go of the steering wheel, only for Yianni to grab hold of it. He stood and leapt out of the four-by-four, over the cliff.

He screamed a whole slew of curses as he flew over the cliff and lashed his rope dart out at the truck. The dart wrapped around a convenient hold on the vehicle, but the silk rope didn't pull him in fast enough, and his side bashed into a clay tile roof of a building on the other side of the road as more tile roofs scraped up his skin while the truck dragged him along.

Through the pain, he willed the rope to reel him in. He slammed his palm into the nearest soldier shooting from the back of the truck and pulled him off, clearing a space for him to hop on.

In close quarters, the gunmen had no chance. Henry became a whirlwind of strikes and kicks, beating down all four of the remaining occupants.

However, as he cleared out the cargo bed, soldiers and Magicians on motorcycles and armored cars began to fall back and surround him.

He ducked as someone launched a bolt of fire at him and someone else shot at him. He pulled his guandao from his ear and used the historically anti-cavalry weapon to reach across to a motorcycle and majorly wound the driver with the sweeping blade. Both the driver and the soldier on the back of the vehicle fell victim to a fiery crash.

Henry stowed the weapon and climbed onto the top of the truck before someone sent the vehicle sky-high with reckless gunfire. He hopped into the passenger seat of another four-by-four, grabbed the diver's wrist, and slammed the soldier's head into the steering wheel's horn, then right through the windshield before throwing him out of the car.

He slid into the driver's seat and, after regaining control of the car, tried to gain some ground towards the girls.

Another car slammed into him from the left, pushing him onto the curb as the road narrowed and the older buildings heralded the winding roads of Kalambaka's old district.

Pedestrians leapt out of the way, while bystanders either watched or screamed.

Henry glanced over to find Josephine riding next to him in her own transport, a gun pointed at him.

He pulsed the brake, misaligning her shot as he pulled the .44 Magnum from his hip.

"Die!" she hissed. But the arcane fabric of her words was drowned out by gunshots and engines. Still, it made Henry lose control of himself long enough for his hand and gun to be tied up with white linen bandages.

The perpetrator was Ramses of Atum Squad, attacking from a motorcycle he was riding with callsign Cleopatra.

Henry jerked the steering wheel of his car, causing it to swerve and bringing Ramses's motorcycle with it as the bindings tried to tug his shoulder out of its socket. He pulled on the now-loose magical bandages and shot at the motorcycle with his revolver. The bike lost balance and skidded across the road, freeing his hand.

He emptied the rest of the revolver at Josephine's car, shooting out her engine block.

The girls were close.

As he stomped on the gas, Henry slammed into two other motorcycles in hot pursuit of Analise and Marion. He was about to do the same to a third until its rider launched three golden bolts of concussive magic that knocked out the driver of one of the few remaining cars and caused it to crash.

"Marion?" Henry yelled from his car.

"About time you caught up, Heinrich!" She grinned.

"Where'd you learn to drive?"

"I own a Vespa!" Marion shouted. "Now, hop on!"

"You hop on!"

"The streets are narrow! Better for a bike! Now—Henry, watch out!" Henry turned to his left just in time to see the truck with the turret on top barrel through the intersection they were passing. Something arcane slammed into the side of his car.

The world went black.

"Henry!"

The voice came through to him, muffled.

"Henry!"

Henry gasped for breath as he sat up, awake.

Alive.

He felt his own body in disbelief.

He was covered in glass, sitting in a crater he had undoubtedly made in a wooden shelf of spices.

"Thank Christ!" Marion said, heaving, her hair soaked in sweat and her face tired with effort. She wrapped her arms around him. "Thank God!"

"What...what happened?" Henry asked.

Marion removed herself from him. "You died, Henry! You...you stopped breathing! I revived you with CPR, but..."

"The coins—"

"Safe," Marion assured him. "But we have to go. We have to move!"

Henry accepted her help in pulling himself to his feet. He was incredibly dizzy, and if not for Marion holding onto him, he probably would've fallen over. He followed her out of the little store he'd crashed into, then around the wreckage of his car.

"He's alive!" Marion said to Analise and Yianni, who stood just outside the store with their backs turned to them.

"Lotta good that does us..." Analise muttered.

Henry put the pieces together as his mental clarity returned.

The four of them were surrounded, and not just by the remaining Magicians and soldiers. They were staring down the barrel of the armored truck's arcane turret. The street was long clear of pedestrians, meaning all bets were off magic-wise.

"Attention, Defectors." Atum's WAC spoke through Henry's earpiece. "If you want to leave Kalambaka in anything other than a body bag, you'll surrender the coins."

Henry stared at all the rifle muzzles pointed his way and found himself matching Analise's despondency.

At least, until he caught sight of the Shell gas station across the street from them.

He took a cultivating breath.

"Marion, get your coin ready. Just yours," Henry muttered. "After that, harass that truck."

"I beg your unbelievable pardon?" Analise turned.

"Yianni...pin down as many of those soldiers as you can," Henry said. "Analise, get over to that gas station. Spill as much gasoline as you can."

"What about you? You're injured," Marion protested.

"I'm gonna take out as many of them as I can." Henry cracked his knuckles. "Either we take the risk now, or all of this was for nothing. Are you all clear on what you need to do?"

He heard no further protests.

"Good. That's your cue."

Marion shoved her hand into the sky, clutching the Wisdom coin, and blinding light shone from behind Henry. The soldiers and Magicians cried out, firing blind for about a second before a tidal wave of brambles ripped through the asphalt road, binding, disarming, or trapping almost all of them.

Analise took the opportunity and sprinted across the street, while Marion fired one of her magic bolts at the truck's turret, throwing off its axis of fire so the artillery strike blew a chunk out of the road.

Henry drew his guandao from his ear, the weapon growing in size as he rushed towards Yianni's bramble and cleaved through both the bramble and the enemies trapped within using Fire Style Wuxing Quan.

Even when the soldiers began freeing themselves, Yianni used more tough dead plant matter to provide Henry with cover from those who were far enough to shoot.

He paused as the scent of gasoline stabbed into his nostrils, glancing up at the fuel raining down on him and his enemies before leaping out of the fray.

Marion aimed her hand at the turret again, but a bullet grazed her, causing her to flinch.

Henry dragged Yianni and Marion out of the way as the truck fired right at their position. His ears rang as the force of the blow tossed all three of them aside, but quickly recovered. He grabbed Yianni's shoulder. "The bramble! Hit them with the bramble again!" he shouted.

"What?" Yianni asked, also suffering from hearing loss.

Henry made a motion like he was flicking water off of his hands, and Yianni seemed to understand, quickly throwing his arms out at the truck, encasing it in dead, dry, flammable bramble.

Henry channeled his will into his newfound pyromantic abilities. He only got the smallest of flames to emanate from his palm, but that was enough.

He whipped his hand out, throwing embers onto a nearby puddle of gasoline.

In an instant, the gasoline, guided by the bramble, erupted into flame.

Most of the individual soldiers and Magicians managed to break away from the fire, running and screaming. They would probably survive, but they wouldn't get in the way.

But the truck exploded with a boom so stark, it felt like Henry's chest had been shattered. He hoped the tinnitus wasn't going to stick around.

CHAPTER SEVENTEEN
The Road of Odysseus

"What do you mean, we have no leads?"

Min flinched as Weiying roared at Zhao's WAC over a video call.

"Fuck!" He hung up and slammed his phone onto the table, then pinched the bridge of his nose.

Luxury resort or not, Min hated being trapped in this hotel with him. Probably as much as Weiying hated not being able to find Henry.

His malicious gaze met hers for a moment before it softened. "God." He sighed. "I just...I just need them to not look at me like I'm stupid. Or talk down to me like that."

In Min's opinion, the WACs hadn't done anything wrong and had been perfectly reasonable. But she couldn't say that out loud.

"Well, they *are* Defectors, Weiying," Min said. "They're good at hiding."

"I know," he muttered. "It's just so...demoralizing. *We're* the Magicians' Circle. *We're* the ones with resources. And yet my fucking assclown of a brother has managed to get all *four* coins! And no one knows where he is!" He tilted his head back and sighed. "Qin Squad is gonna serve my balls on a platter."

Min had to admit he was right to be worried. But instead of moping, she thought he should get off his ass.

"I'd like to see Huangdi do better." He scoffed. "God, I need a drink. Min, go down to the bar and order a bottle of wine up here."

Min furrowed her brows. "What, am I your secretary now?"

"You're my underling." He glared in her direction. "I'm in command here. Go get a bottle of wine. I want to be alone right now."

Min took a deep breath, holding herself back from laying into him with a verbal beatdown. Gathering up what dignity she could produce for herself, she spun on her heel and left the suite.

Going down the navy-carpeted hall, she clenched her fists.

To think she'd sworn to call that entitled prick her brother. Ever since Morocco, Weiying had been insufferable. He did his job, but never without complaining first or blaming something else for anything that went wrong.

After the Greeks found Henry in Plakias first, he'd had the gall to blame his inability on a bout of severe anxiety. Min wasn't sure how she felt about him using that as an excuse, but Qin Squad certainly wasn't happy with it. She figured that maybe he was using it to justify their failure to *himself* rather than to anyone else.

Min stepped into the mirror-plastered elevator and tapped her foot against the wooden floor as it took her down to the ground level.

It was like training all over again—peacocking, whining, and tantrums all the way to Thessaloniki. But at least back then, lives and careers weren't on the line. Back then, there was no risk of the Chaldean Court getting involved.

Min squeezed her eyes shut. "Stop being a moron, Zhang."

She was talking about Henry, of course. In recent days, there had been petitions to the Chaldean Court from both the Coven of Latium and the Hecatean Circle, asking the High Court to condemn Henry and his Defector allies and brand them *Damnatio Memoriae*.

Defectors were criminals of Circles, but by the Court's decree, they were still free agents and allowed to participate in Magician society. Yet if enough Circles felt wronged, the Courtiers who represented them could get someone re-blinded by Solomon's Wisdom—permanently condemned to ignorance of magic.

And more often than not, there were collateral victims. Magicians close to the individual could be blinded to tie up loose ends.

It was the main reason Min was even here, fighting as hard as she could. That and her oaths.

She stepped out into the marble lobby and headed away from the reception desk, towards the fancy-looking bar, separated by the hotel's massive pool by a wall of glass. She walked up to the wooden bar and leaned in under a hanging light as a lanky man tending the place asked if he could help her.

"I don't think I've ever seen you this pissed-off." Mr. Fang chuckled from her left.

"Mr. Fang..." Min stood a little straighter. "What are you doing down here?"

He sat at the bar with a glass of whiskey swirling between his fingers. "What else? Idling until someone gets a lead." He smiled calmly.

To Min, Mr. Fang's serenity had always been infectious. He never took life too seriously, and for that, she was thankful that his mood often impressed onto her. Each member of Zhao Squad had their connection to Mr. Fang. In terms of magic, they had all been personally trained by him.

And after his daughter passed, he'd been treating them more and more like his own children.

Min turned to the barkeep. "I'll have a margarita."

"What troubles you, *Xiao Min*?" Mr. Fang asked.

She turned to him with an unamused look on her face. "Aside from a possible mission failure?"

"Obviously." He chuckled.

"Well..." She sighed. "I'm worried. About Weiying."

"Just Weiying?"

Min looked at his curious expression and shrugged.

"It's like training all over again." Mr. Fang scoffed. He turned to her. "You know, you've spent nearly five years worrying over those boys like you were their mother. At first, I understood. I knew you and Hanying fancied one—"

"We *didn't* 'fancy' each other." Min scoffed, taking her margarita as it was handed to her and letting the strawberry-flavored booze run down her throat.

"You can't say there wasn't a mutual attraction there," Fang said. "I saw you two every damn day. There's no hiding it."

Min just drank in response.

"Well, I understood before Hanying asked you to dinner. But even afterwards, it seems all you care about is those two not getting into trouble." Mr. Fang sighed.

"I'm oathbound to help my brothers, aren't I?" Min asked. "I wanted to help my teammates."

"But Hanying isn't your teammate anymore. And yet all you do is listen to the Chaldean Court's meetings on whether or not these Companions should be Damned." Mr. Fang sipped his whiskey. "Why *didn't* you go out with him?"

"That seems unprofessional to ask, Mr. Fang. And irrelevant," Min muttered.

"As your mentor, I find it to be quite relevant," Fang countered.

As she thought about the question, her mind recoiled from thinking about that embarrassing night.

She was helping Henry study his Civic Sorcery. Fang had asked her to, since Henry and Weiying had gotten into an argument and Henry's punishment was having to pass his beginner set for Confucian magic.

She remembered enjoying most of it. They studied together, snacked, and chatted well into the early hours of the morning. Henry actually managed to pass. But then, after he celebrated his triumph, he'd eagerly turned to her and...well, it wasn't like he kicked her dog or something.

He'd just asked her to dinner. The embarrassing part was the fact that she just sat there, staring blankly at him. She convinced herself that she'd let him down easy by not answering, but that was a lie. Every time she remembered the night, she knew she should've just said no.

But it wasn't nearly that easy. She was so...

"I was afraid," Min said. "I was too scared to say yes, so...I said nothing. Henry probably still resents me for it to this day." She let her head fall into her arms. "God, Mr. Fang." She groaned. "Ever since I've become a Magician, it's like the world has gotten exponentially scarier. And here I thought magic powers would make me feel safe. Hell, I'm afraid of Weiying now! He's gone off the rails..."

She looked at him, pleading for some kind of guidance. Her chest felt like a crumpled-up paper ball.

Fang put a strong hand on her shoulder. "You know as well as I do that's no way to live, Min."

"Well, what am I supposed to do? My oaths won't let me just find something else to do." Min scoffed.

"You can always transfer divisions." Fang shrugged. "Not that I'd want that. It's only thanks to you that Chen Bo doesn't tear Shen in half, *Xiao Min*."

"Then...how do I get this feeling to go away?"

"It's not about what you do. It's about how you think." Fang tapped his temple. "Find some reason other than worry to do your job. Or hate, in Weiying's case. We're on a quest to recover the lost tomb of Alexander the Great. How many others can say that?"

Min pursed her lips. He had a point.

"Don't worry about Hanying or Weiying. They can take care of themselves. Just have fun with this job," Fang said. "If we fail, so what? We'll get a slap on the wrist. They can't afford to lose any of us. You should be more secure in your position."

Min grimaced. He was so nonchalant about all this. At first, she was a little resentful, but she wanted to mirror his take on the chase. His joy in it. That freedom he enjoyed from Weiying's domineering personality, in spite of having to work with him constantly.

Min figured she'd try it, if nothing else.

"Hey, barkeep," she said. "Can you send a bottle of red wine to room 308? Oh, and be sure to spit in it first."

"And...there."

Analise stepped back as the three rings forming the Armillary Ward around the last two coins clattered onto the small wooden table.

Finally able to relax a bit, Henry and the Companions had taken up residence in Cheers Vintage Hostel, a joint with a great balcony view of the slow-moving Bosphorus strait, even when it was cloudy out, and just a three-minute walk from the incredibly massive and old Hagia Sophia. The only drawback was the fact that the cheapest beds were in a funky-smelling basement. While the weather deterred Henry from going into the ancient city, his enthusiasm had come back to him in a wave of curiosity about this whole thing with Alexander's generals.

And now, they had all the pieces of the puzzle.

Or...at least the pieces they knew of.

"And you're sure neither of these are fakes?" Henry lounged back on a cushioned sofa overlooking the coast, resisting the urge to scratch the battle scars he'd gotten from the swarming clouds of mosquitoes around the border crossing between Greece and Turkey.

"They have the same frequency as the other coins," Analise said.

She finished sketching either side of the coin and got to translating before handing it off to Henry. "Well, Mister Historian, what do you think?"

Henry observed the faces on the coin's head side. "Cassander and Seleucus. As expected. The other face is..." He looked at Marion. "Our resident *Iliad* expert want to weigh in here?"

"Hector with Cassander. And Odysseus with Seleucus," Marion said.

"Cassander's coin says, *The Fearful hide behind their scars to avoid true courage* and *The Courageous do not allow the darkness of night to subsume the North Star*," Analise said. "Whatever that means...Seleucus's says *The Fearful obey law to disguise their lack of knowledge* and *The Knowledgeable distinguish between the truths of reality and the delusions of ideas*."

"Honor, Wisdom, Knowledge, Courage..." Henry muttered.

"So, our theory about Alexander trying to make a point against his generals is more or less correct, right?" Yianni asked. "Now what?"

"Now..." Henry unwrapped all four coins, but kept them touching their wraps so they wouldn't let off their signals. "We put the puzzle pieces together. Each of the coins has markings reminiscent of the Vergina sun, the symbol of the Macedonian Empire. If we put them together..."

Henry put the coins together so all their markings shone outwards, leaving a space in the center and having the lines between the coins act as the up, down, left, and right markings on the sigil.

But...nothing happened.

"Enlightening." Analise frowned.

"There has to be more to it," Marion said.

"Well...the whole sunburst design is supposed to have a sun in the middle," Henry muttered.

"Something tells me that isn't happening today." Yianni sighed. "So...what, do we wait for the rain to pass? Or can we use a flashlight or something?"

"I don't see this being much of a scientific process, so I have a feeling that whatever spell we're messing with will know the difference between a flashlight and the sun," Henry said.

"Wait!" Marion reached behind her neck. "My sunstone! It can produce sunlight."

Yianni, Analise, and Henry looked at one another. "That is...highly specific. But it's worth a shot," Henry said.

Marion got defensive. "My brother made it for me. I don't want to hear any lip from *you*."

Each of them took a coin in their hands as Marion held her sunburst necklace up to the sky, channeling magic into the pendant until a beam of sunlight spilled out of the necklace's gemstone center.

The Companions put their coins together around the sunbeam. As they did, shadows began to form in the spotlight.

"Holy shit..." Yianni muttered.

The shadows formed into a map of simple lines and boxes marked by a Macedonian sun. But the longer Henry stared at it, the more familiar it seemed.

"So, we have a map, but...no key?" Analise muttered. "Didn't peg Alexander to be this sloppy."

"It's a map of Troy eight," Henry said.

"Troy eight?" Marion frowned.

Henry pulled out his phone and snapped a photo of the map.

"Wait, can't they track—" Analise started.

"I'm all armored-up on the digital front," Henry said. "Should be fine. I need to check something." He grabbed his backpack from the ground next to him and pulled out his laptop. "I think I know what this is. Need to make sure."

"Thank God you have no life." Yianni patted him on the shoulder. "So, what's Troy eight?"

"Troy is one of those cities that got destroyed and rebuilt so many times over such a long period of time that we have distinct versions of Troy at the archaeological site," Henry explained, sifting through Google's offerings for maps of Troy. "It's been an important thing to distinguish, especially after the guy who found the place did it by blowing the site to hell with explosives. The first Troy was built around 3500 BC, and the area was inhabited until 500 AD. The sixth Troy in the stack is almost certainly the Homeric Troy mentioned in the *Iliad*. But Troy eight is the city that Alexander planned to build that was supposedly never completed. Instead, we have a Troy eight built by Antigonous and Lysimachus."

"So, the city on the map...doesn't exist?" Analise asked as she took a picture of the map.

"Not according to what we know," Henry said. "But that doesn't really matter. Look. This is Troy seven."

He sat back, showing the Companions his laptop screen as they gathered around him. The map of Troy seven was much larger in scope than the hint Alexander had offered. But a portion of the map looked strangely similar.

"The star on the map lines up there." Henry pointed to a marker on the map. "The temple of Athena Ilias. That was the centerpiece of Alexander's construction plans for Troy. That part really exists. Or at least...what's left of it."

"So that's our next stop?" Analise said.

"Here's hoping it's our last." Yianni sighed as he stood.

"I seriously doubt it," Marion said. "We have records of Alexander's body in Egypt. It can't be too far from Alexandria."

"One more thing," Analise said. "We need to talk about what we might be going into. Henry, last I checked, you had no pyromantic abilities. Nor could you command your weapons with a thought. Was it those dreams?"

"Well...it just kinda happened." Henry slid the Courage and Knowledge coins over to Yianni and Analise. "I'm thinking making contact with a coin probably helps. So, take your pick."

Yianni picked up the Knowledge Coin.

"Feel anything?" Marion asked.

Yianni shrugged. "Nothing much."

Henry took the Knowledge Coin and handed him the Courage Coin, giving the other to Analise.

"Whoa." Yianni stumbled back.

"You feel it too?" Analise asked, staring at the Knowledge coin warily.

Yianni nodded as he held up his hand. Green vines bloomed to life out of nothing, curling around his arm. "What is this?"

"Not magic," Marion said.

Analise closed her eyes and held up her coin. "I think each of these...each of these may have been made for us specifically."

Marion frowned. "Meaning...what?"

"Meaning this hunt of ours might not be a hunt at all." Henry's voice grew dark. "I think we're being recruited for something. Some kind of war, if the dreams are anything to go on."

"Am I right to be worried?" Analise asked. "What are you all seeing in your dreams? Is it the same?"

Henry grimaced. "I can't really say one way or the other. I keep being shown historical crises and being warned about Gawgs and Megawgs. There's this guy in bronze armor telling me I'm supposed to prevent some great cataclysm of Western Civilization because I'm...I don't know, just that good at history, I guess."

"I get the same. Although I'm given a different reason. He calls me a...bridge." Marion scoffed.

"That's nothin'. The bastard called me a 'tragic hero.' I don't want that responsibility! Not to mention the snobbishness in callin' yourself that."

"He calls *me* a harbinger," Analise muttered. "I get the feeling he has plans for all of us."

"Well...not much point in worrying about it." Marion shrugged. Henry raised an eyebrow at her. "We were going to go find Alexander's tomb anyway. If he wants us there, all the better. Right, Heinrich?"

"Heinrich?" Analise furrowed her brow.

"This your first time hearing her little nickname?" Henry asked.

A somewhat-guilty smile slowly spread across Marion's face as Analise scoffed.

"Oh, that's not a good sign, lad." Yianni grinned.

"Wait, why are you laughing? Marion, what've you been calling me?"

Analise shook her head, "Nothing bad! Just...It's just the name Heinrich is so...*old*. I don't know a single Heinrich under eighty."

Henry frowned at Marion.

"Hey, don't be so grumpy, old man. These are the best years of your life." She chuckled, softly punching him in the arm.

"I'm six months younger than you." Henry sighed, shaking his head. "Truly hilarious, Marion. An excellent example—nay, a masterwork of comedy. Let's just...get the tickets to Troy."

"Sure thing, grandpa. I think you get a senior-citizen discount." Yianni grinned. "We'll get you a nice seat up front."

"Yeah, and you'll have a disability discount after I shove my foot up your ass," Henry shot back. Marion broke into a fit of laughter.

In spite of his defensive remark, Henry found himself smiling, feeling able to joke with his friends at last.

CHAPTER EIGHTEEN
Beasts and Men

Walking through the entrance to Troy was a lot like walking into a theme park, except instead of a giant statue of the park's mascot, there was a massive wooden recreation of the Trojan horse.

The land around the city was way flatter than Henry had initially anticipated. And all the iterations of the *Iliad* he'd seen had put him under the impression that Troy would be closer to the ocean. But the nearest beach wasn't even visible, somewhere beyond the extent of what he could see past the horizon.

"Hey, why don't we get a group photo?" Marion asked, gesturing to the ten-meter-tall wooden horse.

"And tell the other Circles where we are?" Analise asked.

"This is Troy. Like...*the* Troy. When else would you have come here?" Marion said. "We need *something* to remember all this by."

"We can take a photo in front of Alexander's treasure," Yianni said.

"Get the sticks outta your asses." Henry pulled out his phone. "Half my phone's storage is used to make myself untrackable by the Chinese government. It'll be safe there."

Somewhat reluctantly, the four of them gathered in front of the Trojan horse, allowing Henry to take a photo, though only he and Marion were smiling.

All four of the Companions made their way up the gravel path from the Trojan horse's stone brick plaza to a ruined section of stone wall marked by a sign with the Roman numeral for six on it, then started on the wooden walkway that would take them on the trail around the ruined city.

"This wall right here is what stood during the Trojan war." Henry couldn't keep the grin off his face. To be right where such legendary events took place never failed to make him a little giddy.

"Hey, focus." Yianni snapped his fingers. "Christ, it's like wrangling dogs with you and Miss Mythology over here."

"Oh, come on, Yianni, you can't tell me this isn't cool!" Marion leaned over the wooden railing, nearly touching the Trojan walls.

"Don't be surprised. We all have obsessions here." Analise scoffed. "How'd you break Solomon's Wisdom?"

"I write music." Yianni shrugged.

"Oh," Henry muttered. That explained a lot. Although he wouldn't have expected it from Yianni of all people. The Irishman didn't seem like the most artistic person in the world.

"'Oh?' The fuck do you mean, 'Oh?'"

"Did the Celts never tell you?" Analise asked.

"Tell me what?"

"Breaking Solomon's Wisdom, unless you have magic shoved in your face, is typically an exercise in mastery and knowledge of one's own culture," Analise explained—inefficiently, in Henry's opinion. "An intimate understanding of cultural character by understanding a civilization's story and personality. For me, it was language. For Marion, it was religion. For Henry, it was history. But artists, musicians, dancers, and other performers or creators can also break Solomon's Wisdom through mastery of their craft. But they don't typically bring a conscious understanding of why they broke it."

"Basically, you got lucky." Henry scoffed. "And musicians typically have the least solid understanding of their culture out of the artistic types. They're also kinda full of it. No offense."

"Arse." Yianni sighed.

"Let me guess—your brother was a musician." Analise smirked.

"Art, actually," Henry muttered.

"What kind of music do you make?" Marion asked.

Yianni shrugged. "All kinds. Mostly acoustic stuff with some folk elements."

"Do you have any music out?" Analise asked.

"And let you three listen to my rubbish? Over my dead body." Yianni scoffed.

"Come on, man. What else are we gonna use my speaker for?" Henry grinned.

"Throw it at someone!"

Henry scoffed and turned to find a second wall lining the right side of the boardwalk. "Oh! This wall was built by Alexander's descendants!" He pointed at the right wall, which was constructed of stone blocks that fit together much more tightly than in the Troy six wall to the left, in desperate need of mortar.

"Go wank yourself off with it, Doctor Jones," Yianni muttered.

"Hey, don't be an ass, Yianni." Marion frowned.

"I'll be an arse when I want," he fired back.

"So, you *choose* to be like that all the time?" Henry asked.

"Can we all take this just...*a little* more seriously?" Analise asked through nearly gritted teeth.

"Truce, then. Don't shit on me for history, and I won't go find your Soundcloud," Henry proposed, turning to face Yianni as he walked backwards.

Yianni grimaced. "Fine."

The wall of Hellenistic Troy started to deteriorate as they walked further, heading up a few flights of wooden stairs interspersed by stretches of walkway to a balcony looking over the entire archaeological site and the stretch of grassy plain that surrounded the ruined city-state.

Henry walked up to the bench at the far end of the balcony, shaded by a looming tree. "This...is the temple of Athena Ilias," he said, pointing over the edge at a few weathered waist-high stone blocks, part of a single column, and a few pieces of white marble or limestone in the ground, covered in weeds and grass. Aside from some decently preserved tilework on the floor, it wasn't much to look at.

The other Companions gave him uncertain looks as Analise compared their location to the map the sunstone had revealed. "This place has certainly seen better days." She sighed. "But he's right. This is the spot."

"Christ..." Yianni muttered. "What a shithole."

Henry jumped over the wooden railing, followed by his squadmates. "Spread out and look for any sign of magic," Analise said.

"No need, Velma." Henry knocked on the shoulder-high marble column. He brushed away dust and dirt to reveal an eroded inscription along the circumference of the pillar.

Analise squinted at the markings and began jotting them down in her notes. Henry pulled out his own notes and started to sketch the column and the surrounding area.

"There is nothing impossible for him who will try..." Analise muttered.

"A mantra right outta Alexander's mouth," Henry said almost absent-mindedly.

Marion pulled away some bramble covering the pillar. "Look at this."

Henry rounded the pillar and found that she'd uncovered a Macedonian sun lightly engraved in the stone, with a message underneath. The center of the sun was of a familiar size.

"Ptolemy," Analise translated. "I take it the Honor coin goes here."

Henry pulled out his coin and tried to put it in the center of the sun, but realized that the coin's wrap would have to come off.

"There's another one back here," Yianni said.

"Okay." Henry held them up. "Let everyone get in position. Then we'll lose the wrappings at the same time and put them in place."

Analise went about translating the names for the suns, each of which faced in one cardinal direction: Honor to the south, Wisdom to the east, Courage to the west, and Knowledge to the north.

The Companions pulled their coins out and partially unwrapped them.

"Ready?" Henry asked.

His squadmates all gave confirmation.

"Alright...now!"

Henry let the cloth fall and shoved the coin into place. It fit perfectly.

But having all four coins in one place unleashed enough magical power to nearly fry his magical senses and sent all four of them to the ground with nausea and vertigo.

"*Fuck!*" Yianni cringed through the sudden assault on his senses as Marion screamed a whole river of German obscenities. Analise wretched, spitting up a mixture of bile and drool as the blast made her sick to her stomach.

Thankfully, as Henry was dry-heaving to high heaven, the column seemed to absorb the absurd amount of power and used it to activate mechanisms that caused the floor to shake, dirt to shift, and roots to snap.

The column began to rotate, grinding against stone as parts of the temple floor began to lower.

Slowly, Henry caught his breath again and let the kinks in his suddenly stressed respiratory system work themselves out.

By the time the Companions staggered to their feet, a spiral staircase leading into an abyssal darkness had dug itself into the stone. The coins were missing from the Macedonian suns.

Henry and the Companions stared down into the darkness before looking at one another.

"I guess the only way to go is down," he muttered.

The way down was longer than any staircase had a right to be. But as Henry and the Companions finally got to the bottom, he understood why.

A strange ambient light cast the massive cave they found themselves at the mouth of in dull, azure light.

"Jesus Christ..." Yianni gasped.

"I think the one you're looking for is Zeus," Henry muttered.

Inside the cave was a full, almost perfectly preserved Greek temple made of marble. It had to be as big as the Parthenon itself, yet didn't even take up a fifth of the cave's space.

And it was still painted. On the sides of the cavern were four large, columned, temple-like facades that led to...somewhere. The nearest and furthest pairs were equidistant from the entrance and formed a symmetrical pattern around the temple. A moat of groundwater encircled the temple save for the earthen ramp to its entrance, surrounded by tiny green and blue crystals.

Marion asked the question that was on all of their minds. "Is this it? Is this his tomb?"

Scattered around the cave were painted statues of a myriad of figures, though at this distance, it was impossible to tell who they were.

The Companions stepped onto the rocky terrain of the cave floor, slowly approaching the temple's entrance.

"Nope," Henry said. "This isn't a tomb. It's a temple to Alexander. As a god."

In the shadows of the columns, the Companions approached the towering wooden doors. Henry and Yianni each took one of the portals and exerted themselves in pushing them open.

Two and a half thousand years' worth of dust wafted out from the temple's entrance.

Braziers of fire bloomed to life, illuminating the contours of a statue in the back of the temple. It was Alexander, posed like a god with a lance in one hand, his helmet in the other.

The temple was empty aside from the statue, the podium it stood on, and plenty of murals, both reliefs and paintings on the walls behind the interior set of columns. Each of them depicted one of Alexander's great battles or adventures: The Battle of Issus, where he met Darius for the first time. The Gordian Knot. The taming of Bucephalus. The trek to the Siwa oracle. The Siege of Tyre. The Opis Mutiny. The Battle of Gaugamela. His meeting with Diogenes.

There was only one painting Henry couldn't place. It was an image depicting Alexander overlooking the construction of some kind of wall in the mountains.

Albeit a familiar-looking wall.

No, not a wall.

A gate.

In all of Henry's research, he'd found only one source describing this event. While the others were noted down in contemporary chronicles, the existence of this gate only ever came out of the Syriac edition of the *Alexander Romance*. And it was a work of fictionalized legend at best.

Nonetheless, the Caspian Gates made their way into Islam. But aside from the gate's existence, those sources said nothing of what was behind it. Just generally "the apocalypse." The man-eating tribes of Gawg and Megawg.

Henry figured whatever was actually behind those gates was not so simplistic a threat. He wanted to know what answers this temple held for them.

"The podium has a message for us," Analise muttered. She was kneeling in front of the statue, scribbling in her journal. "*Those who read my words have proven themselves to be lions in mind, heart, soul, and body. But those who wish to truly ascend from the dirt must prove without a doubt that they are worthy of my Companionship. Tread ground my generals have walked. But never follow in their footsteps. There, you will earn your talismans for a final time and learn the truth at my final resting place after uniting them under my gaze.*"

"I think I may know what he means," Henry said. "Outside. The reliefs of temples carved into the walls. They have to lead to these tests."

"Should we split up, then?" Yianni asked.

Analise nodded. "Keep your radios on."

The Companions left the temple, and as they did, Henry started recognizing the statues. Each relief had statues of the *Iliad* character and the general on each coin. Henry pointed each of them to their respective coins, leaving the one with Ptolemy and Achilles flanking its entrance for himself.

He entered through the doorframe and didn't hesitate to make his way down the flame-lit tunnel behind it.

He was so close. Here was Alexander the Great, giving *him* messages. In spite of his chilly demeanor when speaking to that bronze-clad figure in his dreams, he was starting to believe what he had said.

The tomb was within reach. Just barely.

A few soft twists and turns in the tunnel brought him to a new chamber. The vaulted ceiling framed a massive word etched into the stone wall at the end of the chamber, seemingly covered in char and embers: *Arete*. He wasn't sure what it meant, but it probably had something to do with his coin.

The rest of the chamber was Hellenic in architecture, with columns carved into the rough-hewn walls. Between each column were busts of people Henry recognized.

On the right, there was a bust of Julius Caesar.

Unless someone had found this place and added it later, this bust's existence would be impossible.

On the same side were busts of other anachronistic, out-of-place characters: Belisarius, the Byzantine General. Marcus Aurelius. The Han revolt leader Liu Bang. Cincinnatus. Niccolo Machiavelli. Frederick Barbarossa. The Korean Admiral Yi. Mozart. Boudicca. Cao Cao. Saladin. Khawla bint Al-Azwar. Khutulun. Albrecht Wallenstein. Miyamoto Musashi. Qi Jiguang. There were even some modern people, including busts of George Washington, James Madison, Theodore Roosevelt, T.E. Lawrence, and Bismarck.

That was what Alexander meant by honor—not glory or *kudos*, but a personal standard. A code to live up to. A chivalric honor. In some cases, based on morality, but based on any standard of excellence. That was what Alexander seemed to believe Ptolemy was lacking.

And what Henry needed.

On the left was a very different story. The busts were carved not from marble, but from ebony, making the people depicted slightly harder to determine. But after the first few, Henry got an idea.

Judas was the first. The second was Ephialtes, the man who betrayed the Spartans at Thermopylae. After that was Timur the Lame, a genocidal warlord from Central Asia. Others included Akhenaten, Wu Zetian, Vidkun Quisling, Ivar the Boneless, Wang Jingwei, Ivan the Terrible, Stalin, Caligula, Qin Shi Huang, and other historical figures known for being cruel tyrants and traitors to their countrymen.

They were people who succumbed to fear and paranoia. Men and women who indulged in their basest, cruelest instincts. People who had nothing greater to live for than their own self-deceptions.

Above each side was a single word. On the right, the wall was emblazoned with the word *Hetairoi*. Companions.

On the left, the busts were marked by the word *Gawg*. The missing piece of Gawg and Megawg that the warrior in Henry's dreams never mentioned. He had only ever mentioned the Megawgs.

The last, and probably most important, details of the chamber were the statues of men in Macedonian armor all lined up in a wedge formation at the end of the chamber. The foremost soldiers held up a sword with both hands.

The sword glowed orange, as if it had just been removed from a forge.

An ancient Greek inscription under the massive word for honor started to swim in Henry's vision, morphing into something that wasn't legible, yet was clearly English, Chinese, and Arabic all at once. All three of the languages were the ones he could personally read. There was no need to switch between languages, since they were all there at once.

The inscription read *A lion must possess great strength. But a lion is no match for a man in a war of souls. Only men can understand the truth and join my ranks. I do not employ lions. For lions will give in to their smallest thirsts and desires. They will recoil from pain and bask in pleasure, unknowing of the vastness that surrounds them. They have no ambition. They have no virtue. They have no honor. Those who wish to prove that they are not lions will take hold of the sword and slay the enemies behind them. And they will not let go of it nor run any faster than a steady messenger until it is done. Prove that you and you alone command yourself.*

Henry turned to see the statue of a soldier carved in ebony on the far end of the rectangular chamber. Dread soaked into his chest.

That was red-hot iron in front of him. He didn't even know if Marion could heal a brand like that.

Still...if he turned back now, what would it have all been for? If he didn't take up this sword, he would never find the tomb. Worse, if he let someone else do it for him, he knew that the shame would stick in his mind.

He already had one brand...what was one more?

He could remember it like it was yesterday: The shadows of the chamber. The scorn and disdain on the faces of his higher-ups. The sadistic glee hidden under Weiying's outward concern.

He didn't remember the room. For all he knew, it was a pitch-black void. There was only the fire, the iron brand, the chains, and the audience.

Bent to his knees and his head hanging low, he remembered the anticipation. And he remembered the fury. White-hot and far more potent than the charcoal behind him. And the fear he refused to show his enemies.

He could hear the masked man pick up the brand with his gloved hands. He remembered High Command giving the sentence. But he refused to take it with his head hung in submission. Not like his initiation.

He looked up, his face swollen with bruises, cuts, and swollen welts from beatings he'd taken as High Command tried to get more information out of him regarding his supposed treachery.

He didn't care about the pain. Even as the red-hot brand hissed against his skin like the coldest ice he'd ever felt, melting his flesh. He didn't scream like a cow.

He gritted his teeth and stared at Weiying with a cold hatred. An expression of will, not violent fury. A silent, calm promise: *Never again.*

He remembered thinking that. Promising that.

Weiying's facade gave way to fear.

After all, Henry was taking punishment for betraying his brother. Something that was rightly Weiying's to suffer.

And Henry let the Tiandihui libel him on his skin without so much as a grunt. Because he knew that any less than that stoicism would prove them right. He didn't care about pain. He didn't care about his rage. He didn't care about vengeance.

He knew he was right. He would not forsake himself by giving in to the pain.

He was not an animal then. He would not be now.

Henry closed his eyes and took a deep breath before forcing himself to look at the glowing metal weapon proffered by the soldiers.

Maybe a smarter person would convince someone else to do it. Maybe they would find a way around the mechanism. Maybe they would disable whatever magic was running this test. Maybe they wouldn't need to go on this scavenger hunt in the first place.

But it was more than a scavenger hunt. It was a rite of passage.

This was how Alexander vetted those who searched for his treasures. It wasn't just rhetoric. It was a real test of character—proof that he was as strong as he needed to be to reach the finish line.

Henry's hand hovered above the handle of the weapon, feeling enough heat for it to be painful, even from a foot away.

Ravens could get cars to crack nuts for them. They could teach things to their offspring. They could remember faces. They were certainly smarter animals than lions. But what was either of them compared to a human?

It was the ultimate virtue of humanity, the trait that cultivated self-respect and competence. Discipline. Self-belief. Faith.

That was honor. To hold oneself to a higher standard of excellence than base nature. To resist and fight the weakness of hedonism, pride, and fear.

This was going to hurt. But giving up was going to hurt even more.

Henry grasped the blade.

For one blissful second between grabbing the handle and receiving the pain, he felt relief. And he thought his heat resistance from training Fire Style might save him.

And then the burn seared like ice.

He screamed as his fingers tried to pull away. But he forced his hand to grip the blade even tighter. His skin hissed and boiled, shaking against the red-hot iron.

He took it up and turned to the enemy soldier, gritting his teeth and resisting the urge to cry as the fire burrowed into his hand.

Through haggard breaths, he acclimated to the pain as best he could. It was still like plunging his hand into a cup full of needles or putting it through a woodchipper, but he managed to isolate the pain in his mind. He focused like he'd never focused before. He channeled every ounce of motivation, whether discipline or hatred, into the statue across the hall from him.

No faster than a steady messenger.

He took each step much slower than he probably needed to, letting the sword burn not only into his hand, but his mental fortitude.

He just had to keep breathing. As long he kept breathing, he'd live.

He took a few more steps across the chamber, his eyes never leaving the ebony statue.

Pain is weakness leaving the body. Some words from his time training under Mr. Fang came back to him.

Five more steps.

Don't scream. Don't cry. You're not an animal caught in a trap. You're a hunter pursuing his prey.

He passed the bust of Liu Bang.

He counted each breath to four, steady and slow.

The pain was merely hot now. Instincts to drop the sword and thoughts of doubt as to why he was subjecting himself to this never stopped bubbling up, but he was getting better and better at suppressing them with each step.

On the tenth breath, he was finally face to face with the warrior. His forehead was soaked in sweat. His hand shook, and for a moment, he wondered if he would have the strength to swing the weapon. What would it do to his cauterized flesh, fused to the metal? Would he be able to let go of the sword?

He pushed all those thoughts away. He thought of Alexander marching endlessly through the Gedrosian desert for two months with no hope of relief in sight. Compared to that, his suffering was small.

As he lifted the sword and swung it with all his might, he roared not in pain, but in determination. The impact let the metal touch new parts of his hand, but the statue's stone head fell to the ground, cleaved off in a single stroke.

He shoved the length of the blade through the statue's chest before finally ripping his burned hand away from the sword.

And like that, the pain vanished. The horrible sensation was still etched in his memory, but his hand was perfectly intact as he checked it for damage.

He glanced back at the soldiers on the other side. They were gone. So was the inscription. In its place was a shorter, larger inscription in more swimming, shifting languages.

It read *You are worthy of Companionship.*

He looked back at his hand and found a golden coin in it. It didn't give off any blast of magic. It just resonated with the faintest of wavelengths.

He was a man after all.

CHAPTER NINETEEN
Oathbreaker

When Henry stepped out into the cavern, he found his allies waiting for him on the marble steps of Alexander's temple.

"Someone took their damn time." Analise scoffed, her voice echoing off the cave walls.

"What, did you play a game of Trivial Pursuit?" Henry asked. "I can't imagine a test of Knowledge being that difficult."

Marion stood from the bottom step. "Did you have busts all along the sides of your room too?"

"Was that something all our tests had in common?" Henry placed his hands on his hips.

Yianni nodded. "All of them were obscure orators and petty kings and stuff for me. I think. I've never heard of half of them."

"See? History comes in handy. Especially for something like this."

Yianni scoffed. "Point is, I think it's kinda odd. I mean, what kind of Courage trial doesn't feature any warriors or emperors as role models?"

"I think each of these trials and the busts in them applied uniquely to us." Marion crossed her arms. "At least, that's what it feels like. Wisdom means a lot of different things to different people."

Henry pulled his coin out of his jacket pocket. "Well, we all passed. Let's bring this scavenger hunt to a close."

The four Companions started up the steps to the temple. But rather than being darker than the ambient lighting outside, the temple glowed with golden light streaming from the eyes of Alexander's statue. Henry squinted in the face of the tiny sunbeams as he pushed the doors shut behind him.

The Companions circled up around the spot on the floor where the beams touched marble. Their trials having told them what to do, each of them held up their coins, all unwrapped and humming with far more controlled power than before.

Henry reached out with his coin, touching it to his friends' coins and creating a Vergina Sun out of the markings on each one.

But unlike the last time they'd used the sun to receive a message from the golden disks, sunlight only poured through the middle, unimpeded. The shadows cast by the coins were all full of shapes and blobs of varying darkness.

"Huh..." Henry frowned.

"Wait." Analise gasped. "Henry, stack them on top of one another."

He did as he was told, collecting the coins and stacking them on top of one another with the same orientation they'd had before. He put the four coins under Alexander's proverbial gaze. This time, the shadow was cast through all four coins.

It projected yet another map—a map of Egypt with a sun marking the west side.

"Holy shit," Henry muttered.

"This is...is this it?" Yianni asked.

"That's Siwa." Marion grinned. "The Siwa Oasis."

Analise hurriedly sketched the map out in her journal. "It's slightly south of the oasis. Guess we should book a four by four."

Henry couldn't keep his face from splitting into a wide grin as he looked with giddy excitement between the map and his allies, who were all just as captivated and hyped-up as he was.

At long last, they had it. The location of Alexander the Great's tomb. The location of the great historical mystery that would finally vindicate Henry from—

Radio chatter scratched at his ear. A spike of terror shattered every positive emotion he'd been feeling. All four of them froze, eyes turning towards the door of the temple.

Henry glanced back at Analise as she met his gaze. "It's Zhao Squad," she muttered.

His fists clenched as he cast his gaze on Marion and Yianni. "I don't know about you three...but I think this time, we send them a message."

Yianni grinned, readying his Shillelagh in both hands.

Marion clapped her hands together, drawing them apart as a rod of light appeared between them. She grabbed onto the rod as it solidified into her staff.

Analise pulled her gun around and cocked the bolt.

Henry turned back to the temple doors, plucking his guandao from his ear and letting it grow to its full size.

"Companions." His voice was grave. "Move out."

The wooden doors of the temple flew open as Henry slammed his heel into their center. Taking a cultivating breath, he stepped out from the columns before the stairs, looking down on Zhao Squad.

They weren't wearing the usual black-and-white uniforms that marked them as an arm of the Tiandihui. Instead, they each wore their personal silks—meaning no one else was around to watch.

"Quite the entrance there, Hanying!" Weiying scoffed, brandishing a Chinese *qiang*. It was a nearly three-meter-long spear with a white tassel just under the head. Chinese martial artists called it the King of Weapons.

"How'd you find us?" Henry asked, puffing his chest out.

"All those programs you use to hide yourself from the Tiandihui are pretty useless in the face of cloud sharing." Weiying held up his phone with the photo of the Companions in front of the Trojan horse.

Henry furrowed his brow. There was no way something that stupid had done him in. Right?

"Kidding." Weiying's face became marred with that smug grin of his. "Your rental car's company bugs their vehicles. But you should've seen the look on your face."

Henry grimaced, taking another cultivating breath. "Get out of our way, Weiying."

"Give me the coins, and we will."

"You want what I've got?" Henry raised an eyebrow. "Earn it."

Weiying scoffed. "Your Mr. Fang impression needs work."

Henry glanced at Mr. Fang, who was standing towards the back of the line, looking almost bored. It was as if his old mentor were getting sidelined on his own squad.

"Don't waste your best material so early in the morning. We have a whole brawl to look forward to."

"Did your new handlers teach you to bark?" Weiying readied his spear. "I hope they've brought your bite up to par, *dog*!"

The spear moved before Weiying did.

Henry pumped every ounce of effort into a simple sidestep as the spearhead grazed his cheek. Weiying had never been this fast.

His brother tried to whip the flexible shaft of his spear around to the other side of Henry's head, but he parried the thrust with his guandao and spun it with sawblade-like speed, forcing Weiying back.

"Engage!" Henry ordered, but his allies were already moving on Zhao Squad.

Henry launched himself through the air directly at Mr. Fang. Whatever was going on with Weiying, he'd have to find a solution later. Right now, Mr. Fang was the only one who posed a danger to all the Companions if he wasn't stopped.

Missing his flying knee strike, Henry pivoted and brought his guandao down hard, only for Mr. Fang to snake around it. Not letting up, he followed it with two more spinning strikes.

Fang dodged the first, parried the second, and then slammed an ox jaw strike into Henry's face. Stars burst across his vision as he stumbled back.

Henry's eyes darted around the cave. Chen Bo and Shen were going after Yianni. Lu Ying and Min were after Marion. Analise was keeping Weiying at bay with suppressing fire and a myriad of creatively applied non-combat spells, but she wouldn't hold out for long.

His gaze returned to Fang, who had taken up a stance, but was also observing the battlefield for a moment.

In less time than it would take for Henry to blink, Fang vanished and reappeared next to him, grabbing the collar of his shirt. He was dragged across the cave and thrown into the temple, his weapon clattering to the marble as he slid across the stone.

Fang kicked the doors closed as Henry staggered to his feet under Alexander's gaze. With his weapon lying too far from him, he gritted his teeth for the hand-to-hand match to come and proffered his fist.

"Drop your hands, Hanying." Fang sighed.

Henry snarled and attacked with a flurry of punches and open hand strikes. His head clouded with frustration as Fang parried every move with one hand before sending him flying with a single palm strike to the chest.

He collapsed to the ground, gasping for the breath that had just been shoved out of him.

"I don't want to fight."

Henry pushed himself to his feet again. "I'm not giving you the map! You'll have to take it off my corpse!"

Fang squeezed his eyes shut and pinched the bridge of his nose. "Just drop the act already."

Henry's fighting stance became a little less sure of itself. Act? What act?

"What do you want?" He refused to lower his hands.

"You and your brother can be so similar at times…" Fang muttered, putting his hands on his hips, his gaze cast downward. "Willing to die over some damn treasure. Willing to kill."

"It's not just treasure, old man!" Henry growled. "It's history. I can't let it fall into the hands of a Circle."

Mr. Fang chuckled, spurring an indignant glare from Henry. "It's a noble lie to tell yourself."

"You don't know what the hell you're talking—"

"If Zhao Squad hadn't been sent after it, you wouldn't be looking for this tomb," Mr. Fang said. "You want to succeed where we fail. To prove to High Command you're not some pushover. To make sure they don't try to hurt you. Don't forget I trained you."

"So what? What's wrong with that?"

"You're letting fear control you. Again. You can go back out there and act like you defeated me. The quarry was never the Tiandihui's to begin with," Fang said. "But I'm going to make damn sure you know why you're here. I want you to change it, Hanying.

History, self-improvement, glory, whatever it is...just don't let your own resentment chew you up from the inside."

"Why...why are you telling me this?" Henry asked.

"Because something is deeply wrong with Weiying. More than usual. And I'm not sure what it is. I'm bound by oath to protect and guide you," Fang insisted, his eyes hitting Henry with a steel wall of earnestness.

"I broke those oaths." Henry grimaced.

"No, you didn't," he responded as if he anticipated Henry's response. "You're honorable, Hanying. You act like you're not, but you are. It's what makes you a good martial artist. When I taught you Wing Chun, you never once let any of my beatdowns deter you. You never held those failures against yourself. No matter what, you kept fighting. Being a Wing Chun master didn't matter to you nearly as much as your simple determination to enjoy the art. It's the same with your love of history. Let go of this desperation, Hanying."

"It's not desperation, Mr. Fang. Not anymore. It's ambition." Henry glanced away from Fang, swallowing. His gaze couldn't decide between looking at Fang to have this conversation and back at the door, where his allies needed him.

"Maybe I'm just a doddering old fool. Go help your friends." Fang smoothed out his robes as he sat cross-legged on the marble floor. "All of them."

Henry nodded slightly, walking to pick up his weapon. He grabbed his guandao and pressed his palm against the temple doors, hesitating.

"Thank you for trying," he muttered, voice almost too quiet were it not for the echoing nature of the stonework.

He took a deep breath, refocusing, and pushed the doors open.

Weiying was just about to skewer Analise with his spear. Henry lashed out his rope dart, wrapping the silk around his brother's ankle and yanking him to the ground.

He recalled his rope dart to his wrist as Weiying cursed, getting back to his feet. He looked his older brother up and down and spat. "Useless old man!"

Marion, Analise, and Yianni rallied to Henry as he descended the temple's steps. Zhao Squad formed up behind Weiying. The Companions were all exhausted. Marion and Yianni had each had to take on two Magicians, while Analise had been forced to delay Weiying continuously.

Henry figured he could try to pick up some of the slack.

Chen Bo, with his crescent halberd, and Weiying converged on him.

The heads of their weapons fenced with one another, prodding and testing their enemies. Weiying's flexible spear slithered around and seemed to coil like a snake, while Chen Bo's halberd moved with short, small, darting movements, like the twitching of a praying mantis.

Henry's guandao kept up with them, with the lithe and strong techniques of a raging tiger allowing him to control the area with sweeping attacks and spins of the weapon.

He drew his grip back and flung the reverse spike of his weapon around, knocking one of Min's fans out of the air, then swept the glaive around, forcing her back. He ducked under a swing from Chen Bo and, on his knees, advanced on his opponents as he swung his weapon, catching Chen Bo in the ribs. The blade was blocked by body armor, but the Qi fueling his body sent a ripple of blunt force through Chen Bo that threw him to the ground.

Weiying took the opportunity to whip his spear downwards, knocking Henry's weapon from his grip. He stumbled to his feet as he backed away from another thrust.

Weiying kicked the polearm backwards and chased after Henry. When the younger brother tried to raise his spear to bring its weight down on Henry, he skipped forward and threw a kick at the weapon, snapping it in half.

Weiying stopped in his tracks.

"C'mon, little brother." Henry drew his butterfly swords, goading him. "Where's all that skill I saw in Athens?"

Weiying ripped his jian from the sheathe on his hip and moved like lightning, closing the distance in an instant.

But he wasn't as fast as Fang.

Henry parried the jian's thrust and riposted with a pommel strike to Weiying's chest. He became a storm of blades, but only landed the first two strikes. He kept up the pressure, chasing after Weiying with a flurry of slashes. His brother managed to parry and evade all of them, but he never got enough time to shift the momentum.

That was until Henry decided to kick out Weiying's knees. His brother stepped out of range of his cut kick and spun into a tornado kick that walloped Henry in the side of the head. He stumbled, recovering his senses just in time to weave around Weiying's sword, only to be hit by a sidekick in the ribs.

Henry locked Weiying's longsword in the hooks on his sword hilts, but his brother angled the sword and thrust, slicing his cheek.

He stepped back and felt the stinging wound, his fingers pulling away with blood on them. His throat was ice-cold as he heaved, catching his breath.

"I should've killed you when I had the chance," Weiying growled. "It was a rare mistake for me. I intend on not repeating it."

"You really have gone off the deep end…" Henry muttered. "You hate me that much?"

"As if you don't hate me more!" Weiying snarled. "You know, until your little showcase with the coins, they mocked me. Now, they say I'm the only one who can stop you."

Henry threw his swords at Weiying. He evaded them, but didn't account for Henry himself as he ran up and slammed his knee into his brother's solar plexus. Weiying choked as Henry grabbed his swordhand and twisted it into a lock that forced him to drop the weapon.

He was about to finish this fight, but a flicker of shadow filled his vision. In an instant, his heart rate spiked as vertigo rippled across his sight. The image of a horrible-but-ambiguous creature had been stained in his eyes as if he'd stared at the sun.

Weiying shouted a couplet, calling on Daoist magic to stir the winds and throw Henry into the air.

He landed in a roll and popped up to his feet, but the impact still hurt like a bitch.

"Lost your nerve, Hanying?" His brother smirked.

Henry furrowed his brow at the odd, almost malformed space around Weiying's shoulders, burdened by some kind of darkness. His intuition, for all that it could be trusted, told him that was why his brother had gotten so fast and strong recently.

Weiying rushed at him, neglecting to pick up his weapon.

"Companion 1, nine o'clock!" Yianni shouted through the radio.

Henry caught Shen in his peripheral vision. He grabbed Shen's silks and threw him toward Weiying, but his brother ducked under the surprise and slammed a palm strike into his nose. He parried the next two punches through his star-ridden, swimming vision and countered with a punch that Weiying caught before slamming a knee into his sternum.

Henry collapsed as the wind left his lungs and a bruise blossomed over his ribs.

"At the end of the day, you're just a parasite." Weiying sneered. "Trying to take power from those who deserve it. Even if you win, what will you have accomplished? When the Chaldean Court Damns you, what will you have then? Do you have any idea how much of a disappointment you are to Mom and Dad? To me? Dog! I'll—"

A metallic impact punctuated a swift crack and a flash of gold on Weiying's head.

"Will you shut your damn mouth?" Marion gritted her teeth, holding the end of her staff as Weiying reeled, clutching the back of his head.

"You bitch!" He scrambled to pick up his jian.

"Shut up!" Marion shouted so loudly it caused the others to stop what they were doing. "No one cares! You think we asked specifically to be here? You think we want to keep fighting you? You think that if we had any other choice, we'd still be rolling around in the dirt with scum like you?"

Henry blinked. He'd never seen Marion so flushed with anger. He'd never seen anger on her face, period.

"You're cockroaches with astronomically high opinions of yourselves. Nothing left for you Defectors but desperat—"

"I told you to shut up! Wipe that smug smear of shit you call a smile off your face and fight us! Just shut up!" Marion snapped.

Weiying rushed at her with his jian. Henry pushed himself off the ground and slammed his fist into his brother's stomach before following it up with a knee strike and a hook to the face.

He turned and caught Min's wrist with a bladed fan in hand and trapped her elbow before slamming a backfist into her nose.

Marion raised a shield, and one of Lu Ying's fireballs slammed into the golden light.

Henry lashed out his rope dart and sliced Lu Ying's wrist open. She cried out and grabbed the wound, calling on fire magic to cauterize it.

He coiled his dart and called his swords back to his hands as Chen Bo nearly crushed him with his double crescent halberd. Marion blocked the strike as Yianni intervened with two quick strikes from his Shillelagh. The Irishman whispered something that caused thorny brambles to erupt from the ground and bind Chen Bo's arms to his sides.

Shen came up from behind, but his flaming broadswords were knocked out of his hands courtesy of a pinpoint shot from Analise's rifle.

Henry turned to Min, who should've recovered by now, to find that she was struggling to break bramble bonds around her wrists.

They were all working together. For real. They were in sync with each other.

Henry attacked with unrelenting speed. Marion played defense without faltering, transferring from one threat to the next seamlessly. Yianni tied up the playing field with area control, isolating individual Magicians with brambles and shadows. And Analise kept watch, taking down anything the other three couldn't see.

This was what a real squad was supposed to be.

As Henry fought, he found himself losing the need to think about what was behind him, because it was always Marion, Analise, and Yianni.

He could finally focus fully on what was in front of him.

And he loved it.

Fighting in tandem. Shoulder to shoulder. He felt stronger than ever, not in spite of having to protect and work with those by his side, but because of it.

And then, that shadow returned. Not just to his vision, but his mind.

Time seemed to slow as beads of cold sweat formed on his brow and his palms clammed up. He stumbled as some abyssal form towered over him.

As quickly as it came, it vanished.

Weiying took its place and threw a flying sidekick into Henry's chest, throwing him back. He landed on the steps of the temple, the limestone corners ravaging his back on impact.

With a whirlwind of steel and unnatural speed, even by Five Elements Fist standards, Weiying singlehandedly disarmed each of the Companions and forced them to their knees. One of Zhao Squad's Magicians pinned them down as Henry tried to overcome the ache in his back.

Even if he did, he wasn't sure if he'd have the strength to compete.

It's Fang's words. They're holding you back.

Henry furrowed his brow. What? That was insane.

Rage makes you strong. Use it.

Those couldn't be his thoughts, could they? They felt like his, but he never thought to himself like this.

Henry blinked as the jian's cold metal pressed against his neck.

"Not the way I wanted to win this fight, but...I still win." Weiying grinned, threatening Henry's arteries from on high. "I'm impressed you managed to get one of your own. Now, give me what you found here."

Henry got control of his breathing back. He hadn't noticed he'd lost it. "What did you do?"

"You don't get to ask me questions." Weiying sneered. "Give me the key to the tomb."

Henry didn't move. Not that he had anything physically on him to hand over besides the coin, which was kind of useless in finding the tomb now.

"Henry, just do it!" Min said, pinning a struggling Marion down.

Henry's mind raced. He couldn't think of anything to get him out of this.

"Three...two..."

Any way he moved, Weiying could be faster. Whatever the hell was giving him speed was more than Metal Style Wuxing Quan.

"One..."

Henry squeezed his eyes shut, but no pain came. His neck was still intact.

Metal clattered against the stone somewhere far away. He opened his eyes to see Mr. Fang holding Weiying's wrist up.

Weiying pulled it away. "The hell are you doing?"

"Ending this idiocy. The tomb isn't ours to begin with. And here you are, about to kill your own brother over it," Mr. Fang growled. "Get over yourself, boy!"

Weiying scoffed. "How dare you...I am co-leader—"

"You're a joke," Fang snapped. "Ready to slit your brother's throat without a second thought! And for what? Just so you can get some bullshit promotion from High Command?"

"He's a traitor!" Weiying insisted. "He abandoned his oaths!"

"Do you seriously believe your own lies so thoroughly? In case you forgot in the midst of your ego trip, *you* lost the regalia. *You* fell for the Japanese's trap! And you pinned it on your brother!" Fang snarled. "Hanying didn't betray his brothers! He didn't break his oaths! *You* did!"

The other members of Zhao squad's eyes widened as they looked at the two. Henry felt some remnant of an old pain between his shoulder blades.

"If you hadn't shafted your responsibility and blamed Hanying, none of this would be happening! I'm sick of you acting smug and yelling at us to fix *your* mistakes, you child!" Mr. Fang's voice boomed with all the power of a furious teacher. "Let me tell you this, Weiying: it will *never* be enough unless you put an end to it yourself by giving up on this! I oughtta call High Command right now and tell them to punish the correct traitor, you—"

Henry flinched as a glint of metal swept across Mr. Fang's neck. The old man staggered backward, choking and gurgling as he clutched his neck.

Weiying's sword was bloody.

With his other hand, Henry's younger brother pulled out a pistol. A gunshot echoed off the cave's walls.

And Mr. Fang collapsed, a hole in his head.

CHAPTER TWENTY
The Mark of the Beast

F ang laid still, blood covering the upper half of his face.

"Weiying!" Min shrieked at the same time as Lu Ying screamed.

"What did..." Chen Bo staggered away from Yianni.

Henry looked in disbelief at the bleeding body that had slumped onto the stairs next to him.

Weiying walked away, pointing his gun at the rest of Zhao Squad. "Anyone else have a problem? Anyone else want to break their oaths today?"

Henry sat up on the stairs, his eyes wide and every bone in his body trembling. Was this a test? Was he still in the test? He looked over Mr. Fang's body, flowing with blood. It couldn't be real. He had to be in an illusion of some kind.

But as he cradled Mr. Fang's head in his hands and he felt the warmth of blood on his palms, an epiphany seized him.

"No...no, no, no, no!" Henry grabbed at his own hair, his voice quivering beyond his control. "Marion! Marion, please help!"

He looked over at the healer as she staggered to her feet and rushed over, astonishment on her face as she looked between the body and the killer.

"Marion, heal him. You have to heal him," Henry said, feeling dizzy at the sight.

"I...I—I...Henry...he's been shot in the head," Marion stammered. "I can't heal death."

"There's still time!" He stood and grabbed her, trying to pull her towards Mr. Fang.

Marion tried to shove him away. "Henry, stop! You're hurting me!"

"You have to help him! Please!" he begged, falling to his knees. "Marion, don't do this to me!"

He knew he sounded crazy. What else was there to do but go crazy? His teacher, the man who had taught him everything he knew, was dying. The only one who understood his trials, the only one who encouraged his effort, in spite of failure, was dying.

"Henry!" Marion grabbed his shoulders, shaking him out of his thoughts. "Henry, I'm sorry."

Henry blinked tears from his eyes. "No. No, you have to revive him. Marion, I'm begging you. I'll give you anything." He stood, trying to beseech her. "Help me. Please."

"Henry, it doesn't work—"

"Yes, it does!" Henry shouted. "It has to!"

Marion's brow furrowed in anger. "Henry! I can't do anything! He's dead!"

"Then what the fuck good are you?" Henry snapped, shoving Marion into the dirt.

Regret flashed across the storm of rage and grief under his skin as she scrambled away from him, hurt in her eyes.

He gritted his teeth. Fire consumed his chest as he clenched his fists so tight his vessels threatened to burst and his nails drew blood.

He glanced up at the killer. At his brother. And the people in Zhao Squad who were just standing by.

At first, the fire inside tried to calm him. It tried to embrace him in its warmth. To console him.

But there was no consoling him. Mr. Fang was dead. And Henry had been helpless to stop it. What if it'd been one of his friends? Or Marion? Or himself? He wouldn't be able to do anything, and for that, he couldn't forgive himself.

The world was a cruel, dark, cold place.

Henry wrested control over the flame and crushed it inside him, filling it with his hatred.

He flinched as another gunshot echoed off the stone and a bullet tore through his abdomen.

He placed a glowing hand on the wound. The flesh hissed as heat cauterized it.

He looked up at his brother, the perpetrator.

"Jesus..." Weiying chuckled. "You've gone mad."

Henry didn't care about the pain.

Hate-filled, wrathful fire lapped at his insides. Not an impulse, but a great ball of heat and flame that had been burning far longer. Like a star about to go supernova.

Let go.

His chest began to boil with hatred. The world would be better off without Weiying in it.

Let go...

Henry slowly got to his feet, the drumbeat of his heart slowing down to a steady, murderous tempo. His head was full of fog, like crimson mist on a battlefield.

"H-Hanying?" Min whispered.

Let go of everything...Let me take your pain from you. Let me give you power.

Henry screamed. He knew no words to express his rage.

There is only one way to survive in this world: be darker, crueler, and colder.

Was it his rage speaking to him? Or someone else?

Show the weaklings their folly. Show them they have no power over you. Show them your hard-won strength.

Henry folded his hands out in a Wing Chun stance. The one Mr. Fang had taught him. The one Mr. Fang had perfected.

His hands wreathed in flames, he wanted to give them their own brands. And for once, they could understand his pain.

Betray the world before it betrays you.

"Kill him, or he'll kill us!" Weiying aimed his gun at Henry.

Who knows when they'll do it again? Are you just going to sit there and watch it happen? For a fourth time?

The traitors raised their hands, thinking they could stand against him.

NEVER LET THEM HURT YOU AGAIN! TEACH THEM FEAR! BREAK THEM!

Henry grabbed the killer's wrist and swept his leg out from under him before stomping on his face.

He turned to the next two and hit both with swift punches to the nose before turning to a fourth and catching his punch. He pressed a hand into his shoulder, forcing the enemy down. He hit his face over and over and over and over and over and over, shattering teeth and snapping the jawbone.

Another was coming. He swept out the legs of his current enemy and rolled over his back, breaking his arm at the shoulder joint.

He caught the next one's front kick before throwing a side kick into another's ribs. Rippling power that hadn't been there before sent shards of those ribs through his lungs. With the one he'd caught, he pulled back, forcing her into a split, and stomped on her thigh, snapping her hip.

He reveled in her scream of agony.

This is what happens when you try to hurt me. That was what he wanted them to know. He wanted to see them whimper like broken dogs. To cower in the face of his ability and leave him alone.

He parried a blow and slammed his fist into the next enemy's solar plexus before evading a jumping front kick.

He caught the next one's arm and swept his legs out from under him before unleashing a flurry of chain punches into his chest so hard and so fast it sent the enemy spasming into cardiac arrest.

He looked at the remaining two as they tried their best to kill him.

He fought them both off at once with unending strikes and kicks before slamming his elbow into one of their ears, throwing a knee into his head, grabbing his face, and throwing him to the side.

He turned to the only one still in front of him as she threw a side kick. He caught it and forced her off-balance. She collapsed on her stomach as he stomped on her spine, which would paralyze any normal person from the waist down, before punching her in the back of the ribs and crushing her shoulder with a downward elbow.

He turned to the last one he'd thrown.

It was Weiying.

His brother hesitated in his fighting stance as Henry stepped towards him. But his prideful fool of a sibling wanted the first hit.

Weiying tried to kick him. Henry threw it aside like nothing. His brother tried to strike him. Henry grabbed his wrist and punched him in the ribs before hip-tossing him and locking his head between his knees, angling his face up at his fist.

Henry pounded Weiying's nose and face in, punching and punching without any end in sight. A plume of flames bloomed with each crunch, charring skin and hair.

Weiying flailed and struggled as blood spilled from his face and splattered on each impact, but Henry would not stop until he was satisfied.

Something grabbed his shoulder.

He grabbed the hand's wrist and pressed the shoulder down, ready to break it. Rip off the arm if he had to.

Marion's tear-filled hazel eyes stared at him over her craned neck, pleading...

KILL THEM!

Marion...

No.

Henry let go of a breath he'd been holding since he started fighting. Marion shoved him away, terror apparent on her face as she stepped away from him.

She whispered a curse in German as she cradled her arm, a pink, dry handprint in the skin on her wrist from a first-degree burn.

KILL THEM! IT'S THE ONLY WAY YOU'LL BE SAFE!

His quivering right fist was coated in crimson, the stains unaffected by the arcane flames.

Before him, broken and twisted on the ground, was Zhao Squad. They were still breathing, if barely.

Only through sheer willpower did his fist open, the high fading from his mind.

He glanced to his right and found Analise.

Her gun was not quite pointing at him. But it was ready.

Henry collapsed to his knees, eyes watering with unshed grief. And shame.

The beast within him had won.

The ride back to Canakkale, the city nearest to Troy, was silent.

Analise and Yianni clearly had no clue what to say—or no desire to say anything at all. Marion kept her eyes ahead the whole time, never once acknowledging Henry.

That left him to stew in and mull over his grief. Although he never really came to any epiphanies.

Only once they got back to the hotel did anyone say anything.

"We should book a flight to Alexandria before anyone catches on," Analise said as she put her map down on the room's desk, which was already covered in maps, notes, papers, and posters.

No one commented on the fact that she was suggesting violation of important common wisdom. Magicians never flew.

But the room was too thick with tension. With his teammates' concerns left unspoken, Henry sat on one of the beds and held his head in his hands.

He didn't even realize he was getting blood on the linens. He didn't want to look at any of them and meet gazes full of wariness and fear.

The fire that had wreathed his fists in his rage was still inside him. He could feel its flames lapping at his insides. He wasn't sure whether to relish their presence or recoil away. Whatever they'd done to him before was fading. The fire felt warm again. Comforting.

"I'll book the flights," Yianni muttered. "Four tickets to Alexandria. We all good with Turkish Air?"

"Buy three," Marion muttered.

"What?" Henry was drawn out of his head as he looked at her.

She grabbed her backpack and hefted it onto her shoulders.

"Wait, Marion, what are you talking about?" Henry stood from the bed.

"I'm out," she said matter-of-factly.

Henry scoffed, unable to come up with a response.

"How come?" Analise asked. "We're so close. It's one flight and a car ride away."

"We were all looking for something by going after this tomb. Aside from the tomb itself." Marion sighed. "Respect. Affirmation. Accomplishment. I thought I found what I came for." She hung her head, shaking it just the slightest bit. "Guess I was wrong."

She turned towards the door.

"W-wait! Marion, wait," Henry said.

She paused, half-turning to him.

"Come on." He took a step towards her, only for her to step back. He gulped, not sure what exactly to say. "We...we're a team, Marion. We are. We can't do this without you. I mean, are we supposed to just not have a Companion 2?"

Marion's head bobbed with little nods. "Yeah, well, that's kind of the problem. You want me on your team because I can heal you. Because I'm Companion 2. Because that's all the good I am to you."

Henry squeezed his eyes shut. "Marion, I didn't mean—"

"Just stop." She cut him off, pausing before she glanced down at her burned wrist. "You were going to break me in half, too."

"I—I didn't. I stopped myself, didn't I?" He approached her and, thankfully, she didn't back up this time. Still, he kept his distance.

"That's the kind of mercy you show to your enemies," Marion said, pressing the Wisdom coin into his hands. "Not your friends. Not your family. Not your brother. The only reason any of them are still alive is because you didn't find the time to draw a weapon."

"Weiying *killed* Mr. Fang! He killed him in cold blood! And he would've done the same to us!" Henry jabbed his index finger into his chest as he defended his actions, shaking the Wisdom coin at her.

She didn't take it.

He was right to be angry. He had every right to do what he did. "My apologies that I couldn't act with the mercy and grace of a fucking saint. But don't you dare look down on me if you're just going to run away the way you did from *your* Circle and family!"

She scoffed, fiddling with her sunburst necklace. "Goodbye, Henry. I hope you all find what you're looking for."

Before Henry could protest, Marion left the room and shut the door behind her.

He clenched his fists as he walked back over to the desk and pressed his knuckles on the wood. The fire was starting to show itself, wisps of flames off his skin marking the wood black.

He never could seem to keep good company.

No. No, he would not be abandoned again. She wanted to leave halfway through? Fine. That was her mistake. He'd warned her he would drop anyone who couldn't keep up.

She'd just done the work for him.

The eighteenth liar.

"Do you, uh...want to go after her?" Analise asked. "Or are you just gonna leave it on that unbelievably horrible note?"

Henry shook his head. "She can do what she wants. Just pack your bags. We have a flight to catch."

CHAPTER TWENTY-ONE
Desert Desperation

Henry stared at the night sky of Istanbul, nursing a beer as he sat alone at an old wooden picnic table on the roof of the hostel with no one for company but Milo, the pointy-eared, white-haired dog belonging to one of the hostel's employees.

His chest and throat were aching, though he wasn't clear what emotion was behind it. He just knew it was bad.

He scratched Milo behind the ears as, against his better judgement, he let his thoughts swim.

Why didn't he do something?

Why didn't he go after her?

He'd just...stood there. Helpless. Again.

"I thought I might find you up here."

Henry turned to the stairs that led up here from the bar as Yianni popped open his own beer and set a small ukulele on the table.

"Hey," Henry muttered.

"Analise said we should get to sleep. We have an early flight tomorrow," Yianni said, sitting across from him.

"And yet here you are."

Yianni shrugged. "I can sleep on the flight. Cheers."

Henry knocked his bottle against Yianni's before they both drank. The bitter taste running down his throat felt apt for his state of mind.

"You must've really liked her, huh?" Yianni asked.

Henry wasn't sure how to answer the question, since he wasn't sure what Yianni meant exactly.

"Don't deny it." The Irishman scoffed.

"'Deny it?'" Henry furrowed his brow.

"You always underplay how much you like...well, her, at least," Yianni said. "In whatever way it is you feel about Marion."

Henry scoffed. "What are you, my shrink?"

"I have eyes, mate." Yianni drank.

Henry leaned back, staring over the edge of the balcony. "Well, it doesn't matter now. She's gone."

"And you won't let yourself go after her."

He wanted to deny the understanding about him Yianni believed himself to possess. But part of him had to acknowledge that the Celt had a more objective viewpoint for these things. And it had always been a worry in the back of his mind that people could tell what he really felt.

"It's not worth the...messiness," Henry said. "She's made her choice and...it's not like this is unusual. I always mess these things up. Family. Friendship...Romance. All goes down the shitter eventually."

"Now you're being overdramatic." Yianni grimaced.

"Well, you've seen my brother. My mother made it clear I'm just her backup plan if Weiying doesn't become the success she hoped for. My friends from the Tiandihui take my brother's word over mine and think I'm a traitor. My first love...ignored me." Henry sighed. "So I don't say 'always' lightly, Yianni. I've got the receipts. And one day, I'd like a receipt that proves I can actually do this right. But for now, I've got nothing to go on."

"You're so fuckin' paranoid, man." Yianni squeezed his eyes shut. "I mean...don't get me wrong, mate, you're brilliant. But...how do you live, constantly thinking about shit like...accounting how bad you are with girls? Like, that's the last place I'd want to be thorough in keepin' my books. Sometimes, shit just doesn't work out, Henry."

"And I'm just supposed to do nothing about that? I...I'm just supposed to let myself make the same mistakes?"

"Maybe it wasn't your fault," Yianni said. "Ever think of that?"

Henry raised an eyebrow.

"Like...has it ever occurred to you that maybe Marion's got her own issues? Not that you didn't shit the bed today. Jesus. You gotta admit, you're fuckin' terrifying. And you did hurt her. But Marion's never seemed like the most persistent person in the world. It always felt like she was here for the novelty of it all. Not so much for the actual tomb," Yianni explained. "Life's a two-way street, bruv. And I'm sure you know fear can manifest in some ugly ways. Some of the people who treat us the worst are just...afraid."

Henry drank from his beer, letting the ambient noise of the city fill the silence between the two men.

"You sound like you have some experience with that," he said.

Yianni shrugged.

"So, they're afraid." Henry scoffed. "Lotta good that does me."

"Just...try to remember why you started this in the first place. It'll all be for nothing if you don't get to the finish line," Yianni said.

Henry took another drink. "I *started* this thinking I could get the last laugh against the Tiandihui. Make them feel some of what I felt. If I'd never gotten involved...Mr. Fang would still be alive. This is stupid...This whole thing is—"

"Hey!" Yianni slammed his bottle on the table. "You better not leave Analise and I out to dry."

Henry narrowed his eyes. "What do *you* want with the tomb?"

Yianni's face scrunched up with resistance. "Please don't ask."

Henry furrowed his brow. "It's only fair. Why? What, is it worse than my story?"

"N-no, it's just..." Yianni stumbled over his words. "I...Okay. You're right. I just have my reservations."

"Who among us doesn't?" Henry asked.

He waited for Yianni to gather his thoughts before speaking. "Long story short...I need something powerful enough to break an arcane pact. I think if there's anywhere it'll be, it's Alexander's tomb."

"What kind of pact magic needs ancient power to break?" Henry asked. "Celtic pact magic isn't that hard to unravel. Even I know how to do it."

"It depends on who you make the pact with," Yianni said. "Especially if it's with a Fae Queen."

Henry frowned. He wasn't sure what context he was supposed to be picking up. "I'm not so familiar with the Faeries. I just know the three queens that started the Celt circle: Maeb, the Morrigan, and Titania. And not much beyond their names."

Yianni nodded. "Fair. Well, they don't really get involved in the Celts' affairs anymore. But they still wander around. They still have...agendas." He had less hesitance in his eyes than Henry would've thought as he got into the story. "Got into a car crash some years back with me and my uncle. Saw someone in the distance, and...didn't know it was Titania at the time. I called out to her for help, and she gave it. She only saved me. And in return, she bound me to her forever."

"And now you want out because...I assume she took advantage?" Henry asked.

Yianni shook his head. "That's not even half of it. I was forced to join the Goidelic Congregation under threat of death. Turns out the terms of that contract involved her turning me into something of a human superweapon that she can use as her avatar. So, under Fae law, my body doesn't even belong to me. She can hop in and hop out whenever she wants. Not that she does. But everyone still looked at me like a monster. Like *I* was Titania. Fair enough to them. Maybe I am a fuckin' monster. I'm more powerful than most of them with half the training." He sighed. "But the reason I want out is because I learned that the car crash wasn't an accident from a friend. Titania made it happen. Killed my uncle to trap me in a contract."

Henry blinked. "Jesus. How did that friend know?"

"Didn't ask. But it made a hell of a lot of sense when I put the pieces together. Even if it's false, she's still a cunt."

"And this whole time, Titania hasn't, like...tried to stop you?"

Yianni shrugged. "I don't know what the hell her angle is, but until she takes over my body, I'm gonna keep trying. Don't have much to lose."

"Same boat, then." Henry sighed. He lifted his beer. "To two monsters."

"To two monsters." Yianni raised his eyebrows, joining the toast before drinking.

Weiying heaved, cupping his broken nose as if that would stop the rumbling of his medevac chopper from irritating the injury.

He stared at the medical personnel and healers as they rushed to tend to Min, who was strapped to a stretcher on the floor. Though it wasn't as if he could see. Hanying's attack had left him unable to see out of one eye and blurry in another.

His face was broken beyond recognition, and he definitely had a concussion. It was only thanks to his benefactor that he'd sustained less damage than the others.

His fist clenched, watching the medics attach a *fulu* charm to Min's torso as they tried to reset her leg and snapped hip.

How could this happen?

He was supposed to be *better* than Hanying now. How had his brother found his own benefactor?

Weiying's slowly healing eyes kept flickering to the body bag on the other side of the helicopter. He could feel another pair of eyes staring back at him, as if Fang were somehow giving him that annoying-as-hell look from beyond the grave.

What right did Fang have to judge? He was in the way of their mission. If he didn't do this to himself, it was Hanying's fault for going after the tomb in the first place.

Weiying gritted his teeth as Fang spoke to him in his mind. *You wouldn't be here if Hanying wasn't.*

His hand started to tremble as he remembered the sensation of slashing the old man's throat. The euphoria. And the horror.

He hadn't *meant* to do it. It was almost as if he were moving on instinct. As if he were moving to protect his own neck from being cut.

That was happening more and more lately. He'd say something or do something he didn't mean to. If he'd had control, he would've done things differently, so it wasn't his fault.

But the only thing he could do was double down on his actions.

Once this was over, he just wanted to go back to China and binge a drama series.

Every day was exhausting. When he wasn't trying to track Hanying down, it was endless talk with other Magicians and the Chaldean Court, making him constantly anxious.

But as he looked at Fang and Min again, all that seemed kind of petty.

He'd been the one to pull the trigger and put a hole in Fang's head. Just because he was pissed?

He broke his oath to you. If he wanted to live, he should've gotten out of your way.

A shiver ran up Weiying's spine as he recalled Hanying's expression. It was almost scary. No, it *was* scary. Terrifying, even.

Your brother is an incompetent moron. There's no need to fear him.

But there *was*. Weiying had been a victim of it himself. The reality was right there: Hanying was stronger than all of them combined. If he wanted to defeat his brother again, he needed more power.

If he didn't get it...

Weiying felt like he wanted to cry. He wasn't sure why. Maybe he was just that scared.

Hanying is your brother. How could he do something like that? Shouldn't he look out for you?

Weiying gritted his teeth. He'd broken that oath when he blamed his mistake on Hanying.

He is the traitor. Ever since childhood, he's been negligent at best. He broke that oath the moment he took it.

Weiying clutched his ringing head.

If he wins, you lose. How will you go back to your superiors as a failure? You need more power.

He *did* need more power. No matter what, he couldn't allow Hanying to win. That was the end of it.

I want you to say it.

"I..." Weiying's voice scratched his dry throat, though it was drowned out by the helicopter. "I...please help me."

Say it!

"I..." he said. "I'm too weak on my own. I'm...I'm nothing without you. I need you."

Good.

They were just words. But every time he was forced to say them, Weiying's chest felt a little emptier. His breath became shallower. His mind shrank away, as if letting go of more control over his body.

He could feel himself deteriorating. But what else was he supposed to do? How else was he supposed to win?

Henry stared out at the open, barren Egyptian desert from the back seat of a convertible four by four.

As they drove south from the Siwa Oasis, they were supposed to be looking out for anything manmade. But since all he could see for miles was sand, Henry's mind kept going back to the cave under Troy.

The only man who'd ever had faith in him was dead. He'd beaten his former squadmates beyond recognition. He'd probably given Weiying a concussion at the very least.

And to top it all off, he'd pushed one of the only people willing to work with him away.

The perfect shit cake to end this search with.

There was nothing else to do but throw himself into the hunt.

He toyed with the Honor coin, hoping this was the final stage of the scavenger hunt, though a small part of him hoped for more, thinking it would give a chance for him and Marion to make up.

But his mind was occupied by thoughts of Alexander and these Gawgs and Megawgs.

He still wasn't exactly sure what they were. But his mind kept going back to the shadow he'd seen attached to Weiying and the voice that had spoken to him before he lost control.

"Oi," Yianni said, handing him a cold beer. "You want one?"

Henry accepted the bottle and popped the cap off with the hilt of a butterfly sword.

"I feel like, in between all the almost dying and running from bullets and stress, we haven't taken a moment to realize that we're about to discover the lost tomb of Alexander the Great," Yianni said, raising his own beer. "We're about to get filthy rich."

Henry raised his beer halfheartedly. "To being...filthy rich."

He drank, cringing at the rough taste.

"Ugh. I guess in a country where most people aren't allowed to drink, you can't quite expect the black stuff. But surely they can do better than this." Yianni sighed, looking woefully at his beer. He turned, glancing at Henry. "Still worried, eh?"

Henry shrugged.

"Take that puss off your face, mate. We're about to make history here."

"You did what you had to, Henry," Analise said. "She couldn't finish the job. And at least things are going according to plan for once. We've shaken everyone off our trail."

Henry shook his head. "You're wrong. I coulda handled the whole cave thing in so many different ways that would've been better."

Even with her back to him, he could sense Analise rolling her eyes.

He sighed. "At least this way, we only have to split the treasure three ways."

"Now your suckin' diesel." Yianni chuckled.

"Did you just decide to be *more* Irish this morning?" Analise asked. "I can barely understand you."

Henry took another drink from his beer as Yianni turned around to fire back at her.

Withdrawing into his mind, Henry pulled out his journal, containing his research on Gawg and Megawg. The English transliteration turned out to be Gog and Magog, but he felt the spelling in his head was more accurate to Semitic pronunciations.

There wasn't much beyond stuff in the Bible.

He'd also investigated someone called Dhul-Qarnayn who seemed to be involved in all this. Again, more holy texts. Except that the Quran described Dhul-Qarnayn as a man who built a wall, often conflated with the Caspian Gate to keep out Yajuj and Majuj—Gawg and Megawg.

This figure was associated with Alexander the Great, but was always depicted with ram's horns—an esoteric symbol of enlightenment. And treated like a separate entity. So was the man in his dreams not really Alexander?

The topic had been drawing him ever since his dreams, though it had become more intriguing since he saw that shadow attached to Weiying. But out here, he had no internet to delve deeper.

Besides, it was just a distraction from the real thought on his mind: How had he managed to pass Alexander's trial and yet fail that standard on every level right after? Had he gotten lucky? Or was Alexander full of it?

Henry put his notes down. "Any luck yet?"

The car crested yet another dune, sliding down the sheer slope on the other side.

"In these dunes?" Yianni asked. "What, did they build it from scratch and dig a hole in the sand to put it in?"

"I mean, after Ptolemy's descendants melted Alexander's golden sarcophagus down for coins and stuck him in a glass one, I can't imagine they'd have much cash to throw around," Henry said.

"I can't imagine..." Yianni's voice trailed off. "What the hell?"

Henry looked through the windshield as Analise slowed the car down.

In the distance, backlit by the sun, was a statue lifting a sword into the sky.

"How has no one found this before?" Yianni asked. "We're barely ten minutes into the desert."

"Might be the coins helping us see," Henry muttered. "Let's check it out."

Analise drove the car towards the statue for another five minutes before they pulled up to the base of the statue. As they got out of the car and closed in on it, the statue's face became visible.

"That's pretty definitive." Yianni chuckled as the three of them hopped out of the car.

"That's not Alexander," Henry muttered, peering at the face and general regalia.

"What?" Analise asked. "Who is it?"

"It's Cassander," Henry said. "The Diadochi who took over Macedonia."

The statue stood on a stout rock formation that rose out of the sand, forming a sort of podium of sandstone.

"Look here." Analise knelt down beneath the statue, pulling out a small digital camera from the early two thousands.

Yianni scoffed. "You bought a camera?"

"I'm not getting carpal tunnel trying to sketch everything I see. This way, I can take photos without the other side hacking my phone."

Henry squatted next to her, staring at a small map carved into the stone. It looked new, but it seemed to have just evaded erosion with the use of magic. It was a map of Greece and a bit of Thrace, including a star over Pella, the empire's capital, and a message above it.

"What do the words say?" Henry asked.

"*Help this man believe in his worth again,*" Analise translated.

"Hey, Zhang. Come look at this," Yianni called from behind.

Henry walked over to him and followed his finger, pointing up at Cassander's face.

"On his cape, there." Yianni pointed up at the statue.

Henry narrowed his eyes, taking notice of an empty circular socket in the brooch of Cassander's cloak.

"You think we're meant to put a coin in that?" Yianni muttered.

"Couldn't hurt to try." Henry held a hand out. "Hand me the Courage coin."

Yianni gave the golden disc over before Henry threw his rope dart up, wrapping it around Cassander's neck. He pulled on the rope and climbed the five-meter-tall statue, wedging himself between the statue's raised arm and head, then reached down and put the coin in the brooch.

The ground began to rumble, shaking Henry off. He managed to land gracefully, if at great cost to his knees, as the statue's sword arm slowly lowered to point off into the horizon. The base of the statue rotated ninety degrees, pointing the sword to the east.

Off in the distance, another statue rose out of the dune sea.

The three companions looked at one another.

"I better get my coin back," Yianni mumbled, crossing his arms.

They piled back into the car and drove to the next statue in a matter of minutes. This puzzle was probably a lot more annoying before the invention of the automobile.

"It's Lysimachus," Henry noted, pulling the Wisdom coin out. He fiddled with it for a moment, hesitating before he moved towards the statue.

This statue held a bow in hand, an arrow knocked in a string that the sculptor reasonably didn't bother creating.

Analise found another map at the statue's base. "It's Thrace. There's a marking here on...Gallipoli, I think."

Henry squatted down to take a look at the map. "It's Lysimachia. His capital." He stepped back from the statue. "What does the message say?"

"*Let this Icarus listen to the wisdom of others,*" Analise relayed.

"Listen...Plug up his ears?" Yianni asked, stepping back from the statue. "As counter-intuitive as that sounds."

Henry nodded. He climbed up the statue of the older man and found a perfect circle in his right ear. He took out the Wisdom coin and slotted it in before jumping off.

The statue rotated to the southeast and raised its bow, seeming to draw the arrow back.

Henry looked past the statue for a third.

Nothing happened.

"Shit," he muttered.

"Think it's broken or something?" Yianni asked.

Henry pursed his lips. It'd be really bad if it was.

"It's not broken," Analise said. "How long did it take to drive between the first statue and this one?"

"Like...three minutes," Henry said.

"At an average of sixty-eight kilometers an hour, that's about four kilometers we just went." Analise wrote in the air with her finger, doing math in her head.

Four kilometers was maybe two and a half miles, Henry realized as he converted all the metric measurements in his head.

"On the maps, we just went from Macedon to Thrace. How far is that in the real world?" Analise asked.

Henry blinked. "Oh. Oh, my God. Hang on."

He opened his phone and typed in directions for Gelibou, the closest city to ancient Lysimachia from Pella. Thankfully, his love of geography had led him to download most of Google Maps onto his phone.

"Four hundred and forty-four kilometers. Exactly," he said.

Yianni cupped his chin. "So, every kilometer out here represents a hundred and eleven kilometers in the real world."

"Who was southeast of Lysimachus? What was his capital? How far is it from here?" Analise asked.

"It should be Seleucus. His capital was Seleucia, near to where Baghdad is today," Henry said. "It's a long way in the real world."

"That's what we have a car for." Analise grinned, slapping the metal hull of the four by four.

A minute later, they were back in the car and driving southeast. By Henry's estimation, the site of Seleucia was seventeen hundred kilometers from Lysimachia, meaning the drive would be about fifteen minutes through the dunes with no concrete destination.

But ten minutes in, Yianni spotted the statue.

With Seleucus, it was much the same. The map showed the capital of his empire, and the message told them to let him "see reason" once again, so Henry took Analise's Knowledge coin and put it in Seleucus's left eye.

As he did, the statue, who held a lance at his side, turned to the southwest and raised his arm so it looked like he was throwing the lance in Ptolemy's direction.

Taking the car towards the proportional location of Alexandria, Ptolemy's capital, was shorter than the drive to Seleucia, but not by much.

The statue of Ptolemy stood tall with a shield at his side.

The last map at the base of his statue read *Restore this oathbreaker's honor.*

"Okay, that's less definitive than the last ones," Yianni muttered as the three of them stared at the statue, walking around it in case the socket wasn't facing the front.

They kept at this for about an hour, and the desert heat was really starting to get to Henry. Luckily, all his sweat evaporated, so he was smelly and dry instead of smelly and wet.

"His shield," Analise muttered. "The center of the star on it is indented."

Henry came back to the front of the statue and looked up at it from a different angle. Indeed, there was a small shadow cast by an indentation on the Macedonian sun on Ptolemy's shield.

He climbed halfway up the statue and put his Honor coin in it.

Ptolemy swiveled around and lifted his shield towards the northeast.

"So...where are we headed next?" Yianni asked.

"I'm...not sure," Henry muttered. "Northeast, I guess."

They got in their four by four and drove east, trying to stay as close as possible to Ptolemy's exact position. They even passed Seleucus again.

As they drove, Henry kept track of their proportional distance and where they would be on the maps. They passed by Persia and Khorasan, driving through what would be modern Turkmenistan.

They'd driven nearly half an hour by the time they found anything.

"Up there." Analise pointed ahead at a statue in the distance.

"Jesus, finally." Yianni scoffed. "What the hell is this?"

Henry looked at his map. "Sogdia..."

Yianni twisted around in his seat. "What?"

"This is the furthest edge that Alexander ever had any real control over. The homeland of his first wife, Roxana," Henry explained.

As they approached the statue, he discerned fairly quickly that he was looking at a statue of Alexander on his horse Bucephalus as the steed reared up.

"This has to be it," he said.

The statue stood on a large amount of rock that rose out of the sand, creating some sort of variation to the endless dunes. As the car pulled up to the statue, immediately noticeable behind it were several huge openings and wide gaps that revealed the rock formation to be a cliff overshadowed by strange arches stemming from a shallow oasis below. It explained the sudden incline of the dunes around them.

Henry looked up at the statue, uncoiling his rope dart. "I'm gonna have to borrow your ankle, your majesty." He sighed as he wrapped his rope dart around the statue's leg, then turned to his companions. "I'll check it out. But don't come down until I say so. There's a chance this oasis is just a vat of sulfur, considering what the other springs south of Siwa are like."

He planted his feet on the edge of the cliff, managing the slack so he could rappel down. Though as he lowered himself, he quickly found himself without anywhere to kick off, as the cliff face bent inward into a shaded overhang. He descended by just letting the silk rope slide through his hands.

As the rope started to reach its end, he stopped just above the surface of the bright blue water. It smelled alright. Like water and mud. It probably wouldn't be harmful.

Henry let go of the rope dart, letting himself fall into the water. It was only a few feet deep, going up to his waist at its deepest point before he started trudging towards the shore.

Under the shadow of the cliff, carved into its side was the facade of a Hellenistic temple, flanked by now-recognizable statues of the Diadochi and other important members of Alexander's army.

The facade was rather modest compared to the massive temple under Troy. With only two columns and maybe a two-and-a-half-meter-tall door, the entrance looked more fit for a meager king than one of the world's greatest conquerors. In fact, this *was* the entrance to a meager king's tomb. Henry had seen this facade before in Vergina, the common tomb for all Macedonian kings, including Alexander's father, Phillip II.

The only differences were the sandstone instead of marble and the relief carved into the blocks going across the tops of the columns.

As Analise and Yianni made their way down, Henry stared at the relief in puzzlement.

This was no historical battle being depicted. None that he could recognize. It wasn't even a mythological scene.

The one figure Henry could point out was Alexander himself, lance in hand, riding to the left on Bucephalus, going into battle against a horde of abstract monstrosities, almost imperceptible in spite of their forms being carved into stone, who rushed at a line of men on the right.

The humans were not some ensemble of soldiers. They wore clothes, carried weapons, and had complexions of lands and times completely disconnected from ancient Greece.

Henry could spot depictions of Bronze Age charioteers, warrior monks, knights in plate armor, line infantry from the modern age, and many other anachronistic elements.

Just like the companion busts under Troy, it made no historical sense for this to have been made in the Hellenistic Age.

"Well, this is...quaint," Yianni muttered as he came ashore.

"Figured out how to open it?" Analise asked.

Henry glanced at the actual door. Given the two coin-sized circles indented on each stone door, it seemed fairly straightforward.

He instinctively patted his pocket before he recalled where the coins were. But unexpectedly, his pocket jingled. He frowned, then reached in to pull out all four coins. He walked up to the door and placed each coin in one of the slots.

Something started to rumble behind the doors, signaling their assumption was right.

Dust spilled out of the doors as they cracked open.

"Here it is..." Henry swallowed.

"Is it normal to be this nervous?" Yianni's entire body was tense.

"Probably," Analise muttered, her voice trembling slightly.

It seemed all three of them were excited to go running off into the tomb.

"Ready?" Henry asked. He didn't wait for their response.

Tentatively, he lifted his foot and crossed the line between the outside and the interior, then set it down in the tomb. He wasn't sure what he was expecting, but a sigh of relief left him anyway.

It was finally time to find what he'd been looking for.

CHAPTER
TWENTY-TWO
The Shadow of Macedon

Even with his dulled arcane senses, Henry could feel a profound presence the moment his body entered into the abyssal hall of cut stone.

He, Analise, and Yianni clicked on flashlights as the sunlight quickly lost its influence to two thousand years of darkness.

The halls were adorned with stonework and reliefs carved into the cliff, featuring columns, murals, Egyptian paintings, and hieroglyphics.

Analise started snapping photos of the walls as Henry examined them more closely. It was a strange mixture of architecture, with Egyptian art, Greek columns, and Persian stonework.

The hallway took them downwards at a steep angle until they had to be at least fifty feet underground. At the end of the hallway was a marble door frame three times taller than Henry that led into another chamber with about the same dimensions as a temple's interior, but wider. It was lit by some kind of dim light source emanating from a skylight-esque circular hole in the ceiling outlined by six columns, casting beams of light onto a statue of Alexander. The babbling of water fountains echoed against the stone as small streams ran through hand-wide canals along the floor, creating a circular pattern to match the skylight.

Henry stepped onto the polished marble floor and realized that the red walls surrounding the statue and the circle of columns were actually huge red curtains with golden tassels hanging between a square of stone columns, hiding other statues and twin staircases in shadows on the edges of the chamber.

Henry turned off his flashlight as he stepped up to the skylight and looked up at a Macedonian sun seeming to emulate the real sun above ground. "This is one hell of an antechamber..." he mused.

"Yeah, it's like this lad thought he was the king of the world or something," Yianni muttered.

"Let's not waste too much time with this place. We still have an entire tomb's worth of artifacts waiting for us." Analise gestured to the stairs on either side of the chamber.

She was right.

Henry took out his phone, since there was no service, and took a picture of the chamber.

He flipped his camera around and grabbed a selfie with Alexander's statue in the background. Obviously, he could never post this anywhere, but it was a cool memento.

"Alright. Down we go," he said.

The three Companions descended the stairs behind the curtains. The stairs wrapped around to the back of the chamber and met behind Alexander's statue, where there was another doorway to another staircase that took them under the antechamber.

Braziers on the stone walls bloomed to life with flame and dim orange light as the false sun faded, framing a massive door made from some jet-colored material at the bottom of the stairs. The frame and the double doors themselves were covered in elaborate, intricate carvings of Alexander's life, accented by gilding and gold inlays.

"This is it." Henry sighed.

"You don't think something funny's gonna happen, do you? Like...the door gets stuck. Or it all caved in centuries ago." Analise let out a less-than-confident laugh.

Henry turned back to give her a confused look.

"Sorry. Just...nervous," she muttered.

"Come help me with the doors." Henry put his hands on the left door while Yianni took the right.

They strained as they pushed, causing stone to grind against stone. The doors swung open as they pushed them out of the positions they'd been stuck in for two millennia.

The tomb was a pitch-black void except for one softly glowing light somewhere deep in the dark. Though it was muffled by glass, Henry recognized the source.

A mummy. Alexander the Great's mummified corpse inside a glass coffin five times his size.

Fire sparked to life on either side of the doors and traveled down the edges of a long path of stairs to the main chamber, spreading around the perimeter to give the tomb light and casting shadows against the many marble statues inside.

"Whoa..." Henry muttered.

"Fuck me..." Yianni let out a nervous laugh.

"Well? What do you see?" Analise asked.

"A hell of a lotta gold." Yianni gestured to the piles upon piles upon piles of crates filled to the brim with jewels, precious metals, sculptures, armor, weapons, relics, and anything else Alexander would've needed in the afterlife, including a chariot.

Analise slapped him on the arm. "Get the money signs out of your eyes. We're in the honest-to-God lost tomb of Alexander the Great."

Henry broke out into disbelieving, wheezing laughter. "The tomb of Alexander the Great...The last resting place of history's greatest conqueror. Thought lost to history. Rediscovered after over two thousand years. By me..."

The sound of Analise clearing her throat echoed off the high ceiling of the tomb.

"*And* his charming assistants, who happened to be at the right place at the right time."

Yianni scoffed and punched him in the arm.

"Hey! I said you were charming." Henry laughed.

He sighed, staring into the chamber, somewhat afraid to go inside.

What if it wasn't real? What if Weiying was going to pop out, say surprise, then smugly explain to him how he'd gone all that way for nothing?

He shook his head. He was being stupid.

"Well...let's see what the old king has for us."

Henry started down the many steps, covered in woven violet carpet, towards the sarcophagus.

Statues lined every inch of the tomb's perimeter, and the stairs downwards were flanked by pairs of identical statues. The fire backlighting all of them gave their marble faces an eerie presence.

"Damn...this is a big who's who of the ancient world," Henry muttered, observing the statues. "I'm surprised Alexander even knew about some of these guys."

"Like who?" Analise asked.

Henry pointed at the first pair of statues. "That's Gilgamesh. I think. A weird Hellenistic version of Gilgamesh. The oldest story we have. Next up is Khufu, the Pharaoh who built the pyramids. Then we have Sargon the Great, first emperor of Sumeria and of anything ever, then his daughter, Enheduanna—one of, if not the oldest known authors and rhetoricians. Then we have Hammurabi of Babylon, Queen Hatshepsut, Moses, Ramses II, Achilles, and tons of others. I think I see Cyrus the Great back there somewhere." He listed the figures as they continued down the stairs. "They even have the Chaldeans."

The Chaldeans were the most ancient and powerful Magicians in known history: Hecate, the founder of her namesake Circle in Greece; Solomon, who created the spell that obscured magic and founder of the Solomonic Tannaim; Zoroaster, founder of Zoroastrianism and the Flamekeepers of Arya; Confucius, who codified magic in China and started the earliest known of many successive Chinese Circles; and Nebuchadnezzar II, founder of the Final Survivors of Uruk after he and the other Chaldeans supposedly brought the ruthless and brutal Assyrians to their knees.

"You think they fit into Alexander's Hetairoi criteria?" Analise asked.

"I mean...I guess," Henry said. "But we still don't really know what that means."

"We can deal with all that later," Yianni muttered, staring in awe at the tomb. "For now, just...enjoy the moment."

Alexander's sarcophagus was raised on a waist-high block of stone covered in Ancient Greek. As they finally reached the bottom of the stairs, Henry spied four more statues on the left and right of the main chamber. "Olympia, Roxana, Stateira, and Parysatis," he muttered to himself.

"What?" Analise asked.

"These statues are of Alexander's mother and three wives," Henry said.

"Woof. Three? My uncle could barely handle one." Yianni chuckled, weaving his way through the maze of treasure. "I thought Alexander was gay, though. Or...bi."

"We don't actually know all that much about his proclivities, but I'd say he just cared way more about conquest than sex. But a king's got to marry at some point. And it was tradition for Macedonian kings to have multiple spouses. The secret is to leave them all in Babylon while you travel to India." Henry grinned and turned to Analise, who was kneeling down at the base of the sarcophagus, reading the Greek. "What's it say?"

"Lots and lots of laurels..." she muttered. "We have *King of Macedon, Hegemon of the Hellenic League, Pharaoh of Kemet, King of Babylon, King of Sumer and Akkad, King of Persia, King of Conquerors, Son of Zeus, King of the Four Corners of the Universe, King of Kings, King of All Lands*, et cetera, et cetera."

"How modest," Yianni commented. "So, in spite of all this impressiveness, can someone tell me why I sense *zero* magic in here?"

"What?" Henry perked up. "Nothing?"

Both men looked to Analise, whose Arcane senses were much stronger. "Not that I can sense," she said. "These are all just regular artifacts."

"Wait, but then, why are all the Circles looking for this place if there's no magic?" Henry asked.

"Shit!" Yianni snapped, slamming his fist on a stone column. "So, this whole thing was just...what, was Alexander takin' the piss from beyond the grave?"

"It could've been looted a long time ago." Analise shrugged.

"Leaving all this?" Henry gestured to the treasure.

"This is bullshit!" Yianni gritted his teeth.

"Yianni, calm down!" Henry insisted. "Getting mad won't—"

"Don't fuckin' talk to me about calm, Zhang!" Yianni jabbed a finger at him. "You know why I'm pissed!"

"Fine, then! Be pissed! Just do it over there." Henry pointed to an empty part of the tomb's chamber.

As Yianni spat before leaving the other two be, Analise sighed. "I guess I can't *complain* about being...what is this, maybe twenty billion richer? But I came on this stupid hunt thinking—"

She cut herself off, eyes flickering away.

"What is it?" Henry asked.

"The sarcophagus," Analise said. "It has writing on it, but...it's some kind of semitic language. I don't speak it."

Henry walked up and peered at the massive glass casket. He gasped. "It's Syriac." He brushed some dust away and started to read through it. "*Those who seek to become my Companions, your journey continues. My tenth city holds the weapon you seek.* Tenth city...tenth city?"

In his head, Henry counted the different Alexandrias the Macedonians founded. Troad, Egypt, Ariana, Arachosia, Eschate, Caucasus, Margiana, Orietai, Susiana...Only nine.

Henry turned to his companions and blinked.

They were frozen.

"Guys?" He frowned and snapped his fingers in front of Analise's face, getting no reaction.

She wasn't breathing.

"Oh, God..." He tried to move her body, but she wouldn't budge.

What the hell was happening here? He didn't feel any magic as he scanned the rest of the tomb.

The tomb started to twist and distort, the walls, shadows, and statues melting into a black void.

Though thoroughly disoriented, Henry managed to figure out that what he was seeing was some kind of illusion or dream, as he found himself standing in the empty halls of the

Hengshan Monastery. Back in the Daba mountains, where he'd learned magic. The rough wooden floors beneath his feet and the dim, misty lighting brought back an unwelcome sense of nostalgia.

"Oh, if only I could've seen the East in the flesh."

Henry's eyes glanced over to a black-haired, olive-skinned man who was a few inches shorter than him and was slight of build. He leaned on a wooden railing overlooking the mountain vistas. He wore a simple white tunic and...had a pair of curling ram's horns coming out of his head.

"Oh, I'm sure I'll get to go someday." The man pushed off the railing to turn to Henry. "Hello, Henry."

Henry's eyes widened with recognition. "No way..." he muttered.

Something or someone was fucking with him.

He grabbed at his river stone, but couldn't feel anything.

"This isn't magic," the man said.

"How is this happening?" Henry asked. "Because if you are who I think you are...no...no, that's not possible."

"Who do you think I am?" The man smirked. He obviously knew the answer.

"You're Alexander, aren't you? The vision of him in my dreams," Henry whispered.

"I have not been the one visiting you in your dreams. But I am, in a way, Alexander III of Macedon," the man said. "I am what remains of the consciousness after the death of an enlightened soul. I am all about Alexander that was deified. Some call me Dhul-Qarnayn. Others look upon me and see the spirit of the Earth Mother. Others see my initial incarnation: Gilgamesh. But you may call me Iskandar."

Henry's eyes widened even further. "Wait, so...how are you here? Is it magic?" he asked. "What about the coins? How did you make them so—"

"Henry Zhang, I need you to understand something," Iskandar said, ignoring his questions. "Nearly everything you know about the world is wrong. And I need you to have the openness to reconsider the fundamentals of the universe. Are you willing to hear what I have to tell you?"

Right. They probably had limited time here. Henry took a deep breath, unsure where this was going, but wanting to know more, regardless of his actual feelings on the matter. "That's a hell of a disclaimer. But I've made it this far. Shoot."

"I trust my envoy has informed you of the Megawgs and the coming battle."

"He was very vague, but more or less."

Iskandar nodded. "The night I was born, one of the seven wonders of the world was destroyed—the Temple of Artemis. It was a great sacrifice given up by the ancient mystics to imbue me with a piece of the divine. My life was a quest to discover that divine nature and its purpose for being there. By the end of my life, I believe it was my purpose to begin preparing mankind for war on the material plane."

"Against the Megawgs you mentioned. But...what are they?" Henry asked.

"Remnants of a time past. Nameless demons obsessed with the reclamation of their old titles," Iskandar said. "In the dark past of our existence, twelve thousand years ago, human culture was possessed by entities who subsisted on the energies of the mind, heart, and soul. We called these beings gods. They ruled over us with fear for nine thousand years. The gods of Babylon and Sumer gave no quarter to their subjects. They were gods of nature who, if not satisfied, would unleash their tyrannical wrath on humanity."

"Until the Axial Age," Henry said. "When the Chaldeans learned magic, and religion reformed."

"It was more complicated than that. I cannot explain all of it, but the first Magician was not Zarathustra, as your masters have told you," Iskandar said. "Her name was Enheduanna. She alone was the first Magician."

"Sargon the Great's daughter?" Henry frowned.

Iskandar nodded. "The old nature gods were defeated by Magicians long before the Chaldeans ever came to be. The survivors of that culling are the Megawgs. These are the monsters that seek nothing but the destruction of civilization so that they might reclaim their birthright as the slave masters of the Earth. As I inherited this war from the ancient mystics, you and your brother inherit it from me."

"My brother?" Henry furrowed his brow.

"This is the day when you defeated your brother in a sparring match, and he attacked you with a weapon after the match was over." Iskandar sighed, gesturing to the stormy skies outside the monastery. "Do you recall your punishments?"

Henry nodded. "I was supposed to pass my basic Confucian sorcery curriculum in a night."

"That's right." Iskandar snapped his fingers, and the two of them stood in the corner of Henry's old dorm room, which he'd shared with his younger brother.

He felt his heart skip a beat, then sink with dread as he watched his younger self crack a joke to a younger Min as they procrastinated in the light of shitty bulbs from the forties.

"Why so glum?" Iskandar asked.

"You know why," Henry muttered, averting his eyes. "Not my worst memory, but it's not something I like to think back on."

"I find it intriguing that you feel more uneasy when faced with your romantic failure than your branding and exile from the Tiandihui," Iskandar said. "You admit that the two are hardly comparable, and yet..."

"My exile made me stronger. This..."

"Here, you were vulnerable in the spirit, rather than the body." Iskandar finished his thought. "But despite what happened, this was the first time in a long time you let yourself open up to someone."

Iskandar's encouraging tone emboldened Henry enough to look upon the scene and watch his younger self get to act just a bit normal. Just a bit like the child that he was.

"I notice there are three of you, Henry. Where's...what's her name? The candidate I picked for Wisdom."

"Marion?" Henry raised an eyebrow. "She...she's not...she left the hunt. She's not with us anymore."

Iskandar's posture deflated slightly "I see. I find it incredibly unfortunate that she succumbed to her darkness. Had she the courage not to run, her destiny would've been extraordinary, even among Magicians."

"It was—why are we even here?" Henry asked, suppressing his guilt as it tried to claw its way up his throat.

"This is the night when you and your brother diverged. The first night you spent apart from each other in almost a year of intensive training and study." Iskandar gestured to the younger version of Henry they were staring at.

"What divergence are you talking about?"

"Your inheritance," Iskandar said. "This moment was small, but it started you on a path towards a more...mystical understanding of the world. Not in the sense of magic. But it was the first time you truly allowed yourself to engage with feelings and impulses you didn't understand. Your incessant need to be prepared and to be competent...it fell to the wayside. You allowed yourself to be at peace not knowing. That is the kind of Honor you need, Henry: faith in yourself."

"What about my brother?" Henry asked, now concerned as to Iskandar's diagnosis. Now that he thought about it, Weiying *had* gotten more aggressive since that night. He had just assumed it was his younger brother holding a grudge. But if something more...mystical involving the Megawgs was causing him to act the way he had been...well, it'd complicate things. Mr. Fang had mentioned something was deeply wrong with Weiying. Not to mention that his prowess and ability were much greater than they should've been.

On one hand, Henry would be faced with having to figure out what was affecting Weiying and how to get rid of it, which could be well beyond his current abilities. On the other hand, it might absolve Weiying of responsibility for many of the things he'd done to Henry.

But he wasn't sure whether he could face the prospect of willingly looking at Weiying like a brother anymore. It was easier to say he was a monster of a person and leave it at that.

"Let me show you." Iskandar snapped his fingers again.

They were standing in the rain at night, sheltered only by the canopy of a forest as flashes of a roiling storm provided the only light in place of the moon. Henry didn't feel any of the weather, but he spotted Weiying huddled next to the base of a tree, cupping a small flame between his hands as he choked and sobbed under the pelting rain. He sniffled as his light and heat source dwindled.

Maybe Mr. Fang shouldn't have been so hard on him. Or let him wait until a day with better weather.

Henry had spent all night with the girl he'd had a crush on while Weiying was out here alone. What kind of a brother was he?

"Don't pity him," Iskandar said. "He has plenty of it for himself." He pointed up at the monastery, whose lights were quite visible from here, even through the rain. "He quit five minutes in, but didn't have the courage to face his failure, so he sat out here in the rain, crying over the consequences of his own cowardice in order to preserve the lies he told himself."

"Well, if he went back, they would've punished him even more harshly."

"No, they wouldn't," Iskandar said. "Not if he was penitent. But that's the crux of the issue: he has never admitted his mistake. He has never shown a desire to improve his shortcomings. You know that better than anybody. That is why he's out here. That's why his punishment would be worse if he turned back. Had he completed his punishment, he would've had shelter. Instead, he suffers more because of his choices."

"What does this have to do with Megawgs?"

"I'm showing you so you have context for what happens next." Iskandar put a hand on Henry's shoulder and pointed at Weiying. Or rather...behind him.

Something seized Henry by the chest. Sweat beaded on his forehead as he locked his gaze with the large, distorted eyes of some alien creature he'd never seen before.

And yet familiarity prickled in the back of his mind, as if his DNA knew what his mind did not.

Its black body blended into the shadows, making its form and build a mystery. Yet as lightning flashed through the sky, he could make out the vague contours of a humanoid face. But everything was wrong, elongated and distorted.

It stared directly at him.

"It knows we're watching," Iskandar said. "But it cannot hurt you physically."

Henry's breath was starting to speed up regardless. How did it know they were there? Wasn't this supposed to be a dream? A flashback?

"Don't panic," Iskandar said. "It wishes to play with your mind. Control your fear."

"Why can it see us?" Henry asked, unable to tear his eyes away from its cold, inhuman gaze.

"It is a Megawg," Iskandar said simply.

Henry managed to turn away to shoot a look at Iskandar, who stared at the creature with supernatural stoicism. "That...is not a Megawg."

"The Megawgs are not humans or gods anymore," Iskandar said. "They've lost that distinction. They feed on fear. To submit to one's animal instincts is to exalt them. Now, they themselves are creatures of instinct, hedonism, and deception. And they prey on the spiritually weak."

The Megawg's malformed head split as it assumed a mockery of a smile. It already knew Henry would be there. In the past, it knew someone in the future would be watching. And it smiled at the twisting fear snaking through his body as if it knew exactly what he was feeling.

It stepped out a bit into another flash of lighting. Its distorted head lay on a lanky humanoid body no less than ten feet tall, with limbs like barren tree branches tapping against a bedroom window.

No, the Megawg didn't step. It...glided. It came up behind Weiying without moving a muscle aside from throwing its horrible gaze at Henry's brother.

Henry's hand reached for one of his butterfly swords.

"You can't hurt it either," Iskandar said.

Poor boy...what are you doing out here? All alone...

The monster neither spoke nor thought. The words were there, and then they were gone. No movement produced them. No vibration, no magic.

Weiying perked his head up and looked back, gasping.

I'm sorry. I didn't mean to startle you.

Henry furrowed his brow.

"A Megawg's true form can only be seen by those who know of their existence. Otherwise, people see only what they want to see. Or what the Megawg wants them to see," Iskandar explained.

"It's okay..." Weiying muttered.

Why are you out here in this weather? You could get sick. Do you have family around here? Someone you can go back to?

Weiying grumbled as he drew his knees to his chest. "I do...but I'm being punished. Meanwhile, my brother is sitting pretty in his room, dry, with a pretty girl, nothing but books to read and time to kill. That's what they call a punishment for him."

That's not very fair...He's not a very good brother, is he?

"No," Weiying said fervently. "Although...I was the one who started the fight, I guess."

This is no way to punish a child, regardless of what happened. I'm guessing they did not allow you to explain yourself.

Weiying shrugged. "I guess not. I just...ugh. I just wanted to beat my brother *once*. Just once! If I can't become as good as him, they might throw me out!"

Henry's hand twitched. Throw him out? Did Weiying really have no concept of how valuable an asset he was to the Tiandihui?

What happened?

"I...hit him after the match ended, so now, they're making me run all the way up a mountain and back down by daybreak."

How awful! That's so unfair! You seem like an excellent Magician to me. I bet they're just jealous of you.

"I...wait." Weiying furrowed his brow. "I never said the word Magician."

The creature saved its mistake with a bald-faced lie. *I work in another branch of the Tiandihui. I can sense you from a mile away. But I'll have to have a talk with your superior if they're mistreating you.*

"They *are* mistreating me." Weiying scoffed. "I'm the best Magician in the class, and this is how they thank me for my talent?"

Henry watched in frustrated impotence and morbid curiosity.

I can help you find your way up the mountain. And if you want, I can give you a special magic that will make it so you never lose to your brother again.

"Really?" Weiying perked up. "Wait, that's not against the rules, is it?"

What they don't know can't hurt them. For now, they envy you. But with what I can teach you, they will fear you. I can make failure all but a distant memory for you.

Weiying grinned. "I like the sound of that. But...I'd really rather get out of this rain first."

The rain froze around them.

Henry's brother gasped. "Whoa..."

I can offer you that and much more. Just ask me to teach you, and I shall.

"Please! Teach me." Weiying got onto his knees, an excited-but-sadistic grin on his face. "Teach me...what's your name again?"

The creature turned to look at Henry again. ***Hepom Nepots.***

Iskandar waved his hand, stopping the scene. "Hepom Nepots has been attached to your brother ever since this night, and has been driving him down a road of self-destruction. Possessing him."

Henry made a conscious effort to breathe, not really sure what to think. He glanced away from the creature, not wanting to look at it any longer than he had to.

"Your brother is what we would call a Gawg," Iskandar said. "A puppet of a Megawg. Halfway to spiritual death."

Henry turned to him. "There...there has to be a way to save him."

"There may be. Part of it is up to you, but the rest is up to your brother," Iskandar said. "You have to understand how much of a threat they are. The Megawgs have already wormed their way into the highest positions of society through their puppets. They infest your culture with decadence and decay. With each generation, the people of the world become easier targets for their manipulation. They hardly need to intervene anymore. The population of a new generation would be completely pacified even if they sat back and did nothing."

Henry nearly looked back at the Megawg before forcing his eyes to stay on Iskandar. He was right. With the advent of godlike power inherent to industrial society and the internet, neither of which any culture had really figured out how to use responsibly, it was absurdly easy to get people to fall to their base desires for pleasure and fame.

He and his Companions were living proof: Marion to her lack of conviction, Yianni to his monstrous self-image, Analise to that anger bubbling just beneath the surface, Henry to his fear.

And in spite of that, it seemed the four of them had been selected as the most fit to fight against this influence. Henry could hardly believe there was no one better than them out there.

But at the same time, he could easily see that being the case.

"How do I fight them?" he asked, more interested in attaining the power to kill the one attached to his brother.

"In a way, you have already made yourself resistant to Megawg manipulation. By passing my tests, you have proven that you have the base foundation to resist them on your own. Not to mention the fire that now burns within you," Iskandar said.

Henry didn't want to tell him about the failure in his resistance that followed immediately after. But it did make him think that perhaps the tests weren't as thorough as Iskandar assumed.

"As for pushing them back...you must go to Alexander's tenth city: Alexandria-Chaldea."

"Chaldea...so, near Babylon."

"That was the plan. But no," Iskandar said. "It's under Ptolemy's capital. My sarcophagus has a map to it, which you will be able to see with the sight your talismans have given you. Find your way there, and you will have access to every arcane weapon I have collected over my lifetime. But when you get there, you must absolutely do one thing first: you must open the box that keeps my copy of the *Iliad*. It will turn your fire into something that can be used against the Megawgs. However, your Companions must be there. They too have seeds within them that need watering."

"Your copy of the...but how will I—"

"We are out of time, Henry Zhang. When I send you back, do not try to save your brother until you have opened that box. If you try to battle a Megawg now, both you and your brother will die," Iskandar said hurriedly. "Good luck, *Hetairoi*."

Henry opened his eyes. He was in the exact same spot in the exact same pose as when he'd first touched the sarcophagus.

"Nezha!"

He blinked and turned to find Analise and Yianni with their hands up. He looked towards the entrance of the tomb and found Atum—along with the rest of Atum Squad and fifty Egyptian soldiers with rifles trained on them—marching down the stairs.

He grimaced. "Shit."

CHAPTER TWENTY-THREE
The Tiger's Quarry

At gunpoint, Henry, Analise, and Yianni were forced to the side as Atum and his squad got their chance to marvel at the tomb.

"What beauty..." Atum murmured, taking his fedora off as he looked upon Alexander's sarcophagus.

"Turn over your weapons," Ramses demanded, towering over the soldiers.

Henry met the eyes of a dozen men with their fingers on their triggers as he slowly pulled out his revolver.

"The guns..." He cursed as he set the firearm on the ground for Ramses to collect, along with their other guns and close-quarters weapons. "You tracked us using the guns."

Atum chuckled as he continued to look at Alexander's sarcophagus. "As someone who's walked this earth for over a thousand years, I understand the perks of playing the long game. Those enchantments you rubbed off the first night you got them were a ruse. We put a tracking spell on your weapons and caused some division between the other Circles. After that, we just had to wait for you to find the tomb. At the end of the day, we get the tomb, our weapons back, Minoan texts, and the sweet taste of victory, all for a few thousand dollars."

Henry gritted his teeth as he forced his arm to his side, not pulling his guandao from his ear.

Cleopatra approached them. "Hold out your wrists."

With little other choice, Henry and his squadmates obeyed, and as she clamped Nullifier Bands with rubies on them on each of their right wrists, he felt what little arcane sense he had vanish.

They'd cut off their abilities. Most of them, at least. He could still feel the tether between himself and his swords, meaning martial weapon enchantments were unaffected. Nonetheless, their weapons had been taken too far away for him to call them back and not get shot immediately.

But he still had his guandao hidden in the crook of his ear. He just had to wait for an opportunity to strike.

Ten soldiers were left to threaten the Companions as the others started picking up the chests of gold while dust rained down from the ceiling. Henry glanced up to find more soldiers removing a slab of stone, over which they'd erected a mechanized winch. The machine lowered a lift to the tomb. Other soldiers began stringing wire up around the perimeter of the tomb, high above the canal of flames that lit the place.

"What are you doing?" Henry demanded.

"These artifacts are property of the Supreme Council of Antiquities and the Arab Republic of Egypt," Atum said.

"You're lucky these are going in a museum, Defector." Cleopatra flashed him a smug grin.

Henry needed to get a look at the sarcophagus. Without it, there'd be no map to Alexandria-Chaldea.

"We had a deal, Atum! You can't just take it all for yourself!" Analise snarled as she tried to step past the soldiers. They threw her back into Henry and Yianni, and two shot the floor around them, spewing plumes of dust from the stone.

"Hey, hey! Calm down, ya fuckin' brutes," Yianni responded.

"Can't I?" Atum scoffed.

Henry helped Analise up, holding her back as she tried to approach them again. "Don't be stupid," he growled. "Atum, what's the wire for?"

"Ah. You see, places like this completely alter the canon of history that the lay people are working with," Atum said. "If we let this tomb be recognized as Alexander the Great's, it may cause a shockwave of people breaking Solomon's Wisdom."

"So, you're gonna blow it up?" Henry snarled.

"This place remains undiscovered, and you all get buried alive," Atum said. "Two birds, one stone, Zhang."

The lift kept pulling up treasure as Henry's mind raced.

They were securing belts and straps to Alexander's sarcophagus.

"Wait!" Yianni spoke up. "Notice there's nothing magical in here."

Atum squad all froze.

"Nefertiti?" Atum turned to the shortest woman among their number, whose straight black hair covered one of her eyes.

"Nothing arcane," she muttered in Arabic.

"What?" Ramses hissed.

"We know where Alexander's stash is." Henry joined the conversation in their tongue. "Let's cut a deal."

Atum narrowed his eyes.

"What do you—" Cleopatra started, but Atum cut her off.

"Don't bother," he said. "In any other time, Nezha, I would've enjoyed working with you. But you are a Defector. And I've read more than enough adventure fiction to know you intend to double-cross me. There can't be anything you know that we can't glean from what we've acquired here."

Henry gritted his teeth as he watched the sarcophagus leave its resting place.

"Right. After this, we should have everything of importance." Atum tilted his chin up. "Cleopatra, if you'd be so kind as to leave our friends here with some good company while we make our exit."

Cleopatra took a deep breath and stretched her arms out. Her fingers flexed as the tomb began to rumble. She spoke some eldritch form of Egyptian that hissed and echoed in the air.

The nine-foot-tall statues surrounding the main chamber started to twitch before Cleopatra's magic fully animated them. They stepped down from their bases and surrounded the Companions, threatening them with giant marble spears and swords.

"Don't let them escape," Cleopatra commanded as she joined her squadmates on the last lift of treasure. The soldiers started running up the stairs.

Yianni turned to Henry and Analise. "So...you geniuses bought your weapons from your competition?"

"I checked for tracking enchantments!" Analise snapped.

"They're Egyptian!" Yianni's eyes went wide. "They don't have tracking enchantments! They probably bugged the damn duffel bag! And now, we're about to be buried alive because you were all too lazy to smuggle your own weapons in!"

"It seemed less pressing at the time. We didn't think we'd be seen as much of a threat! And arguing isn't going to help anyone right now!" Henry shouted.

"Really? I find it quite helpful in coping with my *imminent death*!" Yianni got in his face, only to be shoved back.

Henry took a deep breath and stared at all the animated statues in their cold marble eyes. "Just stay calm..."

"Why? Do you have a plan? Because I'd really like to hear it," Analise said, nervously tugging at a strand of her hair.

"Well...they didn't bother taking our weapons with them." Henry gestured to the pile of guns and swords next to the podium that Alexander's tomb had sat on. "On my signal, run."

He reached into his ear as if he were scratching it, clasping his hand around the pin-sized weapon.

He inched forward, which caused a statue of Ptolemy to aim a spear at his neck.

But he was close enough.

His weapon grew as he shoved his arm forward. The tip of the blade tapped the statue's chest, transferring a disproportional amount of arcane force and sending it flying across the chamber—a new enchantment courtesy of the Honor coin.

On impact, the statue shattered into pieces.

"Now!"

Yianni and Analise sprinted through the break in the line of statues as Henry drew his weapon back and swung it into the thighs of a Lysimachus statue, carving through the stone like warm butter.

He dodged a marble spear, which crumbled into rocks and dust on contact with the ground, and rushed past the slow-moving statues. He called his swords back to their sheaths and coiled his rope dart around his left wrist.

Sparks flashed across his vision as the detonation wire lit up and six simultaneous explosions knocked out his hearing and showered them in dust.

As the debris settled, cracks started to appear in the chamber walls.

"Run!" Henry shouted.

The entire tomb began to rumble as the three Companions rushed up the stairs and out of the main tomb.

They sprinted into the antechamber just as the floor was starting to crack open, and pieces of stone collapsed into the tomb below them. Henry jumped out of the way as Alexander's statue crashed down a little too close to him. "Stick to the side," he ordered, as the pieces of floor in the middle were the first to collapse.

He shrank his guandao and stowed it away before starting to inch along the side of the antechamber. By the time they started moving towards the front in earnest, there was little more than a foot-wide sliver of floor remaining.

Henry flattened himself against the wall as they made their way towards the door. His heart nearly stopped as a piece of stone snapped under his foot. He stabbed the wall with his rope dart to keep himself steady while the piece of floor tumbled at least four stories down.

The rock above them was rumbling now. It seemed the whole cliff they were under was about to collapse, but Henry shoved panic out of his mind and moved at a slower pace, ensuring he wouldn't fall.

He maneuvered himself around as they got near the door. The only problem was that there was nowhere to walk between the right-most side of the chamber and the exit.

He lashed his rope dart out, pinning it into the top of the tall door frame. "Alright, we're gonna have to Tarzan this!" he said.

He pushed off the wall and let himself fall until the slack tightened. His shoulders were level with the floor of the entrance, resulting in a nasty blow to his chest as he collided with the stone, but he grabbed onto the floor and climbed up before throwing the silken rope to Yianni.

"Fuck me..." Yianni muttered before he too swung across.

Henry helped Yianni up and threw the rope to Analise as a chunk of ceiling fell near the back of the chamber. She flinched, grabbing onto the rope like a comfort blanket rather than a grappling hook.

"Come on, Analise!" Henry prodded.

"Oh, God..." She sighed to herself, her breath shaky. "Oh, Goddammit..."

Cracks splintered the ceiling as smaller chunks started to fall away.

"It's now or never! Jump!" Yianni cried.

Analise screamed as she jumped.

A crack caused Henry to glance up just as the top of the door frame snapped off, taking the rope dart with it. He collapsed to the floor and reached out, barely grabbing Analise's hand before she could fall. "I got you..." He panted. "I got you."

With Yianni's help, he pulled her up and coiled his rope dart around his wrist.

Before they turned back to the door, the entire antechamber caved in, and another round of cracks spread above them in the hallway.

Henry barely had time to curse as they ran. The hallway started collapsing much faster, the sound of falling rocks at their heels as they sprinted. They dove towards the sun as the force of the cave-in threw the tomb's doors shut behind them.

Henry rolled over onto his back, staring at the open sky. He panted, trying to catch his breath. "Holy shit..." He swallowed.

"What the hell is that glaive o' yours made of?" Yianni asked.

"The guy this weapon is named after, Guan Yu, had one of these that weighed over a hundred pounds. I gave mine an enchantment that gives it a hundred pounds worth of impact." Henry grinned.

He was immediately removed from his post-adrenal relief as Analise screamed, grabbing at her hair as she doubled over. "Analise, are you—"

"Fuck!" she shouted through gritted teeth. "God...dammit!"

Her screams of fury quickly changed to hysterical sobs as Henry and Yianni glanced at one another. She pounded her fist against the sand. "Those fucking bastards..." She choked the word out into her hands, covering her face in shame. "Those rat fucking bastard!!"

"Hey." Henry knelt down next to her. "Analise, it's okay—"

"No! No, it's not!" She glared at him with tear-filled, enraged eyes. "Again! I did it *again!*"

Henry looked up at Yianni for help. "What's she talking about?"

Yianni shrugged, but stepped forward. "Oi, lass. We still have a chance. They can't be too far ahead of us. We need a driver, Analise. We don't have time for this shite!"

"Screw you!" Analise snarled. "You have no room to tal—"

"Both of you, shut up!" Henry snapped. "I'm taking command. There's a map to everything we were looking for on Alexander's sarcophagus! It's in Alexandria. We just need to find out where. Now! They have to have left someone behind to blow the charge! I'm going after it. If you want to come, you can come. Otherwise, you can stay behind in the desert."

"*Verdammt...*" Analise sniffled, wiping her eyes. "I'm gonna put a bullet between Atum's eyes."

Henry pushed himself to his feet, along with the others, and pulled their coins, which had been left behind, out of the door. They left the small oasis cove, climbing up the sand dunes around it instead of the cliff, given Henry's worn arms.

Indeed, there was one straggling four by four with three men hurriedly packing equipment into their vehicle.

Henry willed his swords to fly from their sheathes and skewered two of the men in their dominant hands, disarming them of their rifles, before calling them back to him. He locked the muzzle of the third's gun in the hooks on his swords and slammed the knuckle guard into his nose, knocking him out.

"Where are they going?" he snarled in Arabic.

"G-gas station! North of here!" one of the men answered. Henry relayed the answer to his allies.

Analise pilfered the keys from the unconscious man and started the car up while Yianni picked up their guns and sidearms. Henry placed his wrist on the Jeep's back and bashed the golden bracelet on his arm with the guard of his sword until it fell off. Then, able to cultivate and use Qi again, he used Fire Style's explosive strength to break open his companions' bracelets.

"Zhang, I believe this is your boomstick of choice." Yianni offered him the handle of a revolver as big as his forearm—a .500 Smith & Wesson.

"Hello, beautiful." Henry grabbed the gun and flipped open the cartridge to find it fully loaded. "Costs five bucks a round to shoot this thing." He closed the cartridge and placed the gun snugly in a holster meant for a .44 Magnum. "Drive north! We'll catch up to them and hijack their transport!"

"What about the soldiers? We don't have Marion to shield us—" Yianni started.

"Just get me close enough, and I'll take care of it. Just step on the gas!"

Without another question, Analise drove like a madwoman.

The Companions sailed over the top of a dune, their landing taking a rough toll on their Jeep's suspension as they sped towards Siwa. Henry stood in the backseat of the Jeep, looking out for signs of the Egyptians as they closed in on the oasis and loading up a KSG-12 shotgun. He filled one tube with Dragon's Breath and the second with slugs. It was a weird design, being able to switch between the two ammo types—but in a good way.

"We've got a welcoming party up ahead," he muttered, spotting two black trucks blocking the road to Siwa. He glanced right, across the sparse fields that took as much advantage as possible of the little moisture offered by the oasis, and saw a parallel road. "Take a right."

Analise swerved onto a dirt path that took them through the fields, then turned onto the parallel road just as the two trucks started following them past where the barricade was.

Henry pulled out the .500 revolver, aiming it at the hood of the closest truck. In spite of the uneven road, Henry's shot, which ripped through the air and nearly took his hand off his wrist, punched through the truck's engine block, stealing its momentum away.

He holstered the gun and brought the KSG around on its sling for the second truck, chambering a round and firing. A plume of sparks and flames spewed from the muzzle of the gun, bathing the truck in fire and causing it to veer off the road, where it tipped over and skidded into the sand.

Analise took a left, off road, hopping onto another road that led into the winding streets of the tourist town. Her driving and Henry's gun sent locals and tourists alike screaming for shelter. They would definitely be blamed for a terrorist attack of some kind before the week was over.

"There's one gas station around here!" Yianni said, showing his phone to Analise. "It's twenty minutes away!"

Henry glanced behind him as the trucks from the other blockade started chasing after them on the main road. "That's gonna be a long twenty minutes." He sighed.

He lifted his shotgun and hit the small switch to the other tube. He fired at the trucks, which weaved through his slugs.

"Yianni, you got something else for me? Preferably something automatic." He held onto a part of the Jeep's frame, trying to stabilize himself.

"Uh...this one has a big clip." Yianni handed him a Czech-made Skorpion.

He threw the shotgun to his back on its sling, taking the submachine gun. "The SKS by your leg uses a clip. This is a *magazine*. And speaking of *magazines*, get some of those ready for me."

Henry emptied the Skorpion's rounds in a spray of fire that actually managed to shatter the windshield of one truck and hit the passenger of another.

"Yeah, whatever. Puts bullets in shite, doesn't it?" Yianni rifled through a duffel bag that belonged to the men they'd hijacked this car from. "I got more."

As the Egyptian soldiers returned fire, Henry slumped down into the back seat to reload with the ammo Yianni offered him.

"Shit!" Analise cried, jerking the wheel as a bullet sparked off the rim of the windshield. "I'll stick the muzzle of my gun up your ass, you bastard!"

Henry threw his arm out and unleashed some suppressing fire on the two trucks, causing the one whose windshield he'd broken to crash into the side of a building.

"While you're looking, see if you can find some rounds for the Magnum." He passed the Skorpion to his left hand and pulled out the revolver, missing the driver, but shattering the windshield and making a bloody splatter out of a chunk in his shoulder. The car flipped over as the injured driver yanked the wheel.

"What do they look like?" Yianni asked.

"Chunky." Henry sat back down. "You know what, just pass me the bag and ready some magic."

Yianni handed the duffel bag over, grumbling, but did as he was told.

Two cars swerved out of flanking side roads and tried to squash the Companions' car between them. Henry stood and pulled his shotgun around, firing a slug at the one on the left, shattering the window and turning the driver into red paste.

The car on the right kept pushing, sending both of them into a spin. Henry collapsed into the back seat as Analise tried to wrestle control back.

The tires screeched as both cars managed to stop. Henry sat up, facing the other car head-on. He swapped tubes on the shotgun and fired a plume of Dragon's Breath to blind them before swapping back and slam-firing the other three slugs into the driver and engine block.

Analise got them back on the road.

The army had no more barricades in the main town, since that would've been about as foolhardy as what they'd just done to the other barricade in front of all those people. As a result, about ten minutes went by unimpeded.

That gave Henry enough time to scrounge for just enough Magnum rounds to load the cylinder again once he emptied it. He also found a few frag grenades, separating them from the rest of the bag and loading the shotgun with buckshot in the empty tube. He reloaded the Skorpion, practically dual-wielding it with the shotgun.

"We have bandits up ahead, Rambo," Analise said as the town started to disappear for more dunes and sparse settlements. There was only one road, and this blockade seemed much larger than the others, made up of six trucks.

"I've got this," Yianni said. He flexed his fingers, and his forearms gained a thorny wood texture and unraveled, growing into a spike-covered shell of bramble over the car.

Henry could hear the sound of gunfire and bullets hitting the thick wood, but as Analise kept her foot on the gas, they were like a giant spiky battering ram. The car violently lurched as they slammed into and through the blockade.

"Why couldn't you have done that earlier?" Henry asked.

"We had options earlier, and now I'm outta steam, thank you." Yianni sighed as the bramble retracted and reformed into his arms. "Mouth off when *you* can use those flames of yours properly."

Henry shook his head as the four trucks that hadn't been demolished got their shit together and started chasing them.

As they gained ground, he hailed them with a shower of bullets until the Skorpion ran out of ammo. He threw the gun at a soldier's head as he pulled a grenade off his belt and primed it before tossing it into the backseat of one of the trucks. The vehicle exploded in a plume of flames and gasoline, slowing down the one directly behind it.

But the other two were still hot on their trail.

"Jesus, how much are they paying these guys?" Henry scoffed, pulling the shotgun around.

Lucky for him, most of their opposition were in the truck beds, so when he unleashed three rounds of Dragon's Breath, it set most of them on fire. The men screamed, throwing themselves off their trucks if they hadn't already fallen off.

He switched to the buckshot and took care of the two drivers, then sat back down in his seat, only for his eyes to grow wide at what was in front of them.

"There's the gas station," Yianni muttered.

Henry looked through the windshield, only to be faced with the titanium hull and four jet engines of a massive Boeing C-17 cargo plane a ways down the road just as the door to the hold was closing.

They were going to use the road as a runway.

"Shit!" Henry sat up. "Analise, step on it!"

"What?" she cried.

"Drive!"

"I know what you said! What the hell are you planning?"

"You want to stop them? We need the sarcophagus!" Henry shouted. "Floor it!"

"Dickhead!" Analise did as she was told, stomping on the pedal, which nearly caused Henry to fall out the back of the Jeep.

The plane's engines started to power up as it wheeled itself into position for takeoff.

Analise managed to get within ten yards or so as the plane started to speed up.

"Come on, just a little closer!" Henry gritted his teeth as the sound of the jet engines deafened him.

He had to get a look at the sarcophagus. If for nothing else than to get the thing attached to his brother off him.

Well, that was what he would've liked to have said.

No, he had to have his quarry. His real quarry.

He wanted to know what Alexander had waiting for him. He had to be in the know. That way, only he and his people had the metaphorical nukes.

Such a realization did nothing to quell the fire of desperation in his chest as Analise got nearly close enough for him to throw his rope dart.

The plane lifted off the ground, receding into the sky at a rapid pace.

Henry drew on Fire and Metal with a breath of Qi, racing to the hood of the Jeep and jumping off it so powerfully he made a dent in the car.

He soared through the air and got just close enough to throw his rope dart around the back landing gear. Wind pulled on every inch of his skin as it started to retract. He pulled for his life, reeling himself into the retracting wheels.

As the plane really got off the ground, he found himself alone in the dark.

He took a few moments to catch his breath, cultivating Qi. Since the landing gear of planes wasn't pressurized or connected to the cargo hold, only by magic would he be able to accomplish his objective.

He channeled Fire Style differently, using it to warm his body and blood. He let the fires dancing inside him grow, fanning them until droplets of flame spilled off his fingers.

His index finger glowed orange like metal fresh from a forge. He pressed the tip into the metal floor just two feet above him, filling the compartment with a shower of sparks. He drew a circle he figured would be big enough for his shoulders and popped the metal out with a surge of explosive strength, then threw himself up into the cargo hold.

If he could just get the sarcophagus a parachute, he could open the hold and jump out.

Weaving around a labyrinth of crates full of treasure, he found the switch for the cargo hold first and pulled the handle down.

The slow introduction of whipping winds forced him to squint. The cargo door set off a loud tone of some kind as the metal slid against itself to open onto the desert, now far below them.

Next was to find a—

"*Ya himar.*"

Henry whirled around as a fist slammed into his left eye. He collapsed, faced with the consequences of his actions as they really started to sink in—those consequences being the vast, almost infinite Egyptian desert.

It helped that his view of the dunes was not through a window, but coming through a wide-open cargo hold thousands of feet in the air. The roar of jet engines competed with the screeching wind to rupture his eardrums.

Stubbornly, swimming with vertigo, he pushed himself off the cold metal floor of the cargo hold and stumbled to his feet with the help of a waist-high wooden crate. The man who'd just punched him shoved the muzzle of an assault rifle in his face, telling him in Arabic to drop his weapons. Two more men in balaclavas and fatigues aimed their guns at him from the front of the hold.

Henry winced as the man holding the gun pushed the muzzle into the side of his head and called him a son of a bitch in Arabic. "Yeah, yeah, okay. Cool it!" he hissed. "*Kol Khara.*"

He grabbed the muzzle of the gun aimed at his head and shoved it out of the way as bullets sprayed from it. He slammed his knee into the soldier's ribs and spun him around like a dance partner, putting the man between him and the other onslaught of gunfire from the front.

He pushed the now-very-dead man out of the way, drawing his .500 Magnum. The blast of his single shot shook the already-rumbling cargo hold as one of the Egyptian mercenaries collapsed in a heap. He dove behind a crate as the remaining soldier yelled for his friends. Splintered wood showered over him as bullets hit his only defense.

He stared out at the Siwa Desert far, far beneath him. What was he thinking?

He squeezed his eyes shut as the faint noise of boots against metal signaled the arrival of more gunmen. Magician or not, five armed men wouldn't exactly be a cakewalk for him on his own.

Henry winced as more gunshots tried to phase through his cover somehow.

He stowed his gun away. If he was counting right, he only had three shots left.

He drew a butterfly sword and threw it, impaling a man's leg as he dove out of cover and hid behind a tower of chests further towards the front of the plane. He called it back to his hand with a cry of pain from the soldier he'd just hit, flicked the blood off the broad flat of the blade, and shoved the tower of crates over.

The mercenaries scattered as chests full of jewels and silver crashed to the ground. Henry rushed into the fray with all the lethality of a pouncing tiger, drawing his second sword. With ruthless efficiency, he cut down three men in half as many seconds, plunging his blades through the gaps in their body armor like a whirlwind of steel.

However, he was forced to dive for cover again as the mercenaries got their wits back. His eyes shot open wide as he heard *more* footsteps. Just how many of these guys could fit in one cargo hold? They were coming out like roaches from a radiator.

Henry cursed in Mandarin as something slammed into the crate he was hiding behind. He realized a bit too late that it was another crate sliding towards the exit.

The plane was pulling up.

The crate he leaned against for cover soon became a load on his shoulders, along with a second and a third, all full of gold and jewels, shoving him down an increasingly sheer, slippery metal floor. He stabbed his swords into the floor, but lost his grip before he could use them as handholds.

He screamed a stream of curses as the crates slipped off the cargo door, held in the plane by canvas straps alone. He grabbed the canvas and pulled himself onto the crates, but just as he did, one of the men shot the rig holding the straps in place. He leapt off the crates as they were swept away towards the sand.

As he began to fall, he threw out his rope dart. The dart punched through the plane's hull. He pulled on the silk rope, climbing towards the plane against the wind as more crates spilled out of the cargo hold and dropped off into the desert.

The plane righted itself long enough for Henry to make a sign with a Hung Gar bridge hand, quickly calling on a small boon from Chenguang Shen, the god of borders and barriers. He threw himself at the hull of the plane, magically phasing through the metal as his rope dart wound itself back around his wrist.

Appearing next to the mercenaries from seemingly nothing shocked them. He called his swords back to his hands from being wedged in the ground and slammed the knuckle guard of one into a mercenary's nose, then used his body as a shield from a small burst of gunfire before slashing his way through three others, but didn't get to the last two before they started firing at him.

He dove for cover just as one of the bullets hit the fuel line or something—he wasn't an aviation expert—and caused an explosion that threw him into the side of the cargo hold.

Henry rolled onto his back, groaning as he struggled to determine up from down.

The cargo hold was on fire. So were the engines.

"Son of a bitch..." He grunted, staring at the ceiling, now filled with smoke.

He pulled out his gun and shot at the two soldiers as they hid, wasting a bullet. As one of them dared to peek out, he hit him right between the eyes with his next shot. Not willing to waste his last shot, he scrambled towards the last soldier before another explosion launched him into a crate, causing a stack of them to collapse on top of the last mercenary.

Henry cursed, cradling his bruising side.

With everyone dead, he needed to get the sarcophagus before the plane went down. He made his way to the very front of the cargo hold as the plane began to rumble, shaking loose more cargo, which began to slide towards the door.

The remaining crates and fires made way for a seven-foot-long sarcophagus of thick, cloudy glass engraved with hieroglyphics, demotic script, and Ancient Greek. It was secured by canvas belts and pinned to the cargo hold's walls by a metal rig and, like some of the other cargo in the plane, had a parachute attached to it. Excellent.

Henry tried to unclip it from its straps, but a sudden jolt threw him into the ceiling, and he landed on the glass casket, knocking all the wind out of him.

Groaning, he glanced about as pieces of the hull were stripped away and the plane tipped into a nosedive.

He pulled his revolver from his belt and used his last shot to blow away the metal mechanism keeping the straps in place.

The sarcophagus started to slide towards the cargo door as Henry encouraged it to leave the plane with the rest of the treasure with insistent shoving.

He adjusted his grip, pulling it forward, but his finger caught the parachute's ripcord as the plane hit another bout of turbulence, causing the canvas life-saver to billow open. The force of the wind combined with the opening parachute threw him out of the cargo hold and into the open sky.

CHAPTER
TWENTY-FOUR
Qattara

Henry couldn't stop spinning.

For the love of God, he couldn't stop spinning.

It was sand, sky, sand, sky, sand, sky, seeming to shake loose every bone in his body with pure centripetal force. His blood rushed to his head and other extremities, filling his eyes with vertigo and aches.

This was a terrible way to lose his skydiving virginity.

He was panicking. He had to stop panicking. Whenever he saw skydivers, they were usually spread-eagle.

He forced his arms and legs out, suddenly catching a flat wall of wind to the face as he stabilized, falling slower.

Okay...that was the first step out of the way. Now, all he needed was a parachute.

He didn't have a parachute.

He craned his neck behind him and saw the parachute for the sarcophagus still stuck in the plane's cargo hold as it came down like a flaming comet.

But there were other boxes that had slipped out with him that he knew had parachutes attached.

He glanced down and spotted a couple crates not far from him. At least, he thought they were near enough.

He folded his arms together and fell faster, gaining on one of the boxes with a parachute strapped to it.

He reached out for it, but sent both himself and the crate spiraling out of control when he grabbed on. He reached for the ripcord as it flailed in the wind and tugged. The chute didn't budge, so he channeled what Qi he had left into an explosive blast of power.

The cord ripped as it should, but the chute limply spilled out, tangled in itself.

He desperately tried to untwist the lines, but to no avail. With the ground rapidly approaching, he had no choice but to draw his butterfly sword, cut through the chute, and try something drastic.

He bit his finger enough to draw blood and drew the Chinese characters for "silk rope" on the wooden crate. He grabbed onto the end of a rope and pulled it out of the wood, causing the panel to fall away and treasure to start spilling out.

He hurriedly wrapped the rope around his waist and shoulders before drawing the characters for "silk canopy." The rest of the wood converted into a layered parachute-like construction of silk that billowed open and nearly slipped from his hands as it slowed his descent.

He held on for dear life and wrapped the pseudo lines of the parachute through the shoulder straps he'd just made for himself, clamping his hands down to keep them from slipping.

He breathed a sigh of relief as the chute slowly made the fall less and less deadly, but as he watched the sand get closer, he realized that he was still going to land pretty hard. Not hard enough to get truly hurt, but it wouldn't be pleasant.

He also realized that he couldn't see anything but sand dunes in all directions.

"Oh, that's just the perfect shit storm to end my day on," he muttered to himself.

A trail of smoke streaked through the cloudless sky above, leading over a few sand dunes as the plane crashed in a fiery wreck that sent shocks through the air, even this far away.

Henry collapsed more than landed, as it felt like he'd just jumped from a two-story building. He shook off the impact as he got to his feet, surrounded by the deafening winds of the desert and the emptiness therein.

He could make it to the nearest road if he had water—something he only had a shot at finding in the plane wreck.

Henry unwrapped the silk harness from his body and whipped the sand out of one of the layers of his impromptu parachute. He wrapped the silk around his head and tied it into a Litham headwrap, like Tasnim had taught him in Morocco. He covered his nose and mouth with a spare part of the cloth to keep the sand out of his airways before starting his trek towards the plane.

Even without the smoke trail, a path of fiery debris and fallen cargo marked the way to the plane, which was little more than scrap metal, scaffolding, and exposed wires by the time he crested the few dunes that separated them.

With its front half buried probably thirty feet or so into the sand, there was no shot at digging anything out of the cockpit. Most of the soldiers, who would've had canteens on them, were strewn across the desert somewhere south. And despite all the crates and cargo that surrounded him, all of it was just Persian gold and regalia from Alexander's conquests.

"Oh, God, the artifacts..." Henry muttered to himself as he took shelter under the back half of the plane's shadow, left alone with several tons of ancient, wonderfully preserved artifacts.

Well, formerly preserved.

Gold, jewels, and broken pieces of clay tablets lay scattered around the wreck, probably never to be found again.

He fell to his knees, his heart sinking in despair.

His one love in this world was the history and stories of the past. And yet this hunt had demanded that he destroy such rare knowledge, never before seen, never to be recorded. First, the Minoan Palace. Now, the contents of Alexander's Tomb.

Not to mention that if Alexander's *glass* sarcophagus had been lost in the crash, well...then, this whole thing had been for nothing.

Henry took a deep breath. "Don't lose your head, Zhang," he told himself.

He couldn't take much back with him, but he could take *something*. He pulled out his phone and started to snap photos of the wreck and the artifacts that had spilled out of the cargo hold. He picked up a few examples of uncommon coins and shoved them in his pocket.

The intact crates could be recovered, but most of the things in this wreck wouldn't see the light of day again. Not unless someone knew about this and funded an excavation.

As he wove through the artifacts and wreckage, he spotted something in his camera. He lowered it and gasped.

Alexander's sarcophagus lay in the sand under a heavy-looking metal plate. Maybe it was still intact.

He rushed over to the sarcophagus and stepped around some flaming debris. He planted his feet and dug his fingers under the plate, taking a cultivating breath. He channeled Fire Style and strained, gritting his teeth as he struggled to lift the titanium plate. Once he had it a few inches above the sarcophagus, he flipped his grip, allowing him to push it off in one burst of strength. It landed with a crash in the sand.

Henry knelt next to the sarcophagus, taking photos of the hieroglyphics adorning its lid.

The longer he looked at it, the more he started to notice the hieroglyphics changing positions whenever he glanced back at one. He stood and backed away as the markings started to move.

They settled into place as a map. A map of ancient Alexandria. The Macedonian sun marking the spot —Alexandria-Chaldea, in this case—was located to the south of the harbor, around the catacombs of Kom El-Shoqafa.

He wrote it in his phone's notes so he wouldn't forget, although he was down to thirty percent battery and he had miles to go before he reached a place with cell reception.

What's more, he only found one body, with a canteen a quarter of the way full. Even if it took three days to die of dehydration, he'd be useless after one day without water.

He needed to start moving if he wanted to have any chance of survival.

It was evening now, which was a good time to get moving, since the cold night of the desert would be less taxing on him than the heat of the day. It also meant the violet and orange hues in the sky directed him towards the setting sun and thus, west.

The question was which direction he'd traveled.

If the cargo plane was flying the treasure back to the Nile Valley, it was safe to bet he'd been moving northeast all this time, despite the plane's westward trajectory on crashing. If he went south, he'd miss Siwa, even if he could walk that far.

Cairo was farther east than north compared to Siwa, so trying to walk west, back to the road they'd traveled south to the oasis on, was sure to get him killed.

That left north. The northern coast on the Mediterranean was probably the direction with the highest chance of encountering civilization of some kind.

So Henry turned off his phone to conserve battery and started north into an endless ocean of sand.

By far, Henry's least favorite climate was wet and hot. Jungles. By God, he hated jungles. Bugs everywhere. Everything was alive and trying to kill you. Your sweat never evaporated, leaving you with not just swamp ass, but swamp entire-body. The air was stuffy, and you could barely breathe.

But the desert was starting to catch up to jungles in his book. Burning hot in the day, freezing cold at night. And dry every hour of every day.

He didn't want to open his mouth for fear that what little saliva remained in his mouth would evaporate. Throughout the remaining hours of heat, it was actually favorable for him to let his body get swampy. The Tiandihui had given him some limited survival training, telling him not to ration water, but to ration sweat. The longer it took to evaporate, the more efficiently he could use his body's water.

But the frigid night made all that cooling a curse rather than a boon. The wind never let up, as there was nothing to stop it.

He rolled down the sleeves of his mandarin jacket and hugged it to his body as he trudged through the dunes. Through chattering teeth, he licked his lips for the first time in three hours. A waste of water, probably. But his mouth was starting to get sticky.

His eyelids hurt from squinting, a necessity for walking against the winds so as to not get a nice blast of sand into your eyes and scratch up your retinas.

What made it worse was the sand beneath his feet. Every step was a question as to whether it would slip down the dune he was climbing. His ankles twisted and turned as he stumbled through the endless sea.

As he got to the top of a particularly high dune, he stopped, looking around from the only vantage point he had.

He turned on his phone to check for reception. Twenty-three percent. Still no signal.

The tracks behind him were more or less straight.

He turned north and looked to the sky, but shook his head. He knew how to find the north star in Iowa, but not in Egypt. "Shoulda paid attention in Intro to Astro." His voice scratched against his parched throat.

Still, the moonlight was plentiful, and the soft glow offered a serene calm to the scenic vista before him—one that heralded mountains and rocky desert on the horizon.

If only he weren't so dehydrated, he could be in some amount of awe at the alien landscape.

Hopefully, the mountains in the distance had lodging for some tour group or a hut or something.

How did people live out here in single huts? Like...what did they do with their lives? Isolated from everyone.

Well...they probably just did what he did. But they had families.

If only he had the same...

He shook his head and kept true to his northward trajectory. That whole "if only blank weren't happening, I could enjoy this" formula had a few too many applications right now.

If only he weren't exiled from the Tiandihui. If only Weiying had told the truth. If only he had a better brother. If only he *were* a better brother. If only he weren't being hunted. If only he weren't hunting. If only he weren't so desperate...

Then he wouldn't be here, stuck in the world's largest desert. And he'd be able to enjoy things like travelling. Or having squadmates.

If only he hadn't been so eager to get on the plane, he wouldn't have used the hood of their car like a springboard, and they could be out looking for him.

But why would they look for him? Especially now?

God, his footsteps were so slow...He couldn't go any faster without falling from the sand's instability or from pure exhaustion. But at this rate, he'd keel over before he was halfway to the Mediterranean.

Maybe he should keel over. Stop the pain.

You have your swords...

Henry shook his head.

No. That was insane. He'd struggled without end in sight his whole life. He wouldn't stop now. And he wouldn't be like Weiying, curling up into a ball when things got tough.

He had one thing going for him: persistence. He wouldn't let himself die.

The whipping winds had been whistling in his ears for hours, but only now did they start to sound like real whispers.

After everything, don't you deserve a break? they seemed to say.

You never get a chance to rest.

It couldn't hurt to lie down. Just for a little while.

He shook his head. Hallucinations in the desert were supposed to be visual, weren't they? He wasn't *that* dehydrated yet.

The sand is soft this far in the desert.

It's not like you'll get out alive anyway.

"Shut up, shut up!" he rasped.

He panted as he kept walking.

"*Lǎn zhā yī chūmén jiàzi,*" he whispered to himself. A wushu form, taught in verse. A dying tradition, but it was noise he could make to drown out his own mind. "*Biàn xià shì shà bù dān. Biān duì dí ruò wú dǎn xiàng xiān. Kōngzì yǎn míng shǒu biàn...*"

The whispers came back once he finished the chant.

Don't waste your breath...

The wind started laughing at him.

He continued.

"*Lǎn zhā yī chūmén jiàzi...*"

Just as Henry feared, day was much worse than night.

Mandarin jacket tied around his waist, he feared the now-burning sand. The only saving grace was that he'd found his way into a range of dry, rocky mountains. They were still part of the desert, and there was no sign of anything other than desert so far. But at least there was shade.

He sat under a jagged red rock formation, trying to sleep just a bit before continuing past the small mountains, with no shade in sight.

But it was no use.

His head just hurt, pounding with a dehydration-fueled ache. His body craved water more than it did sleep. So he stood and kept moving.

He'd downed most of his water in the morning, giving him another day of functioning.

Slowly, the mountain pass took him downwards, below even what he had to guess was sea level. The stretch of land he was making his way towards was absurdly flat, a mixture of gravel and sand rather than a dune sea.

The sun beating down on him made him start to resent both Marion and Alexander by proxy due to their enthusiasm for the celestial bastard that made him want to die every second.

His thick black hair was a curse, trapping and absorbing heat as it tried to leave through his head. Even while covering it with reflective silk, his dizziness only worsened.

He could hardly take straight steps to save his life. And now that he was on solid ground, that was all down to his own fading motor functions.

But he kept breathing. And he kept walking.

He had to. For Weiying's sake.

Henry shook his head. Even now, he was trying to lie to himself.

You're just in it for the power you'll get to hoard, miser...

Or...maybe he wasn't.

He didn't know. Maybe it was both.

Nonetheless, his mind began to wander as his body kept up the same monotonous pattern of trudging north at a sickly pace.

God, if he could just get some water.

Weiying was under constant pressure to do well. To excel and succeed. To fit in. To be the pride of the family.

It wasn't like Henry didn't understand that. The same had been expected of him for a while. It was just that he had never actually succeeded. And as his parents stopped giving him that attention, he'd stopped looking for it. It was a silent agreement. They wouldn't expect much from him, and he wouldn't expect anything from them.

But Weiying...Weiying was always given that attention in spades. He fit into Chinese culture better, even though Henry knew more about it. He was a better student, a better Magician, and he made himself look like a morally superior person. And that was his drug. As much as Henry desperately reached for the safety of competence, Weiying leaned on the false image of himself that others had constructed for him.

In the Megawg, Weiying had found the equivalent of a drug dealer.

If Henry freed him of it...would it change anything? Weiying hadn't changed as a person. The Megawg had just given him what he craved. It had made him even more dependent than he was.

But if he did nothing, Weiying would get worse.

Henry squeezed his eyes shut. His eyelids were starting to crust up, so he wiped them clean.

No. He had a responsibility first and foremost to himself. Put your own mask on before helping others. That sort of thing.

He stopped, squinting at a dark shape on the barren wasteland.

A mirage?

No, mirages were refractory. This one started walking away from him.

"Hey!" he tried to yell, but it came out more like a hoarse choke. He picked up as much speed as he could and chased after the shape as it walked down a slope.

He stopped as it turned to him.

It was Mr. Fang.

He blinked a few times, and the image vanished.

Okay...*now*, he was that dehydrated.

But as he looked ahead, he stopped. There was a lake in front of him. It was no deeper than two feet, but there were plants growing out of the beautiful blue water.

He sprinted towards the shore of the lake, praying that what he was seeing was real.

He slid to his knees through the gravel and dipped his hands in the water. It was so cool. So clear.

He didn't take a second before cupping his hands and bringing the water to his mouth.

He swallowed before he could even taste it. But when he did, he spat it out.

Salt. Saltier than the ocean itself.

"Fuck..." He gasped. "Fuck! God dammit!"

He weakly punched through the surface of the water, disturbing the image refracting through it.

He stood. He couldn't even drench himself to cool off without covering his skin in salt and drying it out. His fire magic would reward the hours of effort required to boil it with no more than a few droplets.

It was a salt marsh, which, if he remembered correctly, would place him somewhere in the Qattara Depression.

An apt name.

He was a long way from the Mediterranean.

Henry's eyes cracked open. He stared up at the blinding sun for a moment before closing his eyes and rolling over onto his stomach.

"Hey."

Henry glanced up, eyes half-closed.

The shape in his vision started to clear up.

"A...Analise?" He could barely make his voice work.

"Come on. Let's get you up." She offered a hand to him.

He took it, and she pulled him to his feet.

He planted his hands on his knees and heaved, his head swaying with exhaustion, pain, and dehydration.

"God...Thank God you found me. I'm sorry for—"

He looked up. She was gone.

He didn't want to move anymore. He barely had the will to keep standing.

But that tiny voice in the back of his head told him to keep pushing. And it would *not* shut up.

So he kept going.

Look at you. Weiying's voice appeared in his head. He didn't have the drive left in him to protest. *You're pathetic. You'll die in vain, searching for a salvation that'll never come. That's another problem with you: You never get results. You're too prideful to do things the way I do them. The useful way.*

Controlling people through fear and abuse was hardly a useful way.

No wonder you don't get any respect. You're useless on your own. You can't do anything right without extra help from Alexander or your "friends" or whoever.

He's right, in a way.

Henry blinked as the bitterly familiar voice reached his ears. He glanced up to find a girl no more than half a year his senior with wavy brown hair, tanned skin, and broad features.

"Marion?" He could barely part his lips.

She placed a hand on his shoulder. It felt real.

He looked into her eyes, relief and confusion flooding into him.

But the eyes he met were...not Marion's.

They were the same color, but he could sense...scheming. An ulterior motive in the driver's seat of her mind.

Henry slapped her hand away and backed up. "What are you?" he growled.

Upon realizing that it wasn't Marion or even a delusional recreation of her, he felt his chest seize up with existential dread and ancient fear—the same feeling he'd gotten when he saw Hepom Nepots.

He stumbled in the sand, forcing himself to breathe through the overwhelming impulse of his genetics screaming at him to tremble and cower.

What are you talking about, Heinrich?

"No!" His voice lacerated his throat as the fire that burned inside him swelled, torching the edges of his fear. "No, you don't get to call me that. I know you're one of...one of those things! Show yourself! Demon!"

Nothing but silence and the desert wind met his ears for a long moment.

You must think yourself clever.

Marion's image shifted. Her skin warped into some kind of white chitin as the world around Henry was consumed by darkness, blotting out the sky and sun. He looked back at where she had been, only to find a pristine marble statue of a woman.

"You...you made me rip them apart! You made me hurt her!"

I did nothing. It was your rage. Your fear. I just gave you the power to fulfill your desires. Don't be ungrateful, Hanying. The voice seemed to emanate from the lifeless statue, its cold gaze boring into him.

"Who are you?"

I witnessed the first dawn of your wretched species. I will witness its final defeat. I am your only hope for the safety you crave, Zhang. My name was ripped from me long ago, but you may call me...Venus.

"Demon..." Henry snarled. "Get—get away! Leave me be!

The Megawg's laughter echoed in the air, in the heat of the sun, and in the weak pumping of Henry's heart.

Who do you think you are? The Conqueror? Let me go, and Nepots will slaughter all of your little friends.

"I'm a Companion of Alexander the Great."

Henry's right arm went for his butterfly sword. He caught his own wrist, realizing that it was no longer under his control.

YOU ARE A COMPANION TO NO ONE AND NOTHING!

"Talk all you want!" he shouted, struggling against himself. "Now that I know you're here, you can't trick me!"

He could hear it laughing again.

Sure, I can't, Hanying. But that means little. I don't have to trick you. I just have to be here with you. And one day, when you're desperate, when you've been left by your flock, when the world betrays you again, when you understand the futility of your life and the bleakness of your future, when you understand that there is no victory, only survival...

You will beg for my salvation.

Venus's ethereal laughter faded into the wind as Henry wrenched his arm down and the foreign presence in his body faded. He collapsed to his knees as if his bones had simply vanished and his legs had become jelly.

It seemed like the demon was gone. But in his heart of hearts, he could feel her darkness over him. Watching and waiting.

He looked ahead and found himself at the edge of a small cliff maybe a story or two tall. If his ability to process the world in front of him hadn't gone completely.

Was that a road?

He thought he saw pavement, but...well, his mind wasn't exactly reliable. But he was so desperate—so thirsty—that he could no longer resist the impulses of his mind. To him, he'd found civilization at long last. He was done in his search. Now, he just had to touch it.

"Heinrich?"

A final moment of delusion before he would either die or get better.

He fell forward.

"Heinrich!"

"Damn that stubborn bastard!" Analise cried at the open desert.

Yianni drank the last drops of warm water from his bottle before opening the cooler to get another. "Anything?" he asked as Analise packed up her components to make an arcane radar.

"What do you think, genius?" She scoffed. "We have God knows how many miles of desert to cover and not a clue as to where Henry is. At best, my radar only covers a few miles."

"Maybe we should quit it with the radar and just, you know...look for him," Yianni said.

"Why are we even wasting our time?" She shook her head. "We should just go back to the plane crash and get the rest of the gold. Cut our losses."

"And leave him stranded?' Yianni looked at her in disbelief.

"Henry never should've left the damn crash site!" Analise snapped. "It's his fault we couldn't follow him to begin with!"

"Right, it's all on him." Yianni scoffed. "And let me guess, your oversight of the tracking method the Egyptians used. Not your fault? No, there could never be a blemish on Moneta's perfect record!"

Analise stomped towards him and grabbed the collar of his shirt. He resist as she snarled at him. "Say that again and—"

"And what, girl?" Yianni glared at her.

She pushed the muzzle of a handgun into his side.

"Alright, shoot me. Leave my corpse out in the desert. That'll fix your mistake."

"Stop talking like you know me!" She slapped him across the face before throwing her gun to the ground. "You know *nothing*!"

"I'm inclined to disagree." Yianni crossed his arms. "You're a tightly-wound, fragile-as-glass wimp who can't handle taking the slightest responsibility for your actions, who's full of herself from the stick up her ass."

Analise's face twisted in anger. "You want to know why I'm like this?"

"Sure, lass. Tell me how this isn't your fault either."

"I killed my own father," she said, straightfaced.

He blinked.

"My dad was a deadbeat. I thought about doing it for ten years. I thought he deserved it—up until it was time to pull the trigger," she said. "From my perch, I saw the kind of man he really was as he was getting the snot beaten out of him by two Latin Magicians. He was pathetic. Not worth the time. But I was already there, so...I figured I might as well give him a break. It was supposed to be a warning shot to the Magicians. But I didn't aim properly. Shot Dad in the leg. He bled out in the hospital because I hit an artery."

"Well...shit, I'm sorry that happened, but you can't—"

"I will *never* take a shot without aiming again," Analise said. "I'm tightly-wound because if I'm not, people get hurt. You saw what one slip-up can do just today. And you're going to judge me for the...Oh, what did you call it? 'Stick up my ass?'"

Yianni grimaced. "Point taken. But that doesn't mean we're leaving Henry for dead. Let's just keep moving.."

She signaled her acquiescence when she hopped back into their four by four as Yianni started the car, driving north on the Siwa road.

"What the hell did that idiot think he was doing?"

Yianni raised an eyebrow. "Oh, like you wouldn't have done the same."

Analise scoffed. "You might have a point there. Even if you are full of shit."

"Well, broken clocks are right twice a day," he said, grinning.

She glanced up.

Yianni followed her gaze to a blockade made up of two black SUVs in the middle of the open road. "Oh, shit..." he muttered.

He caught sight of flashing reflective silk suits as five Magicians stood in front of the blockade. He stopped the car.

"Analise Abt and Yianni Fotelis. Do I have those right?" Weiying Zhang, in his blue-and-black silk suit, stepped forward. "We have a lot to talk about. Most pressing on my mind, though...what is Alexandria-Chaldea?"

CHAPTER TWENTY-FIVE
The Radiant Bastion

Henry sputtered, coughing as cold water flooded into his mouth, along with his consciousness.

He sat up in the backseat of a four by four, hazy. His head was pounding and his muscles were cramping in all sorts of new places he'd never gotten cramps before.

"Hey, hey! Careful."

Henry glanced to his right and came face to face with Marion's hazel eyes. Eyes with no evil behind them.

He looked around. He was still in the desert, but in a vehicle and on a road.

And Marion was holding a canteen.

Before asking how she'd found him or why she was here, he reached for the canteen.

"Cut it out." She pulled it away. "You have to pace yourself, or you'll dilute your blood. I say when you get to drink, understand?"

He frowned, but capitulated.

"The hell are you doing out here?" Marion asked, sitting in the back with him now that he wasn't lying down.

Henry met her eyes, but broke contact after a spike of guilt stabbed into his chest. "I could ask you the same question."

"I asked first."

He coughed. "We...we found the tomb. It's magnificent. Or, at least, it was. Alexander's magical treasures...they're not here. They're under Alexandria. And they're the only key to defeating the...Megawgs."

"Like from the dreams?" Marion asked. He nodded. "But that doesn't explain why you jumped onto a cargo plane full of mercenaries. Alone."

"The map to the stockpile was on Alexander's sarcophagus," Henry muttered. "And my...my brother is possessed by a Megawg. He has been for years. There was even one on me. I have to save him and protect myself."

Marion nodded slowly.

"I sound delirious, don't I?"

"A little."

Henry sighed. "Well, you're all caught-up now."

Marion scoffed. "With you? If there's one thing you're good at, it's making me wait for the full story." She handed him the canteen. "Take a sip. Just a sip."

"Yes, nurse." Henry sipped from the canteen. Even lukewarm, his body craved more water. But he had the self-control to hand it back.

"'Nurse?'" She took it. "I am the esteemed Dr. Gutenberg. Leading specialist in...deserts."

Henry scoffed instead of laughing, since that would cause him too much pain. "I would expect an esteemed doctor"—he grunted as he shifted his position to be more comfortable—"to be a bit more timely when coming to her patient's aid."

"You're lucky I found you when I did. Or that I found you at all."

Henry grimaced. "Yeah..."

"To waste all that fuel for nothing? That'd be a real tragedy." Marion slapped the hull of her four by four. "This thing is...how do you say? A gas guzzler."

"How *did* you find me?" Henry asked. "*I* could barely find myself. I mean...I didn't know where I...You get my point."

Marion took a sip from the canteen herself before pouring some of it into her hand and flicking it at Henry. He flinched, but the evaporating water did a lot to cool him down in the absence of sweat.

"I heard what went down in Siwa in hours. More people are watching the Egyptians than I thought," she said. "I contacted Analise, and she told me what happened. She and Yianni scoured the east part of this road for you. I covered this part."

Henry blinked. "You...you guys looked for me?"

"Well, yeah," Marion said. "Though I haven't been able to get in contact with them since the start of the search, so...that can't be good."

Henry's eyes widened. "No sign of them? At all?"

"Yianni left me on read two days ago." Marion shrugged.

He grimaced. "Do you have a charger?"

Marion handed him the cord to a portable battery. He plugged in his phone, and once it turned on, he opened his contacts.

And called Weiying.

"Take a drink if you're gonna call someone." Marion handed him the canteen, and he took a somewhat-greedy swig before she stole it back.

The line rang.

Then Weiying picked up.

"I thought I blocked you. What do you want?" asked his younger brother.

"To know if you've done what I think you've done," Henry muttered. "Where are my friends?"

"I don't know what you're talking about."

He was lying. Henry had spent too long listening to his brother speak half-truths and flat falsehoods not to know.

"See you in Alexandria, Weiying."

"You better hope they're good guides."

Weiying hung up.

Marion raised her eyebrows. "Was that your brother?"

"I assume he's forcing Analise and Yianni to lead him to Alexandria-Chaldea. But they don't know where it is, except that it's in Alexandria," Henry said, his mind dissociating from his mixed emotions so violently he was able to map the storm in his head. "If they can't find the fortress, he'll kill them."

"Let's get going, then." Marion sighed.

"I thought you were out." Henry narrowed his eyes, a twinge of resentment bubbling up in his chest.

She gave him an unamused look. "You're in over your head. Do you want my help or not?"

Henry nodded. "Right...thanks."

"Thank the car. It's been the one carrying the aforementioned head around this whole time."

Marion moved to get out of the backseat, but Henry grabbed her arm to stop her. "I meant...for the whole desert thing. Thanks for...well, not letting me die, but also just looking for me in the first place."

Her mouth became a thin, stretched line. "I almost didn't."

Alexandria, Egypt was by far the longest-lasting legacy of the Macedonian Empire. None of the cities founded by Alexander had been so influential and so well-known in history. None of Alexander's Diadochi had been as successful as the Ptolemaic dynasty of pharaohs.

The ancient seaside city oozed with two millennia of history, full of ancient ruins, caliphal fortifications, early modern public buildings, Roman monuments, and Cold-War-era buildings clustered together.

Staying in the rustic Ithaka Hostel right on the coast, Henry and Marion had stopped to clean themselves and their clothes and get a good night's rest before what would inevitably be the final length of this race.

The catacomb of Kom el Shoqafa, the working hypothesis for the location of Alexandria-Chaldea, was a necropolis built under Alexandria in the second century. The timing and associated historical figures fit just right to be involved.

At four in the morning, Henry forced himself awake to pitch-darkness outside. They wanted to get in when security was at its most lax.

Bothering only to check that he had all his weapons and magic components, he met Marion downstairs after just ten minutes.

A few minutes later, he parked their four by four on the street across from the entrance to the catacomb. A cast-iron fence surrounded the block, the entrance marked by a Hellenistic-style gate made of faux marble and filled in the middle by more spiky cast iron. Palm fronds and cacti squeezed their way out from under fallen columns and ruined foundations that had once been the proper entrance to the necropolis.

Henry sighed as he looked at the gate. "Any ideas?"

Marion rolled her eyes as he followed her up to the three-meter-high spiked gate.

"The front door. Never woulda thought of that," Henry said.

"Shut up and look." Marion kicked a chain lying on the ground. "It's been cut."

"Shit."

"Shit's right, Heinrich."

Someone had been here before them. But how? Only Henry knew about the map. He would've expected Weiying to chase after something like the ruins of the Great Lighthouse or the Library of Alexandria.

He cracked the gate open for them to slip inside.

"Do we search for the treasure or rescue our friends first?" Marion asked, straightening out her maroon blouse.

"If we don't have whatever Alexander wants us to find, we won't be able to rescue Analise and Yianni," Henry said as they walked across the flat stone slabs making up a small plaza in the middle of several Greek sarcophagi, made from granite. "So treasure first."

"I was being sarcastic," she hissed. "Is that really what you were told?"

Henry nodded. "Without the weapon we'll find in there, we stand no chance."

A cone-shaped white canopy topping a cylindrical gate of fishnet metal marked the entrance to the catacombs, a spiral staircase surrounding a deep open-air shaft.

Henry leaned over the stone wall of the skylight, which was about two meters in diameter. He stared down into abyssal blackness. The stone cylinder had several windows dotted around it so the staircase could look into the empty space. The acoustics of the stone gave off an eerie ambience. He couldn't tell if he was hearing voices, wind, water droplets, or any number of other noises.

"At least the stairs are Roman," he muttered as the two started the trek downwards, each with a hand grazing the wall.

"What do you mean?" Marion asked.

"Greek steps suck to climb. They're always knee-high," Henry explained. He pulled the KSG-12 he'd stolen off the body of a mercenary to his front and flicked on the flashlight at the end. It allowed him to see where he was going, but the stark contrast between the illuminated stone and the areas still enveloped in shadow made the hair on his neck stand on end.

The entrance to the main tomb wasn't at the bottom of the shaft, but about three-fourths of the way down, through a small passage flanked by semicircular niches with benches for contemplation and mourning. Henry swept his flashlight around as they entered into the top level of the rotunda, a circular chamber held up by six pillars.

Their path took them around the circular gap in the center, then towards a smaller straight staircase. At the end of the stairs was a pillar-supported facade of a strange mixture between Egyptian and Hellenic architecture, much like Henry's trial chamber. Coiled serpents flanked each side facade, each carrying a caduceus wearing the pharaonic crown and situated beneath the shield of Athena.

As Henry swept the area, his flashlight landed on a human face. He yelped and stumbled back into Marion before realizing it was just a statue. "Jesus!" she hissed. "Watch yourself."

Henry shushed her as echoes of voices reached his ears. He pumped his shotgun, swapping to the right tube, which was filled with flechette rounds that would cause less damage to the stonework.

He and Marion peered around the corners of the facade into the main tomb. His breath caught as two men speaking Chinese and clothed in tactical gear started to approach.

These were the Tiandihui's private military.

Henry glanced to his right, meeting Marion's eyes. They nodded at each other, understanding that they would each take down one of them.

Henry stood from behind the corner and shot a flechette round at one of the men nearly point-blank, turning the man's torso into a red mist as Marion pumped half a magazine into the other with her MP5.

They waited to see if anyone would respond to the ruckus. But no one came.

Marion lit the funerary chamber up with orbs of golden light, revealing three waist-high sarcophagi filling up each wall, with art depicting Egyptian myths, funerary rites, and some Hellenistic scenes carved into the space above each of them.

Henry canvassed the area. This chamber was just a small part of the necropolis, but something felt right to him about this place. Like the opposite of what he felt when seeing a Megawg. An intrinsic sort of assurance.

"Do you...feel that?" Marion asked, wary.

Henry nodded. "It means we're on the right track."

He turned to the sarcophagus directly opposite from the chamber entrance and stared at the stone slab covering it. At the scrambled text that slowly put itself into readable language, shifting between English, Chinese, and Arabic.

"*Prove the oath upon the emblem of your Companionship. Speak truthfully, and you shall be welcomed home as brother of the King,*" Henry muttered.

"You can read that?"

"No," Henry said. "It's more like...it made itself readable for me."

"Is it because of the coins?"

"You can't read it? Maybe it's because I touched Alexander's sarcophagus."

"Emblem..." she muttered. "Don't the coins have mantras on them?"

Henry blinked. "You're right!"

He dug the coins out of his pocket and tossed the Wisdom coin back to its rightful owner before looking at his and realizing he still couldn't read Greek.

"So...my Greek isn't bad, but..." she muttered, showing him the face of the coin. It was significantly weathered, and a lot of the letters looked kind of vague. "Apparently, Analise is used to reading through thousands of years of erosion."

"Can you read mine?" Henry handed the Honor coin to her.

She peered at it for a moment before speaking. "*The Fearful cannot believe in an Honorable world. The Honorable believe the world kills the Fearful.*"

Nothing.

"Maybe you have to read it in Greek?"

She did so, to the same effect, though Henry could tell she was just sounding the letters out to the best of her ability. Not that he was any better.

"It says you have to say what's on *your* emblem, doesn't it?" Marion asked, handing the coin back to him. "This isn't mine."

She pulled out her phone, which apparently had the translations of the mantras jotted down. "*The Fearful run from what they cannot grasp. The Wise grasp at what they can see.*"

Still nothing.

She cursed under her breath in German.

Henry cupped his chin. "It just said 'prove,' right? Not speak."

"What about it?" Marion asked.

Henry let the fire fill him, the heat rising to his chest and manifesting as dancing orange wisps on his palm.

Marion glanced at the flames warily, remembering the last time he used them. It took her a second to look away. "I...I think I know what you mean."

Henry pressed his hand against the sarcophagus. Marion's hand glowed with bright white light, forcing him to squint. It was far more intense than any light she'd produced previously. She joined him in pressing her hand against the slab.

Something clicked.

When they removed their hands, Henry weakly closed his fist, extinguishing the flames. Marion couldn't keep her eyes off them, even after they were gone.

"So," Henry murmured, shifting his weight slightly, "what made you change your mind?"

"Huh?" Marion glanced up from his fist.

"About...coming back. Finishing this."

Her mouth quirked at an odd angle. "Well...maybe I was a bit hasty to leave. I mean, even if I leave the squad, we're still friends. For whatever blessings or curses that may bring."

Henry grimaced. "For whatever that may bring..."

Silence permeated a moment between them before Marion dug her fingers under the stone slab of the sarcophagus. "Come help me with this."

"Alright." Henry gripped the bottom of the slab with his fingers, channeling Fire Style.

They both started lifting. Even with Henry's supernatural strength, the slab was heavy as hell.

"I always had my suspicions that I was just a means to an end," she muttered, gritting her teeth as she lifted. "I was just hoping you would prove me...wrong."

The two of them managed to get the slab off the sarcophagus and onto the ground.

"I don't see you that way, Marion." Henry sighed. "I just...what did you want me to do? Not fight? We had our backs up against the wall, and—"

"I never said I disapproved of your violence," Marion said, turning to face him. "I want to believe you, Henry. I do. You're not a bad person. But...I don't know if having a friendship is even possible when you make me feel unsafe."

"I know." Henry pinched the bridge of his nose. "I really do. I just...I—"

Marion grimaced. "We should stay focused. Your brother is still ahead of us."

Henry clenched his fists, but acquiesced, even though he knew she was just trying to avoid the uncomfortable topic. For he too had something he wished to avoid, as the shadowy presence of the Megawg in the background reared its head.

The two of them looked into the sarcophagus to find a deep, pitch-black body of water. And shimmering far below, a small light.

Henry shuddered as his thalassophobia reared its head. "Down we go."

CHAPTER TWENTY-SIX
The Tenth City

Henry and Marion fell from the large body of water onto the stone floor of a grand hall, soaking wet and cold as hell.

He sat up just as his flashlight flickered out. "Shit," he muttered through the darkness.

Marion lit the place up with a ball of the white sunlight she'd obtained from her coin, revealing a much, much larger version of the facade from the catacombs. The only problem was the fact that it was blocked by rocks and debris.

"You've gotta be kidding me," Henry hissed as he approached the blocked-off arch.

"Think it was an earthquake? Like that one that sank part of the city?" Marion asked.

"Nah. There wouldn't be a chamber for us to stand in. My guess is Daoist magic. Probably Lu Ying's work," Henry muttered. "They tried to cover their tracks."

He cupped his chin, trying to think of a way around the problem.

"Now, *that* was the earthquake." Marion gestured with her chin to a pile of broken debris from columns that had once stood in the chamber.

In fact, the whole left side of the cave looked as though a landslide had torn through yesterday.

Henry peered at the wall, realizing it was full of cracks and crevasses. He climbed over a fallen column to one of the cracks that was partially covered by debris. He knelt next to it and gasped. "That's wind," he muttered. "We could probably move through here. We just need to lift...this."

He frowned at the massive column blocking the way, then let his gun hang from its sling and rubbed his hands together as he cultivated Qi with his next breaths. He squatted down and secured a grip on the massive chunk of stone before using Fire Style and lifting with all his might.

He gritted his teeth and groaned as the column slowly started to part from its resting place. His fingers slipped, and the column came crashing down from the single inch it had been lifted.

Henry shook out his hands, cursing.

"This has to be a hundred tons at least." Marion put her hands on her hips. "None of us are lifting that."

Henry considered for a moment. "What about your curse? If you transform, the two of us together could lift it," he said.

The mention of Marion's Impaler's Curse soured her expression. "I...I don't think that's a great idea," she muttered, not meeting his eyes. "There's got to be another way around, right? Or, like—"

"It's either you transform, or I take the chances trying to break this thing like a karate demonstration."

Marion's eyes flickered to the column, then to him. She made no move to join.

"Really? Is the curse that much of an—"

"Yes."

Henry sighed, but took a step back and breathed a few cultivating breaths. If he could focus his strength on a small enough point, he could break the column. Then again, he wasn't sure if Fire Style would be enough.

So he wrapped his arm in his flames, screamed, and brought his elbow down on the column with all the force he could muster.

It might've been a little *too* much, as half of the column collapsed onto the floor. The break was clean, but the force of the impact made another, larger crack in the floor.

"Oh, shi—"

It was all Henry could get out before the ground caved-in beneath them.

He hit his side somewhere on the way down before receiving a faceful of ice-cold water. Panic seized his chest as he swam upward as fast as possible. But whatever he'd fallen into had a current. And a strong one.

He broke through the surface, gasping for air.

"Heinrich!" Marion half-screamed, half-gurgled from somewhere behind him.

"Marion!" he cried out. "Marion, I need light!"

He squinted as a sudden burst of sunlight cast harsh shadows through the darkness. She was close to him.

"I'm here! I'm here!" He swam over to her as the current carried them down a winding underground river streaming through a tunnel of jagged yellow-and-red rock.

"*Mist!* Waterfall!" Marion pointed ahead.

Henry spared a glance over his shoulder to find a steep drop into complete darkness. It was much closer than he would've liked and approaching fast.

He scoured the rocks for some kind of ledge and found a cliff running along the edge of the river directly above him. He threw his rope dart, impaling the rock above, and grabbed onto Marion's waist. "Climb!" he told her, pulling the silk rope taut.

She grabbed onto the rope and pulled herself up onto a ledge about four meters up. But when he attempted to follow her, the dart broke free from the rock.

"Heinrich!"

Henry plunged back into the water, his rope dart loose and the waterfall approaching. He pulled on the arcane tether with the dart as hard as he could, calling it back to his hand just as his shoe slipped off the edge of the riverbed towards the abyssal cavern.

He lashed his dart out, wrapping it around a column of stone at the edge of the drop. He let out a small sigh of relief as the rope's slack was pulled tight and he hung over the precipitous way down, white-knuckling the silk.

"Henry!"

"I'm fine!" He panted.

"The column, Henry! The column is not fine!"

He glanced up as the column started to crack. Fucking sandstone. He flung his legs back, agitating the column's breaking, but building the momentum to jump as Marion ran towards the edge of the chasm.

He threw himself towards her. His fingers latched onto the edge of the rock for a moment before they slipped on a layer of moisture and slime, but she dived just in time to grab him by the wrist.

"I have you." She groaned, then pulled him up just enough for him to get a more secure grip on the rocks and pull himself the rest of the way. He laid flat on his back, letting the adrenaline fade from his body.

"Are you alright?" Marion asked, panting.

Henry pushed himself to his feet. "Waterslides are ruined for me. Forever. But I'm alive."

He glanced down at the seemingly infinite drop and shivered as Marion patted his shoulder. "Let's go," she said, starting off as if they hadn't just almost died.

Her avoidance was really getting to him, even as he could feel Venus's gaze on him from afar.

"You're not being fair." He turned to her. "We almost died because you wouldn't use your full strength. Because it reminds you of something. I don't know what, but from what I know about you, your first instinct when shit hits the fan is to run."

Marion stopped, turning halfway to face him.

He stepped towards her. "We *all* have our dark sides, Marion. You included."

She just stared at him. She was so frustratingly inscrutable. For someone who always wore her heart on her sleeve, she was way too good at hiding her expression. Just her piercing gaze alone set him on edge. He didn't even know if she was angry.

Henry pinched the bridge of his nose. "I...I acted like an animal in Troy. I was backed up into a corner, so I guess I...lashed out. It was uncalled-for." He took a deep breath. "What I'm trying to say is...I was scared of losing anyone else that day. Especially you." He muttered that last admittance so sheepishly he wasn't sure she heard it. But he dared to meet her eyes, anxiety stabbing into his chest like a bed of needles.

Downcast, her gaze stared into the dark chasm. Her face now was less inscrutable and more...conflicted. "We..." Her voice broke slightly. "We have a long way to catch up with the others."

Henry's heart sank into a pit as deep as the one behind him. She was even running from this very conversation. But he nodded. "Yeah..."

He followed her up a winding pathway in the rocks, emerging onto a drier, flatter path above that went past the column that had broken on him. He squinted at the ground beneath him, brows furrowed in scrutiny.

"Are these...bricks?" he asked, touching the small, faint lines in the seemingly flat stone beneath their feet. "Like a pathway?"

"There are some manmade carvings here." Marion's fingertips grazed a wall with an Egyptian-style image of...well, Henry didn't quite know what. The image was too weathered to tell. "And those columns seemed carved as well."

"That means we're close, right?" Henry asked, starting forward again.

"I suppose you could call that a shortcut." She shrugged.

As they walked, the cave tunnel around them started to become more polished. Eventually, as the walls became perfectly rectangular and the dry irrigation canals started to have muck, mud, and eventually running water in them, it became clear that they'd found their way into some kind of ancient sewage system.

Marion reduced the strength of her light, as the sewers allowed light to stream through several rusty grates. "What's the point of a storm drain? We're underground," she muttered, voice just barely louder than the flowing water in the canals they walked alongside.

"They aren't for storms. They're for chamber pots," Henry said, theorizing.

Marion gagged.

Henry peered out of one of these grates and grabbed onto the bars. It had probably been at least a thousand years since anyone had inhabited this place, so hopefully the grate was *somewhat* sanitary. He pushed with a little juicing from Fire Style, causing it to pop out of the stone it was built into, then pulled himself out of the sewer before helping Marion.

"Whoa..." she whispered.

Henry's jaw hung half-open as he drank in their surroundings.

It was as though he'd gone back in time.

Never in his life had he seen such a well-preserved array of Macedonian buildings. White-columned pavilions, red-tile roofs, painted reliefs and statues. Terraces and temples and pristine buildings dotted every inch from wall to wall of the...well, fortress just didn't seem right. This place was a city. A buried city under Alexandria.

"This is it, isn't it?" Marion asked. "Alexandria-Chaldea."

Henry closed his eyes for a moment, taking a deep breath. The fire inside him seemed to flare up and prickle his spine. As if they were responding to being here. As if they'd come home.

"You feel that, right?" he asked.

Marion nodded.

Henry took notice of the wide canals and aqueducts crossing through the fortress and traced the origin of their flow to the Hellenistic–Egyptian fusion of a building that sat in the center of all this. The aqueducts sat on high, as if carrying water down from the temple rather than an actual water source.

He gestured to the massive citadel. "I don't know about you, but my money's on Alexander's stash being up there."

"I—" Marion took a step back. "What's that?"

Henry whirled around, following her gaze. He peered around the corner of one building and found a spherical piece of metal lying in the middle of the street.

Furrowing his brow, he picked it up. It was a helmet.

"Some kind of...Macedonian helmet," he muttered. "Or maybe it's Corinthian."

"The make doesn't matter. What's a lone helmet doing out here?"

"Could be a magic item." He handed it to her.

She shook her head. "Can't sense anything."

Henry glanced back down at the spot he'd found the helmet, then towards his left. He blinked as he froze. The helmet clattered to the ground.

"What? What is..." Mairon approached him and fell silent. "Oh, God..."

In the street next to them was a pile—no, a whole layer—of corpses, now skeletons dressed in Hellenic armor.

"Jesus Christ..." Henry muttered, walking towards the pile of human bones, the implications of their presence dawning on him. Some of the ribcages still had spears and swords in them.

He picked up a still-armored torso and peered at the symbol engraved in the metal. It was worn from time, but he could faintly make out an image of an eagle.

"The emblem of Ptolemy..." He set the body back down.

Another shield had the Lion of Lysimachus on it.

"Did someone seriously try to attack this place?" Marion asked. "It's an underground fortress that's brimming with magic. How is that even possible?"

Henry knelt down to find another insignia on another breastplate—a Seleucid anchor.

"I'm starting to think that whoever started the fight had an invite," he murmured. "Let's keep moving."

As they moved through the city, they found more bodies strewn about. Men, women, *and* children. Just how many people did Alexander plan to have living here? And what about this place made it suited for combatting the Megawgs? Or...unsuitable, given the ruins.

But as they explored more of the labyrinth of buildings and temples, it dawned on Henry: This wasn't a city. It was an industrial-scale Magician academy. For every store and market stall, there was a temple, scribes' study, ancient art studio, amphitheater, wrestling ring, or classroom. It was an ancient, underground version of the Daba monastery he had gone to—a giant Magician school.

Alexander had wanted to create an army of Magicians to fight the Megawgs. Henry wondered if that would even work. Theoretically, it made some sense. Magicians attained their powers from being in touch with the reality of their culture. Megawgs seemed to prey on...well, feasibly, their diet could include detachment from reality. That tended to brew quite a bit of fear. But Magicians would also be prime targets for possession, being the biggest threat.

Clearly, it had failed in practice. The dimly lit, dusty, and dead fortress was a testament to the results of Alexander's experiment—if the bodies weren't proof enough.

Henry found emblems from all four of the Diadochi, as well as Antigonus and Antipater, men who were...Diadochi-adjacent.

As Henry and Marion tiptoed around a mess of broken bones, they emerged into a plaza before a ring of walls cutting off the inner city from the outer ring. The plaza's centerpiece was a fountain surrounded by columns and topped with a tile roof, like a Greek gazebo. From the roof of the circular pavilion, several bodies swung from ropes all around the fountain.

All had been hanged.

Marion gasped. "*Mein Gott...*"

"Christ," Henry muttered as he walked up to the bodies.

Only one of them was armored. The rest were in civilian clothes. Some of the skeletons were so small, they could only have been children. The word *Gawg* was scrawled in Syriac onto one of the thin columns in red ink—or, more likely, blood. The one armored corpse was missing its arms and legs, and if its flesh hadn't decayed, Henry would've bet some other choice bits would've been missing.

"Look at their faces." Marion shuddered.

Henry looked at the other corpses and saw that the orifices in their skulls were filled with gold and silver. They'd likely been killed by having molten metal poured into their mouths and eyes.

"Why would they do something like this?" Marion whispered, horrified.

Henry approached the armored figure. He had the hoplite helmet insignia of the Antigonid Kingdom on his breast. Henry peered into the fountain under the bodies and reached into the water, pulling a plumed, corroded iron helmet from the water. Such a helmet would've been common among Satraps or other similarly high-ranking officials in Alexander's former empire.

Considering what he'd seen so far, there was only one person this could be.

"Oh, my God..." Henry whispered. "This is Antigonus the One-Eyed."

"Who?"

"One of the Diadochi. But during the third Diadochi war, the other four allied against him, and Lysimachus got most of his territory in Anatolia," Henry said. "This battle must've happened after Alexander's death. Sometime between 305 BC and 300 BC." He felt like he was starting to put the pieces together. "I'm guessing the other bodies are his family."

"But why?"

Henry pointed at the blood inscription on the marble next to them. "They must've thought Antigonus was a Gawg. Possessed by a Megawg."

"So, the others did...this?"

"If this was built as a fortress against the Megawgs, and one of the people closest to you turned out to be a traitor, well...I don't know. It would make sense to me." Henry shrugged.

"Let's just...move on before I get sick." Marion shielded her eyes from the sight.

They were unable to pass through the petrified wooden gates of the walls blocking in the inner city, so Henry threw his rope dart up the wall and had the two of them climb the ten-meter face of the battlements.

But as soon as they pulled themselves on top of the walls, Marion dragged both of them down, hiding behind the inward-facing ramparts.

"What is it?" Henry hissed.

She jabbed a thumb towards the interior of the city.

He spared a glance around the ramparts and looked down at an alleyway filled with ten or so men in tactical gear, carrying guns. They were speaking Mandarin.

"Guess we found the rest of Weiying's entourage," he murmured, craning his neck as he tried to get an accurate count.

"Look further back." Marion pointed at one of the abandoned buildings just outside the alleyway.

Henry narrowed his eyes, peering through the window in the building's front to find...Analise and Yianni. They were being held at gunpoint, their wrists bound, cut off from magic by Nullifier Bands.

And no sign of Weiying.

"Shit...Change of plan. Friends first." He sighed, sitting back behind the ramparts. He didn't like the idea of giving Weiying time to find the citadel, but he was already late. They had every reason to kill Analise and Yianni whenever. "I'm gonna need you to cover me."

Marion pulled out her MP5 and chambered a round before meeting his eyes and nodding. He sighed, drawing his butterfly swords.

"Hold on," she said. She pulled a runestone from her pocket and handed it to him. "Take this. Just in case."

Henry pocketed the stone with his coin before throwing himself off the wall. The blades of his swords sank into the shoulders of the closest soldiers. He hefted one body up as the others took notice and fired at him, then threw the body into one of the two closest to him before jamming both his swords into the neck and ribs of the second. He spun around and lashed his rope dart out, catching another man in the abdomen. Pulling on the rope, he threw the man into the wall of a nearby building.

Marion provided covering fire against the remaining six as Henry jumped up the walls and drew his guandao from his ear. He brought the polearm down with a heavy crash, cleaving two men in half as the other four fled from the alleyway.

Henry stowed his glaive and called his swords back to their sheaths as Marion jumped off the wall, breaking her fall with one of her arcane shields. He plucked a pump-action shotgun off one of the bodies before the two of them headed towards the building at the end of the alleyway.

It was a circular, open-concept studio of some kind, likely used for sculpting and statue-making, especially given the numerous stone statues that were providing cover for Weiying's soldiers.

Marion created another shield as rifle rounds rained down on them. Henry returned fire with the shotgun, but the magazine ran out pretty quickly, so he dropped the gun and fueled his body with Qi. He launched himself into the studio and shattered a soldier's jaw with a tornado kick. Marion rushed up behind him and fired three concussive bolts into a soldier who had nearly plunged a bayonet into his back with an old Soviet SKS.

Henry drew his butterfly swords and whirled around, the edges of his weapons sparking against a Chinese broadsword. His vision exploded with stars as a pommel crack against his jaw. He stumbled to a knee, but managed to push himself back up. Marion steadied him by his shoulders as he clutched his face.

Shen's shit-eating grin was punctuated by a flourish of his double daos. He dragged the tips of his swords on the stone ground as he stalked his prey. The soldiers formed up behind him.

"Weiying figured you'd come to rescue your friends first." Shen scraped his swords against the ground like matchsticks, causing the blades to erupt in flames.

Henry wasn't sure if he could handle the gunmen and Shen at the same time. Either one would require almost all his attention. Marion could help, but she wouldn't be able to take on either by herself.

Henry glanced at Analise and Yianni near the back of the studio. They were cut off from magic. If he took a risk trying to free them, even a little, there was a chance the Nullifiers would delay them from helping him.

He wanted his Companions to help. But it was mostly up to him. If he wanted to win, he was going to have to push it. Almost like Troy.

Almost.

Henry delved into the fire billowing inside of him and let it swell in a way he hadn't since that day in Turkey. He could sense the Megawg's influence, but so long as he was watching it, it seemed content just to watch him. No bad fuel for the fire.

That was what it was. The fire itself was not a product of his honor. It was neutral—something that could be fueled by the toxic, black smoke of hatred or the eternal fuel of his honor.

Even though the Megawg was still there, relief filled him alongside the fire.

"What's wrong, Hanying? Getting cold feet?" Shen taunted.

Henry flexed his grip on his swords. Marion moved to join him at his side, but he held her back. "Go help them." He nodded towards Analise and Yianni.

"Heinrich, don't be stubborn," Marion hissed. "You can't fight them all!"

"I know," Henry said. "That's why I need you to help them. I'll cover you."

He met her worried gaze. But she nodded and backed off.

"You were always too full of yourself." Shen lowered into a Northern-Style stance.

Henry fueled his body with Fire Style. He stomped on the ground, breaking a part of the stone floor, then kicked up, throwing the dust and sediment at Shen's eyes. Shen stumbled back as Henry hit his mark.

Swapping to Metal Style, Henry threw himself at the gunmen like a twister of steel, making his way around the room in mere moments.

But when he was finished, not a single man had a cut on him. Rather, all their rifles fell to scraps.

Henry turned back to face them as Shen finally got the dust out of his eyes. *Now* he could take them.

"Kill him!" Shen roared.

Without rifles, the men drew knives and handguns and fell upon Henry all at once.

He launched his swords at two men with pistols, skewering them before they could fire, then sidestepped a wayward stab with a knife and broke the arm of the man wielding it at the elbow before throwing him into two other men. He threw himself over an enemy's shoulder to get himself out of the middle, speared another handgunner with his rope dart, retracted it, and spun the weapon around his body to give himself some space.

Henry kicked the dart out, nailing a soldier between the eyes, then called one of his swords back to his hand just as another soldier brought his knife down. The sword slammed into the man's hand with a crunch before he cut the soldier's throat.

He called his rope dart back to his wrist and his second sword back to his hand in quick succession as Shen slashed at him.

Shen wove his swords around his shoulders and ribs, building up flames until he launched two slashes of fire through the air. Wrapped in his own arcane flames, Henry spun around with a hook kick, swatting the attack out of the air.

Shen pounced, coming at Henry with a storm of chain stabs, putting him on the back foot. He parried both swords at once before planting his sole in Shen's sternum. The Magician went flying, giving Henry just enough reprieve to see one of the soldiers grab something that wasn't a rifle from behind a barricade—and, as she was trying to keep to the side of the studio, point it at Marion.

It was a grenade launcher.

Henry threw himself at the man, but failed to close the distance before the weapon fired.

"Marion!" he cried out, but it was too late for her to react.

He had to do something. Flying in the face of all his beliefs about trust and investment, he poured his fire into his soul like he never had before. The flames overflowed from his body, boosting his physical abilities beyond what even Chinese magic was capable of.

What...what is this?

Henry threw his rope dart out, wrapping it around Marion's waist. He yanked as hard as he could, Newton's laws throwing him toward the grenade in the process of pulling her away.

As the grenade exploded on the wall nearby, the blast felt like a truck hitting him. He landed on the stone ground hard enough to knock all the wind out of him.

"Oh, my god!" Marion scrambled to her feet and rushed to his side.

Henry gritted his teeth and tried to push himself to his knees. He looked at her as she helped him to his feet. "Are you alright?"

Marion stared at him for a moment before scoffing. For a few moments, she pressed a glowing palm to his side, where the pain was starting to set in.

The rest of the soldiers took the grenade launcher away from the man who'd fired it and glanced nervously at the Companions.

Henry called his swords back to his hands, causing the soldiers to flinch. Slowly, he walked over to Analise and Yianni, whose eyes were darting between him and the soldiers. He cut them loose and destroyed their Nullifier bands, turning back as Shen struggled to stand.

"Took ya long enough." Yianni chuckled, rubbing his wrists.

Henry readied his swords, but the soldiers seemed unwilling to attack first.

But then they all parted.

"What the hell is going on he—" Min broke through the line of soldiers, followed by Chen Bo and Lu Ying.

Chen Bo readied his polearm as Lu Ying's palm lit with azure flames. Min was slower to pull out her bladed fans.

"You're finished now, Zhang!" Shen snarled.

Henry met Min's uncertain eyes.

"Why are any of you here?" Henry asked in Mandarin. He looked at the soldiers. "None of you are getting paid enough to do this. You four have no obligation here." He looked to his former squadmates.

"We have our oaths," Chen Bo growled.

"To your brothers. Not to Oathbreakers," Henry said. "Zhang Weiying broke his oaths when he lied about me breaking mine. By all accounts, you all still owe an obligation to *me*. But even if you don't believe me, Weiying killed Mr. Fang. Clear as day. That makes him an Oathbreaker."

Chen Bo's weapon lowered slightly.

"We..." Lu Ying muttered. "What else are we supposed to do? Weiying will kill us too. He's powerful enough to do it."

"I'm his brother. I'll take care of him," Henry promised. "So go home."

That goes for you too, he thought at Venus.

The Megawg seemed to flinch in response to the flaring of his fire. **You want me to stay so you can burn me. I'm no fool.**

With that, he felt the Megawg's presence vanish, like a grinding anxiety suddenly being relieved from his chest.

In spite of Alexander's failures to succeed against this enemy, whatever magic was now within him had pushed on the Megawg's sense of self-preservation. So maybe this weapon might actually work.

At the same time, Min closed her fans and stowed them away.

"What are you three doing?" Shen turned, indignant.

"Going home," Min muttered. "Alright, everyone! Pack up!"

Though it took some time for hesitation, the soldiers began to move, weaving around the bodies on the floor. Most of them seemed relieved not to meet a similar fate. In just a few minutes, they packed up their supplies and left the studio.

And Henry felt pain seeping into his body in place of adrenaline. He stumbled, Marion catching him.

"Jesus, are you alright?" Analise asked.

"I'll take care of him," Marion said. "Go arm yourselves. We're going to have to take Alexander's treasury by force."

The other two nodded and left the studio in search of weapons and their arcane components.

Henry's labored breathing softened as Marion sat them down and placed a healing hand above his wounded side. "You're so reckless..." she mumbled.

"I like to think of it..." Henry winced. "As taking calculated risks."

"No wonder you were in the humanities," she scoffed. She took a pause to soften. Henry could feel tension leaving her muscles in her embrace. "Thank you for saving me."

"After all the times you've covered my ass? It's the least I could do." He cast his gaze down at her small hand, holding him up as her other one healed him.

Silence filled the studio as she finished healing him. Henry turned and met her eyes.

"I...I'm sorry," he said. "I was afraid back in Troy. I've always been afraid. I thought that if I didn't care about myself, no one else would. I...still kinda feel that way. When that dark part of me took over...I didn't give you the credit you deserved. It won't happen again. I promise."

Marion gave him a small grin that caused warmth like a hearth's fire to spread through his chest. "I'm sorry too. For what it's worth, the reason I came back looking for...it's because I saw that, even in spite of your fear, you kept fighting. It made me realize that maybe you were right about how I always run. I don't want to keep doing that. As long as you can put your trust in us."

Henry smiled. "Are we square?"

Marion nodded.

They got to their feet. Henry stretched, and the two of them met up with Analise and Yianni back outside.

He turned to his squad, reunited and ready. "Alright, Companions. This is the home stretch. Let's finish it."

CHAPTER TWENTY-SEVEN
Enyalios

The Companions crossed the stone bridge across a moat surrounding the complex, which appeared to be the only way in or out unless you were looking for a swim in quite rough-flowing water.

The water for the moat poured out from the bottom of rigid, symmetrical geometric stone staircases propped up on square Egyptian- or Babylonian-style columns. The water fell through an opening provided by the stone walkway splitting at the end of the bridge and wrapping around to the stairs.

They took the right path. At the top of the stairs, the diverging paths met again, combining into a walkway towards another center staircase that led up to a fairly high foundation, upon which sat the citadel proper, surrounded by four massive pillars at each corner of the foundation, which blazed with electric blue flames. The citadel was like a giant yellow-beige Parthenon without the Hellenistic flair for extra detail and with a very Egyptian smoothness to its columns and roof. On top of the roof was an obelisk half the size of the Washington monument and made of some jet-black stone inlaid with gold in Hieroglyphic script and topped with a solid-gold point.

"You have to admire the architecture," Henry muttered. "In spite of the cultural whiplash." He took a photo of the grand citadel with his phone.

"What I wouldn't give to be a regular treasure hunter." Yianni scoffed.

"Oh, please, you wouldn't last a day doing this without magic." Analise chuckled. She sighed as she looked up at the citadel. "Besides, who else can say they found the tomb of Alexander the Great? Or, for that matter, a hidden fortress under Alexandria?"

The four of them came to a massive set of doors. Exhilaration set in, prickling Henry's ribcage from within.

"Ready?' Marion asked, setting her hands on one of the doors.

Henry joined her as Analise and Yianni put their hands on the other door. "Three, two..." he counted.

They shoved. The wooden doors flung open, releasing a whole cloud of dust. Henry waved it out of the way and stepped into the citadel's darkness.

Braziers lit up with golden flames, revealing not a citadel, but one massive chamber before them—a massive throne room. It was as grand as any could expect it to be, the main path to the thrones flanked by massive painted columns made of smooth sandstone with old banners hanging down between them.

There were seven thrones. If Henry had to guess, the one made of gold and elevated on a smooth block of black stone imprinted with a Macedonian sun was Alexander's. The others must've belonged to the main players after the Partition of Babylon—the four Diadochi in the end, plus Antigonus and maybe Antipater, who had reigned over Macedon before Cassander.

Behind the columns lay piles on piles of treasure and magic so dense that even Henry could feel it. It was a greater horde than even that of Alexander's Tomb. He recognized Egyptian gold, Greek weapons, Indian sculptures, Babylonian tablets, and Sogdian textiles.

It was hard to differentiate between what was magic and what wasn't. But Henry could pinpoint the strongest presence coming from a wooden box that sat on Alexander's throne.

In awe, the Companions approached the thrones and the semicircular expansion of the main promenade nearer to the seats of the Diadochi that allowed space for Macedon's court.

In that court were three of four skeletons clad in armor with helmets belonging to Satraps.

Only one of them sat on a throne—the one nearest to Alexander's on the right. The skeleton was similarly armored, with a piece of yellowed parchment under one hand and a knife in his other.

"What the hell?" Analise muttered. "This is like that well outside."

"That was the body of Antigonus, one of Alexander's generals," Henry explained. "I'll give you three guesses as to who these are." He approached the skeletons, while Marion and Yianni seemed more taken with the magical items.

"The Diadochi?" Analise furrowed her brow. "That doesn't seem right."

"Lysimachus, Cassander, Seleucus." Henry pointed at the three on the ground, eyeing their emblems, then looked at the one on the throne. "Ptolemy."

Analise walked over to the throne and pulled the parchment out from under Ptolemy's hand.

"Can you read it?" Henry asked.

"It's sloppy. Probably written in a panic. But I can make it out well enough," she said. "*To any who would follow in the footsteps of the Companions.*" She began to read. "*Know what happened here so you may never repeat our mistakes. I must write quickly and thus skip over much context. I can already feel her influence on my mind. The Megawgs are a cunning, but vile species. When we brought the idea of Alexandria-Chaldea to our king and brother, we didn't know that one of us had already betrayed the cause. Antigonus was Gawg, servant of the she-devil who calls herself Venus.*"

Henry's eyes widened, but he didn't interrupt as a chill crept up his spine.

"*We killed them, not knowing that all my brothers, even his majesty Alexander himself, had fallen victim to the Megawgs. I believe I am the only one who has yet to lose soundness of mind. But I cannot know.*

"*We have no one to blame but ourselves. Our king gave his life to imprison them beyond the reaches of man, but that still did not stop her.*

"It all started with the Partition of Babylon. When we divided the empire, our bonds of brotherhood, forged on the battlefield, were tarnished by resentment and politics spawned in the court of Babylon. We foolishly thought ourselves immune to the Megawg influence, having become the only men aware of them. Your tests may have convinced you to think the same.

"But no man is safe from the Megawgs. There is no secret to defending oneself against them. No secret weapon to fight them.

"All it took was a bit of paranoia. When Antigonus turned on us, our paranoia grew a hundredfold, and we took matters into our own hands.

"It only invited the Megawgs in.

"The remains of our brotherhood lie dead before me. Our only hope lies in our own Pandora's Box. When the Megawgs take power again, the box and the stories within will be our only reminder of human virtue.

"May my journey across the Styx be swift enough to escape her. All glory to Alexander III. Glory to Macedon. Glory to mankind.

"...Ptolemy I Soter."

Analise put the letter in Ptolemy's lap. Henry shivered, placing a hand on his shoulder as if to check whether Venus was truly gone.

"So that means..." Marion muttered.

"He killed himself," Henry muttered, squatting down next to Cassander. "The old Companions. Alexander's Companions...they were driven mad by the Megawgs. Even Alexander was."

"If Alexander himself wasn't safe from the Megawgs...then what the hell was with all those tests up until now?" Yianni demanded. "He's no better at resisting them than we are!"

Henry took a step back, observing the entire room. "So...after Alexander's death, the Diadochi built this fortress around the same time as the Partition of Babylon." He assembled the full picture. "Antigonus is already a Gawg, but they don't know it yet. Then the first war of the Diadochi breaks out. Barely a year of peace goes by before the third war. I'm guessing the others knew about Antigonus by this point, since they demanded he cede his territory to them in our known records. Antigonus attacks Alexandria-Chaldea, being surrounded in the outside world. He betrays the others and lets this 'Venus' into the fortress. And she starts infecting their minds, using their paranoia to turn them against each other. Ptolemy draws the rest of the Diadochi here and kills them to stop their influence from spreading further. And before Venus can take over Ptolemy, he offs himself."

He scoffed in disbelief.

"These are the men who forged the Hellenistic world. All driven to madness and death by one Megawg. Because of a little bit of fear..."

"It's...unbelievable," Marion murmured.

"How are we supposed to do *any* of what those dreams have been telling us?" Analise asked, her voice quivering slightly. "The ones who knew, the ones who had the best chance, all failed! How are we supposed to succeed?"

"It's simple, really. You don't."

Henry whirled around as Weiying Zhang stepped out of the shadows.

His hair was all a mess, hastily tied in a knot. His eyes were sunken, with dark bags under them. He wasn't wearing his Tiandihui suit, but his white-and-blue silks. His stance was off-balance and sloppy.

Henry's eyes widened as his heart sank. The hunched-over, long-limbed, distorted shadow of Hepom Nepots towered over Weiying, standing with a brambly hand on his shoulder like a predator.

Henry figured that creature knew how to find Alexandria-Chaldea. If Venus had been here before, it wasn't unthinkable the others would know of it.

Weiying, at its behest, stepped forward.

You're not going to let them take what's yours. You earned this. But your brother makes you look like the loser. Are you going to let him make you look like the loser?

Analise and Yianni each started hyperventilating, while Marion stood perfectly still, eyes wide.

"Don't be afraid," Henry said, in spite of his own quickening heart. "They only have power if you're afraid."

Analise leaned on a column for support as she started crying. Just this monster's presence was enough to give people panic attacks.

"Fuck...fuck this, mate. No way. I'm not..." Yianni's words petered out. He grabbed his head and collapsed to his knees, his face pale.

Marion's hands held her arms tight like she was hugging herself, frozen in fear.

Henry was starting to sweat. He had to show them confidence. Even if it was false.

He squeezed his eyes shut and took a calming breath. He let the fires swell.

"Get a hold of yourselves!" he snapped. "Stand down, Weiying. Zhao Squad went home."

So they, too, abandon you?

Henry's face twisted as the Megawg's voice wormed its way into his brain.

"I'm glad I waited, Hanying," Weiying said. "Now, I have all the answers I need. Alexander himself, the man who prided himself on being beyond our reach...he, too, succumbed. As all have. As all do. As all will. You're the ones who should give up. No one here is any match for the Nameless."

Marion, at least, seemed to have gotten her bearings again, though her breathing was labored, as if she had to force each exhale.

"I need you," Henry said. "Can you hold him back?"

Marion summoned her staff.

"This treasure is mine, Hanying," Weiying said. "*I* found it. You'll give it to me, along with your lives. Or I'll—"

Marion let off a blinding flash of light.

Henry pivoted and sprinted towards the thrones.

It was clear he would have to fight Weiying to get rid of the Megawg. And the only way to do that was to open the box.

He leapt up onto Alexander's throne and flipped open the hinged lid of the wooden box. Something burning slammed into his chest.

World-wide phenomena are rare in the course of history. That's putting it mildly. But there are a few times throughout the annals in which the world at large has experienced great suffering.

The crisis of the World Wars being the most recent.

Another example is the seventeenth century, called the General Crisis by some, where Europe was devastated by the Protestant Reformation and wars of religion. The Ottoman Empire suffered from political instability and overextension, struggling to control their newly conquered lands. China experienced desolation and instability with the fall of the Ming Dynasty and the conquest of the Qing. And the entire planet grew colder, initiating the "Mini Ice Age," which made it harder to grow food all over the globe.

In the third century, both the Han and Roman Empires collapsed as institutions nearly in unison. That particular crisis had something special. It was the end of an age, a reboot for the lifecycle of civilization.

And in the late second or early first millennia BC, the Bronze Age Collapse brought every civilization in the Near East to ruin. Similarly, an age-ending apocalypse.

Some historians believe that after this early recorded collapse, a period called the Axial Age followed, where unlinked groups of people innovated philosophy and religion to move away from the fear-based cults of gods who would wipe out cities if they weren't given enough offerings.

Instead, they established religions with gods who would negotiate.

The Hebrews were the first, forming a covenant with Yahweh. The Greeks created new ways of understanding the gods' creation. Zoroaster started his religion in Iran. India reformed their Vedic texts and began to worship under the banners of Hinduism, Buddhism, and Jainism. Confucius and the Hundred Schools of Thought formed Chinese religion as we understand it today.

Karl Jaspers first described the concept as "an interregnum between two ages of great empire, a pause for liberty, a deep breath bringing the most lucid consciousness."

He had no idea how right he was.

Before the Bronze Age Collapse, the world of Magicians was one of fugitives and mystery cults rather than high art and intellectual pursuit. The objective world was an afterthought to the mysteries of chaos. And so all bowed to chaos. The Gods of Nature all across the world viewed humans as slaves to be kept in line by fear and fear alone. Too small, stupid, and insignificant to give any amount of lenience or respect.

So, when the god-kings and emperors of the world lost control of their populations and saw their empires crumble under the weight of their own arrogance, the gods of nature attempted to reestablish their hegemony.

But by that point, Magicians had risen in strength and number enough to parley with the gods of human virtue and the gods who were willing to work with humans rather than oppress them.

In a violent democratization of warfare and magic, the Bronze Age Collapse brought gods low, and the Axial Age that followed was marked by the establishment of new religion, new philosophy, new magic, and the Magicians' Circles, such that no age like the one before could come again.

One of these battles occurred in Chengtang Pass. The Eastern Dragon King had long ruled over the surrounding area from his underwater palace. He and his fellow Dragon Kings wreaked havoc on the people of China whenever they pleased, only to be quelled by enormous tributes and sacrifices.

But even as the Dragon King received plenty of animals, goods, and food as tribute, he hungered for the flesh of young children.

Before, whenever he desired children, he would have them. None would stand in his way, lest he flood the land and unleash scourges of storms.

But this time, he made the mistake of targeting the friend of a boy named Nezha, an impetuous, rash boy with a good heart, but uncontrolled violent tendencies. Nezha defended the children of Chengtang pass with supernatural abilities and aggressive demeanor, killing the Dragon King's men who had been sent in his place.

Assuming Nezha was an upstart Magician, the Dragon King sent his son, Ao Bing, to deal with him. Wielding his silver spear and powers over cold and ice, Ao Bing attempted to kill him.

But Nezha managed to slay the prince, even as a dragon.

The boy didn't understand the consequences of what he'd done. In his ruthlessness, he'd made it untenable for the Dragon Kings to do anything other than destroy Chengtang pass.

So, as the four Dragon Kings threatened to flood the settlement and report Nezha to the Jade Emperor, he offered to kill himself instead.

The Dragon Kings accepted his offer, and Nezha slit his own throat with the blade of his father's sword.

In light of his sacrifice, a Daoist sage brought Nezha back to life with flaming wheels on which to fly, a chakram to fight, an armillary sash to bind, and the ability to give himself three heads and six arms to fight multiple opponents. He rose from the dead as a god of human virtue and, thanks to the belief of those in Chengtang Pass, became a protector god of rebels and those on the outskirts of society.

And now, he lay at the bottom of Alexandria with the other gods of China, as well as countless other pantheons, waiting for someone with a seed of honor ready to be cultivated in them.

Waiting to one day resume battle with the gods of fear.

Waiting for the day the Companions of Alexander would be ready for war with the Megawgs.

Henry woke up not in Alexandria-Chaldea, nor in the river in his dreams. No, he opened his eyes once again to the shudder-inducing sight of miles and miles of desert under a blazing sun.

Except he wasn't alone.

His Companions stood at his sides. And Iskandar stood before them.

"My Companions!" Iskandar's arms swelled out with his voice. "Today, we welcome four new soldiers into our ranks!"

Henry flinched as an army's worth of roars and cheers slammed into him from behind. He turned to find an *actual* army behind them—a horde of soldiers dressed in fatigues and armor from every period of history and every nation on earth, from bronze-clad Mycenaeans and Sumerians, to Macedonians, to Roman legionnaires, to knights in full plate, to linemen with muskets, and even soldiers from the world wars. There were Shaolin monks, Maori warriors, Varangians, Latin American revolutionaries, and every other variety of man or woman wise to the ways of war in history.

But it wasn't just soldiers. He recognized famous artists, writers, philosophers, economists, rulers, and Magicians among their ranks.

Iskandar stepped forward, holding the box in his hands. "Now, the seeds of your virtues bloom into weapons. The droplet you received after completing your trials is a sliver of godly power—to make sure you could handle our only countermeasure to Megawg shadows."

Henry's eyes widened.

"'Godly power?'" Analise muttered.

"The gods of human virtue, whose existence is owed to the defiance of the Megawgs, hold the only way for us to fight this war in the world of the living," Iskandar said.

From the box, he pulled a small glowing orb emitting an emerald light. "Yianni Fotelis, for your courage and desire to break free from subservience, I give you the divine soul of the hero Cu Chulainn."

Iskandar pushed the orb into Yianni's chest. The Irishman gasped as some kind of power flooded into him, though Henry couldn't sense it, even a little.

"Beware, Yianni. For, like Chulainn's hound, you have a monstrous side that you are at times too eager to embrace. Let your journey be one guided by the stars, not the darkness between them."

Iskandar moved to Analise. "Anna-lisa Abt, your admirable desire to see the limits of your own potential and maintain the balance of the world has earned you the divine soul of Moneta, the Roman goddess of memory and mother of the muses."

He pulled a light-blue orb from the box and pressed it into Analise's head. Her eyes widened as she staggered backwards, power subsuming her mind.

"Beware of Moneta's inability to forget grudges. Reorient your strong will to happiness, rather than perfection."

He approached Marion. "Marion Gutenberg, kind and wise beyond your years. Your desire for a place to call home, I hope, has been fulfilled. And with it comes the divine soul of Sunna, the Germanic goddess of the Sun." He pulled a golden orb out of the box and pushed it into her chest, where her runic tattoo was. "Be careful not to let the wolves chase you across the sky as Sunna did. There is no distraction nor excuse from duty that will last forever. The only difference is whether or not you choose to embrace your sacrifice."

Finally, Iskandar stood before Henry.

He basked in the scion of Alexander's radiant confidence and pride. He wished to be as Iskandar was.

"Henry Zhang, your fiery hunger for excellence and iron will have made you into a man of honor. But so has your willingness to let it all go. To trust the heavens with your fate. You are a true warrior. Your road of troubles has not been traveled in vain," Iskandar said.

Elation filled Henry's chest as Iskandar pulled a crimson orb of light from the box.

"For your trials, you have earned the divine soul of Nezha, God of Protection, Fire, and War. Carry this charge and its glory." Iskandar pushed the orb into Henry's sternum. "Beware Nezha's arrogance. Just because you are strong does not mean you are invulnerable to weakness. Do all that you can to battle the fearful animal inside you. Let that which you cannot understand or predict be as it is. Whether they help or harm, have faith that you can face the mysteries of this world, including the Megawgs."

Henry's next breath was a rush of lightning along his spine. The fire in his gut expanded, swirling within his body and burning like a pillar of light in his soul, forcing the darkness of his mind back. Power coursed through his veins, like ice-cold water under his skin. His hairs stood on end as he could fully sense the divine souls in his friends next to him.

His mind carried flashes of memories from another life—an immortal life. They remained distant from his soul, but he recalled rescuing children from the clutches of a dragon tyrant, slitting his own throat for the sake of his village, and being reborn as a god.

Iskandar stepped back and roared, "This is the beginning, *Hetairoi*! The end of the Third Age! And a new war with which to celebrate its life!"

The soldiers and warriors chanted an ancient Greek battle cry. "*ENYALIOS!*"

Iskandar looked off to the desert horizon. Henry, along with the rest of the Companions, followed his gaze to a roiling tide of stormclouds and shadows barreling towards them.

"Look out ahead of you! At the monsters! They would laugh and spit in our faces for our impudence! They tower over our world and strike our very blood with fear! They are our most ancient predators! And they have come to reassert their dominion over the world! To see us weak, sick, and feeble! To see us scared and paranoid! To make the whole world their slaves! And they will not be brought low easily!" Iskandar said. "But let me remind you who we are! Who you ride with! They may look down on us and see weak sacks of flesh and bones—mortals and slaves. But within each of you lives a soul! The soul of a warrior! Cultivated and cared for by ten thousand generations! Clawing through mud! Trudging through the storms! Standing firm in the face of all the world's wrath!"

"*ENYALIOS!*" Henry shouted the war cry with them in affirmation.

"I remind you that we have been fighting this war since the day Prometheus brought the fires of heaven down to man! Since the first day that we exercised power over the world instead of being another one of its victims! Within your souls rage the hopes and prayers of men, women, and children from every corner of this planet, across ten thousand generations! For twelve thousand years, we have struggled! For twelve thousand years, we have held the line! With nothing but frail bodies, vulnerable minds, treacherous hearts, and mortal souls to be our weapons against uncaring gods! For twelve thousand years, our hearts have beaten in defiance of an enemy that hates us simply because we refuse to lay down and die! For twelve thousand years, our path of conquest has never ceased!"

Iskandar mounted his tall black stallion, Bucephalus, and drew a Xiphos sword from his hip, holding it up so the sun gleamed off the blade. "We are no demigods! Our magic comes not from the horrors of the cosmos! We are not immortals! Not abyssal creatures sculpted from the entropy of the universe! We are mere men! Artists and writers! Historians and tacticians! Dancers, poets, priests, merchants, philosophers, kings! And yet it is us who heaven trusts to fight! We alone benefit from the wisdom of our ancestors! We alone inherit this war! We alone know what it means to die with honor! When the time comes to fight, we will fight with more courage, more ardor, more ferocity than any other being in this world or the next! And so I call you to fight, my Companions! I call you to ride with me and make history!"

Henry drew his butterfly swords and roared like a tiger, caught up in the whirlwind of bloodlust and battle rage—not towards humans, but towards the despicable demons who only subsisted on the suffering of others. Who had no names and so had to steal them from dead gods. Who had no joy and no ambition. Who could only live on hatred alone.

"Our enemy is Venus! Mighty Queen of the Megawgs! Matriarch of all our souls' evils! A worthy opponent! Let us show the gods of the past they are no longer welcome to feed off us! Let us show them our human valor! Our inevitable conquest over the future and all time!" Iskandar cried from atop his horse. "*Hetairoi! ENYALIOS!*"

Iskandar kicked the sides of his horse, and his steed broke into a gallop.

Henry broke into a sprint at the king's side, the spirit of the army and the collective unconscious of all humanity filling him with bliss and bravery unlike any he'd ever felt before. He was no longer afraid. No longer obsessed with certainty. No longer suspicious of the people to his left and right. No longer seeking, but content with being.

His Companions ran with him, charging without fear towards the darkness. Shoulder to shoulder, they brandished their weapons and magics, seemingly in sync with one another's souls.

Honor, Wisdom, Knowledge, Courage—all of them were shields against the darkness. They wielded art as their axes, history as their swords, science as their artillery, religion their as spears.

Culture was their weapon. Virtue was their armor.

Iskandar screamed as he charged. Henry joined the choir and the beautiful symphony of their glorious charge.

As he ran across the sands, he felt his feet leave the ground. Flaming brass wheels manifested, hovering beneath his soles, spinning with divine energy and lifting him into the sky.

And his Companions flew with him.

They soared through the air behind Iskandar, their divine souls filling them with euphoria and lust for victory against the hidden enemies of humanity.

The mass of dark, distorted Megawgs swarmed across the desert like a tide of lank limbs and corrupted human faces.

Without the leadership of Iskandar and without their divine souls, Henry knew the sheer terror that would've shocked his heart upon laying eyes on the enemy could kill him.

Hence why they had to fight. Hence why he screamed. Hence why he followed Iskandar to victory.

Like a spearhead, Iskandar pulled ahead and was the first to smash into the enemy line. The collision produced a light so brilliant it consumed the entire desert, and possibly the entire world.

CHAPTER TWENTY-EIGHT
Hetairoi

Henry's eyes opened. He was back in the Kom El-Shoqafa catacombs. The sarcophagus which he and Marion had jumped down was consumed in a storm of light whirling around it, the spirits of humanity's gods all leaving to seek partners to fight alongside them.

He turned to face Weiying under the arch to the graves as the wind whipped through his hair. His Companions lined up with him, shoulder to shoulder.

The fire inside him had changed. It was no longer just a fire. They were divine flames. But they'd gotten weaker.

They were meant to be cultivated. To be cared for and grown in tandem with Henry's own improvement. The power they offered now was miniscule, like a spark about to grow into a flame.

But it was enough to match a Megawg in combat.

Absolute certainty had consumed him. What he'd experienced was a taste of the world beyond the physical. The more of it he could reach out and touch, the more raw energy he would have to fuel his flame.

He could sense the other Divine Sparks alongside him. Cu Chulainn, Moneta, Sunna...

Ao Bing.

All of that divine certainty flooded out of Henry's body as his gaze darted to the Megawg behind his brother. He swallowed his apprehension like a lump of tar in his throat, managing to suppress his ancient fear.

Weiying cackled from across the chamber as frost swirled around his arms. The Divine Spark in him wasn't a spark. It was growing. Rapidly. Months of progress were going by in seconds.

How? How had he received Alexander's gift?

Rage filled Henry's chest. That was meant for a Companion. Someone who had done the work to earn that power. And this accursed creature had just...plucked it out of the air like a falling leaf. Hatred and fear for his enemy began to boil in his stomach.

It dawned on Henry that these sparks would eventually give them the powers of gods. But Weiying's Megawg was doing something to the one inexplicably attached to his brother. It was erasing the barriers, giving him a direct connection to the energy that fueled these sparks. Or, rather, offering a corrupted substitute. Within minutes, he would have all the powers of the dragon prince.

"Weiying..." Henry said, signaling for his Companions to stay back. "That...*thing* attached to you? You can't listen to it. It's poisoning your mind."

His brother scoffed. "Hanying, sometimes you say things that are *so* wrong while thinking you're *so* right. I've never seen more clearly." He glared at Henry. "You can convince yourself you've broken away from your fear. But you're still a slave to the past, Hanying. A slave to your rage. A slave to your so-called 'honor.' Even after Alexander, the greatest among you rebels, completely failed, you still intend to repeat his mistakes."

"Even if I fail," Henry took a step forward. "I won't let myself be consumed by them. I won't give them the world on a silver platter. Even if you're right, and I'm just delaying the inevitable...what kind of man doesn't even put up a fight?"

Weiying barked a laugh.

Henry saluted his opponent with his hand over his fist. Weiying returned the gesture.

Taking a cultivating breath, Henry sank into his Wing Chun stance, proffering his fist as if in challenge.

Weiying stepped out in a circle before proffering his own open hand and hooking his other hand behind him. He spat. "Everything that happens from here on is *your* responsibility."

"Don't act like you never had a choice."

As it had been since Weiying Zhang was born, the younger of the two brothers attacked first.

Henry stepped around his brother's side thrust kick and slammed his elbow into the back of his brother's knee.

Weiying turned the strike's momentum to his advantage. Henry ducked under a sweeping knife-hand strike and parried a spear-finger strike seeking out his eyes, then responded with a palm strike, punch, and elbow in quick succession. Weiying managed to block or evade all three, so Henry coated his fist in divine flames and slammed his fist into his brother's sternum at the same time as Weiying's mist-wrapped kick whipped into his nose. A spike of cold shot down Henry's spine, threatening to lock up his muscles purely from the shock.

The brothers stumbled away from each other.

"I'll give you this, Hanying." Weiying scoffed. "Killing you won't be boring."

Weiying was still within a somewhat-normal range of strength. Henry didn't know what kinds of supernatural abilities his brother had access to, but if he had to guess, there would come a point where he would be too powerful for them to defeat.

Henry motioned to his friends.

Marion readied her staff, while Yianni drew a sword from the handle of his Shillelagh. Analise pulled out a curse tablet and began writing like mad. Soon enough, an ADZ display appeared in Henry's vision, tracking Weiying.

The outline around his brother flickered slightly as he caused a patch of sharp ice to grow from the ground next to him. He snapped off a two-and-a-half-meter-long shard, wielding it like a *qiang* spear as he took a few steps up the stairs behind him.

Henry, meanwhile, drew his butterfly swords. "Companions! Engage!"

Henry rushed at Weiying, fulfilling his role as the frontline fighter. He shattered Weiying's spear, catching his brother off-guard, and threw a tornado kick into his jaw before making two slashes in his side.

Weiying staggered to the side, his outline flickering again as he drew on Ao Bing's power over ice. But Yianni wrapped his arm in vines as a bolt from Marion hit him like a slap to the face.

Henry slammed the knuckle guard of his sword into Weiying's jaw. He went in for another blow, but his brother parried and countered, throwing an ox-jaw strike into his teeth.

Weiying used his free hand to spew a column of white-and-blue ice at Henry, but a flickering golden shield kept him safe. The younger brother changed plans and swept his arm towards the other Companions, putting a wall of ice between the brothers and Henry's allies.

Henry rushed in to subdue his brother, but didn't notice that Weiying had freed himself from Yianni's grasp until the formerly bound arm socked him in the jaw. He tried to block as he received two more punches to the torso and a kick to the head that threw him into the wall of the stairwell. He grabbed the next punch and threw his brother behind him, face-first into the wall, just as the ice burst apart with bramble and vines.

Marion cast a beam of sunlight directly into Weiying's eyes, eliciting a scream, as Henry grabbed him by his silks and threw him into the stairs over his shoulder.

The Companions made their way up to the corridor between the main necropolis and the rotunda as Weiying groaned and scrambled backwards.

"Defect scum!" he snarled, grabbing something out of the mist. The outline on Henry's ADZ display flickered more frantically as his brother pulled a silver *qiang* out of nowhere.

And it wasn't just any spear. It was the signature weapon of the god in Weiying's soul, bursting with so much arcane energy that even Henry could feel its presence.

That was definitely a power he and the others didn't have yet.

Before Henry could prepare to defend himself, a bullet blasted through Weiying's shoulder in a smattering of red. His brother screamed, collapsing to the ground.

The echo of the bolt on Analise's gun told Henry she was right behind them.

When Weiying took his hand off his wound, some kind of substance born of the Megawgs had filled it in, allowing him to fight as though nothing had happened.

"To me, *Hetairoi*!" Henry shouted.

He lashed out his rope dart, catching Weiying in the other shoulder. He cried out and stumbled away as Henry pulled the dart back. Yianni bound his ankle to the ground with twisting vines as Marion and Henry laid into him unrelentingly with their typhoon of physical and magical attacks.

Henry rushed at Weiying and slid into a sidekick to his abdomen, but his brother froze his foot to the ground, cutting the attack short. The other two flanked him, but Weiying's combination of Megawg-enhanced abilities, godly power, and his own magic kept them on the defensive.

Even as Henry freed himself and rejoined the fray, they were barely a match for him combined.

Still, Weiying only had two sets of eyes looking out for him. A blow here and a cut there whittled him down in an agonizingly long storm of combat. The Companions fought like a well-oiled machine, their souls in sync, weaving between offensive and defensive positions effortlessly.

Weiying fought like a wild gorilla, desperately trying to keep up and flailing as he was slowly pushed back to the rotunda. The spear wasn't quite as effective as Henry had initially thought in this narrow space. Once they got past the point, Weiying couldn't maneuver it around to hit them.

That was, until he leapt back and stabbed the spear into the ground.

While his allies moved out of the way, Henry slammed his forearm down on four or five spikes of ice that erupted from the stone, then delivered a flame-wreathed kick to a new wall of ice, shattering it as he chased after his brother, who was running away. He threw out his rope dart, wrapped it around Weiying's ankle, and pulled his balance out from under him.

Weiying turned himself over as he fell and slammed his palms into the ground. Twin icicles shot from the stone, one of them catching Henry in the shoulder.

Before he had a chance to respond, Weiying thrust out his hands. A column of blizzard winds filled the tunnel with biting cold and ripping gales.

Henry squinted in the face of the mini-snowstorm until Marion managed to put a shield up. She strained, holding onto her staff for dear life, but the shield was holding.

"Okay, he couldn't do *that* before." Yianni sighed.

Henry sheathed his swords and looked at his arm. The wound was deeper than he'd like, but the truckload of adrenaline pumping through his veins seemed to be keeping him up to speed. He lit his hand and pressed it to the wound, wincing as it hissed. That would have to do for now.

"Maybe I can get him from here." Analise aimed her rifle down the tunnel and fired, only for the bullet to change course immediately and spark off Marion's dome, causing her to grit her teeth.

"No more of that, please." She groaned.

"I can try to—" Yianni cut himself off.

Henry spared a glance back due to a prickling sensation at the base of his neck. A black tendril ripped through Marion's shield and slammed into Yianni, who collapsed to the ground. "Yianni!" Henry knelt down next to him. "What the hell was—"

As Marion's shield shattered, Weiying's blizzard tore through the air around them, blinding Henry as ice shards chipped away at his skin. He tried to spew a gout of flames from his palm, attempting to push through the storm winds, but it was no use against the whirlwind of ice and snow.

A hand reached out of the obscuring white, grabbing his wrist.

It was Marion.

Henry unleashed his divine flames, forcing them to coalesce with Marion's sunlight in a concentrated ball. The light and heat of their combined power was enough to tear through Weiying's blizzard as the ball expanded, surging through the catacomb.

Able to see again, Henry closed the distance in an instant and overwhelmed Weiying with a hailstorm of fiery blows until his younger brother managed to interrupt his flow with a well-placed kick to the abdomen. He staggered back as his brother leaned against the railing over the pit that marked the center of the rotunda.

Weiying snapped his fingers, causing a shockwave of energy to radiate through the catacombs.

Consumed by momentary evolutionary fear, Henry doubled over, trying to keep himself from hyperventilating. Marion and Analise similarly fought its influence.

"No one can defeat the Megawgs, Hanying," Weiying said. "Not even Alexander. Our very DNA has instructions to bow before them. Our creation is inscribed with their brand. There is no reality in which humans don't serve them."

Henry gritted his teeth. "You're so damn quick to give up."

"I just understand the reality of our situation better than you do." Weiying's outline flashed rapidly as Henry sensed power filling his brother like water in a cup. Except the cup was more like a lake. No, a vast ocean.

Henry's chest filled with dread as Weiying's body began to shift and warp, elongating and becoming paler. His silks seemed to morph into his body as scales replaced skin and talons replaced nails. Deer horns sprouted from his head as his face elongated into an almost crocodile-like maw.

Henry's eyes widened as he realized his brother was changing into a dragon—a Chinese dragon.

Azure fins sprouted along his spine. His eyes opened as reptilian slits, and his body jerked around like a violent snake as his hair became a blue mane of fur.

"*Mein Gott...*" Marion whispered in horror as Weiying roared at them.

Weiying whipped his tail over his shoulder, throwing Analise down the stairs. Henry raised his arms, wrapped in flame, as his brother's maw clasped around his body and he felt the catacomb walls hit his back.

CHAPTER
TWENTY-NINE
The Tiger and the Dragon

H enry's eyes seared with almost as much pain as his body was in as Weiying burrowed through the ground and emerged into the skies of Alexandria. He put every ounce of strength into pushing his brother's draconic jaws apart as he carried them higher and higher.

His breath became short as the air started to thin and the sky began to shift colors.

Weiying was going to take him out of the atmosphere. *Figures. Once someone turns into a dragon, all bets are off.*

Panicking, Henry wedged his arm out of Weiying's mouth and started slamming his elbow into the dragon's nose. Even as his consciousness started to fade, and his head felt like it was about to explode—which might actually happen—he kept hitting.

His gambit actually worked, as Weiying's jaw loosened, and he fell out of the dragon's grip.

Except now, he was thousands of meters above the earth and falling with no parachute or method of making a parachute.

Weiying, in his dragon form, just looped around in the sky, waiting for him to die.

Throughout his free fall, Henry cursed a million different ways, desperately trying to think of something he could do.

No Daoist magic would be enough to slow him down. And even then, the spell might fizzle out. He had nothing to write on for Confucian magic. Nothing big enough to make a silk parachute out of. And Martial magic had nothing to offer.

The earth was rapidly approaching, and Henry was close enough to notice it now. The deserts outside of Alexandria were starting to look pretty detailed.

His Divine Soul was the only thing that might have an answer.

Weiying had filled himself up with power before turning into the dragon. Maybe Henry could try the same.

He closed his eyes and tried to stay calm, not paying attention to how close the ground was. He didn't understand what the power inside of him was, but it was all he could do.

He focused on his flames, fanning them and filling himself up with their heat. He tried to remember what it had been like in the vision.

His friends were counting on him. He was the only thing between them and Weiying now.

Yes...that sense of purpose. That disregard of his own well being for the sake of something more. That willingness to die standing in the heat of battle with the shadows. That completely baseless faith he felt he could safely trust himself and his allies with.

That was what he filled himself with—the euphoria of serving something greater than himself.

He snapped his eyes open as he suddenly came to a stop in midair, ten feet above the ground. A brass wheel covered in fire spun under each of his shoes as he hovered in the air.

The wheels vanished as quickly as they'd appeared, and he collapsed in the sand of a dune sea. He pushed himself up as Weiying's dragon form slammed down into the sand.

When the dust cleared, he'd returned to being a human again. Although...slightly different. His long black hair had become a silvery white. His clothes had changed to white-and-blue robes he hadn't been wearing before. His eyes glinted, gold now, with slit pupils. And two antler-like dragon horns protruded from his head.

It was as though Weiying himself had merged with Ao Bing and become something different.

Weiying twirled Ao Bing's spear in one hand as he lazily approached Henry. "It's not so easy doing this on your own, is it?" The younger brother grinned.

Henry drew his butterfly swords and flexed his grip on them as Weiying whipped his spear around. He parried the overhead swing, but hardly had time to react as his brother started to twirl the far tip of the spear and make stab after stab at him.

He tried to respond by throwing his swords at Weiying, but his brother simply evaded them and stabbed at him. He tried to parry, but was late and came away with a gash in his upper arm.

On the back foot, Henry found himself up against Weiying's *qiangshu*, random ice spikes that would try to stab through his feet from the ground, and blasts of stormwinds. All he could do was parry for his life with flame-wreathed hands.

Weiying began to cackle as he kept pushing his brother back.

Much to Henry's dismay, Weiying managed to catch him with a torrent of frost unleashed from his breath. Without time to evade, he was forced to block. His muscles strained against the violent force of the winds, his divine flames keeping some of the pain at bay as ice shards lacerated his arms and torso.

The last thing a Wing Chun practitioner wanted to do was block. It let Weiying keep the pressure on and gave him no opening to work with.

Nothing he could do was strong enough.

The younger brother shouted with sadistic joy. "This was always how it was going to end! With you beneath my boot!"

"Would you say the same about Mr. Fang?" Henry asked. "That it was always going to end that way? That you had no agency in the matter?"

"I was with him longer than you were!" Weiying made a rash decision to let up and attack head-on. Henry called his butterfly swords back to his hand and cleared the spearhead. Their weapons locked together, grinding against one another. "You think I enjoyed killing him? If it weren't for you! If it weren't for you, he'd still be alive! He wouldn't have turned traitor!"

"'Traitor?' You're the one who lied to banish me, you dense, oathbreaking coward! Do you really believe your own bullshit so wholly?" Henry screamed. His fire flared up within him, filling his body until the divine flames overflowed with a combination of godly power and his own white-hot rage.

He pushed through Weiying's defenses and unleashed a storm of steel and flames. His brother fell to the sand, bleeding and burning.

But Henry didn't expect him to morph into a dragon just to slam his serpentine head into him with a nasty crunch.

He landed in the sand a few feet away, clutching his ribs. He didn't know if they were broken, but...he didn't like his odds. His breath was ice-cold against the back of his throat. His lips were dry, and he was sweating like a dog. The cauterized wound on his shoulder was starting to ache from the abuse.

It was like wandering the desert all over again, but this time, he was getting beaten up as it happened.

Weiying approached his older brother and stomped on Henry's gut, causing a new shock of agony and a wave of nausea. "You made me do this, Hanying!" he roared into Henry's face as the edges of his vision started to darken. "How does it feel, brother? To be down in the dirt? To have no one to rely on? To not have a country? You were always too American for the Tiandihui. Too meatheaded to be a Magician. Too full of yourself to join the other meatheads. You're a disgrace. You have nothing and no one. And that's all you'll ever be: Alone. Unloved. Scared. Now, you have a hint of how you made me feel."

Henry noticed something blue start to glow in his jacket pocket. Despite all the pain and blood loss, he grinned. "Wanna bet?"

He pulled the runestone Marion had given him in the tunnels under Alexandria out of his pocket and sat up as a flash of light sent Weiying stumbled back, clutching his throat after Marion slammed the butt of her staff into his windpipe.

She knelt down next to Henry, but instead of healing him, she rubbed her fingers in one of his wounds and licked up the blood. She *allowed* her Impaler's Curse to take over.

"Marion, what are you—"

"Returning the favor," Marion said as her body morphed, though with a magical pulse behind it. Her eyes opened, black and gold as she whirled around and leapt at Weiying.

Henry's relief was short-lived, as the battle became a storm of shadows and blizzard winds too fast for him to keep track of. He needed to use this time.

He closed his eyes and tried to focus on his Divine Soul. Instead of just filling it like a panicked coal-shoveler into a train, he needed to delve into it for a technique—something that could help him.

He first slowed his breathing, regaining control over his body. Then he isolated his emotions away from his thoughts, controlling his heart.

The most difficult part was gaining control over his rushing mind, especially as Marion seemed to be on the backfoot. Weiying was overwhelming her as she tried to hold the line between the two brothers.

He was snapped out of his focus as the squelch of flesh pierced his ears. Weiying had stabbed her straight through the abdomen with his spear. He tore it out with no regard for her.

Marion collapsed, but Henry caught her before she hit the sand.

"Oh, my God..." Henry's breath quickened along with his heartbeat. Anxiety rose up through his chest and into his throat.

He looked at her wound. It wasn't a simple in and out. It was torn through her gut.

"Marion...Marion, you need to heal yourself!" he said.

Marion coughed, though thankfully, no blood came with it. But her *Nosophoros* was fading. "You know that's not how this works, *Arschloch*."

Then why didn't you heal me? It was his first thought. He could've helped. He could've protected her.

Henry's face drained of heat as he realized the position he was in again.

One of the few people who believed in him was dying in his arms.

And he was helpless to do anything but watch.

As firmly as she could, Marion said, "Stop panicking." She groaned as blood seeped into her blouse and started spilling into the sand. "Just...burn it shut and get back to it. I wasn't gonna let you...leave this mess in my lap. You need to finish it. You can do this, Henry."

Henry closed his eyes and swallowed. He nodded before placing a flame-wreathed hand on Marion's wound. She groaned as the flesh hissed, but the bleeding stopped under the handprint-shaped burn on her abdomen.

Henry turned back to his brother.

Strangely, it was when he came to peace with the idea of his friend's death that his mind finally rested. He was going to defeat Weiying by any means necessary.

If he died in the process...so be it.

Henry poured his flames into his soul the way Weiying had, allowing them to overflow. He knelt into a sprinter's position. It just felt right as his flames consumed him the way they had when he'd banished Venus and saved Marion.

But now, instead of having nowhere to go, the flames sank into his flesh.

Four fists slammed into the ground next to his hands—fiery apparitions of extra limbs that soon solidified into flesh and bone. His mandarin jacket collar plumed around him as if the fabric were trailing off into crackling flames, and a red silk sash wrapped around his three pairs of arms.

It was the transformation. Same as Weiying's, but a different god.

He could feel it in his soul. The bridge to the other world, providing him with the fuel of life.

Henry looked up with immolating eyes and burst forward, propelling himself on the flaming wheels beneath his feet faster than Metal Style could ever imagine.

Each of the brothers' weapons scraped against each other as they tried to probe or break through the other's defenses. Henry matched Weiying's immense speed by having his other sets of arms attack with his guandao and rope dart. It was a strange experience for his mind, but the muscle memory was still there.

Henry, having more experience with his weapon, broke Weiying's guard and slashed him three times before his younger brother threw himself back and attacked from afar with a storm of ice shards.

"Running away?" Henry scoffed as he cut through every shard that was in danger of hitting him.

"Just buying some time." Weiying slammed his palms against the ground, causing two columns of blue and white to explode from the sand.

No, not columns.

Dragons.

Henry's chest sank with despair.

The serpentine creatures slithered through the air symmetrically as they turned and rushed at Henry. One of them knocked him into the air with a blast of icy breath. The other snapped its jaws around him.

He spewed a torrent of flames into the dragon's fleshy maw, forcing it to free him, then flew around the creature on his flaming wheels and slammed a tiger-claw strike into its back, the resulting explosion of fire shattering its vertebrae.

The dragon crashed as Henry leapt towards the other, pouring more of his willpower into the flames, summoning the immolating brass wheels beneath his feet. Kept afloat, he plunged his guandao into the dragon's side, cleaving it almost all the way through.

He barely had time to get back to land before Weiying cracked the shaft of his spear on his temple and punched him in the back of the head. He dropped his weapons as he fell to the ground.

And with his collapse went his transformation and the fragile connection powering it.

He didn't have time to build it again before Weiying turned him over and wrapped both hands around his throat.

Henry struggled against the thumbs pressing into his Adam's apple and the hands crushing his veins and windpipe, but to no avail.

After taking a moment to assess his situation, he slammed his arms down on Weiying's elbows and threw as much force as he could muster into a double-fisted blow to his brother's chest.

Weiying flew off him, landing in the sand.

Both brothers wearily got to their feet. One was far wearier than the other.

"What's that look for, brother? We're not finished yet." Weiying readied his spear.

"The spear?" Henry sighed. "Why don't you just...turn into a dragon and kill me? With how much power you have now, it'd be easy."

He placed his hands on his knees, trying to catch his breath a little. He didn't want to believe he was done fighting. But if he could just get a break...maybe he could find the strength to keep pushing.

"Where'd be the fun in that?" Weiying asked.

"So, this is 'fun' to you? Killing your family members is 'fun?'" Henry scoffed. "Was Mr. Fang '*fun*?'"

"Shut up!" Weiying snapped.

"That thing attached to you, Weiying...all it does is lie to you. It makes the worst parts about you stronger and cripples your best traits." Henry looked his brother in the eyes. "It literally can't survive without human suffering. It subsists on its hatred for us. Or our fear."

"How would you know? Are you suddenly an expert on the cosmos?"

"I had one, Weiying," Henry said. "In Troy, in the desert. Probably before that. I had one attached to me. Venus."

He caught a glimpse of a little shudder in the shadow of the Megawg looming over Weiying. His brother's brow furrowed. "You...you did," he muttered. "But that's not possible. Where'd she go?"

"Once I could see her, I shoved her away with this." Henry lifted his flaming hands. "You can do the same. You have the power."

Weiying threw down his spear and readied his fists. "Bullshit! Come on! Fight me! If you don't fight, I'll finish her off!" He glared at Marion, who was trying not to agitate the burn keeping her wound in check.

Henry's fists clenched.

Weiying attacked him with a series of spear-finger strikes, all of which Henry parried, then countered with rapid-fire chain punches.

Weiying tried to create distance with a combination of spinning kicks, but Henry blocked or evaded each of them.

And once it was back to hands, Henry was on the attack.

But it was in the midst of combat with his brother that he came upon an epiphany, somewhat by accident.

Weiying could easily stomp Henry into the ground with his divine and Megawg powers. It would be over in seconds.

So why hadn't he?

Henry let Weiying shift the momentum, putting his older brother on the backfoot. He landed a well-placed push kick to Henry's chest using some of that extra Megawg strength, sending him stumbling over.

Henry stayed in the sand for a while, catching his breath.

"Come on, get up!" Weiying demanded.

Henry sighed and sat back. "No."

"So, you're admitting defeat?"

Henry shook his head. "You haven't defeated me."

"Then get up and fight!" Weiying's frustration grew far more quickly than Henry had been expecting. "Or I kill the girl!"

"No, you won't." A part of Henry didn't like the risk he was taking, calling his brother's bluff.

Weiying scoffed. "Wanna bet?"

"I wanna see you kill her and somehow get me to fight you because of that. Why would I give you *anything*, much less the very thing you want, after killing one of my closest friends?" Henry asked. "Think about that for a minute."

Weiying started towards Marion's half-conscious body.

"Or, better yet, you want to defeat me, right?" Henry called out. "Hit me!"

Weiying whirled around. "What?"

"Hit me, tough guy! I'm wide-open! You want to defeat me, why don't you just hit me?" Henry continued to antagonize his brother, and as he did, he suspected his theory was proving itself right. That would put him at, what, one for two? Wrong on the whole world being out to get him. Right about what lies Weiying was telling himself.

He'd take it.

"You chicken?"

"How dare you, you little piece of—"

"Or is it something else?" Henry asked. "Maybe if I just sit here on the ground and do jack shit, you can't do anything!"

He probably should've expected Weiying to prove him wrong with a goal-scoring kick directly to the face. His vision exploded with stars as his brother gathered cold divine mists around his hands.

"I will put you in the ground like I did Fang," Weiying snarled.

"Do it." Henry sat up and narrowed his eyes, blood trickling down from his nose. "But know that you'll never, ever, ever get to see me acknowledge your victory. And that's what really matters, isn't it? You *can't* kill me. Because if you do while I refuse to fight with you, I win. All I have to do is nothing."

Weiying stopped in his tracks, his frustration slowly being replaced with confusion.

"Are the bullshit rules to your own game finally dawning on you?"

Is he calling you stupid?

Henry scoffed. "Oh, come on, it's not even trying anymore! Don't you see how it's goading you?"

"Don't talk to me like I'm a kid!"

"You are! You're a child! Seventeen! You said so yourself! You sure as hell act like it! If you don't want to be condescended to, grow the fuck up!" Henry slowly got to his feet, tentatively touching his probably broken nose.

"I'll kill her!" Weiying threatened.

Henry just folded his arms, giving off a disappointed facade more than anything else. Granted, underneath his face, his mind was screaming with suppressed panic at all the uncertainty he'd gotten himself into. He really hadn't thought this through too well, but it seemed to be working. And it was better than nothing.

Weiying looked down at his hands. His lip trembled as if he was about to cry.

"What...what am I doing here?" he murmured.

Henry uncrossed his arms.

"I...I killed—no, no it made me! It made..." Weiying's face became hollow. "I did it. I killed Fang." He met his brother's gaze. "Hanying, why did I kill him?"

Henry took a deep breath. "Because you let that thing into your head. You gotta stop listening to it. It's the only way to fix this."

"Fix it? How do I...Oh, God!" Weiying grasped at his hair as the silver was traded for black, his Godform receding. "I never meant for this to happen. I just..."

"Use the soul, Weiying."

"It's been with me for so long, Hanying. I don't know if I can..."

"You can and you will. Come on, Weiying!"

Weiying slowed his breathing. "Okay...okay...I'll try." He swallowed. "Leave me be."

The Megawg made a noise halfway between laughter and otherworldly screaming.

"Look at me, Weiying. It's just a parasite." Henry met his brother's eyes intently.

Weiying took another deep breath. "Hanying, I...I'm scared."

Good.

"Hey, eyes on me, Weiying," Henry said, trying to keep his attention. "Don't listen. All it does is lie."

You're not enough on your own. You know that. You've always known that. And here he is, the one that's always been the favorite, telling you it doesn't matter. How convenient for him.

"Weiying, don't listen!" Henry shouted.

But his brother's eyes kept flickering between him and Marion, the hesitation and fear plain on his face.

He's trying to take away what threatens his own status. He's trying to declaw you. He wants you to amount to nothing so he can get all the glory. All he cares about is his own honor.

"It's trying to make you afraid! It's lying! You don't need that thing!"

Weiying shook his head. "Hanying..."

"Weiying, don't do anything rash."

Henry's brother sighed, regaining his composure. Or maybe a composure forced upon him. "There is no real Weiying, Hanying. Just the Gawg."

Weiying created a spear in his hand out of ice and reared his arm back, aiming at Marion.

Henry drew his Magnum revolver from his hip and fired without thinking.

Weiying stumbled to the sand with a scream, clutching his leg as the shot tore a chunk out of him.

Henry heaved, his mind racing as his grip on the gun loosened and Weiying writhed in pain.

Are you not going to finish the job?

The creature loomed over Weiying's squirming body, grinning with an inhuman smile, its eyes completely void, almost like sockets.

What happened, Companion? Where's your courage?

Henry froze, and his gun dropped out of his hand as he collapsed to the sand. He tried again and again to force himself to get up, but every single nerve in his body insisted on trembling as he looked upon the eldritch creature that had possessed his brother—a shard of fear incarnate.

Where's your...honor?

Henry wanted to vomit.

He was suddenly aware of how weak he was. How dangerous and bloodthirsty the world around him was. He needed to get stronger. He needed to become better. He needed to keep himself safe before anything else. The Megawg could offer the power he needed...

It was as though upon staring into the cold death and meaninglessness in Hepom Nepot's eyes, he was being infected by his own obsession with prowess and his greedy brand of fear.

No!

Henry stared into the void, only to find a second, darker divinity to clash with his first. To weaken him. To erase who he was.

You are a part of something greater. You are in command of your destiny!

Was that...Iskandar's voice?

Don't let flaws and doubts throw you from your purpose! Don't let that demon convince you to abandon your honor! Trust your strength to carry you! For once!

No. It was his own voice.

Henry's breathing slowed.

Henry stumbled to his feet, never breaking eye contact from the Megawg.

"My honor," he growled, "is in my purpose. In my mission! In my place as a man, as a Companion, and as a human!"

The Megawg scoffed. **Men are brutes. Companions are failures. And humans are weak. You have no place. You will never be Chinese. You will never be Western. You will never be Tiandihui. You are wrong for this earth! And it will forever remind you of that every time it betrays you. Submit to me, and I will give you the safety you crave. I can give you power. I can give you love.**

The creature's face split into a too-wide, too-white smile. *Let go, Hanying. I know you hate him. And he deserves it. Kill this failure. He made his bed. Make him sleep in it.*

Henry staggered, his head a swirling cyclone of conflicting thoughts and feelings. His fire raged against itself, the divine clashing with what had fueled him in Troy.

You have suffered so much injustice. Kill those who have wronged you. How else will you make sure the rest stay away? How could it be wrong if it feels so good?

Henry gritted his teeth. "No!" he snapped, glaring up at the creature.

His divine flames twisted with conflict. But not for long. And not with the dark tendrils of fire that made him nearly kill his old squad.

The flames surged in his chest, the cup of water overflowing as the connection reestablished itself. Four fiery phantom limbs unfolded from his arms, hands positioned like a Bodhisattva. He lowered into a combat stance with his Godform.

"The world doesn't owe me a damn thing," he snarled. "Nor do I owe it. But I won't let you or anyone else chase me into hiding from the world again! I was chosen to fight your kind and defend my own. I have more than enough faith in myself for that task. I don't need to start placing it in your poisoned words."

The creature recoiled as the concerted spirit of Nezha's power blazed in bright-orange glory across Henry's skin.

"I am Henry Zhang, Commander of the Companions," he declared. "Wielder of Nezha's flames. Heir to Alexander's war. You're just a parasite you got out of his cage."

He took hold of his brother's shoulders and sank all thirty of his fingers into him.

Hepom Nepots screamed an unholy noise that belonged far, far away from this planet.

Henry gritted his teeth and, with the might of his six-armed form, ripped the abomination from its place. He couldn't alleviate his brother's addiction, but he would kill the dealer.

The amorphous black entity squirmed and shifted from shape to horrifying shape as it tried to escape Henry's grasp. But the light of the Third Lotus Prince burned into the distorted, vile creature. He pulled it in and slammed it into the ground.

And the Megawg revealed its true form. Or at least, a *truer* form: a hairless human man without an ounce of color on his distorted, warped body.

Henry pinned the Megawg to the sand as he drew back his right sword, igniting it in Nezha's flames.

Your friend is dying. If you want to save her...you'll have to let me go.

Henry shook his head at the creature's desperation.

Release me! Release me, or she'll die!

"You have a place on this earth. Behind the Caspian Gates."

Henry plunged his blade into Hepom Nepot's chest.

The creature screamed and cried like a child as its voice vanished into dust with its body, burned to ash by the fire as he sent it back behind the wall in his dreams.

He staggered to his feet, heaving. The arms vanished, the flames receding inside of him.

Marion.

He had to help his friends.

But before he could turn around, someone tackled him to the ground, disarming him.

It was Weiying, still trying to attack him in spite of his partially regenerated wound. "What did you do?" he roared. "Where is he?"

Henry pushed Weiying off him, but his younger brother just tried to attack again. He slammed his fist into his brother's sternum and aimed his fist at Weiying's throat. "Stop it!' he shouted.

"No..." Weiying growled. "Not yet, dammit!" He tried to kick his older brother.

Henry had been pushing it away until now, but the display made his chest ache like never before.

"I almost..." Weiying swung.

Henry parried the weak blow and shoved him back. "Weiying, stop this."

"I almost had you!"

Henry blocked and tripped him. "The fight's over, Weiying!"

Weiying took several ragged breaths before roaring in frustration as he got to his feet. "Come on! *Come on!*" he screamed.

Henry picked his gun out of the sand and pointed it at Weiying's head.

His brother scoffed. "What are you gonna do, kill me?"

Henry pulled the hammer back.

Weiying looked at him with pleading eyes, tears streaking through the dirt on his face, glistening under his tangled strands of hair.

Henry had wanted for so long to teach Weiying a lesson. To make him understand his wrongs. But even now, he was that same child who came with him to the Daba mountains almost five years ago.

Henry couldn't teach that to him. No amount of talking or beating would teach him.

"Leave," he said.

Weiying scoffed. "What? In this desert? You want me to die of thi—"

"I said leave! And never let me see your face again!" Henry snarled. "Or I won't miss twice! If I see you again, and you do anything hostile to me or my allies, I will—again—not miss twice. Now, go."

Weiying stumbled back in disbelief.

"Go!"

Weiying turned and hurried away as fast as his limp could carry him.

Henry never took the muzzle of the gun off Weiying's silhouette as he limped up the nearest slope of sand like a frightened animal. His finger never left the trigger.

When his brother had finally vanished behind the dunes, he dropped the gun in the sand before collapsing to his knees.

It was done.

It was finally done.

CHAPTER THIRTY
A New War

U nder an umbrella posted up outside a restaurant, Henry Zhang smiled at his view of the Parthenon from Monastiraki Square. With all the choice in the world and more than a little profit from his escapades, Henry didn't even care how hot Athens was right now. No Circle wanted to admit they lost to a group of Defectors. So while they pretended not to care, Henry got to enjoy being in Athens for real. The food, the history, the weather. He could take his time to soak it all in.

He sat at a small wooden table outside a dingy but reputable gyro shop, reading his way through *The Lonely Crowd*, one of several volumes on the societal trends of this age.

In the days since Egypt, he had expanded his interests from history into macrosociology and anthropology. All three subjects proved to have a lot of useful information about what made the Megawgs so powerful. To a certain degree, he accepted that he would never fully understand the Megawgs. But that didn't mean he wouldn't prepare for the battles to come.

Reading was his way of doing that, since he hadn't been able to use his Godform for more than a second or two since that day.

If he did ever see Weiying again, he would like to be as prepared as he could be to help him.

But for now, he simply wanted to enjoy travel.

"Have you ever gotten a Turkish bath?" Marion asked as she joined him at the table, dressed in a white blouse and black shorts, her wavy hair tied in a bun behind her head.

"Can't say that I have." Henry marked the page in his book.

"When we were in Istanbul, I went and got one after we left Troy, and *my God,* it's incredible. They were so gentle with me. You should try one next time we go."

"Don't believe a word the lass says." Yianni chuckled as he and Analise came back with their drinks. "It's different for boys. They beat the hell outta ya before sliding you on the floor like a malfunctioning mop. It was like I killed the gobshite's mum."

"Maybe we'll see how much you like it with that hole in your gut." Henry grinned.

"Hey, no one gets to joke about the hole but me," Marion said.

For a moment, Henry thought she had ordered herself two beers to start, which wouldn't have been out of character. But then she handed one to him. "For me?"

"For you to learn to like beer." Marion chuckled. "I expect you to buy me one in return."

"Did everyone buy a ticket for the tour tomorrow?" Analise asked.

"Oh, I still have to do that," Marion muttered sheepishly.

"Marion!" Analise exclaimed. "Come on, we've had this planned for a week."

"I'm not exactly a plan-ahead type of traveler. You know this."

"Right. You're a wait-till-the-last-second traveler." Yianni scoffed. "I'm starting to wonder how the hell we survived with your shite-for-organization."

"I'm good at organizing other things!" Marion exclaimed defensively.

"Just buy the ticket and hope it's not all sold out," Henry said. "You don't wanna miss out on Mycenae."

"And *I* wonder why we need a tour if we have this guy to give us all the information." Marion poked a thumb at Henry before effortlessly opening both their beers with the edge of the table.

"Hilarious," Henry muttered as he drank the vile-tasting liquid. Granted, it wasn't quite piss-water anymore, but it wasn't great either. "I should be getting paid for all I tell you three."

"We *would've* gotten paid plenty." Analise frowned. "If not for Alexandria-Chaldea shoving us out the second we opened the good king's box."

"If I ever see that bastard again, I don't care how inspiring his speeches are," Yianni muttered. "I'm gonna give him a good punch to the face."

"I mean, we're not *empty-handed*," Marion said. "There's the gold we recovered from the plane crash. That's a billion at least."

"I don't really care about the money." Yianni sighed.

"We'll eventually find something to deal with your pact," Analise said. "Promise."

"Do you...do you ever think about whether the other gods released from the box went and found hosts?" Henry asked.

"It's possible." Marion shrugged. "But aside from your brother, who was cheating with that Megawg, it's not as powerful a blessing as it seems."

Henry furrowed his brow. "I'm inclined to disagree."

"Why do you ask?" Analise sipped a cocktail of some kind.

"I've just been wondering...what are we going to do? Like, what are the Companions now?"

"An excellent question."

Henry turned around, along with his allies, to find a fair-skinned, stern-faced woman who had to be like a head taller than him standing over their table. She wore a yellow dress with a sun hat covering her long brown hair.

"Can...we help you?" Analise asked.

The woman pulled up a chair from another table and sat at the edge of theirs. She pulled out some kind of black leather wallet and opened it, revealing a government ID belonging to...an agency Henry had never heard of.

His fingers danced along the handle of a butterfly sword under his jacket.

"My name is Agent Gina Harris with the Agency of Arcane and Occult Incidents," she said, her voice lowering to a barely audible whisper. "I've come on behalf of the United States government with a proposition for you."

Henry chuckled. "Okay, so, you're crazy."

"We've known about the existence of Magicians' Circles for over a hundred and fifty years," Agent Harris said. "But never has the need risen for America to get involved in the arcane world until now. Magicians are popping out of the woodwork like termites, and some of them are reportedly showing signs of immense power, including the ability to fly."

Henry glanced at his Companions before looking back at the agent.

"The AAOI feels it's necessary for us to have a finger on the pulse of arcane happenings that might cause disruption to the public and the world at large in the near future. The only thing is that America, as a divergent culture, is not yet old enough to develop its own variety of magic," Gina said. "We heard about the exploits of you four. And we wanted to make a pitch to you."

"That being?" Henry asked.

"The AAOI wants to sponsor the Companions, turning them from a squad to a full Circle," Gina said.

Henry's eyes widened. His Companions wore similarly surprised expressions.

"You would have the resources available to go toe-to-toe with the other Circles, who are undoubtedly hunting you now. You'd also have access to much more manpower, as Magicians of multiple backgrounds tend to show up in America more often than anywhere else."

"And the catch?" Analise asked. "I suppose we'll be under the thumb of your government? Act as proverbial spies in the arcane world?"

"No," Gina said. "You'd more or less have complete freedom to operate as you wish, so long as it does not involve unprovoked attacks that might implicate the American government. In terms of information, only the AAOI needs to know. No one who hasn't broken Solomon's Wisdom naturally will be informed. Not even the CIA."

Henry pursed his lips, considering it. This was all really sudden. And the deal sounded pretty nice. Be backed by the American government? They could certainly do worse.

But they wouldn't be able to have much control over the recruitment process if a government organization did it all for them.

Then again...wasn't this what Alexander had originally wanted for the Companions? Wasn't that the point of his tests?

"Brings us some of these new recruits first," he said. "Let's see who they are and what they're capable of. Then...we'll think about it."

Gina nodded and stood. "We'll be in touch."

As she walked off, disappearing into the crowd like a Magician, his Companions gave him scrutinous looks.

"Are you seriously taking that deal?" Analise asked.

"If you're asking whether I trust that girl or whatever organization she's a part of? Hell, fuckin' no! They're the government. Of course I don't trust them," Henry said. "But that doesn't mean the idea was bad. The Megawgs are everywhere. My brother and Alexandria-Chaldea are proof of that. Who else is going to fight them but us? The Chaldean Court is useless. The Circles don't give a damn. If we can establish some real numbers, we could have a chance at stopping them. So I'm definitely stealing that idea. Will I opt in to get a little government funding? Eh...We'll see."

"Not even Alexander could kill them. He couldn't even resist them," Yianni said. "And whatever it is you did, well...we can't be sure. But I don't think that thing's gone for good."

"Someone has to succeed where Alexander failed," Henry said. "Why not us?"

Analise grimaced. "Well...I guess I don't have anything else going on right now."

"Plus, we're all stuck with each other." Yianni sighed. "It's not an unsound move."

"Alexander tried to literally bury himself underground. To protect himself and his army by hiding in a fortress," Marion said. "If we want to fight the Megawgs, *we* have to be on the attack."

"I couldn't agree more." Henry lifted his beer bottle. "Let's have a toast. To a new generation of Companions."

"Hear, hear." Yianni lazily raised his drink.

Henry swallowed a mouthful of less-than-piss-water with the other Companions. "For the next time we do something this stupid, I'm gonna teach you guys how to shoot like Americans." He grinned.

"Oh, God." Marion chuckled.

"What? Look, before anything else, no member of the Companions is gonna look at me weird ever again when I ask them for Magnum rounds."

"Oh, my God, that was *one* time!" Yianni exclaimed, slapping his thigh in disbelief.

"I can shoot circles around you, Henry Zhang." Analise scoffed, sipping her drink.

"Yeah, when you have a football field between you and your target and time to aim. Ever tried shooting someone at point-blank? And succeeded?"

"Well, no, but—"

"Aha!"

"And here I thought I was only going to have to almost die *once* for you." Marion shook her head.

"Hey, don't even joke about that," Henry said sternly.

"What, did you think I was going to die?"

"Wha—I..."

"He absolutely did," Analise said in a mocking tone as Yianni gave him a look as if to question whether that was true.

"He cried, you know," Marion said.

"I didn't cry." Henry scoffed.

"You absolutely did."

"You were barely conscious!"

"And you were crying at the thought of my death." Marion chuckled. "I assure you, it's very sweet."

Henry pouted. "I'm going back to America."

"What? No!" Analise exclaimed with faux disappointment.

"Oh, yeah—now, you miss me, huh?"

"You really wanna go back to your cornfields, mate? Naw, come live here, where it's either blazin' hot down south or rainy as shite up north."

Marion gasped. "Who am I supposed to make fun of if you're gone?"

Henry shrugged with a shit-eating grin on his face. "I don't know, maybe try crying about it."

"Oh, shut up."

Iskandar's Game, Book 2
THE CATHAR'S CRUSADE

Coming Holiday 2025

Shilling

Thank you for reading! Going to the trouble of leaving a review of the book on Amazon or Goodreads would be greatly appreciated, as well as any other way you wish to spread the word.

See what other projects I'm working on and join my emailing list at authoralexanderhill.com.

If emails aren't your thing, we have a discord server for the same purpose.

About the Author

Alexander Hill is an author of all types of fantasy, but will always find a way to work in his chronic addiction to ancient and medieval history. He decided to write his first novel at 15, after getting concussed by a spin-kick to the head, and never stopped writing. He's been a martial artist all his life, specializing in Wing Chun and Wushu, competing as an athlete on the Ohio State University Dragon Phoenix Wushu Team. Among his vices is a liking to international solo travel, especially when done on a shoe-string budget. His first of such trips inspired his first published novel, *Iskandar's Game: The Shadow of Macedon*, and those he's taken since are likely to inspire many more. While he dips his toes in many fields, such as philosophy, theology, sociology, anthropology, and geopolitics, his true love has and always will be history, as evident on his YouTube Channel, where he uploads loosely structured ravings about history. He's also incredibly bad at putting real focus into things he doesn't think matters in the big picture. So it's likely this bio will change in the near future.